ACCLAIM FOR BILLY COFFEY

"Unforgettable. Evocative as memory, haunted as the South. *Some Small Magic* is big story magic written on the heart. Don't read if you're not prepared to be broken and awestruck at once."

—Tosca Lee, *New York Times* bestselling author

"On one level, this novel continues a long line of appealing road books, as three adventurers hop trains, scrounge meals, and sleep in barns as they cross the rural South. But *Some Small Magic* is also a tale of a journey from doubt to faith, and from hardscrabble despair to the highest form of hope. It's a vivid and compelling read, with characters so alive you expect them to step out of the pages and say hello. The final pages are so beautiful they hurt a little."

—Stephen Kiernan, author of *The Curiosity* and *The Baker's Secret*

"Rich, vivid language and description make up Coffey's latest. Bobby's voice is intense and rich. His flaws cause him to stand out against the colorful characters who surround him. An inventive, intricate plot, cleverly written and filled with humor, *There Will Be Stars* is a truly engaging, entertaining read."

—*RT Book Reviews*, 4 stars

"In the first line of the book, Coffey's hillbilly narrator invites his accidental guest (that would be us, the readers) to 'come on out of that sun' and set a spell. The spell is immediate. We are altogether bewitched by the teller, by his lyrical telling, and by the tale itself, whose darkness is infernal . . . Everything is at stake in this battle between good and evil—including the identity of the narrator, revealed at last. To Christians and non-Christians alike, this roaring tale will leave a powerful mark."

—*BookPage* on *The Curse of Crow Hollow*

"Coffey spins a wicked tale . . . [*The Curse of Crow Hollow*] blends folklore, superstition, and subconscious dread in the vein of Shirley Jackson's 'The Lottery.'"

—*Kirkus Reviews*

"An edge-of-your-seat, don't-read-in-the-dark book with amazing characters . . . Coffey takes readers on a wild roller-coaster ride without ever going over the top."

—*RT Book Reviews*, 4½ stars, TOP PICK! on *The Curse of Crow Hollow*

"Conjures a sense of genteel Southern charm . . . this creepy tale will delight enthusiasts of Tosca Lee's *Demon* and other horror stories."

—*Library Journal* on *The Curse of Crow Hollow*

"With lyrical writing and a rich narrative voice, Billy Coffey effortlessly weaves a coming-of-age story into a suspenseful, page-turning novel. *In the Heart of the Dark Wood* is a beautiful journey that takes the reader down a road filled with Southern gothic characters and settings; perfectly balanced with redemption and triumph of the human spirit. Allie is a courageous character that is sure to capture any reader's heart. *In the Heart of the Dark Wood* is not to be missed."

—Michael Morris, author of *Slow Way Home* and *Man in the Blue Moon*

"Coffey pens a coming-of-age story about the tribulations of the heart that is profoundly believable. The dialogues between characters are intensely rewarding to follow, and readers will anticipate the danger ahead; they will not pull away from the novel until it is finished. Suspense and mysteries of spirit make for a winning combination for any reader."

—*RT Book Reviews*, 4½ stars, on *In the Heart of the Dark Wood*

"*The Devil Walks in Mattingly* . . . recalls Flannery O'Conner with its glimpses of the grotesque and supernatural."

—*BookPage*

"[*The Devil Walks in Mattingly* is] a story that will hold your attention until the last page."

—Jessica Stringer, *Southern Living*

"Billy Coffey is one of the most lyrical writers of our time. His latest work, *The Devil Walks in Mattingly*, is not a page-turner to be devoured in a one-night frenzy. Instead, it should be valued as a literary delicacy, with each savory syllable sipped slowly. By allowing ourselves to steep in this story, readers are treated to a delightful sensory escape one delicious word at a time. Even then, we leave his imaginary world hungry for more, eager for another serving of Coffey's tremendous talent."

—Julie Cantrell, *New York Times* and *USA Today* bestselling author of *Into the Free* and *When Mountains Move*

"Coffey (*When Mockingbirds Sing*) has a profound sense of Southern spirituality. His narrative moves the reader from Jake and Kate's false heaven to a terrible hell, then back again to a glorious grace."

—*Publishers Weekly* on *The Devil Walks in Mattingly*

"[A]n inspirational and atmospheric tale."

—*Library Journal*, starred review of *When Mockingbirds Sing*

"This intriguing read challenges mainstream religious ideas of how God might be revealed to both the devout and the doubtful."

—*Publishers Weekly* review of *When Mockingbirds Sing*

"Readers will appreciate how slim the line is between belief and unbelief, faith and fiction, and love and hate as supplied through this telling story of the human heart always in need of rescue."

—*CBA Retailers + Resources* review of *When Mockingbirds Sing*

"Billy Coffey is a minstrel who writes with intense depth of feeling and vibrant, rich description. The characters who live in this book face challenges that stretch the deepest fabric of their beings. You will remember *When Mockingbirds Sing* long after you finish it."

—Robert Whitlow, bestselling author of *The Choice*

"*When Mockingbirds Sing* by Billy Coffey made me realize how often we think we know how God works, when in reality we don't have a clue. God's ways are so much more mysterious than we can imagine. Billy Coffey is an author we're going to be hearing more about. I'll be looking for his next book!"

—Colleen Coble, *USA Today* bestselling author of *The Inn at Ocean's Edge* and the Hope Beach series

SOME SMALL
MAGIC

OTHER NOVELS BY BILLY COFFEY

SOME
SMALL
MAGIC

BILLY COFFEY

THOMAS NELSON
Since 1798

Some Small Magic

© 2017 by Billy Coffey

Published in Nashville, Tennessee, by Thomas Nelson. Thomas Nelson is a registered trademark of HarperCollins Christian Publishing, Inc.

Thomas Nelson, Inc., titles may be purchased in bulk for educational, business, fundraising, or sales promotional use. For information, please e-mail SpecialMarkets@ ThomasNelson.com.

Scripture quotations are taken from the King James Version. Public domain.

Publisher's Note: This novel is a work of fiction. Names, characters, places, and incidents are either products of the author's imagination or used fictitiously. All characters are fictional, and any similarity to people living or dead is purely coincidental.

Library of Congress Cataloging-in-Publication Data

Names: Coffey, Billy, author.
Title: Some small magic / Billy Coffey.
Description: Nashville : Thomas Nelson, [2017]
Identifiers: LCCN 2016044576 | ISBN 9780718084424 (paperback)
Subjects: | GSAFD: Christian fiction.
Classification: LCC PS3603.O3165 S67 2017 | DDC 813/.6--dc23 LC record available at https://lccn.loc.gov/2016044576

Printed in the United States of America

17 18 19 20 21 LSC 6 5 4 3 2 1

For Salina, who went west and found home

PUBLISHER'S NOTE

Billy Coffey's novels are all set around Mattingly, Virginia, and can be read in any order. If you've read previous Mattingly books, you may be interested in knowing that *Some Small Magic* takes place after *There Will Be Stars*.

Enjoy!

Well I am Death, none can excel
I'll open the door to Heaven or Hell
Whoa, Death someone would pray
Could you wait to call me another day.
—LLOYD CHANDLER

No one knows whether death, which
people fear to be the greatest evil,
may not be the greatest good.
—PLATO

PART I

HOME

-1-

It isn't the horrible thing he's done that bothers Abel, nor that he knows exactly why he did it, nor even that what began as the perfect plan frayed to tatters even before Mrs. Heizer chirped her whistle to end the last recess of the school year. No, what bothers Abel is that fate must always be so cruel.

Most of the last hour not spent watching the girl beside him on the bench or figuring what to tell his momma he has given over to this notion: how it is that things never seem to work out for him the way he envisions. That he now understands he was warned early this morning to simply leave Chris alone provides little comfort. But it's true—Abel was warned. The morning train had seventy-six cars. Seventy-six is an even number, which usually means good. But seven and six add to thirteen, and thirteen is the unluckiest number of all.

What makes things worse is that the bench Mrs. Heizer
has left him upon is dangerous. The wood is too unforgiving
for his back and hips. Sharp edges wait on all sides like traps
rigged to spring. The carpet is too far from the seat to offer
cushion should Abel fall. He wants to tell someone about
this, Miss Ellie or the girl beside him. Wants to warn that
making him sit here like a criminal may well end in disaster.
But Miss Ellie is huddled with the four teachers who have
gathered around her desk, and the girl has scooted all the
way to the other end of the bench, leaving him alone. No one
would hear him over the ringing phones and high chatter and
distant yawps of children. They are happy sounds—the noise
of things ending, if only for a little while.

The glass door beside him swings open. A scent like flowers follows another teacher who joins the little crowd on the
other side of the counter. No student is supposed to go back
there, though sometimes Miss Ellie lets Abel sit at her desk
when there's no one around to tell. Abel watches her now, the
way Miss Ellie's eyes smile even bigger than her lips and how
her blond hair sparkles when the sunlight catches it through
the window behind her. He's pretty sure he loves her. Once,
Abel did a trick so good that Miss Ellie's face turned the color
of a rose and she laid her hand on his knee for six whole
Mississippis. That had been a good day, even though Abel
had gotten hurt again.

The girl beside him won't act like he's here. She was
already waiting on the bench when Mrs. Heizer brought
Abel in, and she scooched over like what was wrong with him
could catch. Abel thinks she's a third grader, then amends
that when he spots the report card jacket on her lap—fourth
grader now.

Shouting from the office down the hall. Abel leans his

head forward some to see, though not so far as to risk a toppling. Principal Rexrode's door is still shut. He sighs and scratches at the cast on his right arm.

Abel's own report card is back at his desk, though the golden apple sticker for A/B honor roll (barely, he concedes—this time there were a whole lot more B-minuses than A-pluses) won't do much for his cause now. Nor will asserting that at least part of the reason for doing what he did can be laid at Mrs. Heizer's feet. Then again, she could have scrawled *You suck eggs, Abel Shifflett* instead of *Enjoy middle school, Abel!* and things still could have turned out this way. Abel still would have given Chris the present that morning, and Chris still would have squatted behind the monkey bars and blown through his pants a few hours later. Mrs. Heizer still would have seen it, and Abel would still be on this wood bench in the office where all the current delinquents / future convicts sat and waited.

He leans toward the girl, making sure not to bump his cast, and says, "What you in for?"

She keeps her head steady and pointed forward, then tugs at the left side of her hair—long and the color of garden dirt, utterly beautiful—and moves it over her eye.

Normally that response would signal the end of things. Yet if Abel has learned nothing else this day (other than never to carry out a plan, even a perfect one, when the morning train promises ill luck), it is that the last day of school provides a unique opportunity to do those things one would otherwise never attempt.

"You hear what happened?" He cocks his thumb, the good one, down the hall to where the shouts are coming from. "All that's 'cause a what I did."

The girl doesn't look his way—won't—but whispers,

"Leave me alone," in an angry voice that sounds anything but a third (*fourth*) grader's. She scoots even more, stopping only when her body meets the armrest. Even more hair covers her face now, though Abel can see she is pretty in a way that will one day place her far from his grasp. Chris Jones says the only sort of woman Abel will ever marry is someone like the lunch lady, who has a lazy eye and four black hairs growing from a mud-colored mole on her forehead. The girl is wearing blue jeans that look new and tennis shoes that lie flat on the carpet. Abel looks down at his own shoes, a ratty pair of knock-offs his momma plucked from the bargain bin last summer. They dangle far above the carpet like dead things. He scoots down until his toes touch the floor, wincing as the wood cuts into his back and neck. His arm is itching bad now. Just below the elbow, where Dumb Willie wrote *WILE* in scrawling orange letters.

"Hey."

No response.

"Hey, you got a pencil?"

"Go way."

"I can't. I got in trouble. You hear what I did?" He reaches into his pocket and then out with a motion quicker than required, given the girl isn't paying attention. "You got a pencil?" he says again. "I'll pay you for it."

He makes the switch and lifts his left hand out to her, thumb up and palm out, the nickel hidden in the fleshy part of his thumb and forefinger. Holds it there until she peers from between the strands of hair to see Abel's fingers empty. He flicks his hand outward, throwing the nickel forward and snatching it from the empty air. Her full lips part as her eyes widen in a moment of glory, bringing a smile to Abel's face before it begins to fade as the girl's gaze drifts from his hand

4

to the rest of him—the mop of blond hair that cannot manage to hide his broad forehead; eyes dull at the irises with whites not the color of milk but a pale blue; the stained, brittle teeth; one shoulder wedged higher than the other, giving the appearance of a boy forever locked in a confused half shrug; the compact, dwarfish body. The last bell of the year sounds through speakers already gathering dust in hallways and classrooms, but to Abel it is more than a notice of freedom. It's the alarm going off in the girl's mind as she registers the ugly truth of the ruined boy beside her.

Abel's sleights of hand have seen him through his six years of schooling, won him three Mattingly Elementary School talent shows, and produced no small measure of *oohs* and *aahs* from classmates enchanted by his ability to produce something from nothing. But those tricks have never bought him their love. Love is a magic too powerful for even Abel to master.

The girl leaps up and shoots for the door, scurrying to safety just ahead of the teachers filing out, and all Abel can manage is to remain half-prone with his feet on the floor and a nickel in his hand as the school empties for summer. Behind the wooden door down the hallway, the yelling continues. The words aren't from Principal Rexrode, which is good. But they're from Chris Jones's daddy, which is certainly bad. Abel winces and tries to fool his mind by scratching again at his cast. Pain is something to which he has mostly grown accustomed over his eleven years, but not the itching. It always starts at a place he cannot reach and ends somewhere deep inside his brain.

"Here go."

Miss Ellie has come around the counter. She crouches in front of Abel and slips a pencil into his good hand. He jabs the sharpened end down between his wrist and cast, shuddering with pleasure.

"Thanks, Miss Ellie."

He grins now, drawing her gaze as the fingers of his good hand push the pencil deeper. They slip off to grasp the plastic stick hidden inside. Abel draws the stick out with a flourish and twists his wrist at the last moment, producing a fake daisy. The yellow center and each of the white petals is caked with dead skin and lint that Abel's sweat has rolled to tiny gray balls. He offers the flower to Miss Ellie anyway, who accepts it with a chuckle. She puts her hand to Abel's knee

(One Mississippi, two Mississippi, three Miss—)

and tilts her head toward Principal Rexrode's office. "Sounds testy in there."

"You hear what I did?"

"Honey, whole school heard what you did." She flashes a smile before wrangling it down, but not before Abel can tuck that memory away. Maybe all he'll manage to marry someday is a woman like the lunch lady, but Abel will lie down with her every night thinking of Miss Ellie's smile. "Not that I'm condoning it," she says. "That was an awful thing you did, Abel."

"No awfuller than what he's done to me. I ain't scared a them."

"Well, I know who you should be scared of, and right now she ain't waiting tables at the diner, she's fighting a gaggle of wilding kids to get in here and handle the mess you made."

"Think Chris made all the mess," Abel says. He grins, can't help it, and finds Miss Ellie grinning too.

"Don't you be so smart." Miss Ellie glances up through the windows.

Abel imagines a river of children churning past behind him, laughing and yelling as they share what they're doing for summer, trips to the beach and sleepovers and adventures, all those things he won't do.

"Your arm just itch? Or does it hurt? I can get you something out of Rachel's office."

"No," he says. "Momma catches me taking drugs, she'll skin me alive."

"Don't think aspirin counts."

"It's okay. I only itch."

Miss Ellie glances up and makes a grin. "Here she comes. Gird your loins, Abel."

The door swings wide to a new smell—not flowers, but cooking grease and cigarettes. The brown bun that Lisa Shifflett tied her hair into this morning has gone sagging now, pressed down along her stooped shoulders from the weight of the breakfast rush, the first of the lunch crowd, and the life Abel knows they both struggle through. She is pale in spite of the June month, waiflike with her skinny arms and legs. Deep lines have formed beneath her eyes. Streaks of gravy and meatloaf are stuck to the front of her apron, a preview of what Abel knows will be their supper.

She bends low and runs her hands over Abel's body, checking his good arm and then his bad one, his chest and legs and feet. "What's wrong?" she asks. "Abel? Did you get hurt again?"

"I'm fine, Momma."

Miss Ellie says, "Nothing to get worried over, Lisa. I'm sorry I had to call you down, but Mister Rexrode insisted. There's been a little trouble."

"Trouble?" Abel glances up to find his momma's eyes have caught a spark. "Chris? Was it Chris again?" She sighs

7

like she most often does and lays a hand to her forehead, pressing back tears and rage. "You'd think that boy'd let Abel be on the last day, Ellie."

Abel says, "Well, Momma . . . ," thinking this may be the only chance to tell his side of things, but now here is Principal Rexrode's door opening and Principal Rexrode stepping out, telling Lisa hello and y'all come back, let's get this thing straightened out. Abel hears his momma say come on, she's got to get back to the diner before Roy fires her for good. He picks himself up off the bench and follows. The walls tilt with each step, hurting Abel's back and hips and his bad arm now where the itch was, and what Abel is left with is a feeling of doom and sadness—still not for what he's done to Chris, but for whatever is about to be done to him.

He glances back toward Miss Ellie. She stands as though her heart is full to breaking, like she is the maiden who will wait in purity and prayer and Abel the knight off to battle a great dragon. Her hands are clasped at her flat stomach. She winks.

Abel turns back and waddles on. He wishes he could disappear.

That's never been a trick he could master either.

-2-

Lisa Shifflett cannot count the number of times she's made this walk to Charlie Rexrode's office. Too many, she knows. And yet this time, which she understands will be the last— next year it will be the office at the middle school and after that the one at Mattingly High and then, she supposes, the dean's office at some college (ha-ha)—things feel different somehow. It's as though someone has added an extra forty feet to the hallway since she last visited, or as though Lisa has stumbled into one of those dreams where she's running from something but her feet are stuck in sand. She needs to hurry, yet everything is happening slowly.

People tell her it's not all that different, raising a son like Abel, but they don't know. They say it's no different for any momma who must raise a boy on her own. Always with a tinge of guilt in their voices as though they know their words are a lie, leaving her a small stack of quarters or the occasional dollar bill for a tip—just like that tone in Lisa's voice when she answers *Thank you* and *I appreciate your prayers*, her own praying long past. But it *is* different. That's what Lisa wants to tell them but never does. It's different because Abel is special and none of you can know that because none of you are like him, and that's why none of you will ever understand and why it'll always be us against you. Me and Abel standing alone against the stiff wind, my boy and his momma and no one else, because we're all we have.

That's what Lisa ponders as she steps into that measureless hallway with Charlie Rexrode's dimpled face way at the end. Not how Roy was mad because she had to leave her tables again or that the tips Lisa would miss were to be set aside for their bill at the market, but that a day that dawned as one more fight of attrition has now skewed toward full-on battle. Her hand reaches back and meets Abel's fingers, her arm swaying, her shoulders dipping and jerking in time with his uneven hips.

Charlie Rexrode steps aside. Lisa ignores his smile, her eyes too full of the god-awful boy slumped in the last of three folding chairs laid out in front of the principal's desk. Chris's daddy, Royce, stands behind him, three hundred pounds

of fleshy rolls and a scowl beneath his beard. With Royce
is Rachel Barlow, the school nurse. Already Lisa is yelling.
She cusses Chris Jones for whatever thing he's done now and
cusses Royce for siring such a demon of a child, her voice
shifting from the tired though happy one that is her usual
to the raised one of work, the voice that calls out orders of
scrambled eggs and chicken potpie to Roy. Screaming at
them, at Chris, this boy from over the hill who has been
Abel's torment since kindergarten. The cast was on her son's
leg then, not his arm. It was red instead of yellow.

"What'd you do to my son now, you little—"

The last word is cut off, not by Royce's hard glare but by
his boy's appearance. Chris Jones has always been a big child,
fat and strong like his daddy, everything Abel will never be.
Yet now he looks feeble, hunched in the chair like a trapped
animal half-starved. His face is the pale yellow of the sunlight leaking through the windows. His brow shines sweaty
and slick.

Lisa asks, "What in the world happened to you?"

"Your boy," Royce answers, "that's what. He near killed
my son."

Charlie Rexrode clears his throat and moves from the
door. "Now let's not get all dramatic here, Royce. Lisa, sit on
down. You too, Abel."

Abel sits in the chair next to Chris. Lisa takes the other,
leaving Royce to stand. Everything is happening slowly again,
only this time the sand isn't on the floor, it's in the air. Even
breathing comes hard.

"Sorry again, Lisa," the principal says.

Royce huffs. "She ain't the one needs apologizing to,
Charlie. Ain't her boy been upended."

"Shut up, Royce"—still smiling, Charlie's always doing

that, even though Lisa sees a weariness behind that smile she knows well—"already gave you my sorry. Won't be another."

The worn leather chair behind the desk wails as it takes the principal's big frame. He reaches into a drawer and pulls out a torn and empty box that he places at the center of the desk. Everyone regards it but Abel.

"Excuse me," Lisa says. "Will someone please tell me what's going on?"

"I know Abel's had his problems," Charlie says.

Abel looks up—to his principal, not his mother, though Lisa can still see the expression on her son's face. There is no anger there, more a hurt, as though Abel has just been offended.

Charlie corrects himself. "With Chris, I mean. Lord knows these two been in here more than once, and Lord knows it's always Chris's doing."

Royce opens his mouth. Charlie shuts it with a single pointing finger.

"But this time, Lisa, I'm afraid Abel was the instigator."

Chris squirms in his chair, bringing Nurse Rachel to life and causing Royce to step backward. Lisa cannot make sense of Rachel's hand on Chris's back and why she's whispering a question of if he needs to go. Why everyone but Abel is looking terrified and embarrassed at the same time. And that word Charlie used to describe her son—*instigator*. It's as though Lisa's mind cannot process what that word even means.

Charlie says, "Abel came to school today with what Chris believed—and Abel said—was a peace offering. Chocolate. Quite a bit of it, actually. Isn't that right, Abel?"

Abel shrugs. He reaches into his pocket and draws out a nickel that flutters between his fingers.

"We don't have chocolate in the house," Lisa says. "Can't afford it." Somehow this seems to her the only explanation needed.

Charlie taps the empty box on the desk. "Found this in Abel's backpack. He must've taken them out before giving it. Chris ate it all before Missus Heizer knew. By then, things had . . . commenced."

Royce explodes: "Your little runt poisoned my boy. Fed Chris a whole box a *laxatives*."

The slow motion of the room unfolds in hours rather than seconds: Lisa's mouth dropping wide, her head shaking no, fingers searching for something to grip. Chris doubles over at the word—*laxatives*—as though he will blow right here and now. Rachel's eyes go to moons. And Abel, looking at no one, making that coin appear and vanish, appear and vanish. He rests his cast on the edge of Charlie's desk, thumping it hard against the wood. Trying, Lisa thinks, to drown Chris's wailing. Asking them all without saying it, *What about me?*

"I wanna know what you're gonna do about this, Charlie," Royce says. "My boy needs satisfaction."

"What your boy needs is a roll of toilet paper and some privacy. I'll not have you telling me my job, Royce. Abel, you got something to say to Chris."

Somehow Lisa finds the presence of mind to do what she must. She forces her foot through the thick office air and finds that air not thick at all. The slow-motion world drowned in clear molasses must exist in her mind alone, because her kick propels Abel's chair into Chris's. Abel flinches and squeaks a "Sorry."

Charlie raps the desk with two fat fingers. "Royce, you get Chris on home. He'll be fine by morning and probably five pounds lighter. You want, get him over to Doc March.

He'll tell you the same. Dumb Willie's already disposed of the underwear. I'm afraid it didn't survive the ordeal."

Royce says, "What? Charlie, this ain't—" then stops at the sudden dawning of some hazy truth. He folds his arms across his wide chest, covered in sawdust from a morning's work felling trees. "I see how it is. My son gets laid upon, but the cripple gets off. You'll fawn over the little bastard boy."

Now the slow turn of time gives way, bringing everything to happen at once. Lisa shoots from her place a hairsbreadth after Abel does the same, pushing him back into the chair just as Charlie tries to corral her, his purpose being clear: Charlie Rexrode seeks not to protect Lisa from Royce, but Royce from Lisa and Abel. Royce snatches his boy up too fast. Rachel backs away as Chris's insides rumble. The sound of him breaking wind reminds them all that they are in the presence of live ordnance.

"Get. Him. Out," Charlie says.

Royce turns his boy by the shoulders as Rachel moves to open the door. Chris's face has gone from the yellow of the sun to the white of the walls. He walks with a ginger step that would draw his own mockery would he witness it in Abel. For this split second, Lisa allows herself the belief that Chris Jones has received what he deserved. Chris bends low as he crosses past Abel, as though gripped by another spasm. Lisa watches as he whispers into Abel's ear. She wants to say something, demand Chris repeat what he just said, but her eyes are fixed upon her son as Royce retreats into the hall. Abel sits broken and defeated in his rage. It's as if all light in him has gone silent now, blown cold and dark.

*

Charlie exhales once the Jones boys are gone and says, "I'm sorry about all this, Lisa. I am. Please, y'all sit back down here."

Lisa's hands are clenched at her sides, her posture rigid. She sits and produces a pack of cigarettes from her purse. Charlie opens his mouth and shuts it at her glare.

"Momma," Abel says. "I—"

"Nope. Not right now, Abel. You'll have plenty of time to talk to me later. Right now I'm going to have a conversation with Charlie, and you can just sit here and be quiet. You can listen while we talk honest. We're going to talk honest, aren't we, Principal Rexrode?"

Charlie leans back in his chair. The corners of his mouth curl into something of a smile. "Honesty ain't a virtue bandied about much around here, Lisa. Especially from that side of my desk. But sure, let's be honest. Off the record. Last day and all."

He opens another desk drawer, this time with a key hooked to a chain in his pocket. The empty box Abel brought from home is whisked aside. In its place appear a bottle of whiskey and a single glass.

"Shouldn't be doing this," the principal says. "With y'all here, I mean. But then, you're sitting here in abeyance of the law by sucking on that cancer stick, so I figure I can at least do this. You could say it's a tradition of mine, one I've come to take a shine to. This bottle sits in my drawer a hundred seventy-nine days a year. I never touch it. Not once, Lisa, and you got my word. But come that hundred and eightieth day, after the last bell rings and all them kids scamper out for three months?" He shakes his head and pours. Half of the glass disappears in a swallow. Principal Rexrode shivers like he's come in from being in the cold a long while. "Christ A'mighty, this job's killin' me slow."

Lisa rubs her eyes. "Charlie."

"Apologies." He holds out the glass. "You want some?"

"No, thank you." But she does. "It's just lunchtime still, what's left of it, and . . ."

Principal Rexrode glances at the clock above the door. His eyes squint and then bulge. "Shoot, Lisa, I'm sorry. I know you got to get back." He turns the glass up again, winces, then smiles. "I don't care you did it, Abel."

Abel blinks, as does she. Lisa would blame the alcohol for what Charlie said, but she knows from experience it takes time for drink to go from the mouth to the stomach and then all the way up into the head. Sometimes it takes near half an hour before Lisa lets slip things she doesn't mean. Or things she means but wouldn't otherwise say.

She talks low and slow: "What you mean, Charlie?"

"Just what I say. Off the record, of course. Me being honest. On the record, I'd tell you Abel near sent a classmate to the hospital today—I don't know, get his stomach pumped or something. Even though I reckon Chris's stomach's 'bout near empty as it can get now."

He snorts—the whiskey, Lisa knows. Now Principal Rexrode goes quiet and still, staring into that glass like he's thinking to himself. Almost in a whisper, he says, "Don't y'all look at me that way. I'm a tired man, Lisa. Come to this job thirty-five years ago, thinking it was my time to do some right in the world. Most the people in this town come through me. All their kids. I done my best with all of them, including you, Abel. Good kids, mostly. You get the usual stuff thrown in, 'course. Fights on the playground and taking peeks off each other's tests. Talking back to the teacher. Get all these kids' parents thrown in too—mommas and daddies and step-thisses and step-thats, grandparents near the end of their days having to raise up their kids' kids instead a walking down some beach in Florida, enjoying their golden years. Awful. Seems like every year gets worse. Like they ain't got no *center*, you know? No foundation. Nothing kids can cling to when the world goes bad."

Lisa can't seem to line up the right words with her thoughts.

"Good kids," Principal Rexrode says again. "Like I said. But then you get ones you know been spoilt the minute they walk in here. Not spoilt like they been given everything, but like whatever good they came out their mommas with is gone already. Torn-like, I mean. From the *inside*. And it don't matter how much you try and stitch them back, it won't hold. It's like their pieces don't fit together no more. Chris Jones is one a them spoilt ones. Half the kids here are scared to death to be caught in the same part of school as him, Lisa, much less the same grade. Much less the same *class*. He's the guy you'll see on the six o'clock news in a few years, getting caught for something that'll make people like you and me shake in our boots and wonder when the Lord's coming back." He pauses, swallows again. "Off the record."

Abel scrunches his eyebrows, which look like two thin strands of hair taped to his wide forehead. When he speaks, it's as though the only conclusion he can reach is one he has neither planned for nor considered. "You mean I ain't in no trouble?"

"I know what that boy's put you through. Ask me, it's high time somebody gave Chris a taste of his own medicine. 'Sides, it's the last day of school. You'll be moving on, Abel. Won't even be back here in the fall."

Lisa, who has gone from angered to screaming to silent in a span no longer than it would take to clear one more table and pocket one more dollar, can only let her Marlboro Red smolder in her hand. Half of her is trying to decide if Charlie means what he says and there will be no trouble. The other half is beholding the offended look that has grown back on Abel's face.

"But I done wrong," Abel says.

Charlie looks at the tiny yellow cast. "Known you six years now, Abel. Seen you in all your pain and discomfort. I've lifted you up in prayer even though I know your momma'd skin me for it. I know your grades slipped this semester. Maybe Chris had something to do with that, maybe it's something else. But we're being honest here, Lisa?" He waits for her nod, which arrives after a long pause. "Well, if I'm honest I'll say punishment does no good here. It's grace Abel needs, and grace is what I'm bound to give. All things considered, son, you been punished enough."

"But you gotta."

"Maybe, if it were any other time. But my conscience forbids it just now. I'll give you a little advice, though. Don't let people like Chris get to you, Abel. You're a good boy, a smart boy. And you're—"

(*Don't say it*, Lisa thinks, *please, Charlie, don't say it*)

"—special," Charlie says. "That ain't no bad thing. But you keep away from Chris Jones this summer. Give him time to calm down, maybe he'll forget all this before next year. And I'll give you some advice too, Lisa. If you'll hear it."

She'll take anything just now, so long as they can get out of here with the lunch crowd still at the diner and without Charlie calling Sheriff Barnett. Lisa can't think of what charge would be levied. Improper use of an over-the-counter medication maybe.

"I know this is a hard time," Charlie says, "for the both of

17

you. It's a struggle for a single mom. Now, I'm not one to get religious on anybody—"

Lisa holds up her hands—

"—but there's revival going on tonight—"

"Charlie, I don't think—"

"I know, I know. But this is different, Lisa. The preacher they're bringing to speak?" He shakes his head. "I've heard stories. He's got the true gift. It's up at the old barn off 42, across the hill. Seven o'clock. Just follow the signs. Or everybody else."

"Across the hill?" she asks.

Principal Rexrode shrugs, then smiles again. "Lord loves all kinds, Lisa. Even the hill folk."

*

There is only silence on the ride home. No *What the world was in your head, Abel?* or *Let me explain, Momma,* just Lisa smoking and Abel pointing his nose out of his open window and letting the wind play in his hair. She knows the smoke bothers him and keeps the cigarette pointed near the vent. People would say it's child abuse, that's fine. Wouldn't be the first time Lisa Shifflett was accused of that, and besides, they don't understand.

Some days (this one, for instance) Lisa thinks she doesn't much understand either. Not anything. Some days she thinks understanding has always been a thing short in supply and long in demand, at least as far as her life is concerned. In spite of what the majority of town might say, their hardships cannot be laid to Lisa and Abel alone. She works hard at the diner and does all she can to provide and nurture. Abel had no say in the course given him—his *specialness*, a word that makes Lisa wince just as much as it does her son, even when spoken in the privacy of her own thoughts. So why must their days then be spent on love alone, rather than with some of the finer things thrown in? Why must it always seem a struggle, one foot in the grave and the other on muddy ground?

In the shadow of the hill that divides Mattingly not only by geography but class and reputation, Lisa's little Honda veers onto a narrow way known as Holly Springs Road. She has always considered the name too pretty for a stretch of dirt road that fronts a smattering of single-wides and a long field stretching to the railroad tracks beyond. Dust here is a constant enemy, stirred up from spoiled ground by winds that blow unceasingly from the mountains and left to cling to clothes and cars alike. Abel coughs (*From the dust,* Lisa tells herself, *not the smoke*) as they wind their way over potholes and ruts to the little trailer last on the right, where the road dead-ends.

Mister Medford Hoskins is the man who owns their trailer, a crotchety old miser who believes the one thousand eight square feet of living space contained therein plus the acre of land it sits on is well worth the four hundred dollars a month Lisa pays in rent. It is the only house Abel has ever known, which Lisa had once promised would be "their new beginning" before she came to understand that every promise made is sworn through a curtain of the unknown. People everywhere begin a thing with hope and certainty in equal measures only to find those things are not stolen so much as they simply fade. Now "their new beginning" is a broken-down and mouse-infested trailer not their own, set in a yard where chicory and dandelions overwhelm the tall grass and where everything leads to a dead end. But it is home, and it is theirs, and as such a castle wouldn't mean more.

The car stops when the gravel driveway meets a worn path leading to the front steps. Lisa grinds the transmission into reverse and waits for Abel to open his door.

He keeps his gaze out the window and says, "Guess you're going back to work."

"Got to. Lunch rush. I've already missed most of it."

"Because a me," Abel says.

"I think that's a fair way of putting things."

"Are you mad?"

"Yes. That's kind of what mommas get when their sons do something like that."

"You gone punish me?"

"I about have to, don't you think?"

"I could work it off," he says, still gazing out toward the weeds. "Clean the wreck room, maybe. Or cut the grass."

"You know better than go in that room without me, and you know you're not fit to cut the grass. I think it's best you go on inside, Abel. I think what you need is to keep in your room and think hard on what you done, because what you done was inconsiderate. Not just of Chris, but of me."

"Think I'd rather mow," Abel says.

"And I think I'd rather not gotten wind of a deed sprung from a thought I believed could never grow in your heart."

"I left my book bag at school," Abel says. "It's got some of my best tricks in there."

"I'll get it after work. Maybe Willie will be there."

"Dumb Willie left at lunchtime. His daddy had to get him in the garden."

"Principal Rexrode then, though he's like to be duly sloshed. Now get on."

Abel opens the door.

"Wait," Lisa says. "Sugar me."

He turns that perfect face and looks at her with those perfect eyes and grins through those perfect teeth, then leans his perfect body over to peck her cheek.

"Lock the door. I trust Royce Jones no more than I do his idiot boy."

"Okay. Toots love," Abel says, which is what he's always said.

"Toots love."

She backs out of the drive and forces the gear from reverse to first, which creates a sound deep in the Honda's bowels that reminds her of a dying sow. Lisa waves as she pulls away. Abel stands alone in a yard of blooming weeds as though weighing past and present and future in scales of his own devising, only to judge all three as wanting. Through the rearview Lisa watches as he picks a dandelion from the grass and twirls it in the fingers of his good hand, holding the fluffy top high to the sun. Lisa watches her son blow and blow, scattering wishes to a dry breeze.

-3-

Next time I see you, you're dead.

That's what Chris whispered just before he left. He bent down like his stomach was hurting again and stared straight at Abel, eyes hard and empty, and that's when he said it.

Next time I see you, you're dead.

This afternoon was not the first time Chris Jones warned of murder. Near to every kid at school has lived under that same sentence of death at some point, which Chris distributes between boys and girls equally like some modern, enlightened bully. The promise alone is enough to send the most stalwart child cowering to the nearest teacher. That the closest Chris has ever come to going through with his threats are boxing a few ears and pantsing some poor kids on the playground matters little. What matters is he *could* do it— Chris is mean enough that he *could* murder—Abel has even heard a teacher say those very words—and so in the minds of the town's children, it's only a matter of time until Chris *will*.

And there is this: Abel can't ignore the feeling that something is different this time. It was the way Chris whispered his threat, how it had been in a voice somehow not his own. Gone was the deep and menacing tone perfected in empty hallways and lonely playground corners, one that not even Abel's magic could keep away. Their first day together in kindergarten, Chris demanded lunch money that Abel didn't have. Abel tried reasoning, saying they was poor and his momma said the school would pay his lunch for him, though reasoning never worked with Chris Jones, not then or since. To pacify the big kid (even then, Chris was the size of a monster) or perhaps even make a friend, Abel proceeded to make an acorn appear from behind Chris's ear. Chris responded by thumping Abel in the neck, thereby cementing one of the many truisms Abel Shifflett would obtain while working at education: bullies cannot be charmed. Chris did little more than growl at Abel from that first day on. Yet the way he had spoken in Principal Rexrode's office carried a sense of *sureness* to it, like Chris had in a matter of seconds jumped forward in time to witness Abel's death outright and jumped back to report the deed. It was no threat, what Chris said. It was rather a promise. One made by a boy who in the span of a single morning had crossed the threshold from bully to something worse, a human wholly spoilt.

Abel doesn't guess that's what his momma had in mind

when she said stay in your room and think on things, but that doesn't matter. What Chris said

("Promised," Abel whispers)

is all he *can* think about. What Chris said, and how even if anybody else had heard it, nothing much would have been done. Abel's momma was too mad about what Mister Jones had said, that part about her boy being a bastard. Principal Rexrode wouldn't have cared; all he wanted was to get into his whiskey and talk about how bad the world is. And Mister Jones? Shoot, all Mister Jones would've done is pat Chris on the back and say, *Atta boy, son. Don't you let the little bastard freaks of the world ever think they're anything but what they are, them Shiffletts is plain country trash even more than us.*

And so Abel lies on his bed for most of the afternoon, broken arm across his chest and good arm behind his head, wondering if passing off a bunch of laxatives as chocolate so the school bully would mess his pants right in the middle of recess was worth this trouble. Nothing else seems of consequence. He is some afraid of what his momma might do, but that fear pales against the terror Chris Jones kindles. His momma won't do much more than maybe yell a little bit and say how disappointed she is, because Abel knows deep down his momma thinks all Chris really got was what he deserved. There will be no spanking; Lisa Shifflett has never raised a hand to her son and would never, even if Abel did not walk around in a glass body. Nor will she ground him; Abel never goes anywhere, not unless Dumb Willie goes along.

That thought gives Abel pause. His momma *could* keep him from Dumb Willie. Could call an end to Abel going through the cut in the trees where the road dead-ends and walking the woods to Rita and Henderson Farmer's place. No more visiting Dumb Willie and no more Dumb Willie visiting, no more fishing and roaming in the woods or taking rides on the tractor when Dumb Willie's folks are gone, maybe for the whole summer. That would be awful, and for more than the obvious reason of Abel having to live the next months without his only friend. If Chris means what he said—and Abel knows Chris does, all he has to do is shut his eyes and he hears that spoilt voice all over again—Dumb Willie will have to be kept close. Shoot, Dumb Willie will practically have to move in.

Abel's vow to shelter in place as his momma instructed holds just over four hours. Three, if he doesn't count the bathroom breaks and the time it took to eat his peanut butter sandwich. It is the distant whistle that calls him, coming soft and building from the far edge of town and over the trees behind his house and now around, to the porch and the bedroom's open window. Abel doesn't have to look at the clock on his dresser to know it's past five, nor does he need to move from his bed to know the train is a long one. The low and hard grinding of the big diesel engines is proof enough.

It's a risk, going out. The grass is tall in the yard and taller in the field. There are rocks, big ones that lie buried except for their thick tips, but even worse is that Abel knows his momma will soon be home. She'll catch him out and call him a liar for going out of the house. One thing Lisa Shifflett never abides is lying. The trouble Abel would find himself in then would be even worse than the trouble he's in now.

But it's a train, a long one, and Abel has to see it. He has to.

The pocket notebook is still on the desk from this morning. Abel grabs it along with the nub of pencil by his lamp, then restocks his pockets with a few of the tricks he took out earlier. Just the rubber band and the ring, the playing cards,

and a few of the smoke bombs. He runs (or tries to) down
the hallway and straight through the back door, keeping one
eye to the ground for those tricky rocks and the other to the
road. Watching for Chris Jones's bike, or a puff of dust made
by his momma's car.

*

Three trains make daily runs through Mattingly: the morning one that passes just before seven o'clock, the evening one
sometime after four, and the late train, arriving in the full dark
between eleven and midnight. For years, Abel has been present for as many of them as he can.

Lisa is gone by six each morning to ready the diner for the
breakfast crowd and isn't home until well after the evening
train rolls through, leaving Abel alone to stand at post for their
passing. Usually she is present on the weekends, sometimes
making a picnic for them both to sit in the field along the
tracks while the big engines pass, always making that pulling
motion with her arm so the engineer blows his whistle. The
night train is different. Lisa doesn't know Abel snuck out to
see it, though only once and to great disaster. Otherwise he has
lain still in bed instead, squinting his eyes and flexing his ears
as he marks the pages with hashes, trying to judge the number
of cars by the heavy clunking of the rails.

His daddy once drove a train, back before he died. That
was when they'd lived in North Carolina, before Abel was
born. Some nights Abel and his momma will sit out by the
wobbly little table on the wobbly little front porch of their
trailer and she'll tell him stories. They're all like tall tales, how
Abel's daddy once drove a train from one end of the country to the other and how not even snowstorms or hurricanes

could stop him, how he was the strongest man in the world and the most handsome too, which accounts for Abel's own pleasant face. And he was kind, Lisa tells him, a kinder man than the world has ever known since. When she says it there are always tears in her eyes, like the memories are so sweet they pain. Abel counts all this as reasons for his obsession, that quivering he gets inside whenever he hears the whistle call. He would walk through a field of fire to get to the curve in the tracks where the trains slow as they pass by the backyard of the trailer. Some old weeds and rocks won't scare him, not even now. There have been occasions when Abel very nearly did not make it back in time, mornings when Mister Houff was just about to pull away in the short bus. He doesn't think his momma would mind if he missed a day or two of school for the train. Just a day or two. Not when she knows her boy is out there looking at those cars roll by. Not when Abel is pulling his good arm so that a man who is like his father once was can wave and blow the whistle.

Though he's told no one, not Dumb Willie and especially not Lisa, that is why Abel snuck from the house on a Friday night two weeks back to witness his first night train. It had been one of those close-to-the-end days at school, when all the testing was done and everyone (including Abel, including Missus Heizer) had decided they could bear no more learning. Since Father's Day loomed, Missus Heizer suggested the class make cards with notes inside. She'd handed out construction paper and glue and pledged her help with any wording, then watched as everyone got to work. All but Abel, who could only stare out the window and try not to cry as Chris Jones and everybody else cut and pasted and raised their hands to ask if "love" was spelled with an *o* and an *e* instead of a *u*.

That was why Abel had gone out that night, to feel a

comfort that the trains were still coming through and men like his daddy still drove them and not everything in the world was so bad after all. He'd seen every rock in his way, including the one he tripped over. He'd screamed, wailed, screamed again; the train whistle drowned it all. And after that there was nothing left to do but make the long walk back inside, clutching his right arm and knowing it was broken. Just like before, like his other arm and the one leg and both feet before. He changed back into his pajamas and woke his momma. Both tasks proved excruciating, though in different ways. What Abel said was he'd fallen out of bed. Lisa wrapped him in a blanket and carried him to the car, saying he was the only boy in the history of everything who could hurt himself sleeping. Off they'd gone to the hospital in Stanley. All of that, and Abel never had gotten a glimpse of the train.

But he sees the evening one now, way far in the distance, and hears the slow unwinding of the engine as it peeks in and out of the trees. The tracks curve at the edge of the field, where the trains always slow to near a crawl before gathering speed for the hill country and the mountains beyond. This is where Abel stands for his counting. He digs for his notebook and pencil just as the lights of the engine appear, three white lamps in the shape of a triangle, flipping through the dates and marks until he finds a blank page near the back. The date goes on the top line, *Evening Train* beneath.

The whistle calls hard. Abel stands afar off and pulls his good arm, making the screech go again. Here comes a snake of iron and steel, head as black as night and smoking, cutting its way through quiet country. The air gathers. The ground beneath his feet quivers as the rails begin to sing, and even as he fumbles for the notebook and pencil as the first engine approaches and the second and third—a third!—and the long stretch of cars behind, Abel's eyes are drawn to those three glowing lights and the black space that fashions the middle of their triangle.

Six cars pass. Abel marks them with four hashes, a diagonal, and another hash. Chemical cars and flats, hoppers pregnant with Appalachian coal, boxcars of every color, their doors wide to the day. One page filled, another.

On and on this dark line stretches, past the curve and beyond, two pages becoming three. Abel's lips are moving—*ninety-two, ninety-three*—his good hand beginning to shake. Because not only is there a genuine caboose on the end, faded red and clacking on the rail, that caboose makes one hundred cars.

A hundred even. One-double-zero on the nose.

As the sound of the engines fades toward the hills, Abel can only stand in wonder. The air of this early evening has taken on the calm of a thunderstorm freshly passed, hanging heavy and thick. And that thing, that sense of possibility that carried Abel from this very field not ten hours before to play a trick on Chris Jones, returns. It is a strange thing. A lovely thing.

It is a thing of terror.

-4-

Twenty dollars. Twenty dollars is all Lisa carries home.

Even that is rounding things up, her halfhearted attempt at what Roy calls "seeing the light in the shadow." That's what he's always saying—*You got to see the light in the shadow, Lisa*—whenever days like this come around. Lisa herself prefers a more realistic (and cynical, she admits) view of circumstances. For instance: it's not really twenty dollars in her apron pocket when she hands the rest of the diner's supper crowd over to Nadine Heatwole, it's nineteen and change. Nickels and dimes mostly, though Lisa knows better than to complain to Roy. *You got to see the light in the shadow* has got to be the most inane expression in the English language. *You got to see the light in the shadow* is too stupid for even one of those dime-store cards they sell down at the pharmacy.

This day, she thinks, *is of a kind that will end me.*

The car reeks of meatloaf and mashed potatoes, reeks like her. Near everyone in town stops by the diner at least once a week, drawn more by the promise of gossip than good food and good service, the opportunity for some to ruminate upon the trials of others if only so their own seem less. Their wagging tongues are kept lubricated by endless cups of coffee. A waitress can do okay at a place like the Shoney's in Camden or the Cracker Barrel in Stanley, but not so much at Roy's Diner in downtown Mattingly. Not when most of your tips are for either regular or decaf. Not when it's just you paying the bills and the kid waiting for you at home, your sweet and beautiful only child, can't get from point A to point B without a side trip to the emergency room.

Often and in her private heart, Lisa has given herself over to the very sense of pity and rage she long vowed to put away forever. The pity is directed inward, to what has come of her life. The rage points outward and up to some undefined section of the heavens, toward whoever is supposed to be up there looking down, for allowing things to be this way. But those times are tempered by the quarters and dollars she finds wedged under the saltshakers on the diner's tables, which are never much but more than Nadine takes home, left for her in no small part by simple guilt.

There was a time when many in town believed Lisa beat her child. That was the best explanation for the flurry of Abel's ailments, all those casts, until of course the truth of things came out. Now these very people are quick to ask how he fares, how they both are getting along, and Lisa will smile and say they are well and thank them for their charity. In a heart more private than the one that mourns herself, Lisa is fine having a child in such tenuous physical shape. Is even happy with it, though that truth is crammed low inside and kept even out of her own sight. Because a boy like that, so helpless and so meek, will always need her. A son like Abel will never leave.

That is why it does not matter much, bringing home only this paltry little bit that was supposed to be much more and bound for the bill at the market. Nor does it even matter that five dollars out of that sum must be fed into the gas tank or Lisa's car will never make it home. That leaves fifteen.

And change—seeing that light.

She stops at the school to pick up Abel's things and finds Willie Farmer (Willie to her, Dumb Willie to the rest of the town, Abel included) indeed gone as Abel had said, off to slave away in his parents' garden. Charlie, however, is still there and still drinking. He lets Lisa into Mrs. Heizer's room and reminds her again of the great healing going on tonight over the hill, then wraps his meaty arms about her when Lisa begins to weep.

Darnell Givens is in the post office when she pulls into the lot. He's at the counter and Lisa can't go in; she's supposed to have made forty dollars today and taken most of it to him at the grocery to pay her credit. There's nothing for her to do but sink down in the seat and hope he doesn't see. She shakes her head at what must be a pitiful sight, this poor piece of white trash hiding from her creditor. He doesn't spot Lisa's grubby little Honda this time, but that may not be the case tomorrow. That's the thing about small towns—no one can hide forever. She waits until Darnell's truck is gone before slinking into the lobby. That familiar sense of weight presses onto her shoulders. The mailbox key is in her hand. Lisa doesn't realize how slippery it feels.

It's a low box, which means she has to bend down to peer inside. The tiny window reveals something inside. Quite a few somethings. She breathes deep, inserts the key, and opens the door.

If there is one decent thing to be found in the midst of such a bleak day, it is that Lisa finds little of consequence inside. There is a catalog she can dream her way through but never order from, bills she can't pay, an overdue on the electric. But no letter. In fact, there hasn't been a letter for close to a month now. Lisa nods, manages something of a smile as she leans against a row of mailboxes. Thinks maybe it will be over for a while, maybe he's given up or gone. She knows this possibility is a lie, but perhaps this lie will be enough to carry her through what promises to be a hellish night.

Begging is an indignity she has refused to suffer even in the worst of times, but that's what things have come to. There really is no other choice.

*

The house is locked when she arrives. All is quiet inside. Abel's bedroom door is shut and he doesn't come out, which is best.

31

Lisa could use some time alone. She sets her purse and Abel's backpack on the kitchen table (hard, in case he didn't hear her come in) and takes a beer from the refrigerator out to the small table on the front porch.

They sit here often in the evenings, talking and even laughing about the day. Abel will say all he learned in school, which is usually more from his library books than his teachers, leaving Lisa to sit and stare in a kind of pensive awe. Her mind thinking, *Lord, this boy is smart. Hearing him's like listening to a grown man with an education,* even as her heart breaks against some unwritten cosmic rule that her son can possess a strong mind or a strong body, but not both.

The screen door opens. Abel peeks first and then moves onto the porch, taking a seat next to her. It is a rare awkward moment between them, one filled with a silence heavier than even the humid air. In the trees that mark the lane's dead end, a mockingbird calls. Lisa looks that way, since looking at Abel would be too hard. Abel does the same, no doubt preferring a clump of branches to the disappointment he must fear is on her face.

He says, "I'm sorry," getting it over with. "About what I did. I'm sorry about what I did."

Lisa takes a swallow of beer. "I appreciate that, Abel. I do. So long as you mean it, that is. So you need to be honest here. What's our first rule?"

"No drugs," Abel says.

"And our second?"

"Always tell the truth."

"Just so. We might not have much but we're rich in that, and there's not much we can't get through so long as we keep things that way."

Abel thinks that over. He scratches his cast and then stops

to pull a filthy pencil out from the bottom near his thumb. If that's one of his tricks, Lisa thinks he's got better ones.

"I'm not sorry about Chris," he says, "because he's mean. Principal Rexrode says he's spoilt. That's as good a word as I can think. He's been mean to me the whole time I've been in school, and you know what's worse? Chris is the only kid who saw me. All the rest ignore me because a what I'm like. But I'm sorry I made you upset. I'm sorry I'm gonna get in trouble, even though Principal Rexrode says I shouldn't. He knows how Chris is."

"I know how Chris is," Lisa answers. "I known people like Chris Jones all my life. You think the kid versions are bad, wait till they grow up." She smiles, tries to anyway, and rubs his cast with her fingers. "There'll always be people like that hovering about, and it don't matter if you're healthy or not, rich or poor. You ain't the only one in the world's got to suffer through the days getting picked on and called names. Yes, I got upset. I still am, and that's being honest. But what got me riled isn't what you did to Chris, it was that all you really did was show a bully how much a bully *you* can be. Do you understand that?"

"Yes'm," he says.

"You're getting to be a man now, Abel. My man. Middle school's a tough time for any kid, and I don't want you to get lost along the way. You can grow to be kind or just turn sour, and at some point there's nothing I can do about it anyway. It'll be your choice. Light calls to light and dark to dark. It's an important time for you now. This is what will make you what you'll always be."

She thinks Abel would have preferred to just be punished than to hear something like this, though it needed saying. That look is in his eyes again, the same one he flashed while sitting in the principal's office. Offended.

He goes quiet awhile, staring at his cast, and doesn't even look up when the mockingbird calls again. Then he says, "Sometimes I can't take it anymore."

Lisa's son says this, her eleven-year-old boy. Her heart crumbles at the words. Not only because no child should ever be cursed with the sort of life that forces him to say such a thing, but because of the way he said it—with neither pity nor desperation, a mere statement of fact.

"What can't you take anymore?"

"Everything, I guess. Do people call you names because they used to think you hurt me?"

"What?"

"You said I'm not the only one gets called names."

"No," Lisa says, "not because of that."

"Then is it because I'm a bastard boy?"

"Don't you ever use that word."

"But I am," Abel says. "That's why they say stuff. Because you got a kid but ain't never been married."

"That's nobody's business. Man who was your daddy died, Abel. Nothing anybody can do about that."

"Yes'm," he says, though this time that mash-up of words doesn't sound so convincing.

"There's meatloaf and potatoes inside. Why don't you go on and eat, then get your good clothes."

"Where we going?"

She sighs and drains the last of her beer. "Punishment, I suppose. For us both. Charlie says there's revival over the hill. And not a word from you, please."

It looks as though Abel has plenty of words, though he keeps them to himself, except for the ones that say, "I'd rather not."

"Me neither. But unless you can do a trick to make a

few hundred dollars pop out of the air, I think we're gonna have to."

He says, "Maybe Dumb Willie'll be there."

"I don't doubt it. From what Charlie told me when I went by the school again, this is something Willie's folks would never pass up. Now get on. Food's getting cold, and we'll have to leave soon."

Abel stands with as much dignity as he can muster. He pauses at the door. "Momma?"

"Yes?"

"I wanted Principal Rexrode to punish me. Everybody acts like I ain't even alive. I did that to Chris because he'd always be mean to me if I didn't, and I did it so I'd get punished just like anybody else would. But Principal Rexrode didn't do anything. He says it's 'cause it's the last day, but that's a lie. I know you hate lying, Momma. I hate it too, and that's why I got so mad. Principal Rexrode won't let me be like the other kids at school on account he says I'm special."

"You are special," Lisa says, and wipes a tear.

PART II

REVIVAL

-1-

Trees numbering more than Abel can count crowd both sides of the road, blanking out a waning sun. Folk say night comes to the hill country long before town. To Abel, that's the appeal of these hidden hollers in the mountain's shadow. He can't see his momma's face, just her one hand on the wheel and the other hand smoothing the wrinkles in her Going Out dress, a faded blue jumper that once hugged her curves but now would slip off were it not for the straps sinking into her bony shoulders. She mutters to herself more than to him about how many cars there are, says it's like driving in a city instead of the country.

Abel sits still in fear of wrinkling his best jeans and a white oxford that he struggled to button himself all the way to the collar, looking out the window. The two of them have often come to the hill country on Sunday afternoons, the little car winding among ridges and meadows mostly forgotten but for those who call this place their own. For the scenery, Lisa will say, because fresh air and bright sun are good for Abel's bones. And yet their gaze will always linger more upon tiny homes that are barely livable and the near starving people in them than on the long view of the valley below, leaving Abel with the notion there is a higher purpose to the trips. Their drives to the hill country serve as reminders that the world holds people lower than themselves, and with troubles deeper and worse.

He sees the family in the car in front of them, how the man is looking through the rearview and saying something to the woman beside him; the kids in back, three of them, turn to stare. It's been like this since his momma fell in with the long line leading here from Mattingly. Abel knows what the town thinks of them, how they are still looked upon by some with suspicion. Not only because the man who was Abel's daddy died before his momma could marry him. Not even because most of Mattingly (and all of Mattingly's kids) view Abel's being born with soft insides the judgment of that sin.

Up ahead come the first of the signs. The name *Reverend Johnny Mills* is spray-painted on the side of a wooden pallet turned up on its end. A black arrow points upward. Abel supposes that means keep going straight and not that Reverend Johnny Mills is presently on his way heavenward.

"Don't sit there," his momma says, "sulking like that. This'll all be okay. I don't want to be here either, Abel. We just don't have a choice. So we'll make the most of it together, and you just do what I say when I say it. And be kind. Don't pay no mind to how anybody treats us. They mean well."

Mostly it's because they're unsaved that the Shiffletts are treated as different. Abel being a cripple is some and Lisa being an unwed momma is more, but neither amounts to much when set against the fact they are bound for hell. And Abel grants that he and his momma are never treated *badly*, except for when Chris Jones gets extra mean, or the customers at the diner skip out without leaving a tip, or when Mister Medford Hoskins raises the rent again. They are merely treated *different*, like everybody's keeping the same secret and Abel and his momma are the only ones who don't know.

He has long suspected it began for his momma the day she showed up in town with a baby but no husband. For him he knows it began in kindergarten, when his momma told Principal Rexrode she didn't feel it right to force her son into attending what's called Weekly Religious Education. *Let him make that choice*, she'd said, *when it's time*. And so once a week from then on, everyone in Abel's class walked out across the back lot to the little white trailer just off school grounds to learn about the glories of the Lord and the sins of man while Abel remained behind alone—first in his own empty classroom and then, from fourth grade until now, on one of the playground benches. The playground had been Principal Rexrode's idea. He said if Abel couldn't get any of the Son he'd at least get a little of the sun, and then he laughed. Abel hadn't understood how that was funny, but he'd gone along.

That's where he'd met Dumb Willie Farmer, right on that playground bench three years ago. Of course Abel had known *of* him. Everybody knew Dumb Willie because he helped the janitor and because he was so dumb, struck that way ever since he'd fallen from a wagon as a boy. It had been Dumb Willie's lunch break ("munch break" is what he called it) and he'd sat with Abel because Abel was alone and so was he. Abel hadn't minded the company, even though he'd had to put down his book and struggle through that first conversation. Talk turned to trains soon enough. Dumb Willie lived with his folks on the farm just beyond the patch of trees that made the dead end at Abel's road, so all the trains cut through Dumb Willie's place too. Turned out Dumb Willie loved trains near as much as Abel did, a fact that pleased Abel to no end.

And then had come the trick.

Miss Ellie had given Abel some of her sweet tea from home and dumped it into a Styrofoam cup that he'd taken out to the playground. By the eventual ebb in his conversation with Dumb Willie, that cup had been all but drained. Abel kept talking as he poked a hole into the back of the cup. He'd said, *Hey, watch this*, and then gripped both sides, easing his thumb into the hole and angling the cup upward, hands easing away from the sides now, making some small magic.

Dumb Willie had sat transfixed and pronounced it a miracle of the Lord. From then on, Abel had in his possession the very thing any boy of good sense longs for in his deepest heart—a fan.

They have been inseparable since. Dumb Willie sometimes came over in the evening for supper once his chores were done. Abel's momma made sure to bring extra food from the diner. They fished and skinny-dipped in the pond at the far edge of the woods. Dumb Willie would take Abel flying in the pastures, which was just about Abel's favorite thing, and Abel would visit Dumb Willie's house if he knew Henderson and Rita Farmer were gone. Those two were trouble. One time Lisa said some in town believe Dumb Willie didn't fall off that wagon at all, that Henderson beat his boy about the head instead, only there was never proof. Abel doesn't need proof to figure that's how it happened. Their meanness toward their son was apparent that first day on the playground when Dumb Willie offered Abel a bit of his lunch: half a bologna sandwich that had gone green, a few crackers, and a half-rotted apple. Abel believed then that Dumb Willie's folks were trying to murder him by starvation. He believes so still.

What they usually talked about was whatever Abel had learned that day and what the janitor had made Dumb Willie clean up—puke mostly, which Abel believed the most awful thing in the world but which Dumb Willie approached with neither a wince nor an ill word. He talked about God too. Abel would listen, trying to think of himself as special in the best way *special* meant, because all the kids in his class had to sit in some old moldy trailer to hear about What Comes After but *he* got to hear it out in the sunshine with the birds and the breeze.

Wasn't ever enough birds and breeze in the world for Abel to abide hearing too much of that, though—Dumb Willie going on about things no man (and certainly no man like him) could know. Sometimes when he got to going so hard that the words started mixing and spittle began raining from the corners of his mouth, Abel had to fight the urge to interrupt. Ask if God was the one who'd made him sick like he was because his momma lay with a man not her husband, or if God had been the one to whisper in Henderson Farmer's ear those years ago to beat his baby boy half to death and all the way senseless, so that the only future his son had was mopping up puke.

*

The signs begin to change about the time Abel's ears begin popping. At the fork in the road his momma veers right, following the long line of cars toward a soft ridge in the distance.

Reverend Johnny Mills and his arrow are replaced by phrases Abel takes as from the Bible, reminders that all things are possible so long as you put away all logic for a minute. A wide meadow opens up ahead to the left. Here, all the vehicles pull in like a herd of cattle setting to graze.

Lisa chooses a spot in the middle rather than along the edge. When Abel looks at her, she says, "People got to see us here, Abel. They got to see us plain."

The folk who pour forth mix with those already arrived, old ones and young and the not-quite-either, people Abel knows from town and many more he's never seen. A few look healthy and prime. Most either are hobbled or appear to be standing in death's reaching shadow. All are adorned in their finest, whether new suits and dresses off the rack or thread-bare clothes that have seen too many Sunday services and Monday burials. And everyone, even those Abel takes as the most feeble and lame, is smiling. It's as if they already believe themselves in the grip of a miracle.

Lisa turns the key, letting the engine die slow. People are staring. Abel sees Sheriff Barnett and his family, Mister Givens from the market, and the Fretwells from the pharmacy. He even sees Dorothea Cash, so old she hardly ever comes out of her house anymore and so broken of mind that all she wants to tell folk is how time is a circle. She's walking with a woman Abel knows is a preacher in town but can't remember her name.

"All these people are poor," he says.

"That's all the hill country is, and about all of town. Why they're here. Every poor family needs a God they think can save them, or at least One they can blame for their troubles."

"That why we're here?" He looks at his momma, panic flashing over him. "You ain't gonna find Jesus, are you?"

It's not a smile that spreads on his momma's face but close, that pretty grin that wakes him every morning and leaves him at every good-night.

"We ain't here looking for the Lord, Abel. We just need the ones think they already found Him. And the only Jesus I know's the little Mexican that Roy lets clean up after the diner closes. Now, let's get on, before I tuck tail and run back home."

He gets out of the car and meets the sweet scents of unspoiled earth, pine and honeysuckle and greening grass and all things good. Abel has come here unwillingly, accompanied by his own prejudices. And yet here is the first sign that all of those judgments should perhaps be laid aside, because this place smells of possibility. He draws in his misshapen chest as far as it can manage, wanting to breathe that air, but is set upon before he can manage it.

*

It's as though the pious turn as one in that single span of time and notice the two heathens among them. Those from town and those not descend upon Abel's momma. Welcoming her, grinning as they enfold Lisa into their arms like some reclaimed wayward child. For once, Abel finds invisibility a blessing rather than a curse. He makes himself even smaller and crouches down between his momma's feet as Sheriff Barnett and Darnell Givens gape in a mix of shock and elation. Even the strangers seem attuned to the notion that Abel and his momma are fruit ripe for the harvest, as if the two of them have arrived bearing the mark of the lost upon them, visible only to the found. It frightens Abel, all these smiles. This onslaught of love.

He crouches deeper as Lisa places her hands on his shoulders and eases him up. Her words crack with strain—"We just felt led to be here"—and yet the effect on the others is instant. Darnell even speaks an "Amen," like what Lisa said was a kind of prayer.

At the meadow's edge waits a wide trail of grass worn to dirt. Where it snakes off is the largest sign yet, near billboard-size, tied to the side of a rusting cattle hauler: the smiling face of Reverend Johnny Mills looking down on them all. Abel follows his momma, the two of them the center of a circle made of chatter and high hopes. The trail ends a few hundred feet on at a faded red barn so tall that it looks to scrape the sky. Dozens stand here, what looks like hundreds. The chattering of their little group yields to the steady buzz of the greater throng, all of whom walk or sway or merely move their feet in place, as though the building excitement is too great for them to hold steady. Gone is the quiet peace of the meadow. Here at the barn the air feels like coming thunder, the way it does just before a train rumbles by, when the crickets and the summer birds pause for a song greater than their own.

Even the barn itself appears a living thing, pulsing with some inward light of life that fills the gaps between the boards. The long front doors are shut. Those nearest press their faces against the chipped wood before turning to speak in high tones. Those behind then turn to repeat what they've heard like ripples in a pond of flesh.

A pudgy, milk-colored hand shoots up from the middle of the crowd. It moves toward the place where Abel and his momma stand, weaving among shoulders and heads until it grows shoulders and a head of its own. Principal Rexrode beams as he breaks through to the outer ring of worshipers.

The hand he raised upward now flattens into an embrace. Of Lisa first, now Abel.

"I'm so happy y'all come," he says. "So very happy."

Abel feels a poke at his shoulder.

"We just felt led to be here," he says.

Lisa says, "Abel's right, Charlie. You showed us a kindness this afternoon. We're glad to be here. After what you said, I thought it best. About that foundation. Isn't that right, Abel?"

But Abel can't answer. He looks up and can't hide the hurt in his eyes, his tongue tied in a knot because of what his momma said. This is why they've come? Not for punishment, but because of the grievous state to which his heart has sunk?

Another poke.

"Yes'm," he manages. "That's so."

Principal Rexrode smiles with every one of his teeth. "What kindness I show you is only due to the kindness given me, Lisa. But I appreciate it. Y'all in for a treat, I promise it. Rev'rend Johnny Mills is a name that's moved all along these parts. Man's touched by the Spirit. He's a genuine healer."

"Healer?" Abel asks.

"That's right, son. You'll see miracles tonight. I can feel it."

Abel's momma won't look at him. She's saying, "Well that's just fine, Charlie. Do you know how many other pastors are here tonight? I'd truly like . . . ," but Abel doesn't care. All he wants is to run back to the car and hide because his momma didn't bring him here for a foundation. She's brought him here for *healing*, that's how bad things have gotten.

He decides he will do just that, hide in the car and lock the doors until it's all over, but before Abel can move he hears his name called somewhere among the midst of the truth seekers. He stands to the tips of his shoes to find the face. His name carries again, stilted and mush-mouthed, as if the two syllables and four letters have been pulled from a sea of slobber in the last seconds before drowning. The giant who steps forth wears BibAlls too short for his long frame. A white T-shirt (his finest, even with the tear on the right sleeve) flaps in the mountain breeze like clipped wings that can no longer fly. His scalp is bald but for the thinnest layer of auburn, slick with a sheen of sweat that coats his entire head in a glow not unlike the one seeping through the barn's walls. His voice booms, "A. Bull, A. Bull," as those big arms wave.

Lisa remains in deep conversation with Principal Rexrode concerning the ecclesiastical makeup of the gathered, and so Abel feels fine in shrugging himself from her grasp.

"Dumb Willie's here," he says.

"Go on," she tells him.

The big man keeps calling, repeating Abel's name and then his own with such fervor that those closest pause in their anticipation. They stare as the huge man stands in a kind of wonder, the way he most often does. Dumb Willie reaches down and grips the sides of Abel's bony arms, lifting him, careful of the cast and those bones either broken or never truly whole. He never bends in Abel's presence, choosing instead to raise Abel to his own height—an act born merely of a simple mind, yet one Abel has always regarded as an act of respect.

"A. Bull."

"Hey, Dumb Willie."

The big man turns Abel in the air, gauging his sides and back as though a slab of beef. "I din't know you'd be. *Here.*"

"Momma brung me," Abel says. "It's a punishment. Or a judgment. Or a wish-upon-a-star."

"Naw it'sa. *Preecher.* Inna barn."

"I know. Where's your folks?"

"Here."

Dumb Willie offers nothing in the way of specificity, leaving Abel with no direction to look. Yet he feels Henderson and Rita Farmer's presence nonetheless, in the same way one feels the only black cloud in an otherwise empty sky. Dumb Willie would never be this far from home alone. He is twenty, some say. Others say closer to twenty-five, though only in body. In mind Dumb Willie will never get much past the first grade, which means of course his folks are close and of course they'd bring Dumb Willie up here. Having a "healer" (Abel can't help but put quotes around the word) this close must seem an answered prayer. It's only too bad that Henderson and Rita would come seeking a remedy for their boy and not themselves.

"You gone. *Come?*"

"Don't see as I got a say," Abel answers. "I guess Momma's flustered at what I done to Chris. Or disgusted. Both, I guess. She thinks my heart could get bad. You can put me down, Dumb Willie. Everybody's staring."

Dumb Willie says, "Chris. *Stunk*," with a seriousness that brings Abel a grin.

"I know. Sorry you had to clean all that up."

"It'sa *preecher*. In 'ere. Da'ee say he can make me . . ." He stops, gritting his teeth. "*Healed.*"

"Ain't nothing in there heal you, Dumb Willie. 'Sides, I think you're fine."

"He can make. *You* fine."

Abel looks over his shoulder to where his momma stands, still talking to Principal Rexrode. "I don't believe none a that stuff," he says. "That ain't no magic, that's just tricks. I seen the train this afternoon. You hear it?"

"Yeah."

"Know how many cars there were? I counted. Guess how many?" He leans up and in, wanting to whisper because that would bring greater effect, even if it does sound like a dying frog: "A hundred."

Dumb Willie blows the air from his mouth. A brief shower of saliva pelts Abel's shoes.

"I ain't never seen a hundred, Dumb Willie. Not in my whole life. It scared me. I think something's gonna happen."

"What gone. *Happen?*"

"I don't know," Abel says. "Hey, Dumb Willie, let's fly. You wanna?"

He picks Abel up again, to eye level like before and then on up, high over Dumb Willie's head. Abel settles his legs around a neck of pure muscle and grabs hold of Dumb Willie's ears, careful not to tug on them too tight.

"Ready?" he calls.

"Rey. Dee."

Abel uses the fingers of his good arm to poke at Dumb Willie's head, pushing imaginary buttons to work the flaps and throttle. Then he turns to a random farmer beside them and snaps a salute.

"Take off!" he screams.

Dumb Willie does. He beats a path through the crowd, running full-bore, weaving among awestruck children and adults driven to silence, old men and older women who grin through tobacco-stained teeth. Faster and faster, Dumb Willie gripping Abel's ankles (not too hard) and Abel steering with a tug on one giant ear and then the next, himself taller than anyone, heads above the rest. Watching his momma grinning and Principal Rexrode mouthing, *Not too fast, too fast,* but Abel wanting Dumb Willie to go even faster because this is what flying must feel like, *real* flying, and this is as close to that as Abel will ever manage.

Dumb Willie slows and then stops, his breath no more strained than if he were sitting on a porch and snapping beans. Abel tries one ear, then the other. Pushes more buttons.

"What's matter, Dumb Willie? I think we stalled."

Dumb Willie says, "It's the. *Time*."

He maneuvers Abel toward the big barn doors easing open, creating a rush of moving bodies and raised voices. A man steps out and closes the doors again before anyone can get a peek inside. His white suit has gone tan with sweat, his cheeks rosy from the heat. He grins through two rows of brown teeth.

"Friends," he calls, "brothers and sisters. Y'all hush up now and look this way. There in the back. Y'all hear me?"

He waits for a wave of "Yessirs" and "Uh-huhs" before smiling again.

"Now that's fine. Friends who don't know me, I'm the Reverend Earl Thomas Keen, pastor at the Trinity Gospel Assembly of the Redeemer, off State Road 33. Me and my fellow pastors is who organized tonight's meeting, which we promise will be a blessing to your souls and a balm to what weariness brought you here. Let me tell you we all met the man inside, the one you come to see. We spoke to'm, prayed with'm, and I for one can say outright that this man is a true soldier of the everlasting God and one touched by the power of Christ Hisself."

A cheer rises, a chorus of "Amens" as the crowd pushes forward. The Reverend Earl Thomas Keen holds his Bible as a shield. He drives them back with a polite wave and a plea to just hang on.

When the noise subsides, Dumb Willie shouts, "A. *Men*."

"Yes," the preacher says, "amen and praise God." He settles his tone from joyous to near grave, marking the reality of what is to come. "There will be miracles tonight, friends. There will be signs. And there will be wonders fit to wrench the devil hisself from what hold he has upon you. Don't you doubt it."

Now the smile again. Abel has never seen such grinning folk. Nor has he ever known such a man as this Preacher Keen, whose presence commands respect but whose voice carries the soothing lilt of the men who knock at the Shiffletts' door sometimes in the evenings, peddling their wares. He half expects to hear next *How many you good people suffer under the aggravation of stained carpet?*

Instead, the preacher steps aside as the barn bursts to music, piano and banjo and tambourine. The tune is foreign to Abel but not to the rest, not even Dumb Willie, who begins swaying to the melody. Abel turns to find his momma attempting to match Principal Rexrode's rhythms. Abel alone remains still—ignored as always, only this time among a crowd of marionettes whose every movement is surrendered to something perceived as greater.

"You'll find a bucket just inside," Preacher Keen says. "Have your love offering at the ready. For the infirmed and the troubled, there are prayer cards available. Please state your needs plain and deposit them at the altar."

With that, Preacher Keen turns and slides open the heavy doors. They rattle and squeak and pierce the air like a sinner's cry. The gathered rush forward. They enter with their ones and fives at the ready and even the occasional ten, the bills folded and placed into a metal pail hung at the end of a rusting screw, a pail already filling. Beside are stacked plain strips of paper and the sort of pencils that Abel uses to count his trains. They are snatched and the papers scribbled upon and folded.

A voice calls Dumb Willie's name. Henderson Farmer stands at the door beside Rita. Both have chosen black clothing for the occasion, both stare from eyes that seem dead things full of hate set deep in their gaunt, expressionless faces. It is a look Abel has seen upon many of Mattingly's farm folk, who dig and reap what hard life they can from ground even harder. Yet there is something even more unforgiving than the soil in the way Dumb Willie's parents carry themselves, something that never sows and yet reaps and reaps still.

Dumb Willie lowers Abel to the ground, laughing. "It'sa *preecher*," he calls, then goes after them.

A hand comes to rest on Abel's shoulder. He kisses it by memory, lips tasting his momma's cracked fingers.

"Come on now," she whispers.

Principal Rexrode ushers them inside. A new melody erupts, hands clap, praises to the Lord. Abel watches his momma pass by the overflowing pail without adding a tithe of her own. All she offers the Lord this night is what she scrawls on a prayer slip that she folds in half so Abel can't see. He waits, alone and forgotten, as she walks toward the altar.

-2-

He stands silent and still in a darkened corner that keeps himself hid but all else visible. It is a wonder, this barn. When the Preacher Keen first reached out to him (that is the way things go now, the name Johnny Mills is big enough that preachers call upon him rather than the reverse) and said Mattingly's hill country needed a dose of the Lord, the invitation was nearly rejected. Nearly. There were too many other towns weighed under by the same need, Spirit-starved people long on hurt and short on hope. And yet something— the Lord, perhaps—said, *You go on up there, Johnny. I might show you something never been seen before*, so Johnny did. Met the Preacher Keen right here at this barn not four days back, Keen saying this was a place of some renown in the town's history. Johnny had only grinned at that phrasing, him knowing a thing or two about renown. And yet when the Preacher Keen had slid open those big double doors, Johnny's doubt gave way. There was power here, sure enough.

Now this place looks even more transcendent. More *magical*, if Johnny allows the word. Preacher Keen and his flock have taken great care to bring not only the Lord here but a whole mess of the wanting. Lanterns hang high in the rafters and along the walls. A stage, wide and long, though not far from the floor, has been erected along the back. The floor itself has been swept clean, the old tractor and an assortment of forgotten tools and equipment moved out, leaving only an empty expanse of wood boards that have mostly survived the years. Reverend Johnny breathes deep, giving himself over to anticipation as the people stream inside.

Benches have been set from the front of the stage all the way to the doors, a dozen long rows to one side and a dozen more to the other, placed at a V to create a wide aisle down the middle just as Reverend Johnny has asked. Two narrower aisles are spread along the sides. Even now the people come in limping, struggling up these aisles, but they will go out dancing. Oh yes, they will. They will dance all the way back to their poor and forsaken lives, and they will never forget this night. This will be more than a full house, this will be a *happening*.

The bustle and music provide the power, Reverend Johnny the current. He does not know the players on the stage. Some of Preacher Keen's flock, decent people from the small time they spoke before the service. And they are slick to a person. The old man whaling on the piano sits unmoved on the bench, yet his hands fly over the keys as though possessed. A young woman on the banjo stands in front of him, fingers wild at the strings. Beside her dances a boy trying to shake the life out of a tambourine.

Reverend Johnny casts an eye toward the front and the overflowing pail hanging by a rusted nail to the right side of the barn doors. A long line of people snakes toward the foot of the stage, bearing slips of paper in trembling hands. Each is deposited in a large wicker basket that has seen nearly as many miles as the man who owns it. A youngish woman comes forward in a faded blue jumper. She does not mingle with the others, nor does she possess any of their fervency, tossing rather than placing her slip into the pile. A pretty woman, Johnny believes, at least once upon'a. She drifts away into the sea of moving bodies and disappears.

Those still outside struggle in and arrange themselves into the makeshift pews as if by some secret design. None sit. They rather dance, driven to near frenzy by the fast beat of the old mountain hymns and the glow of the lantern light and their own singing, forgetting both sense and inhibition. Johnny smiles in his corner of darkness. He praises the Lord who has brought him to this place, to what is no longer a gathering of individuals but a single, mad organism with a multitude of arms and legs and voices that cry out in a praise as sorrowed as it is rapturous, singing and singing as the piano plays and the banjo thrums and the tambourine boy skips from one end of the stage to the other.

He nods at Preacher Keen, standing close but in the light. The holy man from the hills then retrieves the basket of papers and places it at Johnny's feet.

"You brung the Spirit here tonight, Rev'rend Johnny," he says.

Johnny smiles. "Yessir, believe I did."

Preacher Keen smiles and moves away, up the stage as the music fades only a little. His voice is raised above all others even without the benefit of a microphone. Leading them, inspiring them as soldiers to battle. Johnny begins sifting through the untold dozens of papers, reading an endless collection of names and ill conditions. He tries to find the slip placed there by the woman in the blue dress, wondering why he should.

Now comes a collective "Amen!" that shakes the barn's very walls. Johnny looks up to see Preacher Keen ready, arms held out. It is time.

The Reverend Johnny Mills steps onto the stage, beaming as the crowd drinks him in. He is younger than the pictures on the signs, clad in faded jeans and a white oxford shirt, brown cowboy boots scuffed at the toes. His hair, as black as a crow's eye, is slicked back from a widow's peak. He yells a "Hallelujah!" and dances a jig across the stage that whips up the people even more. He feels it, this power. This thing he does. This life that allows him to visit the far-flung and hidden places of the world, that lets him stand here as if he owns this stage and this barn and every soul inside it.

"Amen," he shouts, and Johnny Mills is amenned back with a force that parts his lips. "I feel the *Lord* here tonight," and they cheer and stomp. "I feel'm, knew I would, Him'n me travel all over these mountains as one, friends, *one*, and don't you think the two us is here this night by chance's decree.

Nosir, don't y'all think that for a seccent. Was your *faith* brought us here."

The roar bursts forth.

"Lord's gone with me all over this country, once so blessed but now so in need. And He has touched me, friends. Oh yes. He has given me a holy gift of healing, of peering into the very darkness that haunts the souls of men and shining a light into that deep night. I have healed, brothers and sisters. The sick are made well by the power given me. The lame walk upright and free. I have hurled out demons who dare stake claim to what is rightly the Almighty's alone. I have stared into the devil's very eye and told him he has no claim *here*."

Stomping. Stomping their church heels and their farming boots, stomping in shoes worn to tatters and ones handed down and ones stuffed with old newspapers or bound by duct tape to keep them on. Johnny Mills—Reverend—feels this noise in his teeth.

"Now your Preacher Keen here, he's a fine man."

"Amen," they cheer, making Preacher Keen both blush and puff his narrow chest.

"Preacher Keen called me out, said Lord's leanin' heavy on his heart askin' me to come. He says to me there's a flock of good believin' folk down here in Mattingly."

"*Yes!*"

"Folk who live right and do good and love the Lord with all they heart, and I know that's true."

"*Amen.*"

"But he says to me, 'It's a hard life here, Reverend Johnny. Terrible hard. Some a us is afflicted and poor in spirit, and what we got to have here's a little'"—his foot taps at the stage—"'*charge.*'"

"*Yessir.*"

"Gotta get us some . . . *powah.*"

"*Yessir, that's right.*"

"Need a dose a the"—he dances again, shifting across the stage as if riding a cloud—"*Spirit.*"

"*Yes!*"

"GottagetaWORDfromtheLawd."

Voices raised, hands and heads and eyes.

"What y'all need here, brothers and sisters," Reverend Johnny says,

("*Yesyesyes!*")

"is a *miracle.*"

The piano takes off, banjo and tambourine, and there rises such a holler that Johnny Mills feels the air stolen. He dances arm in arm with God Himself, calling down Jesus and the Holy Spirit and all that great and powerful heavenly host, and Reverend Johnny shouts, "*I need hands, good people. Let me see who will witness the miracle of God in this holy place.*"

Johnny finds his first of the night as the air fills with hands raised high. He says, "Come on up, don't you be shy, go on and let them good folks help you." The crowd strains toward the two men and one woman helping an old man to his feet. His skin is the color of dried leather, cracked by the sun and as dirt-stained as his shirt and jeans. A Mountain Dew ball cap rests cockeyed on his head. Those with him (family, Johnny supposes, given the resemblance) struggle getting him to the walker near his seat. They struggle more to get up the two short steps onto the stage. His back has gone bent from years in unforgiving fields, giving the impression that here is a man who began with nothing and has since managed to hang on to most of it. Reverend Johnny coaxes him forward. He waves the old man up as the crowd cheers and sings and then points to a spot on the stage, a circle in the wood only he can see. This is the spot where they'll stand tonight.

"Right here," he calls. "Right here by me, friend."

The old man takes the walker and leans forward, face red and straining, and makes the few steps to where Johnny stands as though scaling a mountain.

"Yessir," Johnny says. "Yessir, that's fine. What's your name, brother?"

The old man gives it—Rogers. Lewis Rogers. "Back's gone," he says, in case there is some doubt as to what ails him. "Can't abide the pain no more. I've gone cripple."

"A hard life," Johnny says. He says this often, more times than he can count, and every time true. He lowers his voice, though not enough to render those in the back deaf: "Lord brought you to me, Lewis. You believe that?"

Lewis nods.

"Do you have faith, Lewis?"

"I'm a farmer, Rev'rend. Faith's 'bout all I got."

The crowd chuckles—knowing laughs.

"Amen, brother. And do you know the Lord and Savior Jesus Christ, Lewis? Do you believe He came to die for you and was raised up on the third day? And do you hold as truth that the Lord God claims dominion over the powers and principalities of this world, the demons of death and sickness and wearied backs?"

"Yessir," Lewis says. And louder, "Yessir, I do."

"Then Brother Lewis Rogers, I call down the *Spirit* upon you."

Johnny reaches out with the fingers of his right hand. It is this moment that always seems to slow in his mind, even if to everyone else it resembles the strike of a copperhead—fast, lightning fast, seen more as a blur of many movements than a single act. And yet it is this act by which his livelihood is earned, one that promises either success or failure in a span more brief than an eye's blink, and he knows even as his fingers near the sun-soaked skin of Lewis Rogers's forehead that he must believe. Oh yes, Reverend Johnny must. Faith is required by those for whom he heals, but that faith pales against what is required of himself.

"Be *heeaalled*," he screams. Demands it, and then he touches a spot just below the farmer's cap.

The crowd gasps. Lewis jolts as though stung. He screams out (it is fear, Johnny knows, and there is never a more welcome sound) and stumbles backward, letting go of the walker's worn handles. Propelled away not by a shove of Reverend Johnny's hand but by the brief yet brilliant flash of light from the tips of his fingers.

Lewis stands dumbfounded. He rubs the spot above his brow and stares at his hands. Now his feet. Now he realizes he is standing higher than he must have managed in years. His arms and back are straight, hips in line with his shoulders. And when his gaze meets that old walker cast off and a grinning Reverend Johnny half the stage away, Lewis Rogers begins to weep. He begins to weep and then to dance.

Every voice shouts. Lewis raises his hands in praise to heaven and runs—oh yes, he *runs*—to embrace his healer. He poses for a picture taken to mark this momentous occasion, healer and healed, which Reverend Johnny says will be available after the service for a small love offering. Lewis's last act before leaving the stage is to offer a swift kick to the walker, sending it tumbling and the crowd into a frenzy.

Johnny calls others. He summons a woman laid barren and touches her stomach, the flash of light against her womb kindling more than tears, but hope. He heals a young man of asthma and a girl of fever. Cures are passed to both present folk and those who could not make the journey, sending their sons and daughters in their stead. Pictures and pictures, more pictures. And in between the healings come what Johnny Mills has branded miracles even greater called his *words from the Lord*—messages of comfort spoken via direct line from the One who knows all to those Reverend Johnny has never met, those stricken by secret hurts never uttered, longing for peace. He casts out demons and disease by calling upon the Lord of light, moving his hands with such swiftness that they defy imagination. He punctures the skin of the afflicted with his fingers alone—that holy light—leaving their sides and arms and scalps bloodied and his own hands filled with the gore and entrails of the wounded demons he casts back to hell. He makes strong women wail like babies and imbues frail men with courage. He makes them all swoon, slain in the Spirit.

And as full dark takes hold on that lonely ridgetop, Reverend Johnny begins to feel his hold fade. He calls forth a final healing and says he can do no more. Power from heaven is inexhaustible, yet the bones of men are weak. Voices call out, begging. A man in a black suit stands, waving his arms as if drowning. He lifts the arms of the one beside him, a boy no older than twenty whose body swells with muscle. Johnny looks away when he sees that boy's eyes, empty and without knowledge, and his dummy's grin. Scanning the crowd, searching for one who will set folk to talking not only for this night but for always.

A boy who appears no older than seven steps into the wide middle aisle. He holds a broken right arm aloft. Yet what centers Johnny's attention is not the bright yellow cast but the woman reaching to draw the boy back. It is the almost pretty one, the lady in the blue jumper. The boy sidesteps her grasp. Johnny's vision begins to tunnel, all the clamoring and wailing of his name reduced to dull wind.

This one. This one will be the last.

Then Johnny's eyes shift from that hardened cast held high to the soft and weakened body beneath—as dumb as the idiot's grin across the room, only different.

A shame, Reverend Johnny Mills thinks. Children are always best healed and most received. Though near children are the old, who are sometimes even more believed. That is his comfort as he calls the last wounded soul of the night to join him upon the stage, an elderly woman whose arthritis has maimed her such that she can no longer care for her grandbabies, and she's all the momma and daddy they got.

-3-

It looks the same tired world that greets Abel as his momma leads him out. All that seems changed are those who go out with them. He sees it first in the way the congregation turns in unison after Reverend Johnny releases them and Preacher Keen offers his final prayer. Like they've all decided with a common mind that what trials and troubles they carried up the trail to this barn can now be carried back down in joy thanks to the mystery they have witnessed. They leave their benches in a coordinated dance, silent but glad. Tired, though in the way that makes you feel like working awhile more instead of lying down. He has never felt the same as everyone else. In this instance, Abel has never felt more alone.

A few storm the path leading to the meadow and the better life they believe waits. Many more linger to embrace and shake hands as they talk in the glow of the lanterns. And here beneath a crescent moon and a sky bursting in stars, Abel learns his final task of the night.

His momma stops him midway between the barn and the head of the trail. Slicks back Abel's hair—a thing she never does—and straightens his collar. "Need you to stand right here, okay? I'll be back in a bit. We're almost done."

"Where you going?"

"Talk to some people. Don't you mind."

"You gonna go find Reverend Johnny?" he asks. "I don't think he'll make me better, Momma. I don't even think he wants to."

A group of women near the door burst into song, still overcome:

Well, some come crippled and some come quick;
There's a higher power.
Till the healin's done, we ought not quit;
There's a higher power.

He feels his momma's hands at the nape of his neck, her lips on his head.

"Sweet boy," Lisa says. "Now stay here. How's your arm?"

"Fine." And it is. Strange enough, Abel's arm hasn't hurt all night.

"Good. But now I need you to do me a favor, and I need you to not look at me sad when I ask it."

"What?"

"Just for the next little bit, act like your arm's killing you fierce."

She pecks his head again and leaves, winding her way toward the glows and the happy folk, most of whom Abel does not know yet has decided to mildly hate. The women keep to their singing *(You'd better let signs follow you around;*

There's a higher power) as others drift by without a pause to notice him there. His momma is talking to the Preacher Keen. There's Dumb Willie, walking away from the barn with that hag he calls his ma. Abel steps aside and deeper into the night as they pass, not wanting to speak because Rita looks too mad. Trailing behind is Henderson, head low, the third of that ruined family. The way the lanterns strike his black suit make him appear to wink in and out of existence. Abel turns his eyes downward, thinking as a child would—*If I don't see him, he can't see me.*

"You doin' here, boy?"

Henderson Farmer is not old but looks it, with the same leathered skin as the old man Reverend Johnny made walk and two eyes that look like a snake's, half shut, like he's considering things. His every word drips with equal handfuls of hate and hurt with little regard for the ears of those who must hear them—Abel's most of all. For that, Abel has long avoided crossing Henderson's path. It matters not the man's meanness is couched in phrases like *Lord willin'* and *Blessed be* in order to keep his good Christian name to those townsfolk he sees as customers. To Abel, Henderson's mouth always sounds the way venom would feel.

"Momma brung me." Abel looks to where his momma last stood. Now she's talking with the preacher woman from town. "I don't know why. Guess she wanted to get me healin'."

"Healin'," Henderson says, then spits on the ground. "That man seen Dumb Willie. Looked right at'm. Did he call *us* up? Give us some . . . *mir'cle?*" He spits again, like the word tasted bad coming out. "Only mir'cles you get in this life's the ones you go after on your own."

Abel doesn't think about Dumb Willie or Henderson, how they raised their arms to get called for the night's last healing. He's thinking only of himself. How he and his momma had gone in there thinking this was a gathering of fools looking for a God to blame. And though he knows his momma has altered none of her mind on that, a part of Abel admits a bit of his own doubt slipped when that old farmer man got changed. It was that flash—that spark of light from Reverend Johnny's fingers. Abel's never seen a thing like that, never thought it possible. And though his momma had only chuckled as all the rest praised, saying, *That's all just a trick, Abel, no different from the ones you do yourself,* her boy wondered. He wondered enough to step out into the aisle, if only on the hope that someone would see him. And Reverend Johnny Mills had. He'd seen Abel and yet turned away.

"Maybe Reverend Johnny just got tired is all," Abel says.

"That man don't know tired, boy. Don't know trial. Don't know what we go through ever' day."

"You mean Dumb Willie?"

"Gives a *damn* about Dumb *Willie*," Henderson says. "I mean *me*. Raisin' up a child got a man's body and don't know his head from a hole in the ground. That boy's an evil. Stains our good name."

"He ain't evil, Mister Farmer."

"You shut up." Henderson raises his hand, making Abel jump, then lowers it. Wouldn't be good for business, striking a boy in front of Christians. Stain his good name. "Oughta smack you for talkin' to things you don't know. You ever had a daddy, you'd know better. Dumb Willie's a curse. It's a monster inside'm. Anybody knows that, should be you."

"You don't mean that."

"Shut up," he says again. Then softer and tired, like he's got no strength left in him to speak a threat: "You shut your little bastard mouth."

Henderson walks off, muttering to himself. Far down the path, Abel can hear Dumb Willie's crooning. More folks pass. The crowd in front of the barn begins to thin as Lisa re-appears. She glances around as though embarrassed and shoves a wad of money into Abel's hands.

"Stick this in your pocket," she says.

"What's it for?"

"Us," she answers, and when she takes in his eyes she says, "Don't think bad of me, Abel. Please. I didn't make as much today as I should've. Darnell's glad to see us up here, but not so much he'll forgive our debt at the market. That hill preacher didn't have much, but the lady one from town handed over a dozen coffeepots worth of tips." She grins. "Guess all these people were right. Miracles happen."

Abel can't decide which is worse, that his momma is depraving herself or that he is the cause.

"What'd that Henderson Farmer want?"

"I don't know," Abel tells her. "Nothing."

"Well, you stay here, there's one more preacher I want to talk to. Don't know if he's got much charity to give, but he's staring. You hang on to that money, Abel. I can't let'm see I already been given to or I'll look greedy. And you hang on to it tight, or this whole sorry night'll count for nothing."

"Yes'm."

"Good, then." Lisa squeezes Abel's good arm (not too hard) and smiles before swaying off in her blue jumper. She turns back when he calls.

"Do you wish I was healed?"

"Nothing would make me happier. Stay here now. Toots love."

"Toots love," Abel says.

He remains in place more from shame than obedience.

His right arm is throbbing now. Reverend Johnny sticks his head out from the barn door and inches his way toward the side, where he disappears around the corner. No one—not even the singing women—sees.

It's a trick, Abel thinks. *All of it.* The healings, that flash. He's seen no miracles this night, only weakened people who expected such because they believed themselves deserving of it. Folk will believe most anything they think can help. Or heal. But still.

But still.

He watches the darkness at the corner of the barn, wonders what's there.

Lisa is talking to a man holding a Bible in one hand and her fingers in the other. She's smiling.

You stay here, she said, but Abel moves anyway. He has always done his best to obey and be no more a burden than he must. Yet now, this night, he decides that burden is one that must be shared. His momma shouldn't be the only one who must beg.

Besides, the only miracles you get in this life are the ones you go after on your own.

*

There is no dark like country dark, and that is the sort Abel finds around the side of the barn. The trees grow thick here and close, swallowing the sky above and the voices out front. What glow is cast by the lantern light fades. There is no path.

He scoots his feet along the uneven ground rather than raising them so as not to stumble. A hint of what may be a man's cologne hangs in the thick air, sweet and damp and woody. Abel passes this off as another of the mountain's aromas instead, believing the scent too pure to be bottled. No sign of Reverend Johnny. It is as if the traveling preacher has vanished, returning to the very strangeness from which he emerged. For not the first time this night, Abel ponders what in fact he is doing, what it is exactly he wants. He decides it is proof, nothing more. Proof of Reverend Johnny and maybe, maybe, a chance to learn.

The first trick ever taught to Abel came out of a library book. *One Hundred and One Magic Tricks for Boys* was the title, plucked from a shelf on a whim by his momma. It took him over a month (which seems a year when you're only seven) to learn how to make a quarter disappear well enough to shock Lisa to a yelp, but that shock and yelp were enough to hook Abel since. It isn't so much that he *believes* in magic, just that he *does* it. That he imparts only for a moment, long enough to turn a trick, the sheer notion of possibility in the hopes that he, too, may be reminded of its fact. That things aren't always what they seem and that life, the world, everything, is not as dull and gray as he sometimes fears. It is a belief he has never been capable of putting to words but has always felt—that the unseen fringes of all he sees are laid in bright and flowing hues and sometimes those hues leak to the center, not giving new life but rendering the life already there somehow *more*.

That, he thinks, is what happened tonight inside that barn. In the end, that's all magic really is: a shot of color into a dying world.

He runs his left hand along the barn's outer wall, afraid that if he loses hold he will be lost forever in deep woods. Time and place warp with no means of direction. Each shuffle brings him a step farther into the unknown. It is as if Abel makes his way not from one side of the barn to the other but from this world to another hidden alongside, leaving his mind to quarrel with his heart. One shouts, *Turn back*, the other, *Push on*, his desperation caught in the middle.

The wall ends at an abrupt right angle, leaving Abel to grope for it in panic. Here the trees yield to a wide field bathed in the faint light of moon and stars, tall grass rustling as though hiding some unseen army. A lone whip-poor-will calls from the bank of trees at the far edge—what Abel takes as the only living thing here other than himself until he spots the rusting sedan parked against the back of the barn. Both the trunk and the driver's door are open, leaving the dome light to surround the few feet around it in dull amber. Reverend Johnny is there, loading bags into the back. He slams the trunk and sighs hard as he leans against the bumper. Abel hears a clicking sound. Sees a flash, not like the others, spark in Reverend Johnny's hand, smoke rising like a prayer's ghost. His other hand holds a wad of cash he sets to counting.

Abel steps out from the side of the barn. Turns back. Steps out again. He speaks with as much force as his lungs will allow before fear can win him again, hoping the squeak can carry this distance between them:

"Excuse me, sir."

Reverend Johnny jumps so quick that his cigarette goes flying into a bit of trampled grass. The money disappears into his pocket. "Who's 'at?"

"It's me," Abel says. "Abel Shifflett? I seen your show."

The preacher looks to relax, though only some. He picks up his smoke from the edge of the dome light's arc, puffs twice, then snuffs it under his shoe. "You liked to scare me to death, boy. What you doing back here?"

"I seen you leave. You snuck, but I seen you."

"Then you got good eyes." He leans right and left, peering

into the black spaces behind where Abel stands. "Anybody there with you?"

"Nosir. My momma's around front selling her soul. I did something bad."

"And your daddy?"

Abel shrugs. He doesn't think Reverend Johnny can see. "My daddy's dead."

"Well then, maybe you should go keep an eye to your momma, Abel Shifflett. Service is over. All my healin's done."

"How'd you do all those tricks in there?"

"Tricks?" Reverend Johnny steps forward, easing Abel back. "You think that's what they are, then? Don't seem like tricks'd bring you all the way back here risking a momma's wrath. Come on over here, son."

Abel moves far enough that the moonlight catches him.

The preacher nods. "Tricks, you say. Didn't look to me you thought it was tricks when you stood out in that aisle and lifted your hand."

"You seen me," Abel says. "I knew you did, but you didn't call on me. I know a man named Dumb Willie. You didn't call on him neither."

"Dumb Willie? Believe I know the man you mean. Lots folk in there in need of healin' tonight, but I am only a single soul. Pains me that I can't help'm all. Is my burden, you see. One of many. You don't need me to set that arm right no way. It'll heal on its own."

Abel says, "Ain't my arm I need set right."

He sees Reverend Johnny's head dip down and up. "You got a condition," he says. A statement of fact rather than a question. This, Abel knows, is neither trick nor magic. No one has need of powers to know something is wrong about him. "You think I didn't call you up because I can't heal you."

"Thought that's what my momma wanted. I still think it, even though she don't believe."

Reverend Johnny leans down, hands on his knees. "And what is it you believe, boy?"

"I don't know," Abel says. He's never pondered such a thing. "But I can do tricks. Not as good as you, but some."

As proof, Abel slides his left hand into his pocket for the nickel he'd used to impress the girl on the bench. Which didn't, he concedes, though this time it isn't merely a nickel that Abel conjures, but the grin on Reverend Johnny's face. "I was hoping you'd teach me."

He chuckles. "That ain't half bad, kid. Not half bad at all. But here's your mistake—you think all the healin' I do is by my own hand. It ain't, son. Lord's One gives me that power, just as He gave me eyes to see plain. I can't teach you that. It's a gift not mine to bestow. All I do is heal."

"You heal for real?"

"You seen that in there," Reverend Johnny says.

"Can you heal me? It ain't selfish. It's for my momma as much as me."

The preacher leans in close, studying things. "There's too much doubt in you, Abel Shifflett. Takes faith to be made well."

Abel is ready for this line of protest. "That shouldn't matter none," he says. "You're the one doing the healing, so you're bound to be the one needing more faith than me. Which you got."

"Afraid that ain't how things work." The preacher stands back up, folding his arms. "What you want here, son? You ask me to heal what God Hisself made to be broke, that needs faith. More faith than you got, maybe even more than was in that whole buildin' tonight. Ain't a person this world can find

69

faith like that in the time it takes to walk from the front of a
barn to the back. Sorry, Abel Shifflett. I can't help you, and I
got to be moving on. Road's ever long."

He turns back toward the car. Abel stops him. "What
about one a those words, then? Like the ones you gave all
them others. I need to believe to hear one a them?"

Preacher eases back around. Abel inches near all the way
to where the dome light reaches. Letting Johnny get a good
look at how pitiable the boy in front of him is, Abel hoping
guilt can manage what begging has not.

"A word?"

"I hear something good, maybe then I'll believe. Something
that'll help."

"Help what?"

"Me and my momma. We're dire."

Reverend Johnny measures his words as though weighing them on a balance. "Might be so inclined as to give you
a word, son. One that may well be a boon to your happiness
and alter your very life. It is a gift no less precious than the
healing your doubt will not allow, and one that takes no faith
to receive. Just ears to hear is all that's required. But even a
gift comes with a price. This here's my livelihood, you see.
Puts gas in my car and food in my belly. I can't give it free,
even if it's just you and me here. Wouldn't be proper."

The preacher stands waiting for an answer Abel can give
until the idea finally comes. It is a terrible thought at first, a
thing he knows if followed through will lead to a whole new
sense of dire the likes of which he and his momma have never
seen. And yet Reverend Johnny's words hang like fruit ripe
for picking, and Abel has never been so hungry.

He reaches into his pocket and draws out the money his
momma gave him to hold. Lofts it high so Reverend Johnny

can see. For once, Abel is glad for his tiny hands. They make the cash look even more.

"I give you all I got," he says.

Reverend Johnny grins. He whips out a hand and snatches the money away, leaving behind a tingle in Abel's fingers. "This'll do. Yessir, this'll do just fine." He glances again behind where Abel stands. "Have to be a quick one, though."

Abel readies himself. He expects Reverend Johnny to do out here just as he'd done inside, and that is how things at least begin. The preacher raises his hand (to the stars this time rather than some old cobwebby ceiling) as though to beg quiet, cocking his ear for a voice small and still that only he can hear. Waits.

"You getting something? Momma'll be waiting. She told me not to move."

"Hang on your britches. This ain't like dialin' Verizon."

"Okay," he says. "Sorry," he says.

Still nothing. Abel leans his neck back, trying to see. There is the moon and most of Orion, other dots of light he and Dumb Willie have long stared at from the field behind his house but never really seen, never considered. Far away comes the sound of engines starting. He hopes one of those is not his momma, so fed up with the boy her son has become and so disappointed that he wasn't healed that she now feels it best to leave Abel up here to rot.

"Abel Shifflett, the Lord says He knows you hurt. He knows it, that's what He's telling me." The preacher coughs once, excuses himself. His shut eyes clench. His mouth winces like he's stepped into a cow pie. "He, uh, says you're special—"

"He better not be saying that."

"—and that He—" Reverend Johnny coughs again. Tugs

at the collar of his shirt with the hand not raised up to call down heaven. "Sorry," he says. "I ain't. This ain't right."

"What do you mean it's not right?" Abel asks. "I don't got any more money."

The preacher's chin, tilted toward the moon, now tilts higher. Tears fall to his cheeks as his Adam's apple begins to rise and fall like he's choking on something that will go neither down nor up. Abel can see the tendons of his neck strain, making tiny valleys of skin down through the narrow part where Reverend Johnny's shirt is unbuttoned.

"What's wrong? Reverend Johnny?" Abel cannot hide the panic in his words. "You ain't got to do no tricks," he says as the preacher's feet set to dancing, his heels turning in the dirt and now rising up, putting him on his toes, Reverend Johnny struggling, a *haaaaaah* coming from his mouth as Abel's panic yields to full-on fear. "I said no *tricks*."

Reverend Johnny's boots lift from the ground. One inch, then two, now six. His body floats free of the hill country earth as his head lolls back at an angle wholly unnatural. One arm rises slowly. The other, the one he had lifted so as to ask for quiet, lowers itself. The two level straight out at his shoulders, leaving a conclusion both impossible and undeniable—Johnny Mills is about to be raptured straight to heaven.

Abel steps back, stumbling as his feet get confused. He wants to scream for help but cannot form the word, wants his momma or Dumb Willie or even Principal Rexrode, but the corner of the barn is so far away and they are all so far away.

That sound again—*haaaaaah*—draws him back. The preacher's neck snaps forward. His feet remain unchanged, free of the grass, his arms still stretched like a bird's wings, but Reverend Johnny's eyes are gone. The irises, the pupils. Only the whites have been left to show, afire with a light that burns so clear it looks blue and so bright that Abel cringes before its power. Those eyes taking in all around them, wide and unblinking. Seeing tree and mountain and sky as though these were foreign things unknown until this moment. Looking down and beholding his own flesh and fingers.

"Reverend Johnny?" Abel croaks. "You ain't got to do it this way," he tries. "You're scaring me, and I just want to get on now. I want to—"

"Abel."

The voice is not Reverend Johnny's. All this night he has spoken in the soft drawl of the Southern mountains, adding letters to some words and taking other letters away, his tones as lilting as land. But this voice comes deeper yet softer somehow, and with a music underneath that sounds like rain and feels like the sun that follows after.

"Abel." He speaks again—not Reverend Johnny, but the thing that has stolen him.

A feeling comes over Abel to kneel or at least bow his head, one he resists. He does raise his good hand as if to remove a hat he does not wear, leaving it hanging like an awkward salute. His lips tremble.

"What is it, Reverend Johnny?" Staring at those eyes, how the thing inside the preacher has filled him to near bursting. That gaze of ecstasy and agony at once.

"Find your treasure, Abel. Your treasure will be your healing."

"My healing?"

"The treasure must bring healing. The healing must bring reward. The treasure is yours should you seek it, though go in haste and do not turn away. Your time has come."

Abel shakes his head, afraid to say the thing he must. "I don't understand."

73

"Do not turn away," the thing that is Reverend Johnny says, "for the way is dark. It is dark."

The light in his eyes narrows to a beam. Johnny Mills remains aloft only a breath longer. He is then jerked higher, far above the car, and it is as if he is flicked away like a nuisance by a great and unobserved hand. His body buckles forward before being flung into the darkness. Abel hears a cry of shock and pain and lets loose one of his own. He spins, hobbles his way quick to the side of the barn. Nothing of him feels guilt at leaving the preacher there, alone and broken in the night. Nothing of Abel begs him to turn back and offer what aid he can. He only runs. He runs and runs, cursing legs that do not work and hips that make the world tilt and tumble.

PART III

TREASURE

-1-

It is with a glad heart that Lisa Shifflett greets this morning. Early sun floats through the window looking out onto their little backyard and the field beyond. Light puddles into a square spot on the kitchen table that frames the day's first cup of coffee and a half-eaten bowl of oatmeal. Dare she admit it, the word she finds to describe what she feels is one she's struggled with these past years:

Hope.

She is not proud of what happened last night, though she cannot argue with the results. Not only has she secured enough charity to pay off the bills at both the market and the pharmacy, there is even a good bit left over. To hide away or (she smiles again) maybe splurge on something nice. A new Going Out dress, maybe. New shoes for Abel. Maybe even a momma-son date to the movies in Camden. The matinee, of course—no need to get carried away.

Her mood only dampens some when she glances down the narrow hall to the first closed door on the left.

It was strange the way Abel acted last night. Not that Lisa believed their trip would result in any other behavior from her boy, and really she would be bothered much more if Abel hadn't acted strange at all. She has long heard of the revivals that go on in the hill country but took them all as a bit of truth stretched long. That opinion has since changed. All the dancing and cavorting, that singing. *A mob mentality* is the phrase Lisa finds, which is just what people like the Reverend Johnny Mills need in order for their tricks to work. And then Abel stepping out into the aisle at the end. What had that been all about?

The way she'd found him after finishing her talk with that last preacher, that had been strangest of all. Standing there trembling as though he'd been racked by cold, pale as chalk dust. Silent all the way home and not a word when he went to bed, not so much as a "Toots love."

Lisa knows the reason for that: because she went begging. It's because she took advantage of people all fired up to do the Lord's work in bringing healing to the world by putting herself and her boy right in front of them all. And was there really anything wrong in that? No. Abel may think so, but Lisa knows different. Knows better. All of those people had wanted to help—Lisa had batted an eye here and there but had twisted no arms—and she was in need. Her *son* was in need. And in the end everyone came out happy, the ones who had given and the ones given to. That's what she'll tell Abel. It's good for the boy to know how things are. No sense letting him grow up wrapped inside some innocent fantasy. The world is a hard place, and always will be.

All that will be for later, though. Tonight. For now, Lisa

sips her coffee and eats her breakfast and relishes her sense of victory. This day has found her bright—*hopeful*—and yet one morning of cheer isn't enough to rid Lisa of a tiredness that has long soaked her bones. Her apron is wrinkled, still stained with yesterday's meatloaf and gravy. The familiar bun in her hair, held tight by an assortment of pins and a white bow, makes her feel older than her years.

Yet even this exhaustion carries a kind of ease. She is alone for now, isolated from the crowds at the diner and from Abel as well, leaving her precious time to be only herself. These moments come few—the ride to work and back, the few breaks Roy allows, those seconds in the post office before turning the key and hoping not to find another bill she cannot pay and no letter from Fairhope—but these are when Lisa Shifflett is free to adopt the persona of her truest self. She must always bear a countenance of strength with her son, thin and fragile as it may be. She must push through or climb over whatever obstacle wedges itself between her and the better life she craves. Some, she knows, would call that pluck. Lisa considers it more a defiance against her own past and present, against her everything.

She hears the hardwood snap and looks up. Abel's door is open only a crack. A single eye peers out.

"There you are," she says. "I was gonna let you sleep in. First day of summer and all."

The door doesn't open wider. "Guess I got used to getting up early."

"Guess so." Lisa pushes the chair beside her out with a foot and pats the table. "Wanted to talk to you a minute anyway. Thought it'd wait till tonight, but I guess now's best. This way it won't be on my mind all day."

Abel remains in place. The door opens only a crack more,

as though he is weighing options that aren't there. He slumps rather than walks to the table. Limping (as he always will) as he passes the pencil marks drawn into the corner of the wall that have measured his height, one line dated and then another and another, then ones so scrunched together that the dates couldn't fit.

"Want some breakfast?"

"No'm."

"You okay? You didn't say much on the way home last night. Not much at all."

"Tired, I guess," Abel says.

"Looked more than tired to me. I came back, you was white as a ghost."

He shrugs. "I don't remember much."

A lie. Lisa knows it the second Abel speaks. The boy has never lied well and knows the truth is the second rule they have—always tell the truth.

"Probably best." She takes a bite of oatmeal and touches Abel's arm—the good one, which will probably be the bad one sometime soon. "I know that was a trial, Abel. Especially after what happened at school. I wasn't counting on going up there even after Mister Rexrode invited us. Then I went back to get your things, and he invited us again. More I thought about it, the more sense it made. Folk around here, they're giving. They'll empty their pockets right along with their minds when the mood's right. I know that sounds mean. I had to have you there so folks could see how in need we are. It rankled my pride and I know it did yours. But there's no harm in asking for aid when aid is needed, and I don't got to tell you it's needed right now."

Abel only sits, staring at the table.

It is as if a noose has been slipped around his neck and a foot stands ready to kick the chair from beneath him.

"You didn't take me up there for healing, then?" he asks.

"You think that's why we went?"

Abel doesn't say.

"I'd give anything in the world for that to happen, Abel. I would. But it's just not going to. I just went for help."

"It's okay," he says. "Asking for help."

"I'm glad you see it that way. I was worried you wouldn't. Spent all night tossing and turning, thinking how scared you looked. Must've been hard on you."

"They didn't see me. Hardly anybody did." This, unfortunately, is no lie. "I didn't mind it much. It was fine."

Lisa chuckles a "Fine? Don't know about fine," and takes another bite. When Abel shrugs, she stops chewing but holds her smile. "You didn't really believe all that stuff, did you?"

"I don't know. Did you?"

"Only thing that was last night, Abel, was a show. Just Reverend Johnny and Preacher Keen up there waving their arms around like they're conductors and everybody else instruments. People like that, they peddle sin. They sow it. Don't always reap it as they should, but they sow it."

"What's sin?"

"I don't know," she says. "All those things we do that we know is wrong but can't help it, or sometimes can. Bible says there's all sorts of sin."

"You don't believe in the Bible," Abel says.

"Don't need to believe in religion to believe in sin, sweetheart, or where to spot it. All them people healed last night? They might be better today or the next or the one after, but what desperation made them walk up that stage'll come back. It always does."

Lisa decides to end things here. Speaking more might only frighten Abel. He already looks awful pale, though maybe that's just his arm hurting.

"But that's none of our problems, we got our own. I never got a cent from that young preacher man last night. Only thing he gave me's his phone number, which I'll never call. Said it was for 'praying purposes,' can you believe that? Only hands that man wants to lay on me ain't got healing in mind. But I got enough from Preacher Keen and the woman one from here to get us sitting pretty for a while. Where's it?"

Abel can't look at her.

"I looked in your pockets last night," she says. "It wasn't there, and you were so wore out I didn't bother asking. But go get it real quick. I need to stop by the market after work to square things with Darnell, then I thought we might take in a movie. What you think? Bet there's some superhero thing playing."

"I gave it all to you," Abel whispers. "Last night on the way back."

"No, you didn't." Lisa's smile yields to something between a grin and a frown. There is fear and panic in her next words and a fervent hope that somehow this is all a misunderstanding that will soon be made right. "Abel, you didn't give me that money."

"I think I need to go back to bed. My arm hurts."

"Abel—"

"It was a lot." He still can't look at her. "You gave me that money and it was a lot. That's a big responsibility for a kid. How was I supposed to know all that was for our bills?"

"Oh my god, Abel. What did you do?"

"You could have given it to anybody. You could have kept it. Nobody was gonna go through your pockets—"

He flinches at the sound of Lisa's hand striking the table, rattling her cup and bowl and spoon. It sounds like a chair being kicked out from under somebody.

Her voice comes soft and shaking: "Abel, please. What did you do with our money?"

"I gave it to Reverend Johnny."

It appears as though Abel can't decide which surprises him more, that he has said it with such ease or that he has said it as a scream through a curtain of tears. Now he looks at her. Not so as to punctuate his confession with a defiance of his own but so she can see his hurt. Lisa, however, sees none of it. She only stares at her balled fists, vaguely aware of the bit of oatmeal clinging to her bottom lip.

"When?" she asks.

"After the show. I seen Reverend Johnny sneak off. I thought you took me up there to get me fixed, that's why I stood up. But Reverend Johnny said I don't got belief. He said he'd give me a word because that don't need belief at all, just money, and I thought a word was good enough"—spitting it all, wailing the words—"and then something happened to'm, like something got *in*'m, and it scared me so I ran."

For a long while Lisa thinks the two of them will remain that way forever, her frozen in place with that dangly bit of oatmeal, him bawling into his cast. It would be her own hell. A person doesn't need heaven to know hell, just like a person doesn't need religion to know sin.

"It's gone?" she asks. "Our money's gone? How could you do something like that?" Not yelling it, Lisa would never yell at her boy. It's more a whispering of the words and a fear of his answer. "How could you do something like that?"

And now Abel says something so ridiculous, so utterly incomprehensible, that Lisa can barely translate it in her mind:

"There was a hundred cars on yesterday's train."

"What?"

"There ain't never been a hundred cars, Momma."

Anger builds now. Lisa tries to swallow it but finds it only leaks up again, stinging the backs of her eyes, making Abel's face shimmer. "I don't understand what that means."

"I thought it meant something. I thought it was a magic, like Reverend Johnny."

His explanation—if it can even be called such—produces in Lisa the very opposite of what she knows Abel hopes. The first tear falls wet and hard.

"Magic? Abel, *magic*? Do you see any magic here?" She points to the stack of mail on the table, all those bills. "Do you see it here?" To the refrigerator he must know is empty and the cupboards more bare than not. "Abel, we needed that money. They're going to take everything from us."

"Maybe we can find Reverend Johnny," he pleads. "We can get it back."

"Reverend Johnny's probably as clear from here as anybody can get."

"Then maybe the preachers can give us more."

"No, they won't." She swipes at her eyes, not caring that Abel sees, that he's worried and afraid. "You think they'll give me more today after giving me all they had yesterday?"

She folds her arms across her chest, right where the meatloaf has dried, and bows her head.

"I'm sorry, Momma," he says. "Please don't cry."

She moves for her purse and keys. "I have to go to work."

"Momma."

"I have to go."

The last noise that shakes the Shifflett house this morning comes when Lisa slams the front door. Her tears come harder now, a weeping so fierce that she begins to fear for her own fragile body.

Far away, the morning train whistles.

-2-

He stands as tall as he can manage in front of the door. Far away, too far for him to either notice or care, the morning train calls.

The task of cleaning begins only when Abel realizes his momma will not be coming back anytime soon, cheeks wet and eyes a painful red, to say she's sorry. Nor, he guesses, should she. Sometimes he thinks he's being slowly changed into another person, someone wholly different, with a heart full of impossibilities and a brain just large enough to believe them. Yesterday morning it was Chris. Then Reverend Johnny last night. Abel handing over all that money they needed for what may as well have been magic beans.

Clean, that's the only thing he can do. Yard work (especially anything involving a whirring metal blade) is forbidden by Lisa, though she is more than appreciative of the dusting and vacuuming and straightening up that Abel provides. The dusting and straightening up part is accomplished in little more than an hour. Vacuuming takes a bit longer—not easy, given only one good arm.

The phone never rings. A part of Abel thinks it will, or at least hopes. There has never been a day he has not longed for his mother's voice, the chime in it and the way only she can make him laugh, but what he wants even more than those things now is to know he is not the burden he feels himself to be. To know he isn't the reason why they struggle so and why they're so poor, why his momma always looks so tired. That it's the world does those things to them because it's so big and so mean, and not the fact that he was born broken.

By eight thirty, both the entire front of the house and Abel's room sparkle, but even the sheen of sweat in his hair is not enough to budge him from despair. He cleans the kitchen next, then the bathroom. Then sweeps the front porch. Lisa's tiny bedroom is last. He's tired by now and in need of a good rest or at least a visit to Dumb Willie. Still, he pushes on. It is, Abel knows, his way of saying he's sorry. Sorry for losing that money (though not for asking a word from Reverend Johnny; Abel is still unsure what exactly happened behind that barn last night, but he knows it was something worth paying a hefty price to witness), and sorry for what he did to Chris.

But here's the thing—Abel knows none of it will be good enough. He could clean every trailer on Holly Springs, it wouldn't make anything right.

There's this as well: one room remains a mess. The wood door across from his momma's bedroom is dented and scratched and hangs off center so that the top edge always sticks to the jamb. Abel hasn't been in there for months—Christmastime, if he remembers right, when he and his momma dug out the tree.

Abel can't go in there alone. That's the rule. Lisa allows her son free range of the kitchen and living room and every-where else, even the yard and garage, both of which are filled with all manner of sharp and tangled things. Never here, though. And Abel has always obeyed. It is not the threat of what will happen if he breaks that rule that keeps him away, but the fear of what could get broken in a single wrong step. Yet Abel also understands there are times when rules must be broken so a greater point can be made. Or, in this case, a bigger apology.

The knob turns easily enough, though the door itself budges only when he levels his shoulder against it. Inside, the air is stale and dark. Abel keeps his feet in the hallway and reaches in with his good arm, feeling for the switch. He hears a clack before light bursts from a single bulb hanging from the ceiling.

It has always been a play on words, this place that seems to exist in every home but goes by a myriad of names. Dumb Willie calls his family's version of it the *junk room*. Abel has heard others refer to such rooms as the *spare room* and the *storage room* and even the generic *bedroom*, all of which he discards as an utter lack of imagination to describe the place where families hoard the detritus of their lives. He himself came up with *wreck room*. The phrase possesses a subtle humor that Dumb Willie is not able to grasp and Lisa has never seemed interested in, though Abel is satisfied that his momma has adopted the term. And really, what better name can there be for a place that contains such an eclectic arrangement of discarded toys and outgrown clothing, old receipts and broken pieces of furniture, and so many boxes stacked along the walls that they appear as walls themselves?

He sinks to his knees, knowing that will force him to navigate with extra caution. The carpet is an ancient brown that hides most of the dirt but none of the smell. A wide enough path has been created through the room to the window. That is his first task. He yanks hard on the shade, drowning the walls in morning.

It is amazing how much even poor folk can accumulate. He sits and begins slowly, separating the piles and boxes into what can be reused again and what is ill suited for even a yard sale, the reason coming not long after for why this room has never been cleaned. Though nothing here can be considered valuable in a monetary sense, everything holds a story and therefore meaning—a worth known only to him. Abel cradles a stuffed giraffe with a missing eye that saw him through too many hospital visits, runs a finger over the mud-stained Matchbox cars he once played with in the backyard. Here are cards from doctors and nurses who had become friends, telling Abel to *Get Well Soon!* and bidding him happy birthdays and merry Christmases. A bike with training wheels that somehow never made it to the garage. Old dishes that Abel remembers him and his momma eating from as they watched reruns of Carol Burnett, both of them laughing so hard that the sofa swallowed most of the food. Papers from school, long-ago renderings of a stick-figured mother and child holding hands and smiling in spite of the rectangle shapes of casts on Abel's arms and legs. And pictures, so many pictures, boxes of ones of his momma and him and the two of them together, pictures of their house and the mountains, baby pictures and first-day-of-school pictures and class pictures, always with the teacher standing off to the side and Abel banished to the end of the back line, hidden but for half a cheek or a tuft of hair, a sliver of a false smile.

And somewhere in all the time that passes and all the mess he digs through, Abel comes to the realization that this is no mere room filled with wreck. It is instead a history of his life laid jumbled and dust-ridden, memories he can touch as proof they had once been real.

Perhaps it is this notion that memories are true things

mostly, stained yet not colored over by time, that draws Abel's thoughts to the night just past. The image of Reverend Johnny being hoisted from the ground is still fresh in his mind (trick or not, Abel knows he will never be free of its effectiveness) and the words that the preacher spoke, Abel's time coming and treasure to be found, haste and dark ways.

And healing. Healing most of all. The greatest bit of magic Abel has ever fathomed.

Words wholly unlike ones Johnny Mills had offered the others until those words yielded to screams. Abel remembers his own screaming, running back through the darkness along the side of the barn without care of getting hurt or lost, so long as he got away. And now the rest, rushing back as well: Dumb Willie's daddy spitting at the ground; *Only mir'cles you get in this life's the ones you go after on your own*; that young preacher man touching Lisa's fingers and the sad look in her eyes, like she was doing something wrong; *There's too much doubt in you, Abel Shifflett. Takes faith to be made well. What about one a those words, then? Like the ones you gave all them others. I need belief to hear one a them?*

"Abel."

He flinches at the sound—another memory, Abel knows it can be nothing more. Only this memory that seems to call out his name came not from a corner of his mind but a corner of the room, way in the back where the closet sits. His heart thrums as he stares at that spot. Breath stopped. Listening. The voice does not return.

The sound of it, though. Deeper yet softer. Music that feels like sun after a long rain.

Nothing in that part of the room presents itself in any way as different from the rest. There are more boxes piled high against the wall, along with a collection of more old clothes. Yet as Abel peers harder into that corner, he does spot something that looks out of place. A round container mostly hidden by a stack of boxes laid in front and a leaning pile of envelopes and files marked *Taxes* to its side. The dimensions of the cylinder remind Abel of the popcorn tins Roy always gifts Lisa for Christmas, which she in turn always brings home as a gift to Abel. This one, however, is old. He can tell by how the paper around it is faded and flaked and the dent near the bottom rusting.

"Just junk, like the rest"—him, not the voice.

But of course it *isn't* junk, it's stories, and that means whatever in this room doesn't hold value to him is likely to hold at least some to his momma.

A section of the lid is chipped and bent. From being opened over and over, he guesses. Not all the way, since that would require a shifting of all the boxes and papers piled around it, but enough to allow something to be taken out.

Or slipped inside.

"Probably nothing in there."

The voice, if it had been a voice, does not answer.

But as he rises from his spot across the room, walking now instead of scooching, it is as though Abel is convinced that what he is about to find won't be nothing at all. It's something in that old tin, not just papers or pay stubs from the diner or old report cards with *Abel needs to work on his social interactions* in the comments section and an I for Incomplete next to *Gym*. This is something more. Something important. Abel doesn't know how he senses this. Other than the voice he heard—or thinks he heard—came right from where the popcorn tin has been hidden from his notice.

Might be so inclined as to give you a word, son. One that may well be a boon to your happiness and alter your very life.

88

"I shouldn't."

His good hand already shoving aside the boxes.

"Momma hates snooping."

Taking the papers off the top and sides.

"Almost as much as she hates lying."

But now Abel's good hand has already turned the tin around to face him, and what else can he do?

He discovers two things. One is that this really is an old Christmas present. The faded paper on the front reads *Harper's Old-Fashioned Kettle Corn*, and Abel shakes his head at the *Closeout* and the *.99* stamped beneath. The other is that something is indeed inside, and it isn't popcorn. He pries the lid with his fingers and tilts the tin forward.

The avalanche of envelopes that spills out is enough to cover Abel's meager lap. There are dozens of them, more, each opened and then resealed with tiny sheets of folded paper inside that are covered in black ink. He holds up the envelope on top, angling it toward the sun streaming through a billion motes of dust. Reads the name and address in the center:

Abel Shifflett
PO Box 57
Mattingly, VA 24465

Now the return address:

213 Kable Street, No. 11
Fairhope, NC 28573

He knows no one in North Carolina. Abel barely knows everyone in Mattingly, much less places beyond. He looks at the pile of envelopes covering his legs, tilts the popcorn tin again to see more inside. It's got to be a hundred.

I ain't never seen a hundred, Dumb Willie. Not in my whole life. It scared me. I think something's gonna happen.

He opens the envelope in his hand and unfolds the paper inside. It's smaller than what he uses at school, what his momma would call "letter writing parchment." The date at the top right is four weeks prior to this day. The words themselves are a mix of cursive and print, but legible. So legible, in fact, that Abel at first believes them typed rather than written. There are no smudges, no mistakes. Not a single thought has been crossed through. At the top left is Abel's own name, followed by a comma and *Things in Fairhope are the same. I won't complain about it since it's so pretty. I can look out my window and see blue mountains and green trees and flowers of every color I can imagine (and some I even can't). It's beautiful here.*

Abel lays down the paper and looks at the others. All appear written by the same hand. He continues:

I wish I could enjoy things more than I do, but I try to keep busy. I wish you could see it here, Abel. How pretty it is. Sometimes I think about that happening (I can't help it!). I think about you being here with me and that makes me smile and makes me sad too. I guess that's what love feels like. I think if there was more of that kind of feeling, things would go a whole lot better for everybody.

I'm scared for you, Abel. I know it isn't safe for you there. There is too much you don't know and can't see. I worry about you just about every day. No matter what's going on with you, I can make it better. So write back, okay? I'll write again soon. Hope you get this. Take care, kiddo.

Here, the letter ends. Abel blinks his eyes hard and quick, thinking that will keep the lock tight on the deep place inside where he's shoved down the tears from this morning, even as those tears bang and knock to be let loose.

He reads the date and his name and stares at the comma after, how that makes him feel as though what follows is nothing less than a conversation begun long ago. But none of these things is what finally brings those tears to fall. None of that is what renders him a weeping mess upon the soiled and foul carpet of the wreck room. It is instead that Reverend Johnny speaks once more, promising a treasure to be found. And it is the two words Abel finds written at the bottom, four letters that end with another comma and then three letters beneath:

Love,
Dad

-3-

From his place behind the pulpit, Reverend Earl Thomas Keen can look past rows of pews and the four chairs in back where ushers bide each Sunday sermon, to where the open doors allow a view of the trees and road beyond. He prefers the entry unobstructed as the weather allows. Church should be an invitation, as he sees it. For the weary and the troubled, the put out, for any who wander by.

As such, Trinity Gospel Assembly of the Redeemer is wide and welcoming more days than not. Those belonging to his congregation know this place as Earl Thomas's second home (or first, should you hear Lori Keen say it, though she will gladly add it was Earl Thomas's passion for the lost and discarded that drew her to marry him). He is here most days but Thursdays, which are set aside for the hill country's sick and homebound. And he is here this Saturday as he is all others, at the pulpit he has claimed for the last quarter century, polishing his sermon. The robins and mockingbirds, the lowly sparrows, sing beyond the foyer. Earl Thomas greets them as an audience not so demanding as the one that will gather on the morrow in the plain wood pews laid before him. He wipes his brow, sips from the bottle of water beside him, and begins again.

A good preacher will say every sermon is vital; Earl Thomas is no different. Each Sunday is an opportunity for the Lord to use him as a cord woven in strands of grace and mercy to pull the damned into a life of beauty and forgiveness. Still, there have been weeks when the world gets the better of this hilltop revelator, when acedia takes hold and Earl Thomas is left at the end of Sunday service to shake feeble hands and gaze into tired eyes as proof he has just delivered a clunker.

That cannot happen tomorrow. Tomorrow must be special.

Electricity still courses through him, carryover from the blessing of last night. There had been much talk of the traveling healer known as Reverend Johnny Mills in this part of the Blue Ridge. Stories—grand ones—of the wonders he could perform. When a few of the hill country brethren approached Earl Thomas with the idea of extending their own invitation, the vote had been near unanimous. Near, but for a single exception. Earl Thomas had seen healers before, scores of charlatans who preyed upon the needy and pretended to speak for a God they rebelled against in the secrecy of their own hearts. He had cast his no with that in mind, a notion that Johnny Mills dispelled in short order. The strange man from nowhere truly had power. Never in his life had Earl Thomas witnessed such miracles as took place inside that barn, and he knows his pews will be full tomorrow because of it. That is cause enough to have kept him here since this morning. And though it is nigh lunchtime and Lori will be expecting him, that is what keeps him here still.

His finger remains upon the verse in his old leather Bible, one hand raised high to emphasize a particular word:

"*Faith*, good people. *Faith* is what we need. That greater power to see beyond our temporary troubles and know the loving hand that guides them. We say, 'Lord, why must I suffer?' and cry out, 'Father, why must I go without?' But, friends—"

He pauses here, looking up, just as he will pause here and look up tomorrow. Earl Thomas must stare his flock in the eye because it is a true thing he will say, and hard like all true things are.

"I say the Lord seeks not happiness for any of us, nor comfort. They are good things, but not His aim. What He wants most, cares for most, seeks to foster most . . ."

A shadow passes by the doors and lingers, robbing Earl Thomas of his thought. He stares at the black shape edging up the steps.

"Is our souls. It is eternity that sets in His mind, not our fleeting trials, and that is why our eyes must be upon Him, upon others, rather than ourselves. For it is as the writer of Hebrews says, 'Without faith it is impossible to please him—'"

That shadow growing now, easing into solid form.

"'—for he that cometh to God must believe that he is, and that he is a rewarder of them that diligently—'"

And now to the edge of the farthest pew. Earl Thomas

stops, trying to understand what it is he sees. Finishing barely above a whisper—"'seek him.'"

His first instinct is to laugh. Earl Thomas counts it to the Lord that he doesn't, as only the holiest of powers could stanch his reaction to such a sight. The child is done up in the way of the trick-or-treaters who knock at his and Lori's door, children from families too poor for proper costumes and so who throw on anything and everything in order to look as ridiculous as possible. The child's face is hidden by an old football helmet, the face guard stained brown, the strap at the chin cinched tight. The wide girth is an illusion; he (or is it a she?) is not a heavy child, merely one adorned in layer upon layer of clothing. Earl Thomas counts three shirts beneath the catcher's chest protector, along with what appear to be two pairs of shorts under a thick pair of winter sweat-pants. Shin guards are strapped to the child's legs. Part of the same catcher's gear, he supposes. An orange gardening glove rests on the child's left hand. On the right, beginning from the wrist and disappearing beneath a sleeve, is what looks like a bright yellow cast.

"Say there," Earl Thomas says. "I help you with something?"

A tiny throat clearing, followed by a voice like one of the frogs in the creek out back:

"Sorry to bother you, sir. My name is . . ."

Earl Thomas leans over the pulpit, trying to hear. He thinks first the child spoke so weakly that the name melted halfway up the aisle. Now he thinks the child reconsidered and didn't offer his name at all.

"I was at your show last night. Up at the barn?"

"I see."

Earl Thomas, known through these hills as a wise man gifted in tongue, can manage only these two words. He has welcomed many a passerby into his sanctuary, once even chased a hungry deer that wandered through those wide doors, but he has never been confronted by such a mystery as this. The boy doesn't budge from his spot at the edge of the foyer. His gloved hand reaches for the pew in front of him as he begins to wobble.

"I'd ask you to come up here, son, have us a word. But from the look of you maybe I oughta come there."

Earl Thomas reaches for the bottle of water and makes his way up the middle aisle. The boy sits at the end of the last pew and proceeds to unsnap the helmet and lift it away, heaving a sigh. Sweat drenches his forehead. His cheeks are slick and the color of an apple. He takes the bottle of water Earl Thomas offers and drinks half in two large swallows, pouring the remainder over his head. It is at this point that Preacher Earl Thomas Keen believes himself in the presence of one who has never stepped foot inside a church.

"What in the world you all dressed up like that for?" he asks, taking a seat on the pew in front of the boy. "Hot as sin outside."

The boy says, "I had a long way to go. Wasn't safe."

"They a zombie horde out there or something?"

"Nosir. It was just a long ways. And I had to go by the Jones place. You know the Joneses? Their boy Chris wants me dead. I had to sneak through the woods when I went past."

"Am acquainted with Royce. Chris too. You look awful hot, son. How about some more water? Got a fountain in back. Plenty cold."

"I appreciate that, sir," he squeaks, "but no. I'd rather just get on with what brought me here. It's an issue of time."

"I accept that," Earl Thomas says, trying not to grin. "Time's a funny thing. We always think we ain't got enough of it, but we can usually scrounge up enough to waste. Don't recall seeing you out this way before. You from around here?"

"Nosir. Like I said, it's a long way. I had to ride my bike. I ain't done that in a long time on account of I got a condition." He nearly spits the word. "But I had to come, because something's happened. I thought I might fall off or get run over, so that's why I wore all this stuff. And because of Chris. This all comes from my friend Dumb Willie," he says, patting the chest protector, the helmet, the shin guards. "He finds it left over from school sometimes. Nobody claims it, he gives it all to me. I'm not sure why since I can never use it because of how I am. They call him Dumb Willie for a reason, but he's my friend."

He pauses. To breathe, Earl Thomas thinks, since all of that has come out in what seems one long statement of fact. The boy stares at the room around him.

"I ain't never been in a church."

"Well, ain't nobody perfect, son. That what brought you all this way? You in some trouble?"

"Nosir, not exactly. I been upended."

"Sounds serious."

"More than I can say. I found something."

Earl Thomas cocks his eye. "What'd you find?"

"Reverend Johnny here?"

"No, afraid he's gone. Snuck out last night before I could say good-bye and give'm my thanks. People like him, they don't want attention. They're happy doing the Lord's work."

"But you're sure he's gone?" the boy asks.

"I don't know what you mean, son."

He looks down. Shrugs. Flicks at a bit of wood on the pew in front with a shaky finger. "Just don't mean nothing, I guess. Can get scary sometimes up here in the hill country, though."

"Can. But I promise ain't nothing happen to him. Closed up the barn myself last night, and Reverend Johnny's car was gone. But I bet I can help with whatever problem you got."

"Don't think so," the boy says. "Reverend Johnny gave me a word."

"He did? Don't recall seeing you up on the stage last night."

"That's because nobody sees me. And it wasn't on the stage. I seen him after, out back. Reverend Johnny was getting ready to leave and said the road's ever long, but he gave me a word anyway. I had to do something I shouldn't've, that's the only way I could get that word, and now Momma's heart's broke on 'count of I cost her and I'm a burden. But now I think Reverend Johnny was right. It didn't make no sense to me what he said and I thought it was all magic beans, but now I don't think it was. Because I found something. I found treasure, Preacher Keen. Like he said I would. And that means there's healing next and then reward. But I need to know it's true before I go on and hope. That's why I come. I remembered you said what church is yours and where."

"I see. Well then . . . ?"

Earl Thomas waits. It's a fine trick he's learned through the years, wait and let that silence fill until the person you need something from can't take it anymore. Usually works. Works now too.

"Abel," the boy says.

"Abel"—nodding as he says it. "Fine name. Biblical. You know that? Abel was one of Adam's sons. He made an offering of the things most precious to him and found favor."

"I don't think that counts for much. My momma named me. Or maybe my daddy. Momma thinks all Reverend Johnny did was tricks. Like that light in his hands? I do tricks too but I can't show ya. I got all this stuff on and about all I could do is let a smoke bomb off. Which I won't, since it's church."

"I appreciate that," Preacher Keen says.

"Momma says all them people Reverend Johnny healed are gonna come up hurting again, only this time not just in their bodies but in their hearts too. That right?"

"I guess it's all the Lord's will, Abel. His ways are mysterious."

"It was a powerful thing Reverend Johnny did to me, Preacher Keen. He scared me so bad I still can't stand it. I even tried telling myself it was all a trick, all the way to this morning I did. But I think the only reason I wanted to think it was all a trick is because otherwise . . ." Abel shakes his head. "Well, otherwise it means I don't know anything. So I need to make up my mind either way. A lot depends on it. Maybe even my whole life."

Now the smile is gone from the preacher's face.

"I'm not sure what you're tellin' me, Abel."

The boy sits and studies his hands. "I guess I don't know what to believe. That's what it is. Reverend Johnny tells me one thing and my momma tells me another. But my momma lied, Preacher Keen. I can't believe she did because she loves me, but there's no other way 'round it. That makes me think Reverend Johnny's telling me the truth. And that scares me."

"Why's that scare you, son?"

"Because it means I got to do something I can't. Not can't in my heart," he says, then raises up that one busted arm, "but in my body. But I got to do it, because then everybody will be better. So I guess I just need to know if Reverend Johnny's real. If you hold to miracles. I guess you got to, you being a preacher and all. But I mean truly. For real."

"Who's your momma, Abel?"

"Don't guess I'll say. She's a good momma. I don't want you thinking she ain't. She just don't believe. I think it hurts her too bad."

"Well, if I just knew a little more about what's happened . . ."

"It's private," says Abel. "If you forgive me."

"I will." He leans back, studying the boy. "Son, ain't a soul ever walked this earth didn't crave more than the ground he trods and the sky he looks to. It's a longing, and it's in us all. There's some that gives themselves right over to it and others that go all their lives trying to either ignore it or explain it away. That's the choice we all got to make before we can move on from this life, and it's the one eatin' you right now."

Earl Thomas Keen wonders where in the world these words are coming from and thinks maybe they ain't from this world at all, and wishes he had a pencil and paper to copy all this down.

"Now, you ask me if I believe in miracles. I do, and I ain't ashamed to say it. Reverend Johnny Mills made me believe them even more. Just like you want to believe, else you wouldn't come all this way carrying a broke arm and a hunnert pounds of clothes. I ain't never seen what I seen last night. Was the Spirit moving. Some people can look on a thing like that and find comfort and joy enough to carry them far. Others like your momma find just as much comfort in denying it's real. But I don't expect there's much in the way of joy in denying it. You tell me this life's all there is, just rocks and trees and atoms, and all we are's a sack of bones so we might as well do what we want. That don't sound to me like a recipe for joy. Now, I don't know what's going on with you, Abel. Nor will I ask again. But I'll say this: no matter what it is, I been where you are. I have. I've had doubts and pains and still do. It's what you do with them that counts in the end. Whatever this is you're feeling, if Reverend Johnny led you to a road, it's one you're meant to take."

Abel fiddles with his helmet. "What if that road's a dark one?"

"Most is." Looking at him, because it's a true thing Earl Thomas says, and hard like all true things must be. "'Specially the ones that hold a light at their end."

The boy nods slow, like it's an answer he didn't seek but will accept. "I appreciate your time," he says. "I'll let you get back to your preaching."

"You sure?"

"Yessir."

Earl Thomas reaches over the pew and places his hand on Abel's good arm. "How about I pray a minute with you before you go?"

"I don't guess so."

"Well then, how about I pray for you on my own, then?"

Abel shrugs, still not looking. "I ain't got a say in what you do with your private time."

"You'll be first on my list, then. Promise you that. I got one more thing to ask. Come on back here in the morning. Bring your momma with you, and your daddy. You'll find good people here, Abel. Ones asking the same questions as you."

"My daddy's gone," Abel says. But he says it with a smile on the end that shines as mystery. "Maybe we'll come, but it won't be tomorrow."

"And why's that?"

"Because I got a long way to go."

He stands in slow motion like his legs are tired. Earl Thomas walks him back out into the sunshine. An old bike not fit for riding leans against the edge of the steps.

"I can take you home if you want. Be my pleasure."

"Nosir, Preacher Keen. I should go it alone. Need the practice."

"Where you headed?"

"Away."

"Well then, you be careful. Here, let me at least help."

He cinches the helmet back on Abel's head, checks the chest protector and the shin guards, smiling all the while because the boy looks three times his real size. He wants to offer the bottle of water for a ride he suspects is farther up into the mountains, poor as the boy looks. Instead, Abel heads east. Toward Mattingly.

Earl Thomas watches as the boy struggles away, raising his broken arm as a good-bye. Won't he have a tale for Lori when he gets home. He returns a wave of his own and lets his hand hang in the air as a sudden urge compels him to call Abel back. Reason with him, plead, hold the boy as prisoner so long as Earl Thomas can keep him safe. But in the end he doesn't, and that feeling fades.

Boy'll be all right, Earl Thomas says to himself. *Abel's got a path to walk same as everybody else. And just like everybody else, the only one who can walk it is himself.*

-4-

Whether the heat or the clothes or simply because there is too much for Abel to consider, the ride home feels twice as long as the ride to Preacher Keen's.

He keeps his head down and body bent forward, willing
his legs to work the pedals up one hill and over another. Even
on the downslopes, he can manage no faster than a crawl.
The brake on the back tire sticks just enough to make a burning smell that turns his stomach. It is as if all of creation has
conspired to slow Abel so that he will fully consider what
he will do next. And the more Abel pedals and sweats and
the longer the road ahead grows, the more his mind recalls
another truism, this one, too, born in the dark hallways of
Mattingly Elementary: knowing you *have* to do something
isn't nearly the same as knowing you *can*.

That is his chief problem now—not *should*, but *could*.
Abel didn't need Preacher Keen to tell him he *should* run
away. That had been decided early on, though whether early
this morning when Abel realized he'd broken his momma's
heart or late last night when Reverend Johnny broke down to
convulsions out behind that barn, he cannot know. Maybe,
he thinks, the decision came sometime yesterday afternoon
between committing his evil act toward Chris and sitting
with his momma on the front porch.

When Abel began to realize just how much of a burden
he had become.

Regardless, it was only upon finding his daddy's letters
that his path was seemingly laid clear. No longer would he
be running *away* from all the mess he's made of his life and
his momma's. Now he would be running *toward* something.
Fairhope, to be exact. Preacher Keen's role was merely to
settle the question of whether that destination was the right
one, the treasure Reverend Johnny had promised. Abel
merely wanted to know if Reverend Johnny had done some
small magic outside that barn, or if it had all been a trick.

As he pedals, wincing from how the chest protector

chafes his shoulders and how the breeze makes a constant swooshing sound inside the football helmet, Abel decides there remains a lack of hard evidence in that regard. Preacher Keen possessed no real proof beyond his own opinion. All he could say was how the Spirit had moved and people had been brought to believe in more than rocks and trees. Which, Abel must admit, sounds to him now like words spoken in a circle, never going anywhere or saying anything.

It's all so depressing, which only serves to make the going slower: Abel has come all this way looking for answers, and all he's found are more questions. Preacher Keen would probably smile if he heard something like that. He'd say there are always going to be more questions than answers because that's how things work. Because it all comes down to believing.

Maybe everything comes down to that. Abel hopes not. If it all comes down to believing, he'll never get anywhere.

Not that the past hours can be counted as utter loss. Far from it. Even with Preacher Keen's admittedly biased position on the matter, Abel has gotten what he most needs: a confirmation of something far greater than a miracle. Preacher Keen managed to say everything Abel has come to feel ever since sitting in that pile of his daddy's letters in the wreck room, his every motivation and the source of a fire that still burns hot. Not for something so cryptic as faith, but for a chance to even glimpse the joy of which Preacher Keen spoke. The kind that lasts and holds up under the hard things.

Hope. That is what Abel needs now. Hope is where that dark way Reverend Johnny spoke of will lead. Hope is the light at the end.

And not just hope—*Fair*hope. Was there any coincidence

in that, or was the name of the town his daddy was in (and in *alive*) some small magic as well? One more way of someone or something telling him he should go?

"What happened to my daddy?" he says to the birds and the trees along this empty stretch of road. "That's what I'm worried about. Because he's supposed to be dead. Momma's always told me that. Daddy was a railroad man and then he died because his heart gave out. Only he didn't die. So he must'a left. But why would he leave, since Momma says he loved her and she loved him?"

A quiet whisper rises from a place deep inside him—*Maybe it's you. Maybe that's why he left.*

Abel stops his bike, weighing that thought. He decides no, that's not it, though he can produce no real reason why it shouldn't be the case. But why write your kid a bunch of letters when you never even loved him? Or missed him?

"It's something else," he says. "Something maybe bad." And then this next thing Abel states, which is as much for himself as for the birds and the trees. Three words that settle things: "He needs me."

The issue of *should*, then, is settled. But as to the question of *could* Abel go? That is another matter entirely.

In many ways his ride out this morning has served as much as a practice run as a search for answers. Abel has wandered from Holly Springs Road many times on his own, not only for school but to count the trains and visit Dumb Willie. Those trips have never counted for much in distance, however; neither the field beyond his backyard nor the patch of woods to Dumb Willie's house is so far as to allow Abel a sense of journeying anywhere.

But Fairhope? Fairhope is different.

In those strange hazy minutes between finding the letters

and getting dressed to go see the Preacher Keen, Abel pulled the atlas down from one of his bedroom shelves. Fairhope lay near the southeastern border of North Carolina. A fair-size town, judging from the size of the circle printed on the map. A whole state away

("Practically to the moon," he moans now)

and untold hundreds of miles.

That number had presented itself as huge back at home, the map spread wide over the kitchen table with the popcorn tin of letters beside. When people exaggerate a long distance between things, that's the number they always use—*That place? Shoot, that place gotta be a hunnert miles away.* Meaning not just a hunnert but sometimes two or three, even a thousand. Meaning *unreachable.*

And if a hundred miles ("Or more," he huffs) looks a long way on paper, it feels forever on the open road. Abel guesses he's gone eight miles from home to Preacher Keen's church and halfway back. He's sweat so much on the first leg of the trip that nothing is left to leak out of him now other than a runner of slobber that catches on his chin strap, left dangling in the wind. His broken arm hurts even more than it itches, which is plenty. His legs have gone from burning to sore to numb. At the base of the next hill, he surrenders and begins pushing the bike like it's a horse gone lame.

"Cain't even make it out my own town," he tells the trees. "How'm I supposed to make it all the way to another?"

The answer comes not from the trees but a place born of his own weariness: What if he's just misunderstood everything Reverend Johnny told him?

Abel stops along the road again, weighing that possibility. He lays aside the likelihood that Reverend Johnny is nothing more than a magic bean salesman (a task still difficult, in spite of it all) and embraces for now the notion that a genuine miracle performed by a genuine miracle worker took place behind that barn last night. That Reverend Johnny's eyes going blank and shining and his body being pulled up from the ground and then tossed like a toy hadn't been a trick at all, but *real*, just as his words had been real.

What does that mean?

"Means maybe I didn't even hear right." A robin chirps in the trees, seeming to agree. "Because something like that'd be scary to anybody no matter what they say, and to a kid especially. And I was scared. Trick or not, I was."

It feels good, admitting it.

He pushes on, left hand trying to hold the bike steady up the next hill, right arm high so it won't throb. What if that's what happened really? People almost never hear what's being told them, only the parts they're interested in. And even the parts they hear get so twisted and rearranged sometimes that what you think you're hearing is only what you *want* to hear. Treasure and healing? That's all Abel's ever thought about. And the way he felt behind that barn after enduring such a hard day? Of course he would twist Reverend Johnny's words into something else. Even an invitation to run away.

Your time is come. The treasure must bring healing. The healing must bring reward. Go in haste and do not turn away. For the way is dark.

It is dark.

Cresting a hill, glimpsing another far ahead, Abel's heart begins to sway. He carries no doubt that his daddy's letters constitute the treasure that was his should he seek it. But healing? There isn't a doctor in the whole valley and beyond could promise that. His momma has told him so.

Even if she hadn't, that's a thing Abel doesn't have to be told by anybody. He knows it. And *go in haste* could've been Reverend Johnny's way of getting Abel to leave—not home but the *barn*—just as *do not turn away* could mean keeping to what Abel has been doing his whole life and *the way is dark* could have been a warning to stay in Mattingly, right where Abel is.

It shocks him, the reasonableness of it all.

Likewise shocking is that in a matter of only a few hours, Abel has gone from finding a treasure so precious he considered it life-changing and so powerful it brought him all the way to the hill country alone to now deciding it will change nothing at all. What he will do with the knowledge that his father is alive and wanting him (not to mention that Abel himself may be in some sort of danger, according to that letter), he cannot say. He supposes he'll have to settle on something before his momma gets home.

Pushing the bike along, paying no heed to the little house rising up on his left or the bully sitting on that house's front porch, Abel is forced to acknowledge two things. The first is that it was not so much the letters themselves that brought him all the way here, it was the sense that he had failed his momma to such a degree and had left her so hurting that leaving for somewhere, freeing her, was the best option. The second is that his desire to make things right will never be enough to carry him to Fairhope.

-5-

The fly must have been sick or old to have been caught so easy, probably ready to die anyway. Not that such rationalizing matters. It's survival of the fittest that Chris Jones thinks, which is pretty much the only thing he's remembered from the last hundred and eighty days of fifth grade. The weak exist so the strong can keep alive. They are made as food to eat and tools to use and, sometimes, just stuff to play with.

It makes him strong to kill it slow.

He spent the better part of the evening before on the can, moaning in a way that made his daddy cuss and his momma say it ain't all that bad and shoot, Chris probably deserved it. Well, he didn't deserve it, didn't *nobody*, especially nobody like him. Chris knows he should've questioned that little bastard runt Abel soon as he held out that . . . *chocolate* . . . and said it was so he wouldn't get picked on no more. That's how the weak ones work it. Royce has said such to Chris more times than Chris can count. The weak ones gotta be sneaky and conniving because they know they ain't strong, and so they go around acting like common terrorists. *You ain't careful*, Royce says, *you turn your eyes away for just one second, they'll get you. Then, by god, it's up to you to get them back ten times harder.*

He shifts his weight to the left cheek of his ample behind, which is still sore and feels like it will be sore forever. On a section of plank before him lie a pair of pliers and a tiny mound of body parts—two wings and four legs. The remainder of the fly, nothing more than a dark gray cylinder, rests to the right of its own appendages. The body quivers as though endeavoring escape. Chris tilts his head at the movement. Thinking how stupid that fly is, it don't even know how to die. He could step on it. Flick it down into the gap between the boards and let the ants get it, or maybe set it on fire with one of his momma's lighters. Chris could kill it, but he doesn't. He only watches, waiting for that final moment when life slips away.

His daddy wanted him to come cut wood. That was this morning, after Chris's momma went to work. Chris said no, then refused again after Royce said he could even work the chainsaw. He didn't want to chance getting sick out in the woods, hearing his daddy either laugh or cuss. Would have been great any other day, but not this one. All because of that runt, that little bas—

Something moving along the road catches his attention. It's hard to see through all the trees, but it looks like some-body coming. Some kid pushing a bike. The fly is forgotten. Chris moves to his knees (it's a slow movement, due to what his momma called his *blown gasket*) and peers toward the road. Not many kids out here, especially ones with bikes. Chris would know if there was.

This kid looks almost as big as Chris himself. Then the trees give way—no, not big, just wearing a bunch of clothes. And catcher's gear? He snorts, thinking, *What a idiot.* Thinking— *Maybe I should go on out there and see if that kid* knows *he's a idiot.* Wouldn't matter if he did, ain't nobody home to get him in trouble. Not a bad-looking bike neither. Chris has always wanted one.

It's when he stands that he notices the kid with the bike is limping. Not like he's hurt, but like that's just how he walks.

Now he sees the bright yellow cast.

Whatever slow movement has plagued Chris for the last day vanishes in a rage that blinds him to all but revenge. He leaps from the porch and finds two rocks in the yard, heav-ing the first as hard as he can. The stone smashes into the side of Abel's football helmet, just above where the chin strap is fastened. A crack like cannon fire sounds along the road.

Chris hears Abel's cry (like a baby, a cripple little *baby*) and sees him stumble off-balance. The next rock whizzes past the face mask. The bike follows the direction of Abel's body and crashes into his left leg, knocking him to the ground onto his busted arm.

Good.

Abel screams again and raises his head, eyes bugging in a fear that looks so delicious that Chris's mouth begins to water. He can't move with all those clothes on, can't get the bike off, and so can only manage to kick like a turtle stuck on its back.

Chris runs across the road without even a glance to see if there is traffic. He grabs the bike and heaves it away, then straddles Abel with all his weight. Screaming like a boy possessed, "I'ma kill you, you cripple little wuss. Your momma ain't gonna save you this time."

He smashes a fist into the helmet, clattering Abel's teeth. Both boys cry out from the pain. Abel tries kicking as Chris punches the helmet again, meaning to smash it and Abel's soft head. Punching the helmet and the chest protector, punching between Abel's legs, the blows blunted by the layers of clothing.

"You know what you did to me, you little bastard? *Everybody was laughing.*"

Chris pounds again, again to little effect. And even as his fists fly and pummel, he realizes that Abel has ceased struggling at all. It is as though he has surrendered to some fate, this thing he deserves. Chris reaches for the chin strap and does not see Abel's left hand reaching into the dirt and gravel. Nor is he aware that Abel's right hand is balling into what fist it can.

Both react at once. The dirt and gravel (along with a bit

of glass from a broken bottle, it turns out) meet the side of Chris's face just as Abel's right hand flies out and up in a wide arc that ends with the thickest part of his cast meeting Chris's nose. The result is a wet popping sound, followed by a rain of tears and gushing blood.

Chris rolls away with his hands over his face. He lowers them and sees Abel moving toward the bike, struggling to stand on those two gimpy legs. Running away, like all cowards do. He's digging in his left pocket for something. Chris refuses to let whatever it is get out and stands (wobbling as he does, the little freak clocked him good) before barreling toward Abel at full speed, screaming at him, yelling death.

Abel turns at the last second and raises his left hand. He's got something in his fingers. Before Chris can react, he hears a mighty call.

"Shazam!" Abel screams, just before he throws a small cylinder to the ground between them.

It explodes with a *pop* into a wall of smoke that Chris runs into. The fumes choke him, making his eyes tear up and his lungs cough. His fists flail at the cloud, trying to beat it back. By the time the air clears, Abel's almost to the next hill, pedaling forward as he glances back.

"I know where you live," Chris yells, though with the busted nose and the two hands covering it, the words sound more like *I bow ere you biv.* "I'm gonna kill you. You hear me? *I'm gonna kill you.*"

Blood fills Chris's hands, dripping onto his legs. He watches until the little speck disappears over the next hill. Then he blows out a breath and hobbles toward the house. Reaching the porch, he stops long enough to smash what remains of the fly with his shoe.

Tonight, he thinks. *It'll be tonight.* He knows where the little cripple and his whore momma live. He'll go and watch. Wait.

And if Chris has to, he'll kill them both.

-6-

In a world rife with disagreement over matters large and small, it should be a miracle that folk in Mattingly agree as to which of the townspeople's gardens is the finest. Everybody knows there is no better crop than that which grows in the two acres back of Henderson Farmer's house where the yard abuts his north field. Henderson has long held close the secret of his plot's success, a task made easier by the remoteness of his farm and fields. The farm was his daddy's and his grand-daddy's, near two hundred acres, the little two-story house in the middle framed with wood siding that was white in some forgotten time but has since turned to the complexion of the fields around it, a brown film that streaks in the winter snow and hardens in the summer heat. It is a place of silences. Few visitors call upon this place set along the boundary between town and the wild places to the west and south. Even now the only noises are the few birds singing from high in an ancient oak, the hoe blade slipping into soft earth like a knife, and the clanging chain.

Most of Henderson's wage is obtained by the bulk corn he grows and the livestock he sells, which is always some but never much. Yet in these last years a good bit of Henderson's yearly gross (not to mention most of his good name) has been derived from the produce stand he and Rita run in the town square from late June to early September. Folk say there must be something in Henderson's dirt to make his vegetables grow so ripe and full, or some ancient wisdom that imbues his crop with such life. Even those who grow their own groceries will stop at the stand after the first harvests, hands full of money as they come and arms full of Henderson's tomatoes and onions and peppers as they go, all of which Rita packages in paper bags stamped with words alleged to Christ, the Farmers being good Christian folk.

Yet many would know that notion false were they in the Farmers' backyard now. They would stand unbelieving at first, thinking themselves fooled until they came to know different. For the one responsible for the beauty and goodness of this garden is not Henderson at all, nor the coldhearted woman called his bride, but the unwanted son they keep prisoner to tend it.

Dumb Willie drifts among sprouting rows of what for miles is called Farmer Corn in awed and hushed tones normally kept for gossiping of rich folk. He whispers as he works the hoe, flattering the plants from the black dirt in that clumsy way he talks. The hoe slips again and again into the soil, turning the dirt, Dumb Willie hilling the corn as a chef prepares a meal or an artist touches brush to canvas. Once (only once, and apart from then hardly ever) he clips the edge of a stalk, bruising it—"Boozed it!" Dumb Willie nearly shrieks—at which point he falls to his belly and uses his big hands as delicate instruments to heal what he's broken. Every now and again he pauses to retrieve a weed that he holds close to his eyes before burying it with soil and moving on. His momma's words are often repeated in his thoughts— *Weeds need pullin', else they choke the life out every good thing.* As he moves down the row, digging deep beside the tiny weeds to catch their roots, Dumb Willie considers how he is called a weed too.

There is a quiet grace to his movement in spite of his massive size. Barely a mark of Dumb Willie's passing would be left between the rows were it not for the steel chain fastened above the boot on his right foot. He must measure each step, pausing to hold the hoe in one hand and gather the long links in the other, easing the chain down between the plants so as not to crush them. The other end is soldered to a tall metal pole sunk deep at the garden's center where a sparrow is perched, its head bobbing. Dumb Willie smiles at it. Sparrows are his favorite. The bird lights off and leaves a feather behind, which he retrieves and then tucks into the front of his overalls.

He talks and talks and calls that praying, hilling the corn and making it safe, and he stops to wince at the hot sun beating down and to look long at the edge of the grass where Rita has left a jug he cannot reach. A moving thing far at the side of the house catches his attention. He sees A Bull's yellow cast waving and then sees A Bull. A Bull's waving and he's all dirty.

Dumb Willie shouts the name and his own. He drops the hoe onto a fragile bit of corn and marches from the garden, that long chain jangling, kicking up dust as it winds around the plants and snaps them. When the links reach their limit, he is spilled to the grass. He looks back to the chain and the pole as though seeing both for the first time. Now to the jug on its side that his fingers still cannot reach. Now finally to A Bull, who has stopped his waving and looks on in a sad and fascinated way.

"You're chained, Dumb Willie," he say.

"I . . ." It's a word, he forgets what it is. "Fawled. It's on my. *Fut.*"

"Your folks here?"

Dumb Willie shakes his head. His hands spread and flex in the grass, gathering in the blades. A Bull leaves the side of the house, no longer needing to hide since they are alone. He's limping. A Bull's always limping, he's got bad bonez.

"They'll be gone awhile, you think?" A Bull asks.

"Da'ee say I heel the. *Corn*."

"Yeah, but are they gonna be gone awhile?"

Dumb Willie say they'll be gone awhile 'cause he's chayned. "Can't take you on the . . ." It's a word. "Tractor."

"That's okay. Can you take a break, you think? I got stuff to say."

He pats Dumb Willie's head and then walks down to Dumb Willie's feet, which is a long way for A Bull because he's so short and Dumb Willie's so tall. Jangling that chain and the lock that holds the foot to it, cursing.

"I'm sorry, Dumb Willie," he say. "I cain't get this off you."

"Oh. Kay."

A Bull leaves the chain and goes to where the jug of water is. He lets Dumb Willie drink first and Dumb Willie say thank you for the wadder.

"I got to tell you something, but it's a secret. You know what a secret is."

Dumb Willie nods. He knows *secret* and places a dirty finger over his lips.

"Yeah, that's it. Last night up at that barn? I seen Preacher Johnny after all that was over. I went out back and got him to give me one a them words. He did. He told me I was gonna find a treasure, and that when I found it I'd have to do something."

"It'sa. *Preecher.*"

"Yeah, the preacher. He did something, Dumb Willie. I don't know what kinda trick Preacher Johnny did. I thought it was a trick, but now I don't because of what I got to tell you. You should've seen it, way he acted." He looks at the chain. "Wish something like that'd happen to your folks once."

Dumb Willie doesn't nod in agreement. It's an awful thing what Abel say.

"I hurt my momma's feelings this morning, Dumb Willie. I didn't meant to. I think she's fed up with me, though. I cost her. She got all this money last night from people who want to help us out, but I had to give it to Reverend Johnny so I could get that word. I made her cry. My momma, Dumb Willie. I made my momma cry. That's just about the worst thing ever. I didn't even get to see the train this morning. But then I was cleaning up the wreck room—"

"Sorry," Dumb Willie say, "'bout that. *Trayne.*"

"It don't matter, now listen. I was cleaning out the wreck room and I found all these letters Momma kept hid. Know where they was from?"

Dumb Willie shakes his head.

"My daddy."

"You ain't got no. Da'ee you a bass . . . *terd.*"

A Bull say, "Not anymore I ain't. My daddy's still livin', and I know where at. That's the treasure Reverend Johnny told me. So I didn't know what to do then. I rode my bike out to see Preacher Keen. No way I could tell him everything, but I said what I could and he said I gotta go. I didn't think I could since it's so far away. I thought on it and thought on it, and I was thinking so hard that I forgot about having to cut in the trees when I passed Chris's house. Chris seen me. He tried killing me, Dumb Willie. Just like he promised. And now I think I gotta go. I just got to."

Dumb Willie's eyes shrink to slits. "Chris. *Stinks* Chris a. *Weed.*"

"Yeah." A Bull sighs, and that makes Dumb Willie grin. "Dumb Willie, you got to listen to me. Where my daddy is? It's a long way off. I think I know how I can get there, though. And I got to. If Reverend Johnny was right about the treasure, then that means he's right about the rest. He said that treasure's gonna get me healed." He stops here, talking slow and looking straight at Dumb Willie's nose. "Healed, Dumb Willie. That means I won't be cripple no more. You see?"

Dumb Willie bobs his head.

"And then you know what I'll get? A ree-ward."

"*Ree* . . . ward?"

"Yeah. And you know what that ree-ward is, Dumb Willie? It's my folks. Because I don't know why my daddy left or why Momma say he died, but I bet I can talk to him. I bet I can make him come back with me, and then we'll be a family."

"Fambly," Dumb Willie say.

"And then everything will be okay. Me and Momma'll never have to worry about anything again. Daddy'll get a new job here, and we'll almost be rich. I gotta go find my joy, Dumb Willie. But listen. Are you listening?"

"Yez."

"I cain't leave you here, 'cause there's no telling what'll happen to you. So I want you to come along. To go see my daddy. Momma can't go. I hurt her too bad, and she kept those letters from me so I ain't even supposed to know. But I need to find my joy, and so does she, and neither of us can find it if I stay here. So you think you wanna find some joy? It'll be an adventure."

"Venchure."

"Yeah. So you wanna come?"

Dumb Willie pulls on his chain. "I got heel the corn and pull. Weedz. Da'ee won't let me. Go he say we . . ." It's a word. "Kweer."

"No, we ain't. Your daddy beats on you an' your momma treats you bad. They say you got the devil. Shoot, they even chain you up in the garden. Folk who love don't do that, just craven ones. My daddy'll take care of us, I know he will, and then when we get back here I bet my daddy'll never let your folks do anything bad to you again. Shoot, my daddy might even say you can come live with us. I'll take care a you once I get healed. But it's a long way, and that's why you got to come along. We'll go tonight, okay? After everyone's in bed. You get some food and clothes and stuff and meet me in the field behind my house at eleven. You know eleven?"

Dumb Willie nods, say, "Leven." He knows leven when the news comes on and he's supposed to be asleep but he's not because that's when the trayne comes. A Bull hears the trayne so Dumb Willie hears the trayne because they're . . . it's a word . . . *friends*.

"Good. It's a secret now, okay? You remember that. It's a hush-hush."

Dumb Willie say, "Huss-huss." He says, "We goin'?"

"Yeah. We're going."

And A Bull smiles. It's a bright smile that makes Dumb Willie smile too and A Bull says yes, they goin', and it's a place where there's no stinky-weed Chris Jones and no mean mommas and no daddies that chain and beat. A Bull says the word where that place is and then says the other word it's like, and that is the word Dumb Willie repeats. He repeats that word over and over and softer each time, rolling it in his mouth as though it is dipped in honey. Dumb Willie says that word to A Bull and the tractor and the corn and the sparrow and the hot sun above. Says it again, to himself:

"Hebbin."

-7-

It was in Lisa's mind all day to take the long way home after work. That way she could make sure the tears were cried out and the anger was put away. While she suspects there is still some of both in her, it is not enough to keep her from going straight home. She hasn't spoken to Abel since leaving this morning. That makes almost twelve hours. Lisa's never been out of contact with her boy for such a stretch of time. Anger or not, tears or not, she wants to see his face. Wants to wrap Abel in her arms and kiss his head and get some toots love in return, and then she wants to figure out a way to make things right with her creditors in town.

He's in his room when she comes in, her shoulders rolled forward and her hair free of the bun Roy requires while working. The day's mail pokes out from the unzipped portion of her purse. No letter again today. Trying to see the light. The house smells of pine needles and the little sachet of potpourri that Lisa keeps stuck on the vacuum filter. Abel's cleaned. From the looks of it, he's cleaned everything.

"You like it?"

Abel is peeking out from the corner where the living room meets the hall.

"Sure."

"It took me all morning," he says. "I didn't clean nowhere else. Not the wreck room. Because I ain't supposed to go in there. But I put you a beer in the freezer," he says, "a little while ago. I thought maybe we could talk a minute."

"I think a good talk's in order."

Lisa sets her purse on the chair by the TV and plucks the bottle from the freezer. It's the only thing in there besides what's left of a box of Popsicles and half a bag of corn dogs. She hears the front door open and close, then the sound of a chair by the table on the porch being pulled out. Abel's waiting when she joins him. He's gotten a wire hanger from his closet and is shoving it down his cast, eyes half shut with pleasure.

"Are you mad at me?" he asks. "I mean, still."

"I don't know. Maybe a little."

"I ain't never made you cry before, Momma. Except when I get hurt. But those are always on accident, so I guess that's okay."

"What you did last night," she says, taking a drink, "was on purpose."

"Only because I wanted to make things better."

"Abel." Lisa moves her hand to his own. "There ain't no better for us, there's just getting by. And that's all folks need, really, when you think about it. We got a place to live and a car to get us to town and back. We're warm in the winter and cool in the summer and our bellies are full every night when we lie down in our own beds. I'd call that good living. You'll come to call it that too. But in the meantime, you're grounded. Two weeks. That means no Willie."

"Okay."

Okay? That's all he can muster? No bargaining, no grief?

"I know what I am," he says.

"And what's that?"

He shakes his head and pulls the hanger out, laying it on the table. It smells of dead skin.

"Tell me about Daddy," he says.

"What about him?"

"Anything."

"Well, he was a smart man, just about the smartest man I ever knew. Like you'll be."

"And what'd he do?"

"He drove a train."

"And how'd he die?"

Lisa takes another drink, a long one, and forces her eyes to stop burning. "He died, Abel."

"When?"

"Just before you were born."

"'Cause his heart gave out?"

"Yes," she says. "His heart gave out."

They are the same questions he always asks followed by the same answers he always hears, though their repetition has grown no easier. Then comes this question, one that's new:

"Where is he?"

Lisa sets her beer down. "What do you mean?"

"Is he in heaven?"

"Yes."

"But you don't believe in heaven."

"What?"

"You don't believe in heaven," Abel says again, "or nothing like that. Like Reverend Johnny, you said all he did was tricks."

He's looking at her square, not off into the trees at the dead end like he was looking yesterday. Studying her. Lisa doesn't understand what's happening here. This was supposed to be about Abel, not his daddy.

"That's just what folks say," she tells him.

"Where's he buried?"

"North Carolina."

"What town? Can we go there?"

"I don't think that's a good idea, Abel."

"Why not?"

"Because I said so."

That's not a good enough reason. Lisa knows it, and she expects Abel knows it too. But it'll have to do for now.

"What if things could be better?" he asks.

"They can't, Abel."

"But what if they could? Would you be happy?"

"I'm happy now."

"Maybe you ain't," he says. "Maybe you just been so sad for so long, you think that's what being happy is."

Lisa cannot answer this.

"Don't worry, Momma."

"About what?"

"About nothing."

He gets up from the table and leans in close for what Lisa believes will be a kiss. Instead, he snatches a nickel from behind her ear and places it on the table.

"What's this for?"

"For what I owe. I know it's not all of it, but I'll take care of the rest too."

He walks inside, letting the screen door shut behind him. Lisa can only sit and drink her beer. She fingers the nickel and wonders how long Abel has been carrying that around, wonders what just happened, and whether it was Abel who just got punished, or her.

-8-

He spends the rest of that evening locked in his room and pretending to sulk. What Abel really does is pack his things and try not to say good-bye. His school backpack is big enough to hold everything he thinks he'll need—extra clothes and underwear, a new toothbrush from under the sink, his atlas, and a small first-aid kit he sneaks from beneath the kitchen cabinet. The kit will be for Dumb Willie, should he need it. Abel knows if anything goes wrong with himself, antiseptic and bandages will be about as useful as a hammer.

An appearance must be made at suppertime and just before his momma goes to bed, if only to convince her nothing more is wrong with him than mourning two weeks without Dumb Willie. They watch an old Carol Burnett rerun on TV. It's their favorite and something of a nightly ritual. Abel makes sure to laugh in all the right places. His eyes wander toward his momma's purse, still on the chair. Today's mail is sticking out from one zipper. Abel wonders if there's something for him in there, another letter from his daddy. His momma has always been so insistent on being the one to stop by the post office. Even those times when Abel has been with her, she's made him stay in the car. Now he knows why. He goes to bed right after the cartoon Carol slops her mop into the bucket and scratches her butt. Lisa follows soon after.

At ten thirty on this Saturday night in June, Abel changes from his pajamas, puts on a pair of jeans and a white T-shirt, shoulders his school backpack, and sneaks from his bedroom. He stops by the wreck room and chooses three letters at random from the popcorn tin. Three, no more than that, and tucks them into his back pocket. He has no idea how often his daddy writes. The letters could come once a week or once a month, Abel doesn't know. But it wouldn't do, should the next come while he and Dumb Willie are still on their way, for his momma to come straight here and find the rest of the letters gone. She'd know right where her son was headed and be in Fairhope waiting, likely with Sheriff Barnett.

He does not look in on her, afraid that even cracking the door would break his momma's sleep. Abel merely leans his head against the door and shuts his eyes. He kisses the wood and whispers, "Toots love, Momma. I'll be back soon."

The back door is locked behind him. Abel twists the knob twice to make sure, once to the right and another to the left, and is struck by a sudden sense of guilt that there will not be a man around for a while to tend to such things.

The world beyond lies dark and quiet. No breeze tumbles down from the mountains this night. In the low places of the field, pockets of mist gather and spread like reaching fingers. The sky allows only a little more shine than the night before, a sliver of moon and stars scattered like bright grains of sand, a thick swath of the Milky Way. Abel tests the balance of the bag against his back by stepping off the slab of back porch. Past the rusting swing set and the clothesline and garage. At the edge of the yard he pauses to look back. A lone light burns over the back door.

"Good-bye," Abel says, to everything.

The crickets quiet as he steps among the field's tall grass. Here, Abel begins to relax. Night has never troubled him. Darkness brings a quality of balance. The eyes cannot be depended upon to judge big from small and strong from weak, meaning night is the only time he feels an equal to the things around him—not special, but ordinary. Yet he soon finds he cannot enjoy the walk down to the curve in the tracks as he should. Not merely because of the heaviness of the pack or the heaviness of his leaving, but because of the eyes upon him.

Someone is watching.

He stops, searching the shadows. Abel wants to dismiss the feeling as a symptom of some wider fear but finds he cannot. The feeling not only persists but grows stronger. He moves as quickly as he can manage, glancing over his shoulder as often as he does at his feet.

The place where the tracks curve lies empty. Dumb Willie is late. Abel touches his back pocket, drawing a sense of strength from the letters there. Could be Dumb Willie he senses. He studies the mist, the field, the house, watching for any movement. Abel even whispers a hard "Dumb Willie" into the black.

A shadow stands far off toward the side of the house. It does not correspond to any tree or shrub and seems rather to have sprouted from the ground on its own. Standing motionless near the light above the back door. Staring at him.

To Abel's left, a train whistle calls faintly.

The shadow by the house leaps forward with a speed Abel believes supernatural as the long whistle calls closer. Dumb Willie, it's Dumb Willie, that shadow is too fat to be Abel's momma's. Dumb Willie's gone to the house and not the curve. Abel shakes his head in the same pitiable way most do when in the Farmer boy's presence. He even chuckles to himself as he raises his cast to guide the figure in.

Closer now, the shadow running, Abel lowers his arm as

a bolt of fear surges through him. The figure coming gains in girth as it approaches, but not in height. Screaming Abel's name. Promising murder.

Not Dumb Willie. Not sweet Momma.

Abel cries out too late.

Chris Jones is upon him.

-9-

In spite of his advantage in both size and years, Dumb Willie does not share A Bull's comfort with the late hours. Darkness frightens him and always has. These times of shadow and gloom are when the things that have always haunted him rise from slumber. Every creak Dumb Willie hears in the night is a spurut. Every pop a munster.

These are the things that own the night, just as flesh rules the day.

But there are powers greater than even the dread that grips him now, powers like love, and love is what shines as a light for him along the faint path through the woods to A Bull's house. Dumb Willie sings because that's what he does when there are munsters and spuruts about, mushing the words into a broken, staccato rhythm. He turns every few steps to make sure he has not wandered from the trail. Each rustle of limbs behind is the debbil come for him, scurrying him on with a series of quiet yelps. The sack of clothes and food he's snuck from the house remains slung over his shoulder.

He was quiet when he left, just like A Bull said. Dumb Willie's ma and da'ee didn't hear, they don't know about the . . . it's a word . . . *venchure*. They don't know about the venchure 'cause it's a secret. Dumb Willie's got to go find A Bull's da'ee so A Bull won't be no bass terd no more.

The singing carries him most of the way to where the trees stop at the dead end. Dumb Willie eases onto A bull's porch and looks in A Bull's window but A Bull's not there. Then he remembers. *A Bull say meet me at the curve where the train gets not fast.*

Dumb Willie remembers he forgot, he's so dumb.

He eases off the porch and swings along the side of the trailer, stopping only to peer through the single small window on the end. The glass is so far from the ground that even someone of his height must rise to his tiptoes. Only shadows lurk within. But in that dark there are neither munsters nor spuruts, just A Bull's ma.

He waves though she cannot see. Dumb Willie say, "Gudbee *Lee*. Sa."

There's fog in the field and fog is where the munsters live, but that's where Dumb Willie goes because it's what A Bull said. Far away, the trayne whistles. He turns his face to the curve and sees a shadow there. It's a small shadow from all that way, and thin, and that shadow raises an arm like hello. Dumb Willie raises his arm too because that's A Bull. A Bull's at the curve because they're going to get on that trayne, have a venchure.

Dumb Willie holds his arm high, waving it. He takes a single step and sees another shadow bolting from the backyard and into the field. Running and running, a smudge that crosses his vision before vanishing into a bank of pale mist. It emerges again from the opposite side, aiming straight toward where A Bull stands, and there is only one word in Dumb Willie's fragile mind, two syllables that freeze him in place and make him want to scream:

Mun. Ster.

A Bull screams.

Dumb Willie forgets the sack. It drops into the grass as he goes chasing, plowing through the fog that reaches for him like hands. A Bull screaming again and that munster screaming, the trayne screaming too. Coming around the bend that trayne has one-two-three eyes shining like day.

The munster is on top of A Bull.

Dumb Willie feels his hands turn to fists. His face is hot from the running. A Bull crying, holding his cast high so that it may bear the blows. That munster punching, saying, "Look at you, you even bawl like a bastard," and what Dumb Willie wants to scream at that munster is *You can't be punching A Bull like that, he's got bad bonez*, but Dumb Willie's mouth is shut by the trayne's next whistle and his own rage, and in the next moment Dumb Willie is upon them.

The munster makes a sound like *POOF* when Dumb Willie's fist smashes into the side of its face. Dumb Willie reaches down to lift it from A Bull's body, his hands grasping hold of each side of the munster's head as he lifts it, squeezing that head as the munster cries and squeals and kicks its fat legs, making Dumb Willie even more incensed, making him scream out, *"You leave. Him. Lone you. Stink,"* as he goes shake shake shake and the munster's bonez go crunch.

Dumb Willie throws that munster away it stinks. A Bull is on the ground. His cast is still in the air and his eyes are like a bug's eyes. He's shaking like he's cold. Dumb Willie say, "A Bull Dumb. Willie you. Oh *kay?*" as the trayne sounds hard. Its eyes shine on the munster in the grass, it's all dead like a weed, that munster looks like Chris.

"The train," A Bull shout. "Dumb Willie, get on the train."

Dumb Willie picks A Bull up and carries him like a

football like they do on TV. He runs for that trayne passing. There's cars that don't have doors. A Bull says the doors on one car are wide. Dumb Willie reaches the . . . it's a word . . . rails and runs beside. That trayne is too fast. Those wide doors run away. Dumb Willie reaches, he can't reach. A Bull's pack slips off. It goes under the wheels and that trayne keeps going, going on.

"Run, Dumb Willie, run!" is what A Bull yells.

Dumb Willie runs fast.

-10-

A grief Abel cannot grasp is joined by a terror he cannot stand against as he watches his pack crushed beneath the train's wheels. The noise is unbearable, the scream of the engines and the howling of the rails, the great shaking of the ground. Dumb Willie clutches him tight. Abel's legs dangle from the ground. His head bobs free as an arm the size of a man's leg squeezes against his stomach, stealing his breath. He can't grip Dumb Willie's waist because his arm hurts, the busted one. Now both arms feel busted because of the way Chris beat him.

Chris.

He lets his head fall as Dumb Willie chases the boxcar. Behind them lies the upside-down image of Chris's body. One arm is stretched outward, the other pinned beneath his stomach. Chris's legs are bent as though he's trying to get up, but Abel knows Chris Jones will never get up again. His head is bloodied and caved from the rock Dumb Willie threw him upon. It is of little comfort that Chris likely never felt that hard landing. Abel had heard the boy's neck snap under the force of Dumb Willie's shaking and knew then that Chris was dead. Any doubt he harbored is gone now, at this final glance. Chris lies on his stomach and yet his head has been spun clean around, his chin tucked against his own back.

Abel cannot hear, cannot think for the noise. The cars seem ready to topple, shimmying, the only boxcar with an open door fading into the night. Even here at the slowest point of the tracks, the train moves too fast.

"Run, Dumb Willie, run!"

It is as if something even greater than murder and wobbly trains frightens Dumb Willie, because he looses a yell that pierces the night and finds a final burst of speed. The cars seem to slow as the train lurches and heels. The boxcar draws near again. Dumb Willie reaches his free hand out. His fingers strain for the bottom ledge of the car, almost as high as his shoulders, then draw back as the car eases away once more.

Abel feels Dumb Willie's grip on him loosen. Feels the arm around his stomach slide from there to his hip as another arm settles beneath his armpit, feels himself being lifted high toward the gaping night inside the car. He has always read that time slows and stretches out in moments of extreme peril. Here at the end, Abel knows that to be a lie. The world instead streaks too fast for his senses and thoughts to judge. Even Chris Jones is pushed from Abel's mind, forgotten in the midst of the new and horrible fact that Dumb Willie is about to toss him.

"No," he screams. "Dumb Willie, *don't*," as the bottom ledge of the boxcar inches closer a final time. Abel feels himself being hefted higher and tilted back in the same motion.

Here time does slow, if only for Abel's final breath. The train itself is made silent, the rails and wind. All thought and feeling are gone as Abel takes flight. His arms are outstretched and grasping, eyes wide as he realizes Dumb Willie hasn't thrown him far enough. Abel will not land inside the car, nor will his fingers even scrape the ledge. All things fall away as every memory and sense returns, the sum of his days reduced to a pinpoint in his mind. What fills Abel are not the letters he carries folded in his back pocket or the hungry steel beneath him and around, not Dumb Willie or Chris Jones or Reverend Johnny Mills. It is instead the picture of his momma, how tired she has always looked and how Abel was so wrong in leaving her alone.

His body begins to drop toward the wheels as Abel yields to what is meant. Somewhere far away, Dumb Willie cries out in a noise too full of knowing to have been made by an idiot.

There comes a moment of utter pain and nothingness, a great letting go that ends when two small hands emerge from the darkness of the boxcar. They take hold of Abel's shoulders, lifting him.

The last thing Abel feels is himself flying once more. The last he hears is Dumb Willie, screaming his name.

PART IV

THE TRAIN

-1-

He tumbles end over end into the middle of the boxcar and lands hard on his bad arm. There is no pounding of a broken bone bumped, no searing agony. Only panic grips Abel as he goes sliding. He shoots his left hand over the boards, searching for a gap or knothole, anything to stop his movement. None can be found in this darkness. The pitch and sway of the train drags him deeper into the car, the rectangle of dim light at the door shrinking. And outside, the anguished voice of Dumb Willie, wailing Abel's name.

His foot strikes the back of the boxcar; Abel struggles to his knees only to be thrown off-balance. He sinks to his stomach as a shadow appears at the door's edge. Fear silences what warning he may shout for Dumb Willie to run, to watch out. The shadow reaches down and out in a single motion that ends with Dumb Willie's bulging form pulled inside. He is thrown inside with an odd sort of grace, a perfect somersault that places him in the precise spot where Abel landed, legs straight and arms stretching to the sides, looking the way Jesus hung on the cross inside all the books Dumb Willie's momma has.

"A. *Bull.*"

Wailing the broken word not as a plea for help but as the sound a heart makes when it has been rent and stripped bare. Dumb Willie is crying. Abel has never heard him cry.

The shadow is gone, the wide door empty but for ashen moonlight. Noise floods Abel's senses, wind and iron and the train's squeal as it gathers itself away from the field. Beyond, the night flies, near meadows and distant ridges and all the world Abel has ever known, his momma and their little house. And Abel here in this box of steel and wood, alone but for the company of a killer and the shadow of some something. His perception shrinks to just what he can smell—a rank combination of diesel and what can only be urine.

"A. *Bull.*"

"I'm here," Abel says, and that is all he says, because he is here and Dumb Willie and that something else as well, and Abel doesn't know just now which frightens him more.

Dumb Willie's form sits up and scampers toward the sound of Abel's voice. "A Bull you. *Fawled.*"

Abel feels Dumb Willie's fingers groping for him. He stabs at them in the darkness with his cast, then feels the stroke against his arm.

"*Don't touch me,*" he says, so loud that Abel knows Dumb Willie has heard him. He knows that shadow, that whatever-it-is, has heard him as well.

Dumb Willie jerks his hand away as though it's been burned. Which, Abel supposes, it has been, only by the heat of his words rather than his skin. He regrets saying it as soon as he does. Not only because it has called attention to themselves, but because Abel knows Dumb Willie's feelings are hurt. But he cannot bear that touch for the moment, those same hands upon him that just shook Chris Jones until his neck snapped and all the life in him drained out. It doesn't matter that Dumb Willie's memory of that act has likely been shaken out as well, him being *special* in that way just as Abel is *special* in another. It doesn't matter, because Abel will never be rid of Chris's final moments. That look of rage and hate as he rained down his fists and swore death swirling to the one of shock and puzzlement that became Chris's dying expression. That memory will haunt the remainder of Abel's days.

"I didn't fall," he says. "I'm okay, Dumb Willie."

Around and beneath him, the train ratchets upward into the hill country. Abel climbs to his knees, gathering balance. Now to his feet. He searches the darkness.

In his ear, Dumb Willie says, "Sumthun *got*. Me."

"I know." And softer, "Me too."

Motion at the opposite end of the car, there and now not. The train is gathering speed. Outside, the world is a mass of hard shadows broken by occasional house lights in the distance, shooting stars that blink away too fast to wish upon. They could make it to the door. Jump if they must. Even if for Abel jumping would mean—

From the darkness comes a voice that echoes over the wheels and rails: "Who are you?"

Dumb Willie shrieks.

"You can't be here," the voice says. "Nobody's supposed to be here."

Abel spins his head to where the words have come from, far in the opposite corner, just as Dumb Willie answers, "A Bull. *Fawled*."

"No, I didn't," Abel whispers.

"What's that?" the voice asks. "Who are you?"

No longer in the corner. A spot near the door? Abel thinks he sees a shadow there.

He gropes for Dumb Willie's hand and finds it. Squeezes. The meaning is clear: *Don't say a word.*

"I'm Dumb. *Willie.*"

"Got to be dumb," the voice answers, "thinking you can flip a cannonball like that. What you make me do that for?"

A girl's voice. One tired like Abel's momma's and just as kind, with a sweetness like Miss Ellie's. There's a girl on the train. This frightens Abel even more than seeing Chris dead and knowing the man who killed him is currently holding his hand, scares him more than even his tumble toward the rails.

A light blooms, hardening the shadow near the door to a tall, slender body. Her back is to Abel, the flame hidden. When she turns, the light takes hold and gathers atop a thick white candle in the girl's left hand to reveal the far side of the car and a battered leather bag against the wall there. She is young, older than one of the high school kids but not by much. Her hair is long and auburn, half of which has been tied into a ponytail that hangs over her left shoulder. The rest tumbles down the right side of her face, curling inward just below a narrow chin so that it frames two blue eyes that sparkle.

Most of her hair is hidden beneath a black hat like the ones Abel has seen in the old movies, something a gangster would wear, or an old farmer. Its brim is beaten and its crown holed. The ribbon has gone missing. Her blue jeans are worn through at the knees; her tennis shoes may have once been white but are now as filthy as those on Abel's feet. The shirt she wears matches the hat's color, a black streaked with the gray dust of the boxcar. A row of white buttons begins midway to her stomach. Only half of these are fastened, revealing smooth, tanned skin and the beginnings of two mounds that threaten to loosen Abel's bladder. He pinches it shut before there is an accident.

"It'sa. *Girl,*" Dumb Willie says, his voice awed and low, like he's witnessing a miracle.

"You hush," the girl says. There is venom in her voice, and rising rage.

"You keep away," Abel says.

"Or what?"

"He'll kill you."

Spoken in the gravest possible tone and without the slightest tremble, because Abel knows these words to be true. As an added warning, he glances at Dumb Willie beside him. Most of the big man remains hidden by the night, though the candle reveals a splattered streak of blood—Chris's, it can be no one else's—staining the front of his overalls. Yet where there should be building rage (or at least bubbling fear) upon Dumb Willie's face, Abel sees something else. Dumb Willie isn't looking at the girl at all. He's looking at Abel instead, slack-mouthed, his cheeks flushed and his eyes wide and watering.

Abel looks back to the girl. "You better be scared."

She chuckles, the candle bobbing in her hand. "That a fact? I don't see nothing much to fear. What are you two doing in my house?"

Dumb Willie glances down at his hands, flexing them. He looks up to Abel and says, "Chris. *Stunk,*" before Abel plunges him into woeful silence with a single look. However much Abel longs to see that slumbering monster inside his friend bare its teeth to the stranger across the way, no trace of it appears. Instead, Dumb Willie shifts his look of dream-like wonder, unchanged and whole, from Abel to the figure by the door. It's as though he's never seen a girl before. Or at least not one this beautiful.

"That your name?" she asks. "Chris?"

"I'm Dumb"—grinning now—"*Willie.*"

The candle flickers. The girl shields the flame by cupping it in her hand, forcing the light to cone around her face. Abel reminds himself to breathe.

"We didn't know anyone'd be here," he says. "We're sorry."

"Sorry?" The car fills with a chuckle that sounds more like sadness, like the breaking of a sacred thing. "Sorry don't mean a thing now."

"You can't throw us out."

"Why? You'll kill me if I try?"

Abel doesn't like the question. Nor does he much approve of the manner in which it was asked, with the raising of one brown eyebrow and a smirk that conveys some secret knowing. He wonders if the girl was watching at the curve. If she saw.

"We won't bother you. Ain't that right, Dumb Willie?"

Dumb Willie says, "It'sa *girl*. Over there."

"Can't throw you out," she says. "But if you stay, I'll need rent. You got anything I need?"

Abel thinks of his backpack, now lost miles behind. And given that Dumb Willie's next reply only serves to remind them yet again that Chris *stunk*, Abel is left to believe what provisions his friend brought have been left behind as well, either back along the curve or in the field, tossed away with as little forethought as Dumb Willie tossed Chris. In a night filled by all manner of horrible things, this is the one that collapses Abel's spirit. They have neither rent to pay nor supplies to see them to Fairhope. Worse, it won't be long before Chris is found. Come morning, Royce Jones will rise to find his boy gone. The Farmers will discover Dumb Willie missing, and Lisa will sneak into Abel's room to wake him and find his bed empty. Sheriff Barnett, the whole town. How long before someone gets the idea to search the tracks behind Medford Hoskins's old rental house? How long before they find Chris and find Abel's pack, find Dumb Willie's?

How long until they know?

"We don't have anything. We lost it all getting on the train."

"Sure now?" she asks. "Bet you carrying something of worth."

Her eyes narrow in a way that is less doubt than searching, the candle held high. Abel thinks of the letters in his pocket.

"I'm sure."

She adjusts her hat and neither nods nor speaks, only sits, using the leather bag as her chair.

Abel sits as well. He leans against the corner of the car and pulls on Dumb Willie's arm, making him settle.

"It'sa. *Girl.*"

"I know. You just sit here with me, Dumb Willie. Sit here and don't you move."

They ride for what feels a long while, long enough for the train to crest the mountains and the car to shift such that Abel's end is the one higher. Dumb Willie's chin drops. He raises it with a grunt, flutters his eyes. No amount of elbowing and pleading on Abel's part can keep him present. Dumb Willie sleeps as only the ignorant can, deep and peaceful.

The girl continues her vigil by the door. There is something of her that Abel feels is terrible in a way terrible doesn't mean, much like the flame in her hand can comfort so long as you don't draw too near. Abel stares down at his cast, which has been left dented but whole. He stares and will not look away, because even now he can feel the girl's eyes upon him, those pretty blue ones set inside that pretty face. He feels that look as one that speaks not of friendship, but of options weighed and regrets counted.

-2-

Only now does the world slow enough for the girl to regain her thoughts, consider things, and what she considers is not the boy across the way or his slumbering friend Dumb Willie or even how the two of them came to be in this car. What the girl considers is how this should not be.

The boy moves his gaze away toward something and anything else, finally settling on the filthy yellow cast that covers an arm so small the girl doubts it would even reach past her own wrist. Beside him sleeps the one called Dumb Willie, his snore silent over the grinding rails. That snore is far more comforting than the look Dumb Willie first gave her, one so full of wonder and knowing that she could only answer in anger.

Yes, she thinks. Anger is what she felt. At them, at herself. And it is anger she still feels, though now tempered with the fear of being placed in such a position as this.

It was a mistake, bringing them here. Dumb Willie, but the boy most of all.

Yet as the boy draws his legs inward to make a wall of knobby knees and grass-stained denim between them, the girl believes she has committed no violation. Would anyone be seated where she is now, they would believe the same.

They, too, would have taken pity.

The boy is a frail thing, pale and waiflike, with strange alien eyes and a body that looks pieced together of spare parts—one short leg matched with one longer, a chest too full for his waist, an odd hip alongside an even one.

No harm has yet been done that cannot be repaired.

He glances up, meeting her eyes for only an instant. Now looking away again, to Dumb Willie rather than the cast. His hand slips behind his back in a slow motion designed to go unnoticed but which only calls attention to itself. What does he have back there?

"Thank you," the boy says.

"For what?"

"Saving us. You didn't have to."

"Shouldn't have," the girl says. "It's not meant. Understand?"

"No," says the boy. "Are you a hobo, a tramp, or a bum?"

"What?"

"I read about them. How they sneak on trains. I know all about trains."

"You don't know enough to not try to get on one that's moving. You think something like that can end more than one way?"

"We had to."

The boy grows quiet. *Good*, she thinks. *Let him be still awhile, give me time to think.* Should have thought before, she wouldn't be in this mess now. Should have left what was meant to take its course as she stood in the darkness of this car, looking out on that field. Should have stayed apart even as that strange scene unfolded before her eyes, this boy being beaten by another and Dumb Willie running.

Should have let it be.

But no, she couldn't. Not one more time.

"Hobo," she says.

The boy raises his head. "What?"

"To answer you. Hobo, tramp, bum. Hobo."

"That's good."

She lets the candle flicker, the flame struggle to keep hold. "Why do you say that?"

"Hobos are trustable," the boy says. "Tramps don't work 'less they got to, bums won't work at all. But a hobo works all the time. He travels and he works. Or she."

"You're a smart fella."

"I read it," the boy says.

The girl lets silence sink in again, or what passes for it here. Just the wind and the wheels, the singing rails. She says, "You know all about hobos, guess you know the code."

"Code?"

"Hobo code. Everybody got to have a code, 'bo ain't no different. Like how you got to cause no trouble and how you got to move like a ghost. Not be seen. Like how you ain't supposed to help no runaways."

"I ain't no runaway."

"Well, why you here then?" She points to Dumb Willie, still snoring in spite of all the hollering around him. "Why's he here? Only two reasons anybody's got to hop a train to anyplace. Either it's for what they think they'll find when they get there, or to run from the place they are."

"We're on a mission," says the boy.

"For what?"

He won't answer.

"You in trouble?"

He won't answer that either.

You are, she thinks. *The both of you. Now I am too. And you have no idea how much.*

She settles her back against the car, taking in the two boys across the way. Neither is so different from the ones who've come before, who whether by their own choosing or not reach the end of one thing and have nothing to do but go in search of another. Dumb Willie wears a bloodstain on the front of his overalls. There are no cuts on his body or the boy's. The other boy's, then—the one Dumb Willie killed. Flung him like a bale of hay, left him a sack of lifeless bones. The girl had watched, silent and hidden, as Dumb Willie snatched up his friend and went running for this boxcar. Him screaming and the boy screaming. What she should have done was nothing. Abel went tumbling to the rails, and what the girl was supposed to do was trust what's meant.

But there had been none of that this time. No standing guard, no trust. No code. Because after that fall and in the midst of those cries

(Those cries)

she remembers her own hand shooting out from the dark, taking hold of the boy. She remembers pulling the boy inside even as the deepest parts of herself screamed their protests, and remembers pulling Dumb Willie in as well, shattering everything, unbalancing some never-touched part of her own universe, and why? Why these two, when neither is no different from all those others who crossed her path?

And it is here the girl alights upon an answer, perhaps not the correct one but one that feels close enough to truth: it was because they were no different at all. Because that made them everyone.

"I'm not running away," the boy says again. "I'm out to save my momma. I'm to bring my daddy home. I'll get a reward."

"What about him there?" she asks, nodding toward the hulking form beside him.

"Dumb Willie had to come. I have to keep him safe. That's what friends do. Don't you know that?"

She doesn't. The candle flickers and the train rolls and she doesn't know what *friends* means. She wonders if that, too, had a hand in this thing she's done.

"We have to get to Fairhope," the boy says. "It's important."

"Fairhope? Carolina? Long way to go if you don't know where you're going. That where your daddy is?"

"Yes. My name's Abel."

The girl nods. "Old name. Bible name."

"So I've heard."

"Well, Abel, I'm gonna snuff this candle. Burnin' low, and I ain't got another one. That suit?"

Abel dips his chin and raises it. He reaches for Dumb Willie's hand. "You ain't gone hurt us, are you? Because I don't think you will. I think you're kind."

She laughs, too shaken to do anything else. "Kind? Ain't nobody ever called me kind. But no, Abel. I ain't gonna hurt you. You don't have evil in your heart, do you? Or that man with you? One of you gonna sneak over here in the night and put me on the Westbound?"

"Never," he says. "I won't never do that to you."

"Good, then."

She holds out the candle. There is a *whoof* that plunges the car to darkness. Only moonlight remains, dim and shadowy through the open door.

"Never minded the dark," she says. "Some people's scared in it. Not me. There's things you see in the night ain't no place else. Brings a comfort, don't you think? Makes you face things."

She hears only the wind at the other side of the car and senses no movement.

"You keep over there, Abel. Won't do you no good to fall to sleep and roll right out this car."

"I don't think I'll sleep tonight," comes the reply. "If it's all the same."

The girl nearly smiles to herself. Nearly. The rest of her is too occupied with what she's gotten into and what she must do next. She thinks, *No, boy, I don't guess you'll sleep much at all*, and lowers the brim of her hat, settling her head against the wall. The car rocks them, the *thump thump* of the wheels beneath. The train carries them ever on, safe and sound like a momma's womb.

Too late to make things right now, she thinks. Though sooner or later, she'll have to get this boy home.

It's meant.

-3-

Though Abel is aware he has been proven wrong of much in the last days, he finds a strange comfort when he proves himself right in this: sleep will not come. He shuts his eyes to the darkness and the strange girl who saved them—a girl, he reminds himself, who would not even offer her name. It is a mystery what sort of person would go to all the trouble of saving someone's life (not only his own, Abel recalls, but Dumb Willie's as well; leaving Dumb Willie behind surely would have amounted to a death sentence) and still be so wary as to not even volunteer the most basic part of herself. Maybe that's another part of the code. Abel has never met a hobo, but what he has read of them leads him to believe they are a strange breed, and prone to peculiarities.

He rolls to his side—always the position in which he has

slept, curled into a ball so nothing can hurt him—and uses Dumb Willie's chest as both mattress and pillow, careful to avoid Chris's blood. The faint outline of the girl remains by the door. Abel thinks she's still looking at him. Far from unnerving, her vigil gives him a sense of safety and almost peace. She isn't scary, not anymore. Abel has spent so much of his life in fear that to discern what is truly frightening and what only pretends to be is a simple enough matter, and the girl is not scary. She is odd and beautiful, but not dangerous.

He is in possession of no facts to support this theory, yet the past day has taught him that sometimes facts alone are irrelevant. Sometimes it's the feeling of a thing that matters more, and what Abel feels is that the girl is no different from himself in the ways that matter. They are both wandering now, both unsure of the road they take. That makes them kin in a way. His lips spread at that word—*kin*—and Abel smiles at the notion that one so wonderful as she could share a bond with someone so ruined as him. Yet as his head rises and lowers ever so slightly in time with Dumb Willie's breaths, Abel decides it's true, or at least could be so. He has long seen Dumb Willie as a kind of kin. The strongest of bonds very often have nothing to do with flesh. Sometimes it's longing that yokes people together, and in ways that are not understood but still endure all things.

His mind refuses rest for fear of the nightmares that may follow. Images of his momma and of Chris; of the monster alive inside Dumb Willie and of himself being thrown toward the rails; the girl watching him, who somehow both eases and dismays. Abel's only comfort is the sound of the wheels beneath him, turning on toward someplace other. What portion of him that knows that running may do no good now is silenced by the greater part that says running is all that remains. For himself, but for Dumb Willie more.

However long and dark the road ahead and no matter the joy found at its end, there will be only one happy ending now. Abel can still return home with his daddy, but not Dumb Willie. More even than the restlessness, this thought is what keeps Abel awake this night. Not the long road afore, not Reverend Johnny's promises of Abel's healing, his daddy, his reward. Nobody will ever believe Dumb Willie was only trying to save Abel. Not once they find Chris dead and see how mangled he looks. Not when they all get a good fill of that expression that died on Chris's face. It'll be up to Abel to figure out a way to keep Dumb Willie safe. Right now, that means getting as far from Mattingly as they can.

He shuts his eyes and listens to those turning wheels that inch him farther and farther from the field and a trouble he cannot fathom. He will not sleep, refuses it. Sleep, in fact, is the only thing from which Abel cowers this night. He is afraid if he drifts, the train will somehow stop moving. That it will even somehow turn and go backward, returning him to all that lies behind.

*

He rolls over again to find only the worn wooden floor and morning light reaching into the deepest parts of the box-car. Dumb Willie stands at the edge of the open door, looking out to a world that has moved on from meadows and ridges to endless thick forest. The girl stands with him. Their backs are turned. Her hand rubs Dumb Willie's back in small circles as she speaks in low, soothing tones. It is an act that speaks to Abel of comfort, even intimacy, and flares a jealousy in him before his mind can form a single thought.

"Hey, what y'all doin'?"

Dumb Willie shudders like he's been splashed with water. The girl turns and adjusts the brim of that hat she wears, which remains still even in the breeze.

"Abel," she says. "Mornin' to you. We're just talking on things is all. Filling each other in."

Abel stands. He wobbles less than he did last night, in much the same way he supposes a sailor gets his sea legs. Or maybe that sudden spurt of agility is owed to a fear of what Dumb Willie may have confessed.

"Fillin' each other in on what?" he asks.

"On what's got to happen. To you and him, and to me."

"Dumb Willie, you okay?"

The big man moves a hand to his head and turns, facing Abel with eyes gone wet and red. He wipes his nose and mixes the snot on his fingers with the dried blood on his overalls. In a broken voice Dumb Willie says, "Love. You A. Bull."

"That's weird," Abel says. "Don't say stuff like that." And then to the girl, "What'd you tell him? You done got him all blubbery."

She holds out her hands, palms up, as though feigning ignorance.

"A. Bull you got go. *Home.*"

It is not so much what Dumb Willie says as the way he says it, almost as though there's no choice left to them now—it is the way Chris Jones had talked just before leaving Principal Rexrode's office, when he'd promised murder. Dumb Willie looks a pitiful thing, standing there by the door. So big and strong he shouldn't be scared of anyone, now crying like a little baby.

Yet something in Abel can see in these tears and in this broken, pleading face Dumb Willie's truest self. It isn't the muscles that make him what he is, nor is it Dumb Willie's dumbness that first drew Abel to him that day on the playground. It is rather that Dumb Willie is *good*, he is *kind*, and the world has not enough of those things. He does not look a murderer, a breaker of children. Just after they were pulled to the train, Abel feared his friend for what Dumb Willie had done. Now he can only look upon him with a mixture of adoration and respect. Dumb Willie saved him. It doesn't matter if anyone else will ever believe that, Abel will. And as such, Abel vows here and now in this dusty old boxcar that he will save Dumb Willie right back. That's what he knows his momma would do. Lisa Shifflett doesn't believe in God, but she does believe in sin. After last night, Abel counts himself a believer in wickedness as well—in Chris, in Dumb Willie. Even in himself.

"We ain't goin' home, Dumb Willie. We know that. Where are we?"

"A good ways from where you came," the girl says, "which is how trains do. Not so far as you'd like, though. It's a slow ride on this track. Mountains tend to be tall." She looks from the door. "We're deep in the woods here. Double track ahead. There's another train coming, and it's a cannonball."

"What's that mean?"

"Means it's a fast load. That cannonball's gotta get to where it's goin' quick. It's got the right of way. Happens all the time on this rail."

Dumb Willie still stares. Love is not upon his lips but is spread wide on his face, love and sadness plenty. Abel tries to keep his eyes away.

The girl won't look at him. She's looking outside and

saying, "Train's got to switch tracks up ahead to let that cannonball pass. It'll stop altogether and wait. That cannon-ball'll go by nice and easy before going on its way. Back to where I got you. We need to be on that other train, Abel. I got to get you home."

"Me and Dumb Willie are goin' to Fairhope."

"For your reward?"

"A Bull ain't no bass . . . *terd*," Dumb Willie says.

The girl wrinkles her forehead. "What's that mean?"

"Means we can't go back," Abel says. "We can't go home. Not yet."

"You got no means. No provisions. Shoot, you don't look like you ever been no place. How you gonna get to Fairhope?"

"The train'll take us."

"We're going west, Abel. Fairhope's southway. You jumped the wrong train."

She's still looking from the door and Dumb Willie's still mourning when Abel realizes what's happened. The girl has seen him. Last night it was too dark for that. There was nothing but her candle to go by, and what faint moonlight forced its way into the first half of the boxcar. She heard his voice, maybe got a glimpse of his face, but nothing more. Here in the full light of day, though, there are no shadows in which Abel can hide. Everything of him, every bit of his broken parts and misshapen body, is laid bare. And while sunlight serves the girl well (Abel cannot believe that someone he saw as so pretty in the night could be made even more so in the daylight, but it's true), it only makes himself uglier. That's why she won't look at him. Sending them back isn't part of some code. It's more a rejection.

"Then we'll get on another train," he says. "One going south. You can take us."

The words are out of his mouth before Abel can snatch them back, leaving the girl in silence. He had wanted to broach the subject of her going along as early as last night, though in a far more elegant manner. Now Abel decides he will force it. If she is sending them back to Mattingly simply because they're too unfit to travel on with her—with a hobo, albeit a beautiful one—he will make her say it.

For the first time this morning, Dumb Willie finds his grin. It looks a horrid thing, jagged and devoid of all sense. Abel prefers it to the blubbering.

"I can't do that," she says. "You think I got no sense? Go all the way to Fairhope with a couple Angelinas like you?" She shakes her head in a way that seems to Abel more for herself than him. Like she's fighting something. "I can't do it, Abel. I have to get you home. It's meant."

"It ain't meant," he says, unsure what *meant* means. "A man sent me. He gave me a word and told me to go and so I did, me and Dumb Willie, and he was a holy man. He did magic. Like you did when you saved us."

Dumb Willie lays his hand against the girl's arm. He leans in, nodding as though to clarify things. "A Bull know the. *Magic.*"

"What?" she asks. "You think I'm magic?"

It sounds ridiculous, that's true, at least some of it does, but the parts Abel still struggles to believe about Reverend Johnny and what he said are the parts that matter little right now. And though it sounds ridiculous, the girl isn't laughing.

"I'm saying something happened that I don't know, and then you happened. And I think you're supposed to come."

"No, Abel. That's what you don't understand. I never should have brought y'all this far. We have to turn—"

"We can't," he says. "You don't understand *that*. We cain't go back."

"Why? There something you need to tell me?"

Abel can only stand there as the train begins to slow, wondering where this part of his plan had gone so wrong. It should have been good enough, having Dumb Willie along. Four days to Fairhope, five at the most. Most of that sitting in the same old boxcar hooked to the same old train, having their adventure. He'd figured getting on the train would be the most dangerous part of their trip. Now it's become the easiest. He should have thought things out more, but everything happened too fast. Abel had gotten into trouble at school and had gotten hauled off to revival, had met Reverend Johnny and hurt his own momma, found his daddy's letters—

His daddy's letters.

"I need to show you something."

He reaches into his back pocket and draws them out, folded and wrinkled. The girl's eyes settle there. Abel walks the length of the car with them outstretched in his hand. The one with the cast stretched around it. Abel wants her to think long and hard before sending a cripple and a dummy back to where they came from.

"You asked me last night for rent. Something I got of worth. These are it. I'm sorry I lied."

She takes them in one dirty hand and turns the pages over. Her eyes pass over them quick. Abel wonders if the girl can even read.

"I found them yesterday. They're from my daddy. He's in Fairhope, like I said. I have to find him. Me and my momma ain't getting by. She says we are, but we ain't because there's no joy, there's just trying and trying. That's why I'm gonna go find him. I'm gone bring my daddy back home with me and we're all gone be together. He can work so Momma won't have to so much. But we can't go back right now until I figure things out. Something's happened"—Abel looks at Dumb Willie, who stands at the door looking not at Abel but at the girl as he says this—"and it's something bad. For Dumb Willie especially, but me too."

The train nears a crawl and lurches hard to the right, accompanied by a scraping sound so loud it could mean the whole world's been torn in half. Abel sees two sets of rails from where he stands. One leads on, the other back. He pauses to think what that makes this place, here in the middle of all these trees. He settles on a word: *crossroads*. For him and Dumb Willie, for the girl as well.

She says, "You don't know what you're asking."

And now something, not an idea but more an impulse, gives Abel these words: "I thought he was dead. My daddy. Momma always told me he was and I don't know why. I couldn't ask her because I ain't supposed to go in the wreck room by myself, but I did since I was trying to say I was sorry for what I did. I did something bad. Maybe two things." He thinks that over. "One and a half things. It don't matter. What matters is I been sent. That's all I can say. I got a promise that something good's gone happen if I go. It's like a second chance. Ain't nobody hardly ever gets something like that, but now I got one and I got to go. And you got to come too. Please?"

The girl stares at the letters. From this close Abel can smell her. She stinks of dirt and sweat and all things good. Far off, a cannonball whistles.

She whispers, "I'm supposed to take you home."

"Not yet," Abel says. "Please, just not yet."

-4-

The massive brakes squeal and smoke, shuddering the floor beneath Abel's feet. With no word either way, the girl hands the letters back and peeks around the edge of the door. The train's engines idle to a low groan.

"Can't see it," she says. "Y'all back off anyhow. Dumb Willie? That cannonball comes, I don't want that other driver to see you."

They oblige, Dumb Willie and Abel crowding to one side of the door and the girl to the other, the three of them watching and waiting.

"We might have a bit," she says. "Could be half an hour, could be more. You can tell what'll happen with a train most times, but sometimes you can't. That driver up there, he might be kicking back for a bit until that cannonball comes past. Might be he'll take a little walk, check the connections and the cars."

"What if he finds us?" Abel asks. "Nobody can know we're here."

"Be all right," says the girl. And now she looks from the edge of the door and over her shoulder to where Abel stands. Grinning at him in a way that lets him feel it's true, they really will be all right. "A good hobo is a sneaky thing, and a good driver knows it. We leave them alone, they'll do the same. It ain't like things used to be. Drivers and 'bos get along all right so long as we keep quiet. We're ghosts, you see. That's how we got to act. So long as we do, won't nobody get found."

She sits cross-legged on the boxcar's floor, those two tanned knees sticking out from the holes in her jeans. Dumb Willie's looking at them. Abel wants to say quit that.

"This train's going to Greenville," she says.

Abel wants to look that up in his atlas. He gets so far as to look back toward the recesses of the car for his backpack before remembering he doesn't have it anymore. That got crushed back home along the tracks, right after Chris got crushed too.

"West Virginia," the girl says. "We crossed over before dawn."

"West Virginia? That's the whole wrong way."

"Said you hopped the wrong train. Not every set of tracks moves south, Abel. We'll have to stop in Greenville. Part of this load is feed going to the mill there. We'll sneak off then, find us something going south."

Abel grins at the word—*we'll.*

"You. *Comin'*?" Dumb Willie asks.

"Got to, don't I? Abel says he ain't going home, and the only reason y'all here is because of me. Means I got to see you through. Ain't that right, Dumb Willie?"

Though he has no proof, Abel cannot chase the suspicion that much is passed in the long and unbroken look the girl and Dumb Willie share. He would question them both were there time, but now comes in the far distance the call of a whistle. The cannonball is near, which is of some consequence. And the sun is getting high. That is the bigger consequence and all Abel can think of at the moment, that high sun and what time it must be getting. Most everyone will be up now. Dumb Willie's folks and Chris's. Abel's momma.

He gets up and moves into the soft shadows deeper inside the car. Waddling more than walking, massaging his hips and

155

his broken arm more from habit than any inkling of pain. Which is strange, he decides. Abel can sleep in his bed and then get up with joints that feel like an old man's, but he rolls around on the wooden floor of a boxcar all night and he feels fine. Great, even.

He turns to see the girl staring at him, blue eyes piercing. "You okay?" she asks.

Dumb Willie answers, "A. Bull's a . . . *clipple.*"

"Stop that, Dumb Willie," he says. And to the girl, "Don't stare. I don't like it when people stare at me."

"What's the matter?" she says again.

"Clipple," Dumb Willie answers. He holds his palms out and shakes his head as though adding, *How many time I got to say it?*

It isn't mean, the way the girl has asked it. In fact, Abel has taken her words as something of genuine concern rather than mere curiosity. Not that it makes him feel much better.

"It doesn't matter what's wrong with me," he says.

The girl shakes her head, making her brown hair shimmer in the sun. "It matters if we're all going on together." That hair is better than Miss Ellie's. "We can't be loping all over creation if you want to get to where you want to be. It'll be a hard go. You ready for me to take you home?"

"No."

That sun. It has to be near nine o'clock now.

"What's your name?" Abel asks.

"Never needed one."

"Sure you do. Everybody's got a name. Ain't that right, Dumb Willie?"

"I'm Dumb. *Willie,*" he says.

Abel decides to sit again, though keeping to the shadows. That way she won't dwell on what he is, only what he says.

"What are you doing out here all by yourself?" he asks. "Which reason is it?"

"I don't know what you mean," she says.

"You told me there's only two reasons people hop a train, for what they think they'll find when they get to where they're going or to run from where they are. Which are you?"

She smiles. It is the first time Abel has seen her do that, and it is as pretty and pure as he'd imagined. For the most part, anyway. Her lips spread in a way that makes dimples on her cheeks and her teeth show, though only the top row, which is as brown as his own but not so jagged. The corners of her mouth nearly touch what parts of her hair aren't covered by that black hat. The girl's eyes, though, remain still. There is no greater spark in them from that smile than there is without one, as if the amusement his question has triggered reaches deep but not far.

"Neither," she says. "I just ride. Always have, I guess. Ever since I can remember. I go from place to place and make my way best I can."

"Where's your folks?"

"Don't have any."

"But you got to have a name," he says. "What do people even call you?"

"Whatever they want."

"What do we call you?"

She shrugs. The cannonball calls again, much closer now.

It would give a body shivers, Abel thinks, looking long into those eyes. The day has come hot, baking the inside of the boxcar. Haze clings to the trees outside. Already the front of Dumb Willie's overalls is soaked. Yet the girl remains calm and still, her own clothes untouched by sweat, as though she's seen drier days than this.

"Dorothy," Abel says.

"What?"

"That's what we'll call you. It's from one of my favorite magicians. Dorothy Dietrich? She's the only woman to ever do the catching bullet trick. That's when you catch a bullet in your *mouth*. It's like the hardest trick ever."

Dumb Willie leans forward, putting his face in the sun. He says to the girl, "A. Bull can do the. Magic."

"That true?" she asks.

Even though his face remains in the shadows and even if she can't see, Abel still blushes.

"I'll show you sometime," he says, "Dorothy." He smiles at the word. It is a powerful thing, naming someone. "Dumb Willie, this here's Dorothy. You say hi."

Dumb Willie grins. "Hi Do. Tee."

And Dorothy smiles herself, everywhere but in her eyes. "The pleasure is mine, Dumb Willie. And Abel. Abel the Great."

Abel's cheeks feel so hot he swears they're about to burst into flame. The whistle calls again, this time so close that the walls of the boxcar tremble.

"Come on over here," Dorothy says. "You can watch with me."

She opens her left arm, inviting him. Abel leaves his spot in the shadows and joins her, keeping his head down and trying not to waddle, not wanting to see her seeing him. He squats next to her and shudders as her arm goes around him, then looks to see an expression of longing on Dumb Willie's face.

Only one engine leads the cannonball, meaning the cars behind will be few. It slows with a final call and comes alongside at barely a creep—four tankers, a dozen flats, and two boxcars on the end, their doors wide. Abel watches them all. How easy it would be, jumping one of those boxcars and heading home. Running back into his momma's arms and saying he's sorry, he was only trying to help things. Go inside his own house and walk through his own yard, travel up and down his own little dead-end road. For the first time, he believes he may have done as Dorothy asked if only there was a little more time to consider things. He would have taken Dumb Willie and gone on home, choosing the familiar over the wide uncharted lands before him—just as he'd always done. His daddy would not matter in the end, nor even the healing Reverend Johnny promised. They were things too distant, and the world was far too big for a broken little boy. What waits back in Mattingly would be an awful thing, but Abel thinks he could convince everyone Dumb Willie only meant to protect. And at least that thing is known. That is what matters now, even as Dorothy's arm grows stronger around him.

What lies behind is known, while everything ahead is not.

-5-

It is by Abel's judgment little more than an hour after their westbound train started moving again when the deep woods and ridges yield to a smattering of homes and paved roads and then, finally, the streets and buildings that make up the town of Greenville, West Virginia. The three of them keep well away from the doors now, Dorothy saying there's no sense in risking them being seen. She gathers up her leather bag as the train switches tracks once more and then eases beneath a graffitied bridge, aiming itself toward a hulking mass of steel in the distance.

The feed mill, she says. She now moves to the opposite end of the boxcar and flips the heavy latch on the other door. Abel and Dumb Willie stand with her. She slides the door open as the train shudders to a stop, the gap only wide enough for the three of them to fit through. Dorothy jumps out first, followed by Dumb Willie. They both help Abel. He settles his tiny feet on the big rocks and ties and realizes the last ground he touched was a whole other state away.

"Come on," she says. "And remember, we're just ghosts."

Bordering the tracks on this side is a thick copse of trees. Dorothy leads them there. Abel sees no one about, hears nothing but the whining of the mill's machinery and the distant sound of traffic. Dorothy stands guard at the tree line while guiding them in—Dumb Willie first, Abel following. She has slung her bag crossways, the strap dividing her two breasts. Abel wishes he was that strap. He doesn't know what's happening to himself.

Inside that tangle of trees every way looks the same. Dorothy takes a spot in front of Dumb Willie and leads them on, deeper, until not even the noise from the mill can be heard.

"You sure you know where you're goin'?" Abel asks. "There ain't no path here."

Dorothy looks over her shoulder and flashes most of a smile. "'Course I know. We're being taken care of here, Abel. And you know who's doing the caring? The ones come before. Ain't a lick of land between one ocean and the next a hobo ain't stepped through, 'specially if it's near a rail."

Dumb Willie shakes his head as though he's found a flaw in that reasoning. "Ain't no . . . *trayne*. Here."

"That's so." She stops and points toward one of the dozens of trees ahead of them. "But there's other rails, if you know what to watch."

Dumb Willie scampers ahead to inspect. He circles the tree and stops along its side, hands on his knees. Grinning, though Abel knows that expression may mean little. It's just as like to be a bug sitting there, or a bit of moss. Could be anything other than something.

"A. Bull *look*."

Abel moves forward past Dorothy, skimming the side of her arm with his and mostly on purpose. He has no need of bending in order to see. The mark looks an old one, carved into the trunk at his chest level. A circle with a diagonal slash running from its top left to the bottom right. Beneath there is an X with two small circles to either side. A wavy line has been made across the top.

"Good road to follow," Dorothy says. "That's what the first means. Second means fresh water and a safe camp. Just what we're looking for."

Abel runs a finger over the shapes. "How'd you know this was here?"

"Part of the code. Them marks are most places. All we got to do is heed. They'll keep us safe."

"Sape," Dumb Willie echoes. "Sape's good."

"Safe's very good," Dorothy answers. "Shoot, couple Angelinas like y'all out here alone? I'd give it a day before you both caught the Westbound."

Abel looks up to her. "What's that mean?"

Whatever part of Dorothy's grin that could be called genuine fades. "Means dyin', Abel."

Dumb Willie rubs his chin, eyebrows drawn. Abel pictures Chris Jones on the tail of a long black train, pounding his fists against a darkened window. Wailing for help, screaming as he rides off down the rails.

"Some are plain," Dorothy says, speaking of the signs.

"Most is hid. Lots, really. Things go on all around folk they can't see or fathom. Some can, but they're few." She looks at Dumb Willie. "Special. But y'all come on now. Place we need's right up here, if I ain't mistaken."

She moves off once more, leading them. Dumb Willie places Abel's legs around his neck like they're going flying, only this time they're not. This time Abel thinks Dumb Willie just wants to make sure his friend doesn't get lost in this tangle of trees and shrubs. The traffic noise sounds louder now, like a road is just up ahead, though Abel can't see anything even from this height because of the woods. Dorothy moves among the trees with a grace akin to her slender body, disturbing not a branch. Dumb Willie tramples all in his path.

"A Bull," he says, "this our. Venchure?"

"I don't know yet."

Dorothy dips left and walks ahead some twenty paces, then stops. She turns and smiles, says, "This'll do."

The trees open here to a small stream that feeds into a pond. Willows and cattails surround the water, offering them welcome shade and privacy from the cars and trucks that travel an unseen road that cuts through a hill beyond. It's as though this place of calm has been set aside in the midst of all the noise and thrum, protected by the fact it has been forgotten.

"We'll keep here," Dorothy says. "We got water plenty, and there's food to be had. You hungry, Dumb Willie?"

Abel moves Dumb Willie's head up and down with his hands, careful not to bump it with his cast. Dumb Willie, he's always hungry.

"Next train won't come before tomorrow noon. We'll have to sleep here."

"Tomorrow?" Abel asks. "We got to get to my daddy."

"Ain't no telling trains what to do," Dorothy says. "Don't you worry none, Abel. It'll be nice here. Dumb Willie, we can sleep under the moon. Ain't no better sleeping than that."

"We ain't going to town?"

"Think we best keep from there," she says. "We'll be fine here. Dumb Willie, why don't you go on and boil yourself up in that water. It'll feel good."

Dumb Willie lowers Abel to the ground and clamors off back into the trees, leaving Abel and Dorothy along the bank of the pond. Dorothy shrugs off her bag and sets it on the ground, offering him a seat. He takes it. They look out over the water and the birds that skim from the trees. Fish pop at the surface, eager for a meal of bugs.

"Thank you," Abel says. "For coming with us. And for saving us. I told you last night, but I wanted to tell you again. I know maybe you didn't want to do either."

Dorothy bends her legs and hugs them. "That's no offense to you. I'm used to being on my own. What I did, I didn't even think about. Or maybe I have thought about it for a long time until I didn't have to think about it anymore. Either way, it can't be undone now. We'll get you to your daddy, Abel. Then I got to take you home."

"Because of the code?"

"Something like that."

"Well, thank you anyway. It would've been an awful thing if you hadn't pulled me on that train."

"Why's that?"

He lifts the shoulder that isn't stuck upward, making them both form a shrug. Thinking of Chris again, because Abel supposes he always will now.

"It just would've been bad. Momma'd be alone. That would be an awful thing. And Dumb Willie would have been left alone too, which I guess is a thing even more awful. And I'd've never gotten to see my daddy."

"You think that's true?" Dorothy asks.

"I know it."

She falls silent.

"You didn't see anything, did you? Before you pulled us up."

"Why? There something you need to tell me?"

Yes, Abel thinks. *But I can't tell that, not ever and not even to you.* He waves a hand over the water, wanting to change the subject. "There's places like this back home. Lots of'm. Me and Dumb Willie have been to them all. We fish and swim. Well," he says, correcting himself while holding up his cast, "not so much swimming lately. It's bad news to get a cast wet."

She points to the bright yellow thing on his arm. "How'd that happen?"

"I snuck out one night to look at the train. That's what I do. Momma said my daddy used to drive a train. I guess that's true, I don't know. She lied about him being dead, so now I'm wondering if there was other stuff she didn't tell me the truth on. But I tripped over a rock."

"Must've been a pretty nasty fall."

"Not really," he says.

He looks at Dorothy, sees her looking back. It's that same way she looked at him on the train. That concern. Abel doesn't want to say more—he never wants to say it just like he never wants to say it about what happened to Chris—but she's looking at him and their arms are touching and some of her brown hair is tickling the side of Abel's head and he finds he can't help but talk, can't keep himself from cracking open his heart just to show her a little, because even that little might keep her here beside him.

"I'm sick," he says. "I have a condition. I'm *special*." Tears gather in his eyes. "My bones are soft. That's how I was born—broke. They don't work right. They're weak and they break *all the time*. That's why I'm so small and why I limp, because my back's not straight. That's why my eyes look different and my teeth are bad. That's why I'm not strong like all the other kids, because of my *stupid bones*."

The tears rush now. Abel shakes such that he looks to be freezing in the summer around them. Dorothy's body goes slack next to him. Her posture slumps, head tilted to the side. Abel slumps into her shoulder and feels Dorothy's right arm move around him, now her left, pressing him deeper into herself. It feels something like heaven, her holding him, though Abel recognizes her arms are tense and her body has gone rigid again. Her head is positioned wrong so that her hat goes tumbling off into the grass behind them. It's like Dorothy doesn't know how to give a hug, like she's never done that before.

"Don't you worry none," she says. "Ain't a thing wrong with who you are, Abel Shifflett. I promise that. That was a brave thing to tell me that, and brave's what you got to be. It's a long way yet to go, and the way is dark."

"What?" Abel feels a tremble through his body that has nothing to do with tears. He lifts his head out from her arms. "What did you just say?"

"The way is dark. We got to be careful."

Far to their right the trees shake, scattering the birds. All sense of dread is forgotten at the sound of Dumb Willie's yell. He bursts into sight in the altogether, rolls of fat and muscle rippling at the long strides of his milk-white legs, his member swinging wild as he races past the spot where Abel and Dorothy sit. He leaps into the air and tucks his legs, the call coming "Canna . . . *bull*!" as gravity snatches him downward.

The sound of him breaching the water comes just before the splash, which not only reaches Abel and Dorothy but soaks them. Dumb Willie's head rises from the pond. There is another whoop, a sound of pure release, and a smile that would shake light into even the darkest heart.

Dorothy whispers, "Let's get him." She gives Abel a nudge and leaps to her feet, not bothering (to Abel's sudden dismay) to take off her own clothes as she plunges into the water, splashing Dumb Willie's face and head. Abel swipes at his eyes and joins them. He gets in only as far as his ankles and holds his cast high to keep it from getting wet, though he kicks enough water into Dumb Willie's face to make him choke.

For the first time in a long while and perhaps even forever, laughter fills this small patch of forgotten wood in the midst of a bustling mountain town. The noise is full and whole and worthy of wonder. It is magic, this laughter, and one not so small as to slip through Abel's knowing. The feel of it lodges into the cracked places of his insides where not even his brittle bones dwell, telling him things will be all right now. Wherever that dark road leads, Dorothy and Dumb Willie will travel with him. And Abel's daddy will be at its end, and healing, and the world will be made right. Yes, that is how Abel knows it will be. Just like Reverend Johnny told him and like the Preacher Keen said.

Because most every road is a dark one. Especially the ones that hold a light at their end.

-6-

Never before have so many people come together on this stretch of dirt and gravel. Whole lines of vehicles packed to either side of the road, clogging the driveway, abandoned in front of the Dead End sign and in the empty field across the way. Old pickups caked with mud and manure, faded cars with hand-printed windows, a pale yellow church bus. Sheriff Barnett's black Blazer parked with one wheel in the ditch, evidence of his hasty arrival. And still more are coming. Lisa hears the noise of engines and tires struggling over the potholes, heading her way. Word is out.

She sits at the small table on the porch, a cigarette trembling in her right hand. Men approach the front steps but dare no farther. They hold their hats in their hands. Their lips move. She acknowledges them with an absent nod. The able-bodied among them

(*Quite a word*, she thinks—*able-bodied*)

will go off as soon as they see to her and join the search through town and the outlying woods. The rest—women mostly, mothers themselves—will keep behind to offer their prayers, their company, their silence.

It has not yet been four hours since she woke groggy and tired to find Abel's bed empty. Everything since has blurred into one continuous nightmare. There was no sign of Abel in the backyard, no note on the kitchen table. She called Charlie Rexrode first—Charlie of all people, as though she'd known even then that whatever had happened could be traced back to Friday at school. Roy was next. Then, finally and once Lisa had found something of her senses, Sheriff Barnett. Charlie and Roy never answered. Both were at church by then, readying themselves to worship a God who is supposed to watch after sick little boys. Jake had picked up, however, his Sunday already interrupted. He was over at the Farmer house. Rita had called, saying Dumb Willie had up and gotten himself lost.

The sheriff had questions when he arrived, looking worried but acting calm. By then Lisa's world had begun melting at the edges. Jake wanted to see Abel's room, check for signs of intrusion. Lisa could think of nothing missing ("Except my son, Jake, where is my *son*?") and found no comfort at all in that Dumb Willie was gone as well, nor even Jake's guess (or had it been his hope?) that the two of them had likely gone off together to spend the morning fishing or exploring. Lisa had tried explaining that wasn't possible. Abel always left a note when he was going off somewhere with Dumb Willie. He would say where he was going and when he was coming back, and would always sign those notes *Toots love.*

Then Jake had asked in a soft, embarrassed way if Lisa really thought they could be far, Abel being how he is. Lisa's insistence, yet again, that Abel would never do such a thing without letting her know had brought further questions:

Abel been acting different lately?

Anything going on?

You two having any problems?

Jake not bothering to write down Lisa's answers—no one can transcribe gibberish—only nodding every so often when she happened upon a word he could recognize. School. Chris. Money. Reverend Johnny.

Chris? Jake had asked. *Chris Jones? You mean Royce's boy?*

She'd answered yes, and that was when Jake's act of stoicism crumbled.

Royce called on my way over here. Said Chris is gone too. He wanted to know if I'd send the boy home if I saw him in town.

And so they'd come. Word had gone out and pews had emptied, townsfolk fanning out to the Farmer place and the Joneses' in the hill country to the dead end on Holly Springs. There are faces here Lisa doesn't know, hundreds of them, along with three vans from the television stations in Camden and Charlottesville. Their cameras are up, but the news-people are kept away. Lisa sees women who came to be strong and to comfort and men who gather in small groups, talking to Jake on the radio, dividing up the search. They promise Lisa all will be well even as most arrive with pistols strapped to their hips and long rifles slung over their shoulders, bely-ing the unspoken belief (unspoken to her, at any rate) that something foul has happened. Something other than a mis-understanding and more than a miscommunication. Not Abel trying to wake Lisa that morning to say he's going out fishing with Dumb Willie, Lisa so tired she'd forgotten. Not Dumb Willie seeking a respite from a "ma" and "da-ee" who treat their boy with as much dignity and care as one of their farm implements. Not Chris out doing what spoilt boys do, killing small animals or starting fires.

Or taking revenge.

Lisa curls her shoulders as a chill runs over her, and the women gathered fan themselves in the June heat. Juliet Creech, the preacher woman who two nights earlier had given Lisa fifty dollars in front of an old barn in the middle of nowhere, now brings a glass of water. She places it in front of Lisa and sits in the chair beside. Takes Lisa's hand.

"Don't you worry," she says. "We'll find them. We take care of our own, so you be strong now. You have faith."

Of faith, Lisa has none. But she will be strong. She has always been strong.

In the distance comes the sound of baying dogs, hounds brought in to catch Dumb Willie's scent. Jake has taken men from the Farmer home along the shortcut to Holly Springs. The woods are thick but not vast. Lisa looks up, meaning to follow the sound. She glimpses Abel's empty window instead.

I must be strong, she thinks. *For Abel and for me and for all these women here, these women who not seven years ago went about town whispering I was an abuser because they know enough of living to love but not enough to be weary. I must be strong so they won't know my own wish—that my son is somewhere in those woods hurt, unable to move or call, and not that he's run off because he thinks he's become a burden. He's so clumsy, my Abel. Only child I know can hurt himself sleeping, and if You let me find him, I promise I'll do better. I'll be a good momma. I'll tell him about those letters. I'll say everything.*

Everything.

That howling, louder now. Lisa stands and moves to the edge of the porch as three dogs and a small group of men break through the trees. The men are dragged to the front porch, the dogs' noses pressed hard against the earth. They veer off, barking and slobbering, toward the field at the side of the house.

The women do not move until Lisa leaps down the steps. They proceed at no more than a steady walk; anything more will only reveal the sense of dismay that has crept into them all. In the field, Sheriff Barnett raises a sack the dogs have found in the tall grass. Shouts from farther on, where the railroad comes to a curve.

Now Lisa runs. She tells herself she must be strong and yet she runs. Past a swing set Abel never used and toys long unplayed with, beyond where the dandelions turn their yellow faces to the sun. Stumbling over hidden rocks that surely would have tripped Abel, leaving him hobbled and screaming for his momma even as his momma slept. Lisa runs as the others run after her. She runs and sees the men at the curve, standing glum and silent over the unmoving shape lying at their feet. A boy's body, plump and disfigured, thrown away like the plastic bottles and empty cans that litter this part of town.

Chris, someone screams, and *God* and *No* and *Call Royce*. Lisa lifts her eyes farther up the tracks. More men are there, Jake running from the field. He comes to a skid among the gravel and ties and stands there staring down. His hands rise in an expression of either shock or surrender, knocking his hat askance.

"Abel?" Lisa takes a step in that direction as the others move to where Chris Jones lies, the spoilt boy who in death will no doubt be remembered as precocious and misunderstood. "Abel?"

Quicksand forms beneath her feet, just as quicksand was in the narrow hallway leading to Charlie's office and is everywhere always, at the diner and the house, making her sink, sink. Jake turns his head. He sees Lisa coming and begins running toward her, waving his arms. Lisa hears his screams of *No* but does not listen, the men at the tracks stunned, one of them turning to vomit in the verdant grass.

"Abel?"

A shirt, a leg of blue jeans. The tracks smeared with red paint and litter and no, not paint but blood. Not a leg of jeans but a leg, the litter a tuft of blond hair and—

"Abel? *Abel?*"

Jake slams into her, screaming for Lisa to turn away, but she cannot, she is Abel's momma and *What happened to my boy?* The smell of this place, a coppery, metallic stench. The sound of a million buzzing flies. And here is where Lisa Shifflett's world ends, in this spot of grass and steel that has become a grave. She feels the air taken and the day grow dim. Jake's voice is an echo in her mind. The last thing Lisa sees before she faints is the hardest irony of all.

It is the only unmangled thing left of Abel and all of him she will bury—the arm that lies at the track's edge, wrapped in a yellow cast.

-7-

Whether it is a fact entirely unknown to others or one merely dismissed as absurd, there are things that do not escape Dumb Willie's notice. A great many of them, as it happens, most of which are presented to him with a frequency that borders on the everyday yet that seem to be passed over by most people—smart people—with a stunning ignorance. It is this ability that allows Dumb Willie to see the hidden things that flow and weave at the underside of life. It is also this specialness that has allowed him to bask in a secret sense of pride that extends over nearly everyone. This includes even A Bull (whom Dumb Willie regards as the smartest person he has ever known), even if A Bull is dumb in his own peculiar way. Not dumb like Dumb Willie, but like how people in the dark are dumb because they can't ever see what it is they run into. A Bull's so dumb, he don't even know he's dead.

Dumb Willie smiles at the picture that forms in his mind—people running into things because they can't see. The image is a fuzzy one, as most are, not unlike how the tee-vee gets fuzzy whenever Dumb Willie's ma turns on the blender, yet it remains sharp enough to coax a laugh. It is a high sound that carries across the pond and into the trees, all the way to where Do-tee has gone in search of supper. Dumb Willie's hungry but he likes these woods. He's starving but not afraid.

It's a venchure they're on. Venchures are fun.

"What you laughing for?" A Bull say.

"Nuffin."

They're walking around the pond, exploring. A Bull, he ain't talking. Dumb Willie thinks A Bull is quiet because he leaves no footprints behind when he walks. He looks behind and see his own footprints, pressed down hard into the mud, but A Bull don't have footprints.

Do-tee's got footprints, but Do-tee's not her name. Do-tee's name's a seecrit.

Maybe A Bull's quiet because he's got to walk in soggy clothes. A Bull jumped in the river with all his clothes on, he's so dumb.

Dumb Willie laughs again.

"We should get those rocks from the woods," A Bull say. "We cain't get'm around the water, or else they might blow up. I read it."

"Oh. Kay A. Bull."

Into the trees they go. It's not the ones Do-tee went in but the others, ones on this side of the pond. A Bull says get this one, Dumb Willie, and that one, so Dumb Willie does. He hold the rocks in his arms while A Bull looks at his letters. A Bull likes those letters, they mean he ain't a bass terd.

It's enough rocks they get and so they go back to where they swam. A Bull lays the rocks in a circle while Dumb Willie finds dry wood, which he brings back by the armful and stacks nearby. Now some of the stack is brought into the middle of the rocks. Dumb Willie puts the smaller pieces in first, under a mound of dried moss. The larger ones are next, set against the small like a teepee.

"That's good, Dumb Willie," A Bull say. "Where'd you learn to do that?"

"Da'ee tole me. He say build the . . ." It's a word. "Fyre.

He say build the fyre, Dumb Willie, but I din't . . . *do it* . . . right."

"What'd he do when you didn't build the fire right?"

He whisper, "It's'a. *Seecrit*," and puts a filthy finger over his lips, because Dumb Willie won't say what his da'ee does. Not even to A Bull he won't. It's a bad thing what his da'ee does, and sometimes Dumb Willie thinks A Bull has no business going to find a daddy because some daddies are better lost. He hopes A Bull's daddy ain't one a those.

"It's okay," A Bull say, "you ain't got to tell me." He thinks a little and adds, "You ain't tole Dorothy, have you?"

"Nuh."

"You tell her anything yet, Dumb Willie? Like last night on the train?"

It's a lie to tell him. It's a seecrit. Dumb Willie doesn't say anything.

"I like Dorothy. You like her too, Dumb Willie?"

"Yez."

"But listen here, okay?" A Bull puts his good hand over Dumb Willie's. "We got to be careful, even with Dorothy. People's gone be looking for us soon. We got to get far away 'cause a what you did to Chris."

"Chris. *Stinks*."

"Stinks less'n you, Dumb Willie," Dorothy say, and they both jump. She steps back through the edge of the trees. Dangling from one hand is a dead rabbit, already skinned. "But whoever it is, I bet he ain't near as sweet."

"Where'd you get that rabbit?" A Bull say.

Dorothy holds the dead thing high to her face. "You joshing me? We might be in town, Abel, but this here's still the woods."

"How'd you catch it?"

"Easy. Was its time is all." She makes that grin. Dumb Willie sees it everywhere but in her eyes. It's a pretty smile. "What's wrong with you two?"

With Dumb Willie, nothing. He has witnessed his da'ee skinning many a rabbit and has no room in himself for disgust, hunger claiming it all. A Bull, though, has always been a bass terd. He can only look with shock upon the blood and smooth bits of muscle and fat, naked ears and those wide, blank eyes.

"How'd you get the fur off?"

"Ha!" Dorothy shout. "Shoot, Abel, skinnin' a rabbit's about the easiest thing there is. All you do's grab hold and yank."

A Bull's face goes clear white. There's a shine in his eyes not-Do-tee says is from when he died, but the rest looks sick. Dumb Willie thinks it's funny—here A Bull's gone do like he made Chris, only out the top and not the bottom.

"I ain't hungry," A Bull say.

Dorothy dips her head like she's done something wrong. "Sure?"

"Yeah." A Bull's cheeks bulge. He swallows. They bulge again. "Think I'll just go over . . . there."

He rises up and limps off for another part of the pond. Do-tee shrugs a little and watches, smiling like she knows a seecrit. She walks to where Dumb Willie sits and lays the rabbit there.

"That's a good job there, Dumb Willie," she say, making him grin and the slobber to pool at the sides of his mouth. "Let me get a match."

She opens her leather bag and roots around, brings one out that she lights. A Bull's still a way off, skipping stones into the water as the traffic goes by.

175

"Figured that'd be enough to send him scurrying," Do-tee say. She lights the fire and blows at the flames, making them grow. Next comes the spit, built with four branches pushed into the soft ground. Now a long stick that Do-tee plunges into the rabbit's mouth and down. It reappears from the other end brown and bloody. She smiles. "If not, guess this woulda done the trick. What's matter?"

"You. *Kill* that?"

"No. That ain't what I do. Like I said, was its time."

She looks at him, then over to where A Bull sits. "Do you know who I am, Dumb Willie? It's okay to say it, Abel can't hear."

"You the . . ." It's a word. "Debbil."

Do-tee laughs. It's a good laugh that sounds like birds, like the sparrows sing in the morning. The sparrows are Dumb Willie's favorite.

"No, Dumb Willie. I am not the devil."

He didn't think that was the case, not really. The devil wouldn't be so pretty.

"You a. *Angel.*"

Now she smiles. "Death is no angel, but I appreciate you saying so." She sets the branch with the rabbit growing from it onto the spit, letting the flames lick the flesh. It smells good. Dumb Willie slobbers more, he can't help it. Dumb Willie's always hungry.

"I am what comes, Dumb Willie. The thing that comes for all at the end of their days. I am there at the last breath anybody ever takes. I lead them onward, you see? From the world they've always known to another that waits. Do you understand?"

He thinks he does, but Dumb Willie don't know.

"Like this rabbit here," she says, turning the branch a

little. "I set out in those woods there, I wasn't looking for this rabbit. But I got called to it. That's the only way I know to say. It's like a charge comes into me. I feel it in my head and my chest, like lightning. That's when I know. When I saw the rabbit, all I had to do was wait and skin it. It was a peaceful end, Dumb Willie. And now you get to eat."

She turns the spit. That rabbit's looking at Dumb Willie.

"There's never a time I don't get called," Do-tee say. She's looking at that rabbit like that rabbit's looking at Dumb Willie, but Do-tee's far off, thinking. "I'm everywhere, I guess. Or most places. Wherever there's people, I am. And it's always been that way. I'm called, and I take them on. I come for them in whatever way will bring them comfort, or bring them fear." She glances his way and tries to smile again, but this time that smile isn't in her eyes and isn't on her lips either. It isn't anywhere. "Depends, I guess, on where you're goin'. You didn't tell Abel our secret, did you?"

"Nuh."

"Good. Was a bad thing I did, Dumb Willie. Not telling Abel what's happened to him. I have to take them on when I'm called. That's all I do. But I couldn't with him. I saw him and you and the boy—Chris?—and I snatched Abel up, then you. And I just couldn't do it. I couldn't show the path. I couldn't tell him. He looked so pitiful. Do you understand?"

"Yez," Dumb Willie say, because he does understand this. A Bull always looks pitiful, he's got bad bonez.

"They always look back. Do you know that? After their last breath is done and I come for them. You should see it, Dumb Willie. I guess you will one day, but I mean, you should see it. That path. It looks so beautiful. And I'm there helping them to that path, and they all just look back. Every single one. It's like all of them know they're not losing anything, they're *gaining*, but there's still so much behind they never finished or never did. Like there was so much left to say."

She plucks a bit of meat off, tastes it. Dumb Willie wipes his mouth.

"Abel would have looked back too. He all but told me he would. He didn't want to leave his momma all alone, wouldn't have never seen his daddy. And he didn't want to leave you to the life you have, Dumb Willie. I think it was that most of all. Abel loves you."

"I luv A. Bull," Dumb Willie say.

"I know. That's why I can't take him on just yet. And that's why we can't tell him, okay? It's our secret. You can't tell."

He shakes his head.

"Good. We'll get Abel to his daddy in Fairhope, but that's as far as things can go. I'll be in trouble if I do more." And in a sad voice, she adds, "I'm in trouble *now*."

"Home," Dumb Willie say.

"Yes, we got to get Abel home. He's hanging on to so much, Dumb Willie. That boy has the whole world on him. He wouldn't even tell me about Chris. What happened."

"Chris. *Stinks* he's a. Weed."

"I know. But he's got to face it, Dumb Willie. He has to know he isn't alone in this."

Dumb Willie looks off to where A Bull sits. He's holding his letters and . . . it's a word . . . envelopes. A Bull looks small all the way from here. He looks like he's fading in the dark, like he's not here all the way.

"A Bull's. Dayed."

"Just his body is," Do-tee say. "That's all. That's not Abel's body you see; that's just the mask left to hold his soul until

I take him on. That's why nobody can see him. Just me and you, because you're special. Do you understand?"

Dumb Willie nods. He don't understand.

"Body always dies, Dumb Willie. Even yours someday. But the best part of people? That lives on." She turns the spit, making the meat brown and good, and casts her eye toward the boy far off. "But only for a while, so long as he's kept here and refuses to go home. No mask is meant to be worn forever."

-8-

She has watched them all this evening and supposes that could be called guarding, though in this hidden place at the edge of a bustling town there is not much to guard from at all. It is safe here, and that is why Dorothy keeps them.

The fire, lit more to cook Dumb Willie's supper than to keep them warm, is now nothing more than a thin sheet of orange embers set against the glow of passing cars and streetlights from the hill above. Dorothy and Dumb Willie are huddled close to that faint light and the little heat it continues to give, which punctures the air with an occasional snap and crack. The air still holds the faint scent of cooked meat. Above them shines most of a moon and a smattering of stars. A slight breeze follows over the pond, cool and comforting, rippling the water. Dorothy has removed her tennis shoes and socks. She squeezes her toes into the soft earth and grins at the feeling, grins at Dumb Willie's building excitement, his nudges that are followed by whispers of "Watch . . . *this*."

Death takes the form of many things, but a hobo is among its favorites. There is a kinship there, a bond between it and those whose lives are defined by the steady rhythms of rail and road, who are leaves of flesh and bone caught in a gentle wind that blows in no particular direction, yet brings them still to where they are meant. Death hopes that's the case now, with these two boys.

From the trees comes, "Ready?"

"Ready," Dorothy calls.

Dumb Willie begins to clap. Abel waddles from the darkness with singular aplomb, trying to weave among the shadows and passing headlights in a way that gives credence to the mysteries about to unfold. He stops just beyond the fire's arc and holds his good hand out as an acknowledgment of the applause, then bows low at Dorothy's presence.

He straightens and asks, "Who here believes in magic?"

Dumb Willie raises his hand.

"Me," Dorothy says.

"Who here is willing to plunge into the world of . . ." His arms move in small circles of ever-increasing speed that end with a quiet *snap* that produces a mashed plastic rose in his left hand. "*Possibility?*"

"Oooh," Dumb Willie shouts, clapping again. His face gleams.

Dorothy shrieks with delight (and no small measure of surprise—she had seen the fingers of Abel's left hand slide down into his cast but had been unprepared for his polished practice) and feels a blush when Abel bends to hand her the flower.

"My lady," he says.

"My handsome prince," she answers, which nearly buckles the boy's knees.

He produces a warped deck of cards from his front pocket and asks Dorothy to shuffle them. Then, wedging the deck between his cast and thumb, he says, "Watch carefully, and pick a card."

Abel runs the first two fingers of his good hand along the top of the cards, fluttering them in a steady speed.

"Get one?" he asks Dorothy.

"Yes."

"What's your card?"

"Jack of hearts."

Abel looks worried. "Jack of hearts?" He looks to Dumb Willie. "That's a hard one."

Dumb Willie places a hand over his mouth. Between his fingers, Death hears, "Uh . . . *oh*."

Abel says, "Well, I guess we'll have to rely on the magic of possibility to make this trick work. It's never been the jack of hearts. Never ever. Shuffle the cards again, Dorothy."

She does, handing them back. Abel keeps the cards face-down and kneels by the fire.

He looks into Dorothy's eyes and says, "Now I'm gone start laying these cards down. You look at them and tell me when to stop."

"When will I know to stop?" she asks.

"You just will. That's the magic."

He lays the first one down, then the next. Halfway through the deck, Dorothy halts him.

Abel turns that card over. Ace of diamonds.

"Uh . . . *oh*," Dumb Willie says. His hand is back over his mouth, shocked at this unfortunate turn of events.

"I don't get it," Abel says. He looks at Dorothy. "You sure you saw the jack of hearts?"

Dorothy's grinning. "I'm sure."

"Wait," Abel says. "Wait just one second. Dorothy, what's that behind your ear?"

Before she can answer, Abel leans in close and whips his good hand behind her right ear, just beneath her hat. He draws out a card in his hand and slowly turns it over.

Jack of hearts.

To Dumb Willie it seems the grandest thing he has ever witnessed, nothing more than a miracle. Dorothy's mouth drops in a look of fear and wonder mixed, a look born not from the card in Abel's hand but from the light leaking out from behind his eyes. Where they were a dull blue, there is now a white like snow struck by sunlight—Abel's soul, seeking its freedom from the thin bonds that hold it.

He makes coins appear and disappear and a tiny copper ring to float in the air. Deals a royal flush three times in a row no matter how well Dorothy shuffles the deck. Dumb Willie cuts a piece of string in half with his teeth that Abel somehow fashions together again and guesses whatever number between one and ten that Dorothy can imagine.

And when all the magic is done and the traffic is slow on the hill and Greenville has been laid to slumber, Abel stands apart from them and rests his good hand in his left pocket. He grins a showman's smile and bows once more, then says, "I have one small magic left, lady and gentleman. Just words. Always believe in possibility. Things are never what they seem. Let the magic guide you, because then"—he pauses here, grinning—"*anything* can be real."

He lifts his good hand from his pocket and raises it high before throwing it hard toward the ground. Dorothy spots a small gray cylinder that hits in the center of one of the larger rocks near the fire. There comes a loud *pop!* that makes Dumb Willie yell with glee and then a heavy cloud of smoke. Dorothy follows the muffled sounds of Abel's coughs as he circles around behind them. The cloud thins, revealing nothing but the pond.

Dumb Willie jumps up. "Where he. *Go?*"

"Right behind you," Abel says.

Death cannot help but smile.

*

The light has come to his eyes, meaning the thin covering of what is left of Abel's body is beginning to wear. And yet what is left is still enough for him to manipulate things—cards, coins, even a smoke bomb—which means there is still time yet. Dorothy doesn't know exactly how much (she has never done such a thing as this, keeping the dead held to earth), but it may be enough. Enough to get Abel to Fairhope. Then home. It must be home afterward, because the boy is coming apart from the inside. Even now, staring at her from across the remains of the fire, Abel looks more two than one.

"Did you like it?" he asks. "My show?"

The words come in little more than a whisper. Beside them, Dumb Willie snores. Dorothy didn't think the big man would sleep at all this night, such was his excitement over finding Abel not lost.

"It was the most amazing thing I ever seen," she whispers back.

He beams. The light from his eyes flashes from a glow to a shine. "Really?"

"Really."

"I ain't never done a whole show before. I did a few tricks at school. For the talent show. I got a ribbon. But it weren't a whole show."

"Well, I'm glad I got to be the first."

This looks to please him to no end. He leans forward, putting his cast to the ground as a balance, and draws the letters from his back pocket and turns them over. Where his cast was there are now small impressions in the dirt, barely there. The place where he sits is hardly disturbed.

"Must be some powerful words," Dorothy says, "to get you to take off like you did."

"You want to see them?"

"Wouldn't do me no good. I never did learn to read. Most folk tell you anything you need to know so long as you ask, even if you got to see past their own spin on things to get anyplace near the truth. Guess that's the same with any words, said or writ down. Time I thought maybe I should learn it, wasn't nobody to teach me. Meet quite a few folk in my goings, but it's meant they all move on."

"Road's ever long."

Dorothy lifts an eyebrow. "What?"

"That's what Reverend Johnny told me before he gave me his word. He's magic."

"Well, he was right on that. Road is long. Though every one's got its end."

Abel says, "I don't know what all of my daddy's letters say. There's a lot more than these, but I couldn't bring them all. I was afraid Momma'd find them gone and know where I went."

"So one letter's enough to get you to pick up? Leave home and Momma both?"

"Yes," Abel says. "No," he corrects. "Reverend Johnny's the one made me leave. He said I'd find the letters and tole me what else would come. It's why I left. Me and Dumb Willie. Only way I could was knowing I could bring my daddy back. It's my reward, to have a family again. But now I don't know if we ever can."

Dorothy leans forward.

"Why can't you go back, Abel? We a long ways from Mattingly, so it don't matter to keep it secret anymore. And you need to say it. That's where it all begins."

"Where what begins?"

"Being ready to move on."

"I'm ready now. Longer we stay here, longer it'll take to get to Fairhope. That's where everything is, and not just my daddy. Reverend Johnny said so. He said I'd get healed."

"Healed of what?"

"My bad bones." He holds out his cast as though she needs the reminder. "He said if I left to go find my daddy, I'd be fixed."

Dorothy lowers her eyes. "I don't know if that's a thing that can be had for you now, Abel. Not in the way you want, least."

"Yes, it can. I believe it. There's a reward for me. But something happened. Right when that train came."

"What happened?"

Abel turns the stack of letters over. Unfolds the one on top. He says, "I can't say."

"I spent more years than I know wandering about. Met all kinds. Good folk and bad and others—about all, if I'm true—that's some of both. There's ones so proud they think they can get through life and death with no help at all. Then there's ones who know there ain't a soul strong enough to stand on its own for long. People are built to need each other.

"Out here, all a hobo's got is the kindness of others. None of us'd make it without that. That's always been true for you and Dumb Willie, ain't it? Now you both got me, and

I'm bound to come along—back to home if I have my way, Fairhope if that's your will. But time is precious. We ain't got a lot."

"What'd you mean yesterday," he asks, "when you said the way is dark?"

"Only what I did. You go on and call this an adventure if you want. Ain't nothing finer than an adventure. It's about the only thing that gets folk out of the world for a spell by putting them deeper in it. But you better believe ain't a thing in it gone come easy. Gone need me," she says, then points to where Dumb Willie sleeps. "Gone need him. You can't afford to close yourself up no more."

Abel's eyes move to the page in his hand. His lips move in silence.

"Why don't you go on and read that to me?" Dorothy asks. "Really?"

She smiles again and wonders why Abel looks at her so funny. "Really."

*

27 March 2005
Dear Abel,

It is a cold day here and dreary. I often get sad when the weather is this way (I get sad a lot, but the rain brings it even more) and I think of you. I do that no matter what the weather is.

I looked at the calendar the other day and realized you must be two now. Is that right? Too young to read anything I write. But I guess I'm writing these as much for me as for you because I don't think your momma will ever let you read them. I didn't think I would be gone long, but now I think it will be long and I guess that's why she won't tell you about me. Because she's mad. I don't want you to think bad about her for that, Abel. It's better I guess if you go on not knowing anything about me except for what she says, which might be all of the truth or some or none. It was bad when I left. That's all I'm going to say. But maybe even if you never read the things I send you, she will. I don't have much reason to think so, but your momma gave me this address and said write but never call, and if I called she would up and move and the two of you would be gone forever. But it has to be something that I can send these, right? (Are you reading this, Lisa? Do you remember how we loved each other?)

Abel, there are so many things I want to say but don't know how. It's hard saying it. But the truth has to come, doesn't it? Even if it's forced, the truth must come. Lisa, you know that. Tell Abel. I don't care if he doesn't understand. Tell him I can see what no one else can. Secret things. Tell Abel there is more. I know you don't believe that, Lisa. You have to see things and touch them to know they're real. But I have. I've seen and touched. Tell Abel that.

Tell him it's real.

Love,
Dad

*

The page shakes in Abel's hand. He doesn't look up and says no more, both things for which Dorothy is thankful. There is too much in the boy's letter for him to consider, and yet hearing Abel read those words has brought a light into her mind that had gone missing ever since she pulled the boy from the rails.

"Secret things," Abel says. "What's that mean?"

"Could mean nothing. Could mean a lot. I'm not sure."

Abel turns the paper over, looking for more that isn't there. He stares at the rest like he wants to devour them all, though he doesn't. Dorothy wouldn't have allowed it even if Abel had tried. Those letters will be a kind of nourishment in the next days. Might even point the way. Gorging on them all at once would serve no purpose. Better the boy take small bites.

"He's right about my momma. He said Momma don't believe in nothing and he's right. That's another part of why I'm here. The letters are some, but that's most."

"How's that?"

"There's a boy at school. He was mean, to me most of all."

"Because you're special?"

Abel winces at the word but doesn't disagree. "I did something to get back at him for all the mean things he's done. Then I got in trouble. Momma made me go to a barn church. It was just to get us some money, but I didn't know that then. I thought she wanted to get me healed, because there was a healer there, the Reverend Johnny."

"You thought he could heal you?"

"Not at first," Abel says. "And maybe not ever, I guess. He said he couldn't heal me because I got no belief, but I had money enough for a word. It's like he looks at you and sees your insides, and then he tells you what God wants you to hear. But Reverend Johnny didn't do that to me. At least, I don't think. We were out in back of the barn after. Something come over him."

"Come over him?" Dorothy sits up, forcing her body to move slowly and her voice to carry nothing more than passing interest.

"I can't figure it," Abel says. "I told myself it was a trick. That way I wouldn't have to tell myself it was true. But it was. It's like something . . . got in him. Next day's when I found my daddy's letters."

"Now listen, Abel. I want you to be honest here. This . . . something. That what give you the word?"

"He said my time's come. That the treasure is mine should I seek it, and then I'd get healed and find my reward. But he said I had to go quick and not turn away. And he said the way is dark."

All falls to quiet in this hidden part of Greenville. Even the few cars that pass along the hill make no noise.

"That's what *you* told me, Dorothy," Abel says. "You said the way is dark. How'd you know to say that?"

"I don't know." And this is true, at least so far as Dorothy knows. Yet here is something (a comfort or a fear, only the coming days will tell) that tells her there are forces at play here, and some perhaps stronger even than herself.

"So that's all how I left," Abel says. "Most of it, anyway. And now I don't know what to do but go find my daddy."

Abel's daddy. Secret things.

The truth must come.

"Even if it's forced."

"What?" Abel asks.

"Nothing."

But it isn't nothing, it's something. Abel's eyes flashing that light, the living part inside that dead boy wanting out. Sent by a word. Dorothy will have to learn more of this Reverend Johnny. But before that, it's time for them all to wet their fingers and test the wind. Would Abel's momma be the woman Abel says she is and Dorothy believes her to be, he will have been found by now. And the boy Chris. Dumb

Willie will have been found gone. Such a thing will be news. How they go from here will depend upon how big that news has become.

"Don't you worry, Abel. We'll figure this all out. Meantime, how about we take a little trip in the morning? Train won't be here until the sun's high."

"Where we going?"

"Think we'll go into town. See the sights."

"Is it safe?" he asks.

"So long as you're with me. You tired?" she asks, knowing he isn't. Abel will never sleep again.

"No."

"Well, why don't you come along over here anyway and shut your eyes."

He does, eager to do so, and lays his head on Dorothy's lap. She strokes his blond hair and finds the skin and skull beneath more soft than hard, like running her hand over the surface of the pond. Abel's breath slows. He lays his good hand near Dorothy's foot, barely felt. His words are strange ones she cannot figure, yet spoken with a peace that brings her comfort:

"Sorry, Miss Ellie."

PART V

GREENVILLE

-1-

They gather this morning in the pond with pant legs drawn and rolled to their knees and their shoes lined along the bank. Dorothy splashes water on her arms and face before drying them with a handful of cedar bark. She then turns her attention to Dumb Willie and the bloodstain on the front of his overalls.

Abel receives little consideration, not that he minds. He's happy to boil up without being asked to strip first, and besides it's Dumb Willie who needs all that doting because he's so dumb. Any evidence required for this conclusion can be found in his description of the nightmares that filled his sleep, munsters and spuruts that portend evil things.

"It's . . . trubble. Comin'," he says.

Dorothy keeps rubbing pond water over Dumb Willie's clothes, wishing for a bar of soap in a low voice. She quiets at Dumb Willie's warning.

"Don't pay him no mind," says Abel. "Sometimes it's hard to know what runs through Dumb Willie's mind even when he's 'wake, much less when he's sleepin'. Ain't that right, Dumb Willie?"

Yez is the answer Abel expects, as that is how Dumb Willie answers most every question he is ever asked. Only this time Dumb Willie says nothing and shakes his head. It is a slow motion, forced and quiet, as though he's dunked himself in molasses.

"It's. *Trubble.*"

"We'll be fine now," Dorothy says. Abel believes her. "But we'll have to act our best when we're there. Powerful thing, coming to a town. I had it in mind to keep clear and wait for the train, then you read that letter from your daddy, Abel. He gave me the idea. Now, let's make sure we clean things up good for the next 'bo. That's part of the code." Dorothy stops here. Abel sees a faraway look in her eyes. "Always leave things better than you found them."

She tends to the remains of the fire, spreading dirt over the ashes to make sure they don't catch. Abel picks up the unused portion of the wood.

Dumb Willie offers his own contribution to the cleanup by digging a grave for what remains of his supper the night before. He chooses a quiet place along the pond where he says the birds sing best. The meager portion of bones and most of the rabbit's head go into a small hole. A dandelion from among the trees goes on top. Dumb Willie fills the hole back up and pats the top as one would a pup's head. Last comes a sparrow feather he pulls from his overalls, like his own magic trick. He inserts the tip into the ground as a marker and wipes the dirt onto his chest, undoing all the cleaning Dorothy has done. Dumb Willie now folds his hands.

Dorothy removes her hat at Dumb Willie's prayer, something about Dumb Willie loving rabbits and the woods and Abel and Dorothy too, and how all the world's unfairness can be laid to the fact that all things must pass from above the ground to below. Abel can't understand most of what Dumb Willie says because Dumb Willie's crying, yet he bows his own head as manners dictate. His eyes, though, remain open. He is afraid if he closes them he will see Chris in all that darkness, flashing that look of confusion upon his dying face as he rides off on that Westbound, his head wrenched backward and the skin of his neck rippled and torn.

-2-

No place is the same. That is the lesson Dorothy has long known. The contours of every town and village and city are as unique as the ones who call those places home, the dips and rises, the hidden places known only to those who have grown up on those streets and neighborhoods. The manners of speech. The learned taboos of what never to say and injunctions of what to say always. Customs that seem as inbred as the shapes of noses and the color of eyes. These are all things Dorothy can slip into and out of like old clothes, never becoming one with the great mass of those she shepherds between worlds but mixing herself among them if she chooses. And she chooses now, in this tiny place unknown to most of the greater world. Not for her own benefit and certainly not for her comfort, but so the small, brittle child beside her may finally confront a bit of the truth that brought him to death, and therefore grasp the larger truths that follow.

They make their way from the pond up toward the hill and the road made upon it, following that hot pavement into Greenville proper. Dorothy leads the way, her leather bag over her shoulder.

"Been awhile," she says, "since I been Greenville way. Was an okay place back then so far as places go. 'Course things can change, which is why we got to be careful now. That's the thing. Dumb Willie, you don't cause no trouble. You be quiet and still."

Away in the back she hears, "Kay Do. Tee."

"And, Abel, you listen here." She stops and turns, making sure Abel looks her in the eye. "Best thing you can do is keep to Dumb Willie's side. Don't you talk to nobody, don't draw no attention. You understand?"

"Don't worry, Dorothy," he says. "Nobody ever sees me anyways."

Buildings rise not far on. The road curves ahead to the right and meets another road, making the shape of a T. A work truck motors past there. Two cars. An old dump truck spewing gray exhaust. They stop at the wooden sign at the intersection that reads *Welcome to Greenville, Jewel of the Alleghenies*. A crow perched on top of the sign caws at Dorothy's presence. It flies when Dumb Willie shoos it away, pronouncing it a munster.

Dorothy shrugs off the bag and bends to her knees. Two marks are carved into the sign's bottom. One looks to be an arc with a dot just above the lowest point. The other is a crude cross.

Abel studies them. "What they say?"

"Says town won't give us trouble so long's we only passing through." She rubs the cross. "And if we find us a church, we might get some food. You hungry, Dumb Willie?"

Dumb Willie nods.

"Okay then. Here we go. Remember now, we're just ghosts."

Dumb Willie moves up as they enter the bustling downtown, placing himself between Dorothy and Abel as though wanting to both protect and be protected.

"Trubble," he mumbles.

"It'll be fine," Dorothy says. "All these folks want is to get on with their days. Probably they won't even see us."

Abel reaches for Dorothy's hand. To him and Dumb Willie, this place must be everything Mattingly is not. There is nothing of the gentle transformation from woods and farmland to streets and buildings. Greenville instead seems to rise from the land all at once. It is at one point not there and then there completely, a maze of paved roads and busy intersections and sidewalks crammed with those, too, in a rush to get from where they are to where they're going. Noises—car horns and backfiring trucks, hollers of either anger or elation. More even than their long trip on the train, entering this strange and noisome place is what announces to Abel and Dumb Willie that they are no longer home.

True to the mark carved into the town sign, most who pass regard them either with fleeting curiosity or not at all. They must seem an odd pairing, this homeless-looking girl and the slow white boy with her. Abel remains snug between them, unseen, watching all who pass. Dorothy makes sure to put half of one leg in front of where Abel walks, cutting off anyone who may have a mind to step between herself and Dumb Willie. What results is an intricate dance, dangerous in its consequences. One small misstep, and someone may walk clean through Abel and ruin it all.

Thankfully, no one on this hot June morning manages to come anywhere close. Dorothy's mere presence is enough to drive those in front of them toward the far edge of the side-walk and those behind to allow a wide gap between. It is as if all of them—man, woman, and child—find their normal day suddenly impeded by an unseen shadow. A coldness drifts over them, a shiver that bows their shoulders and a quick sense of anxiety that forces many into a queer sort of chuckle and comments of rabbits running over their graves. Some pause, unsure of this feeling, drifting toward shop windows or ducking into the nearest store without quite knowing why. Others turn back toward where they've come from—making sure they have locked their cars, perhaps—while their hands reach for the phones tucked inside their pockets to call home and make sure all is well.

Death is accustomed to such reactions. Dorothy finds their repulsion an advantage, keeping Abel safe in his igno-rance. Even Dumb Willie seems aware, glancing at Dorothy and nodding in that way he sometimes does, one that implies he is not so dumb as most believe.

"Main drag," she says to Abel, though looking at Dumb Willie. "Busy day."

"Where we trying to get?" Abel asks.

"Church. We'll find the one marked. Plenty churches here. It's a believing place."

Most of a small town's staples are on this stretch but for the one Dorothy is looking for. They pass a hardware store and a smattering of fast-food places, banks and groceries and a pharmacy. Townsfolk and traffic blare around them in city song.

"Seems to me," she says, "there's a church along the next street up. Visited there myself before. Preacher there's kindly. Bet we can get you some breakfast there, Dumb Willie."

They take the next corner down, away from Greenville's

center. Here rests a quiet park of rusting swings and a pond filled with ducks and chattering birds, a wide cemetery beside. Across the street is another gathering of shops. A florist, a bakery. People mill about. The sun feels concentrated, giving everyone an air of aggravation at the long summer ahead. A group of old men linger in front of a barbershop. One, Dorothy sees, has made himself comfortable in a green plastic chair near the door. The day's paper is spread out before him. And there, just down the block on Dorothy's side, rests a gray metal box standing against the curb. To their left is a stately bricked building with two sets of stone steps that lead to a grand wooden door. The sign reads *Greenville Church of Christ*.

Dorothy stops here. "Might be the place."

She circles around back of the sign and bends, pressing a single finger into the wood. A cough hides the burning sound.

Sometimes you follow the signs, she thinks, *and sometimes you make your own.*

"Yep. Y'all come look."

Abel sees it first, then Dumb Willie. The cross is just like the one at the start of town.

"I'm going in," Dorothy says. "Y'all stay put."

Abel's eyes widen. "You mean we got to stay out here all by ourselves?"

"Won't be but a minute, and you got each other to watch over. It's a careful thing asking a preacher for aid. Gotta know just what to say. Best you keep out of it."

The boy remains in place as Dorothy takes the stairs, watching all the way. She turns at the stairs and waves, counting six men across the street at the barber. One is already staring at the strange retarded boy standing alone in front of the church.

"Remember what we talked on, Dumb Willie," she calls. "Oh. Kay Do. Tee."

She pushes on the door, thankful to find it unlocked. Inside is a shadowed foyer and an empty sanctuary beyond. To either side of the door are narrow windows that offer a view to the street.

Dorothy stands there, watching and waiting, then reaches into her shirt pocket for the feather plucked from a rabbit's grave. With a gentle push and a soft blow of air, she sends it flying.

-3-

The people are fewer here, offering a sense of relief in spite of the old men gathered at the barbershop across the way. One of them is staring. Abel shields his eyes with his bad arm and judges his own side of the street. A mother and her little girl approach. The woman stops at a newspaper box half-way down the block to straighten the bow in her daughter's hair. Dumb Willie assumes the stance of protector in front of Abel—feet wide, hands clasped at his back.

"Say, Dumb Willie."

"Whut?"

"What you think Dorothy meant by that? 'Remember what we talked about.'"

Dumb Willie stands silent, his back to Abel's front. It is in fact all the answer Abel needs. He's seen the two of them together, the side glances Dorothy and Dumb Willie share when they think he isn't looking. Their private talks.

"Guess maybe she means all that stuff about being ghosts and all. But now that I think about it, I don't guess that's what she meant at all. Know what I think, Dumb Willie? I think you and her got something going on that I don't know. I don't know what it is, but I think it's something."

The woman and child pass. Dumb Willie breaks his stance when they're close. His attempt to make himself look small only serves to draw the mother's attention. She stares, placing her hand at the girl's neck, and gives Dumb Willie a wide berth. To Abel's comfort, the woman doesn't even look his way.

"Dumb Willie, you got a secret you ain't telling me? Something about Dorothy?"

Now he turns. Only some, and only long enough to say in a small voice, "I'm. *Dumb.*"

"Not as much as you think you are," Abel says.

The gentler rhythms of Greenville may not be apparent but they do exist, a subtler noise beneath the tumult and thrum. Still, this is a foreign place. He and Dumb Willie are now even farther from Fairhope than when they started, and there's yet a long way to go. Abel wishes his momma were here. Better, he wishes for Reverend Johnny and one of Reverend Johnny's words. His mind reaches back to that night behind the barn, if only because that place seemed so less strange than the place he is now. He shuts his eyes and feels the cool mountain air on his cheek, loamy earth beneath his feet as Greenville falls away, leaving Abel too deaf to hear what Dumb Willie says

("A Bull it'sa. *Fedder.*")

and too blind to stop what happens next. He blinks to find himself alone and Dumb Willie down the sidewalk, stooping to catch something blown on the breeze.

"Dumb Willie, what you doing?"

The feather slips from Dumb Willie's grip, sending him farther away.

"Dumb Willie. Dumb Willie, you *look at me*."

A passing car honks. No sign of Dorothy, but the men across the street are watching. Abel stands helpless as Dumb Willie lunges forward, pinning the feather beneath his boot with a "Got. Choo" of victory and his hand upon the newspaper box. Dumb Willie smiles as he lifts the feather from the pavement. He twirls it in his hand and goes to place it in his breast pocket. His face turns toward the clear window beside.

"A Bull."

"What?"

"A. Bull *look*"—pointing at the box—"It's my. *Pitcher*. My pitcher's onna . . . *paper*."

He jumps as he speaks the words, Dumb Willie's thick boot heels barely clearing the cement. The men across the street are rubbernecking, their gaze unbroken even by the passing traffic. Abel feels himself beginning to walk but doesn't know how. His mind is not working his legs. A big man, old and wearing suspenders, points and turns to the others gathered about the barbershop. All of them look now.

There are degrees of stares. This is a fact known only to the freaks of the world. The stares directed at Dumb Willie are not the curious sort, nor ones of pity. What Abel sees in the eyes of those men is fear deepened by suspicion.

"A Bull it's my. Pitcher."

"No, it ain't, Dumb Willie. Now shush."

That idiot's grin, wide and unfeeling. Spittle pools at the sides of Dumb Willie's mouth. Abel reaches the box. He bends to see *The Greenville Sun* written at the top of the paper inside. The words are on his lips—*That's just some man*—until he spies the picture above the fold, a grainy black-and-white copy of the same faded BibAlls and vacant stare as Dumb

Willie wears now. The headline is large and bold and strikes
Abel to his core:

Reward Offered for Mattingly Murderer

Manhunt under way

Across the street, the old man in suspenders steps to
the sidewalk's edge. He turns, motioning for the newspaper.
Dumb Willie waves. A shout—"Hey!"—sets time from pause
to fast-forward, four of the barbershop men now standing at
attention.

How Abel can hear the faint sounds of the church door
opening and closing he does not know, but he knows he
has never before been so thankful for Dorothy. She comes
down the steps looking one way and then another, not seeing them.

Abel sees her turn at Dumb Willie's words: "It's me it's
Dumb. *Willie*," repeated once and again in growing decibels.

"Thought I told you stay put," she says. Her gaze is to
Abel as she walks, though he sees her eyes cut to the men
bearing witness. "What's goin' on?"

Only the first two lines of the story are visible, the rest
hidden beneath the fold. Yet even those few words are ones
Abel cannot bear to read. Dorothy's shadow draws near. She
bends low over Abel's shoulder.

"What's that? Is that Dumb Willie?"

Authorities have issued a reward of $25,000
for information leading to the arrest of William
Randolph Farmer, 22, of Mattingly, Virginia, in
connection with the brutal mur—

"Abel, what's that say?"

"It's me Dumb. *Willie.*"

Abel cannot move, cannot think. This thing he has feared ever since jumping the train is now unfolding, the hope of gaining his reward proven false, all those foolish wishes of a child.

The men at the barbershop point, yelling through the traffic.

Abel turns to Dorothy: "We have to get away."

-4-

Dorothy bends close and studies the front of the day's newspaper. A "Hey!" is shouted from across the street, a man in blue suspenders pointing. He is older, seventy at least, wearing the flushed face of a drunkard and bearing a bulged and hardened gut. The sort of person Death expects to meet face-to-face soon, and one who may have just realized that the simple-looking stranger across the street is a wanted killer.

"What's that? Is that Dumb Willie? Abel, what's that *say?*"

Thankfully, the pointing old man is not the one in possession of the day's *Sun*. That distinction belongs to another man who appears equal in both age and condition, sitting in a faded green plastic chair at the other side of the barber's door. He is leafing through the classifieds by the look of it, likely searching for a steal on a used lawn mower or a pickup bed of mulch, paying no attention to either the picture on the front page or the very possibility that the same man could be no more than fifty feet away, screaming, "It's me Dumb. *Willie,*" in a voice so loud and grating it sounds political.

Abel has gone even paler than usual. His lower jaw is

slack, his eyes two wide caves swimming in gleaming white lagoons. The men are hollering as he stammers, "We have to get away. You have to get us away, Dorothy. We have to go right now."

The dread Dorothy kindles, that shadow unseen yet powerful enough to reach even across the street, is enough to hold the men in place, though not for long. The old man talks fast. One hand points to Dumb Willie while the other motions for the newspaper. Down the corner turns a police-man. Dorothy knows all it will take is that old man seeing Dumb Willie's picture. He will flag down that cop, and then there's no dread powerful enough to keep them safe and Abel's secret hid. All she had wanted was for Abel to see that newspaper, for him to be forced to confess what happened in the field that night. It is a strange thing, Dorothy thinks, that even the schemes of Death can be undone. And yet in these moments of panic she realizes she should not be shocked at all, having strayed from her purpose and done what was not meant.

"I can save us," Abel says. "Dorothy, get ready to run. I'll get Dumb Willie."

The words are nearly out of her mouth ("No, Abe—") when he reaches into his pocket. Abel throws down a smoke bomb and yells, "Shazam!" as it pops and billows, sending the people on the sidewalk running and traffic to swerve and snarl. The men, all of them, jump from their place in front of the barbershop. They run into the road and across as Dorothy reaches for Abel and Abel reaches for Dumb Willie. The policeman, too, is running. And Dorothy, for the first time in her existence, finds in her deepest places something like fear.

She pulls on Dumb Willie, leading him and Abel half-way down the block toward a narrow alley that cuts between two shops. People are screaming, yelling, the men and the cop both now on Dorothy's side of the street. She grits her teeth at how Abel creeps along, knowing that is all he can do. Dumb Willie calls out, "Koose me," to those scrambling out of their way, "That's my . . . pitcher," and "I'm *fay*. Mus," Dorothy shaking her head, because a politeness born from innocence is all Dumb Willie can do as well.

Another holler rings out, this time a man's name. Dorothy lifts Abel into her arms and thinks that name might be the policeman's. She tells Dumb Willie to move faster—"No runnin', that'll just bring more eyes"—saying it full of the panic she feels.

The alley empties into a parking lot. Here, Dorothy chances a loping jog. Her leather bag jostles against Abel's shoulder. His legs swing free against her thighs, yet his eyes remain fixed for the mob he must expect to come rushing behind them. Far away, a whistle calls.

"The train," she says. "We have to get to the train, Dumb Willie. Hurry."

The way they came is cut off from them now—too crowded, too many eyes. That leaves only Greenville's smaller side streets and neighborhoods. They wind their way among backyards and homes and over chain-link fences, ditches filled with mosquito-laden rainwater and empty culverts. Sirens wail in the distance. Abel spots the hill. Dumb Willie points toward the tall metal shafts of the mill, gleaming in the sun.

They skirt the hill, moving slowly along the slopes so they are out of traffic's sight, and here Dorothy can see beyond the pond and patch of woods to the rails and the four men surrounding the train. They stand in brown uniforms with wide hats and sunglasses and shotguns leaning against their hips. Three police cars are spread evenly across the length of the twenty cars hooked to the single engine preparing to leave. Two on the right, Dorothy sees from their vantage point, one on the left. They'll have to go there. In the middle of the line rests a faded red boxcar. Its door is open.

"The trees," she says. "We'll hide in the trees. Right when the train gets moving, we run for that boxcar."

"They'll get us," Abel says. His face is the color of snow. "They can't get us, Dorothy. They'll take me and Dumb Willie away."

She rests a hand to his cheek. "They will not, Abel. Not so long as I'm with you. Dumb Willie, you be a ghost now, you hear? They can't know we're down there."

Dumb Willie stands off, grinning as though he's never had more fun. "Kay Do. Tee."

"Okay then. Let's go."

They inch their way down the slope. Abel remains in Dorothy's arms. He feels as light as air in her hands, though heavy in her worry for him. At the pond they ease into the woods, making their way a step at a time until they reach the tree line. The single police car remains on their side. Officers search the backs of all the cars, their tops and sides. They enter the empty boxcar and carry out what looks like an old coat. Left by another hobo, Dorothy reckons, before she lights upon another idea.

"They think Dumb Willie got here on the train," she whispers. Abel looks up at her. She corrects herself: "That's what they must think. You and him got here by the train."

"Then what'll we do?"

"We'll wait. They won't see us."

And yet they will, she realizes, as soon as the police decide to search these woods.

They'll have to be gone before that.

She sees the engineer and conductor both. They're arguing with one of the cops and saying they got a load to deliver, ain't nobody on their ride. They must be convincing, because the policeman begs off. The uniforms huddle in a tight circle and talk on their radios as the engineer climbs back aboard. He idles the big diesel in clouds of white smoke. Three of the officers peel away toward the other side of the train, leaving one standing at the car.

Dorothy pulls at Dumb Willie's sleeve. "Get ready," she says. "When that cop moves off, you take Abel and run. Run as fast as you can, Dumb Willie, and don't you stop till you hit that boxcar. Okay?"

"What are you gonna do?" Abel asks.

She grins. "A trick."

Dorothy eases from the trees and steps onto the rocks that line the rails. Moving easy, confident. Letting the power grow in her in much the same way as Abel's soul grows in him. The sun is not yet at its highest, casting long shadows of the trees outward over the cars like thin, black fingers. Dorothy puts that shine behind her, letting her own shadow grow outward. The policeman stands facing the train. She hides just beyond the periphery of his sight and continues moving until the very edge of her silhouette touches the heel of his boot.

He flinches. Looks right toward the last car, now left at the idling engine. Now the boxcar.

Death takes another step, bringing her shadow to the back of the man's knees and causing the man to take off his hat and run a hand through his hair, over the back of his neck. He fingers his radio first (just a hunch, Dorothy believes, and so she inches closer still and turns that hunch to a worry), and now he reaches for the cell phone in his pocket.

He sticks a finger in one ear after he dials. Dorothy hears,

SOME SMALL MAGIC

"Honey? Me. Everything okay?" as the man bends low, trying to drown the noise of the train. He cannot. "No, I'm up here at the mill. Something about that guy who killed those kids. I just need to know everything's good there. What?"—pushing his finger in more—"I can't . . . hang on."

Perhaps it is the way Dorothy's shadow is upon him, perhaps it is chance, but the policeman turns right toward the end of the train rather than left toward her. She bolts toward the open door of the boxcar, motioning for Dumb Willie to do the same. He races from the trees with Abel in his arms, those big legs pumping and those boots slamming upon the rocks and ties. Abel's eyes are wide. His good hand is a fist holding a clump of Dumb Willie's overalls, though Dorothy sees that Abel doesn't seem to be jostling at all. It is rather that he's floating, an angel of stillness set against Dumb Willie's flapping jowls and flying hair, and to Dorothy's horror she knows that is because so much of Abel is gone now, and so little remains.

She tosses her bag into the boxcar followed by herself, then turns to take Abel from Dumb Willie's arms. Dumb Willie scampers up and inside. Dorothy has no need to tell them where to go. By fear and instinct, both boys crawl into the faint shadows in the car's rear.

The train comes to life with a jerk, easing the cars on. Dorothy huddles with them in the back corner as the police car disappears behind them. The mill follows next.

Then, miles later, Greenville itself.

-5-

They're over there by the door now, A Bull and Do-tee. They look out as the world goes zoom, but Dumb Willie won't move from his place in the back of the boxcar. Even though he thinks a munster might be lurking about in these shadows, he won't move. There's people out there yelling and chasing because he's faymus. Dumb Willie don't want to be faymus no more.

He wants to tell A Bull to get away from that door. Someone might see. Then Dumb Willie remembers nobody can see A Bull no more because A Bull's dead, caught between places. They got to go find A Bull's da'ee. A Bull thinks it's to bring his da'ee home, but Dumb Willie knows better. Do-tee told him she's taking A Bull there only to say good-bye. Then they got to go home.

Sunlight creeps into the car in thin shadows that end near the tips of Dumb Willie's boots. The shine lights on a million bits of dust and dirt left hanging in the air, making them shimmer as the wind carries them up up up into the shadows where they vanish without a sound. He wonders if that's how it will be when Do-tee takes A Bull away.

Do-tee takes everyone away. One day she'll even take Dumb Willie. He thinks that will be a good day. Do-tee's his friend.

Sometimes A Bull looks behind and watches Dumb Willie, but that look makes Dumb Willie sad. He smiles anyway because that sad is a hush-hush. Do-tee said, *Don't you tell Abel*, and so Dumb Willie won't. But there's a shine in A Bull's eyes now like those bits of dust in the sunlight. His eyes used to be blue like the sky because he was broke there, but now they just shine because A Bull's not broke no more. A Bull's looking at him now.

"Hey, Dumb Willie," he say, "come on up here."

"I. *Can't* 'cause I'm fay. Mus."

"It's okay, we're moving now. Greenville's a long way back. Don't nobody know we're here."

Now Do-tee turns and smiles but not in her eyes. She says, "It's okay, Dumb Willie, I promise," and so Dumb Willie gets up. Do-tee's smart like A Bull; she won't let nothing bad happen.

He sits at the edge of the open door, careful to do like Do-tee say and keep his feet from hanging out so that driver won't see. Do-tee is sitting like an Indian does but Dumb Willie can't do that, his legs are too big. He tries to sit like that anyway, because Do-tee is smart. She's pretty and smart and kind.

Dumb Willie has never thought long on Death, even though he's seen it. The animals die on the farm and the corn dies in the garden, the tomatoes and the onions and the watermelons die, even the seasons die and people too. Some things die and then get born again, like his garden. People go to hebbin or hell. He has always thought Death to be not something that happens but a *thing*, like the cold that chases summer away and makes all the plants die. Like a spurut, or a munster, something to be feared. But now he knows Death is Do-tee, Death has long brown hair and a warm face and soft lady-parts, and Dumb Willie isn't scared at all.

"We have to say something," A Bull say. "Don't we, Dumb Willie."

"Yez," even though Dumb Willie doesn't know what.

"Something happened when we left Mattingly." A Bull's talking to Do-tee now. "Something bad. It was an accident, though, wasn't it, Dumb Willie? You didn't mean to."

"I din't mean. To," Dumb Willie say. Then, "What din't I . . . mean?"

"About what you did in the field." A Bull looks at Do-tee again. "There was trouble in the field. It was awful. I was getting hurt. Dumb Willie saved me."

"Chris. *Stunk*."

"He did," Abel say. And to Do-tee, "That's why Dumb Willie's picture was in that paper. I thought if we got far enough away, no one would know. But I guess everybody does now."

Do-tee moves some of her hair behind her ear and tucks it under her hat. She's looking hard, like she's trying to figure things. A Bull stares at his own shoes. They're muddy and streaked with grass and there's a pine needle sticking out through the laces, and what Dumb Willie thinks is that on A Bull's shoes is all the way they've come.

"They think Dumb Willie murdered somebody," A Bull say. "But he didn't. He didn't, Dorothy. That's not the way it happened."

"But someone went Westbound?" she ask.

The word unlocks something in Dumb Willie's thoughts, a memory of them on the train and Do-tee saying what going West meant. Her eyes were dark in the night, and in those eyes were secrets. Chris died because Dumb Willie made him, and Do-tee was taking Chris to the West even as she stood in that train saying, *Who are you?* It is a strange thought, nearly too big for Dumb Willie's specialness to hold: Do-tee is sitting right here with them now and yet she is other places too, doing what's meant.

"Yes," A Bull say. "Somebody did. And there's a reward for him. That's why those men came running across that road when we were in town. They wanted that money."

Do-tee's eyes flicker. "There's a reward for Dumb Willie?"

A Bull nods. "Twenty-five thousand dollars."

"'Cause I'm fay. Mus." Dumb Willie shakes his head, already tired of celebrity. He yawns he's so tired.

Do-tee say, "Dumb Willie, why don't you go on back

there and try to get you some sleep. It's been a busy morning. Me and Abel need to talk a little."

"It'sa. Munster. Back there."

"No, there's not," she say. "I promise. We're safe here, safest place ever. Here." She takes off her hat and leans past A Bull, placing it on his head. "This will make that monster tuck tail and run."

It's a small hat and don't fit right, but it's good because it smells like Do-tee. It's a good hat. A Bull could pull a rabbit out this hat and Dumb Willie could eat it, he's always hungry.

"It's okay, Dumb Willie," Abel say. "You go on back there and sleep awhile. I'll wake you up if there's something good to see."

"Kay A. Bull."

He keeps the hat on with his hand on the crown, not wanting the wind to take it. There's more light in the back now, but as Dumb Willie lies on the hard floor of the car and eases his head onto Do-tee's leather bag, he decides that doesn't matter. He's got that hat on now.

All those munsters are gone.

-6-

For hours and miles they ride in silence, Dorothy offering nothing but her company and Abel looking out over all that passes, trying to work out his thoughts. It isn't so much what he needs to say. He knows the time has come to say everything, no more secrets, and in fact that time should have come long before. The question is rather how to say it. For now, that answer won't come.

He has never known the world could be so big and wide

as this. Greenville is long behind them, having given way to the chopped mountaintops of West Virginia and glimpses of tiny towns and sad people, endless woods that look to Abel as though no man has ever stepped foot in them, and then flatlands of wheat and corn and grass so green it looks to have been painted. And now rising before them are mountains taller than he has ever seen and could ever imagine, rolling ones and ones with stubbed peaks of pine. Dorothy said they are the Smokies. It's Tennessee they're in now, and that means they're moving south.

He turns to make sure Dumb Willie is okay and is struck by how deeply his friend sleeps. Struck, but not surprised. It is as though Abel can almost see Dumb Willie's memories slipping away each time his chest rises and falls. The old men at the barbershop and their escape, Dumb Willie's picture on the front of the paper, all those stares and shouts, them running for their lives and trying to board this train. To Dumb Willie, all these things will be left behind, washed out and gone. To most in Mattingly, William Randolph Farmer is a dimwit to be pitied. To Abel, Dumb Willie had always been someone to be admired. The world holds few souls who live only forward, their pasts all but erased the moment they drift by.

"I wanted to tell you," he says to Dorothy.

"Tell me what?"

"What happened that night you saved us. I tried to tell you a bunch of times, but I never did. I didn't think you'd understand. And I guess so long as I never told nobody, maybe that'd mean none of it ever really happened. I could outrun it and leave it all back."

"Don't nobody leave anything back," Dorothy says. She's looking out toward the mountains, letting the wind play in her hair and tilting her face to the sun. "It all gets carried right along no matter where you go, and that's the pain everybody feels. That want to lay things down that are meant to be carried, if only for a little while more. If only so you can learn how soft life is. It's hard at the edges and soft in the middle, Abel."

Abel turns these words over in his head. They seem to bump into each other and go lopsided. "I don't guess I understand much of that."

"You will."

"There was this boy I knew, Chris Jones. He was always mean to me because I'm cripple. He said he was gone kill me. Lots of kids say that when you're my age, but they don't mean it. It just comes out, like when grown-ups say they'll pray for you because that's about all they can do. But Chris meant it. He's always calling me a bastard and saying I'll never be nothing on account of the way I am. A freak. That's what everybody calls me."

"Not everybody," Dorothy says.

"Guess you could say I poisoned him. Chris, I mean. But I didn't think that's what I was doing, or at least that's not what I meant to do. I just wanted to get him back is all. But then he found out and said he was gone kill me, and I knew he would. Day me and Dumb Willie left, Chris tried to kill me twice. First time was when I was coming back from the Preacher Keen's. I went there because I didn't know what to think of Reverend Johnny and his power, even though I'd found my daddy's letters already. Chris would've killed me for sure that time, but I was all done up in clothes and catcher's gear."

Dorothy says nothing. Her eyes go from the mountains outside to Abel beside her. Nothing in her face says she's

213

shocked, or even surprised. Abel thinks this is good, because the bad part is coming. The part he has to say now because there's no other choice.

"I told Dumb Willie to meet me at the tracks that night. I couldn't go all the way to Fairhope by myself, and if I left him at home, something bad would happen. Dumb Willie needs me because his folks are awful things. He got the way he is because this one time his daddy beat him all the way stupid. His name's Henderson. He didn't get in trouble because everybody thinks he's a fine Christian man. Dumb Willie was only a baby then, so Henderson's always said Dumb Willie was born that way. His folks never even took him to Doc March. I don't even think Dumb Willie knows that's why he's so dumb, but he knows his folks treat him bad. I couldn't leave him all alone.

"Chris was there at the tracks too. Or he was at my house, I don't know for sure, but he saw me and came running. He was gone kill me, Dorothy, I know he was. I ain't never seen anybody that mad. He had me on the ground and was hitting me, and I can't get hit. My bones'll break if I do. Sometimes Momma won't even hug me hard because she's afraid what'll happen. But then Dumb Willie got there. I don't think he saw it was Chris. I think all Dumb Willie saw was one of his monsters. He believes in monsters and ghosts and all that stuff. He snatched Chris up off me. Dumb Willie just . . . *tore* him. He threw Chris away the same way that Reverend Johnny got thrown. Like it was some kind of thing that's been in him all along suddenly came alive and wanted out."

A tear builds in Abel's eye. The wind swallows it.

"Dumb Willie killed him. He killed Chris. He meant to, Dorothy, I promise it, and I don't even think he remembers. I knew they'd find out. I just hoped I'd be so far from home when they did that it wouldn't matter. Momma must've gone looking for me but found Chris instead."

He leans forward and plucks the next envelope from his back pocket, looks at it.

"I'm so sorry, Dorothy."

"For what?"

"For almost getting you in trouble. Because you were right, and so was Reverend Johnny. The way is dark, and it's because of what Dumb Willie did. And what I did. I don't understand how things got so bad."

"Ain't a thing in this world makes folk slobber more than a killing," Dorothy says. "Especially when it's a child and the killer got away."

"He's not a killer."

"But he is, Abel. Dumb Willie *is*. Doesn't matter that he didn't mean to or he didn't know what he was doing. Doesn't even matter if all Dumb Willie was doing was trying to save you. He's a wanted man," she says, pointing deeper into the boxcar to the hulking body clutching her hat. "Word's gone out. Story like that? Everybody will know. Them old men back in Greenville are like old men everyplace, got nothing to do all day but sit around and flap their gums. But such men are respected. Folk will believe what they say. They state as fact they seen a wanted murderer on their very streets, it'll get taken as truth. And it'll spread."

"But if we get to my daddy, we can take him home. Dumb Willie too. I can tell everybody what happened."

Gone are the smooth lines over Dorothy's cheeks, that gentle upturn of her lips. In their place comes a sad look that settles into her.

"I don't think you can do that, Abel."

"If I tell them," he says, "they have to listen. Everybody

knows what Chris was like. Principal Rexrode does. My momma. My momma will believe me, Dorothy. She loves Dumb Willie. My momma knows he'd never do nothing bad on purpose."

"You can't go back."

"What do you mean I can't? All you been telling me is how you got to get me home."

"That's not . . ." She shakes her head, looking to struggle for the words.

"I was promised," Abel says. "'Do not turn away,' that's what Reverend Johnny said. So I can't, Dorothy. I can't turn away. I'm going to Fairhope and getting my daddy, and then we're all going home. Me and him and Dumb Willie. Even you, if you want. Reverend Johnny said I'd get healed on the way and I'll get my reward."

"You said Reverend Johnny couldn't heal you."

"But something can. He all but said so. If I can get healed, then there must be something to heal me."

"World's full of people who need healing, Abel. Folk aren't going to up and forget what happened to Chris Jones. There's no running from a thing that bad. No hiding it. Folk everywhere will be looking for him. Long as they think Dumb Willie might be hopping trains, they'll be searching every one. We're not safe here anymore. We're not safe anywhere. Folk everywhere will be coming to claim that reward, and they won't care a whit if Dumb Willie's live, dead, or more broke than he is when they drop him back in Mattingly. Any man who ends a child's life?" She shakes her head. "Nobody'd think twice to either fill Dumb Willie with lead or hang him from the closest tree. Twenty-five thousand is more than most in these parts see in a year's wage, maybe even two. More money than they can dream of having. It's easy money, killing a man."

Abel turns the envelope over in his hands, wanting what Dorothy said to not be true. Wanting to believe Reverend Johnny was right, that somewhere between Mattingly and Fairhope he will be healed of all his troubles and then find his daddy, and that his daddy will somehow make everything right. But now all those miles between the place where this train rolls and where his daddy waits are laid with danger, and even when they get there . . . *if* . . . what then?

"I'm scared, Dorothy." It is a hard thing to admit this, especially to a girl so pretty. "I'm scared they'll get Dumb Willie and take him away. I don't know if I can save us again. That smoke bomb was the last one I brung."

Fear strikes him, a great sense of being lost, stuck between two places and yet finding a home in neither. There have been few times in Abel's life that all has been well with his body. No bumps, no bruises, no casts. He has long been accustomed to things fracturing, and yet this thing he feels breaking in him now is no limb or bone but something deeper and more—not a snap, but a shattering. He collapses beneath the weight of it, eyes burning as tears flood and now fall with a speed that not even a wind made of steel and iron can carry away. They leak into Abel's mouth, drowning his rows of brown, jagged teeth. Dorothy's arms enfold him, squeezing hard. He wants to say, *Not too tight*, but knows himself already broken.

"Now you just cry," she says, "you just get it on out. Why don't you go on and read that letter from your daddy."

"Don't be mad at Dumb Willie," he says.

Abel feels her arms loosen but he won't let her go, pinning them to him with his cast.

"It ain't his fault the way he is," he says. "And I know you like him. You give him your hat. I seen the way you two talk, like there's a secret you won't say and neither will he. But he

217

ain't bad. Dumb Willie's just scared, that's why I got to keep him safe. He says there's monsters and spirits and puts stock in things that don't mean nothing."

"Never met a soul does otherwise," says Dorothy. "Why you think the world holds such a sadness? Folk everywhere spend their whole lives putting stock in what don't matter. Shiny things and fancy things, whatever won't last. Shoot, they all like my old hat." He feels her chin resting on the top of his head. "Even you, Abel. You put stock in some preacher you started out not even believing's true."

"Reverend Johnny's different. He proved himself true. He's magic. That's why you don't understand."

"You think I don't know about magic? How you think I got us past that cop? You know about magic, so do I. I know there's big magic and small, and I know it's everyplace but hid to most." She waits, so long that Abel thinks her words are done. "Dumb Willie sees it. That magic. He's special."

"Don't say that. That's an awful word."

"Not the way I mean it. I mean Dumb Willie's special in the only way that matters. There's most in this world go through their every day without regard for the world farther on. They think that world either don't matter or ain't there at all. They're crippled."

"Like me?"

"Oh no. Worse than you. You're only that way in your body. They're that way on their insides. There's others who got their hearts to that world, but not their eyes. They look to it but don't live for it, which makes them better off but only some. But then you got ones like Dumb Willie. They're the special ones, Abel, and you know why?"

Abel shakes his head against Dorothy's chest.

"Because they ain't meant for this life at all. They're so

tuned to that next world that it leaks into this one here, turning it all to a wonder they can't bear up against. You tell me Dumb Willie's pa is the one broke Dumb Willie's mind. I don't know about that. I think maybe it's more Dumb Willie's always been so full of heaven that he ain't got much use for earth. That's how it is for those few blessed enough that their souls point to other lands, but cursed such that they got to live in this one. Folk call them dumb. Call them crazy. But they ain't neither. All they are's closer to heaven than anybody else."

That says it right, Abel thinks. That says it more right about Dumb Willie than he could ever tell in words.

"What about me? Am I special too?"

He feels her hand upon his hair, the way Dorothy's fingers run through it down to his ear, touching the lobe.

"Abel, you're maybe the most special of all."

"Good," he says, "because I love you."

That hand stops. "What?"

"I love you," he says again.

Her soft voice trembles over the wind: "Why?"

"Because you're you," he says, not caring what Dorothy answers, not wanting even that love returned.

Wanting only that she hear the words.

-7-

5 March 2009
Dear Abel,

It's been a long winter, hasn't it? I can't remember one messier, but then I guess that's not saying much since some-times I don't remember so good. But a friend of mine said

219

the same thing the other day. His name is Henry. You'd like Henry, I think, even though you have to be careful with him sometimes. Anyway, Henry said he can't remember a messier winter so I guess that's true. It's been four straight days of rain here. Most everybody's been stuck inside. It's a cold pour like March ones are. Not sleet or snow, just 34 and rain. I told Henry nobody can do a thing about the weather and he said I was right. Everybody complains about things but it's an empty complaining since nothing can get changed. You should probably remember that. It might come in handy someday.

I was thinking today about how I never liked the cold months. Even when I was a kid like you I didn't. The only good thing about winter was sometimes it snowed and there was no school. Plus Christmas break. Do they still call it Christmas break? Do you like winter?

Anyway, I am looking forward to spring. That's always been my favorite time. Everything looks so dead and gone and then it all starts growing back like the world's been holding its breath and this is the exhale. I've always thought spring meant hope. Like it's God's way of saying I know you'll all screw this up again, but let's try one more time anyway. One time I heard that the definition of a miracle is something coming from nothing. If that's true, then I guess spring is the biggest miracle of all.

Here's something else I like about the warm months— the thunderstorms. Your granddaddy (you didn't know him—he died a long time before you were born) used to love thunderstorms. He'd take me outside on the porch whenever one sprung up. You could watch them coming from way off, how the clouds would gather up and turn all black and angry. The wind would stir the corn in the field, and the rain would march right toward you in a long straight line and it would be lightning and thunder. Sometimes it got so bad I thought the whole world was going to end.

But then it was over, you know? The clouds either moved by or gave out and the sun would sneak back and blue skies, and the birds would set to singing again. The air smelled so fresh and clean that it was like spring inside spring. That's what I loved best. But those winter storms are a lot different, Abel. They don't pass by so much as settle in, like this storm now.

I guess what I'm trying to say, Abel, is that most of my life has felt like this last week, only on the inside—34 and rain. I've come to find it's like that for a lot of people, especially around here. Everybody has to face storms sometimes. Sometimes they come and go fast like those Carolina thunderbumpers Daddy and me used to watch, and sometimes it's like this.

It's a cold damp that starts out on your arms and legs and then ends up in your eyes and mouth and finally your soul. And the thing is, I think however the weather is in the world isn't much different from the weather in you.

Both can feel cold and hot or dry and wet.

Both can leave you pining for death or happy for what life you got.

The only difference is if it rains and snows out of the sky you can always find a roof somewhere. It storms that way inside you, though, ain't much you can do. It'll be like that for you sometimes, Abel. It's like that for everybody and that's what I want you to know. And it might even be worse for you because of me. That's what I'm scared of.

My momma (you never met her either) used to always go to the bingo in town. Every week she went. She'd play and play and come home with nothing but clothes stinking of cigarettes, and what Daddy would say is it's no use to ever go at all. He said our family always had bad luck. That's true because we never won ahead on anything. Momma always had fun though. And I think that's what we all have to do, enjoy things anyway because we won't win. Nobody ever wins in this life. It's all 34 and rain.

I don't want to end this letter with something so sad (even though it's true) so I'll just say I hope you're doing well. I hope you're good.

Love,
Dad

-8-

She whispers the words to the wind and the darkening sky beyond, to the small town they pass, unknown to Abel and Dumb Willie but known to Dorothy, because even now she is in a small house not far from where the train passes, taking an elderly man onto the path that leads to a place far fairer than that which he leaves behind. She says those words again, soft so Abel won't hear:

"Thirty-four and rain."

Abel's daddy had said much more in his letter, which Dorothy asked Abel to read aloud not once but twice, making him promise nothing had been left out. She holds that letter now in her hand. The words themselves mean little to her, being nothing more than a collection of squiggly marks and dots. It is the page itself Dorothy wishes to touch, if only to gauge the man who touched it before her.

Because there is something here. Something more. Hidden.

She looks from the paper to where Abel sits, guarding Dumb Willie not from her or the monsters Dumb Willie believes lurk here but from the nightmare that stirred him.

Thirty-four and rain. Why had Abel's father used such words as that? More, why had those words struck Dorothy such? So much, in fact, that she had Abel read those parts over yet again.

She remembers a day such as that, one long past and near to where the train is leading them. Not a city or a town, but a single, forgotten place. How the wind had blown that cold day and the rain had fallen, Death being called. Dorothy being seen.

The page trembles in her hand, shaken not by the train cutting through these lands but by Dorothy's own memories. She looks back to where Abel sits, shining and still. He stares down at a yellow cast that covers an arm no longer broken, rubbing a soothing hand upon a behemoth's chest. Dumb Willie will have to go somewhere safe. They all must, Dorothy decides, else their journey will end and she will have to take Abel on.

The boy said he didn't know how things had gotten so bad. That is a sentiment Dorothy knows well. She has gone against what is meant by keeping Abel in this world, Death so pained that it could no longer bear to take another child from this world, even to paradise, knowing what that child would do once he took Death's hand. That act of rebellion will bring punishment. Dorothy is powerful, and yet there is One who stands over even her, and that One rules all. Even if Abel is delivered on after he finds his father, judgment must come.

But it is to Dorothy's grief that she now finds herself struggling even to fulfill this, Death's very purpose. Dumb

Willie has promised not to tell Abel of his end. Dorothy herself would do that, she'd said, after Abel's father was found. Yet now she knows she could not bear to give Abel this message, no matter the comfort and joy he would find once freed of this world. Not because that comfort and joy would mean the end of Abel's dream of a life with both father and mother. Not because Abel would leave Dumb Willie behind to sit alone at a table of consequences.

Because Abel loves her pure and whole with a noble heart filled with innocence, and that is a thing Death has never been told.

She looks at the page again and settles her eyes upon the marks that Abel said were the ones he had to repeat:

Thirty-four and rain.

They cannot stay on this path. It is too dangerous for Dumb Willie and so too dangerous for Abel. The wilds beyond would not keep them. It must be her, then. The woman on the farm.

There is nowhere else for them to hide.

-9-

It is not sleep that takes Abel this night, nor can he say he remains awake. He is rather caught in a dark place between the two, where memories whisper and pictures flash—his momma and his bedroom, fishing with Dumb Willie, walking among the tall grass and hidden rocks of the field behind his house as a distant whistle blows.

They are comforting scenes that come without the sharp lines and bright dyes of the near past. These are dulled and sepia-colored snapshots of pictures taken long ago and left to fade inside boxes stuffed in moldering attics or scrapbooks shoved into the nether regions of an old hope chest.

These images swirl toward darkness inside Abel's mind before flaring again to pictures of Chris's face, twisted in rage with a runner of slobber oozing from the corner of his mouth. The feel of the hard ground of the field at Abel's back. His cast flailing in shocks of yellow light as he tries to parry Chris's blows. Dumb Willie's voice—*You leave. Him. Lone you. Stink*—and Chris being flung upward as though yanked by the same force that had taken Reverend Johnny. Dumb Willie picking Abel up and racing toward the train. Abel being lifted high and thrown to where the boxcar rolls, that feeling of flight

(I'm flying, I'm flying for real)

toward that wide black mouth and now that wide mouth moving farther from reach. Abel tumbling to darkness, left to fall forever and never land, caught between two worlds—

What this is, this in-between place, shatters at the sound of scraping metal. He feels the boxcar shudder around him and lifts his head from Dumb Willie's chest. Night has descended beyond the door where Dorothy stands. Her leather bag is slung over her shoulder.

"Abel," she says, "time to get up. And wake Dumb Willie too. We have to go."

"Go where?"

"We have to get off this train. Cars are being dropped. Now's our time."

"I don't . . ."

He rubs his eyes and tries to wrangle his thoughts as to what is dream and what is real. Dumb Willie stirs beside him. He rises up like a mummy from a crypt and rubs his own eyes, says, "I'm. *Hungry.*"

Dorothy says, "We'll get you some food soon enough, Dumb Willie. Right now it's time we find somewhere safe for you. Not for long, only a few days."

Abel looks beyond the door. "Where are we?"

"Just to this side of North Carolina. I know it don't seem far, but it is. For a freight train, it is."

"Carolina?" he says. "Are we there? Are we in Fairhope?"

"Not just yet. It's a ways more." She leans her head out the door. Checking, Abel supposes, to see if the conductor has gotten out of the engine.

"We gone wait for another train?"

"No, Abel. Trains aren't safe just now. Nowhere's safe, really."

"'Cause I'm fay. Mus," Dumb Willie says. He offers a smile of victory at Dorothy's nod.

"I know a place," she says. "At least, I think I do. We can hide there."

"What about Fairhope?" Abel asks. "We got to get to my daddy."

"Fairhope's down the rails, Abel." Her eyes are dark but soft and full of kindness and something Abel cannot reckon. Sadness, he thinks, or a feeling close to it. "Another train, and likely more. The more trains we have to jump on and off right now, the more apt Dumb Willie will get seen."

Abel feels a lump sprout in his throat. He dips his head to nod and finds he cannot lift his chin. He feels Dumb Willie's hand on him, hears, "Be oh. Kay A. Bull," and spots the tops of Dorothy's shoes when she walks to him. Her hands are on his shoulders. She bends down.

"Fairhope's a ways yet, Abel. We're here. Now, maybe here leads to there just like you say and like your Reverend Johnny foretold. But between the two's a wide space even I can't see through, and so what's left for us is the only thing I know, and that's to keep you and Dumb Willie safe. Things got off-balance. I'm trying to set them right, but there's not much time. Do you understand?"

"Yes," he whispers. And she's right. "We have to keep Dumb Willie safe. But we can keep him safe while we go on. I went the wrong way when we left home. This feels like we're going the wrong way again."

"We're not."

But we are, he thinks. *It feels like we* are.

She lifts his chin with a finger. "What you told me last night, Abel. That was a brave thing. Telling the truth is always brave. And for that, I'm going to tell you the truth too. I saw what happened that night. Chris dying. I saw it. Then I pulled you and Dumb Willie up into the car, and that's when the balance got lost. I shouldn't have done that, Abel. It wasn't meant. But I did because I wanted to and I'm glad it happened. Because I'm fond of Dumb Willie, and I'm very fond of you."

Very fond does not sound like love to Abel, but it does sound close.

"I don't know how it can be that I feel that way," Dorothy says. "I'm a stranger to most, and most who see me are afraid of one thing or another. Those who pass my way do so for only a bit before they're off to what's next. Not you, though. Not Dumb Willie. You I saved, and I don't want a bad thing to happen to you because of it."

"You saw?" he asks. "Then why'd you make me tell it?"

Her words sound strange and spoken not by her lips but from that thing in her eyes Abel cannot say, that sadness: "Because I don't want you looking back. I couldn't bear it if you did that, Abel. And keeping close a thing like that, something so horrible. You would look back, just like all the others have."

"What others?"

"Don't you mind that just now, and don't you worry. Do you have your letters?"

"Yes."

"Keep them close. Those letters are special, Abel. I don't know how or why, but I think they're pointing the way. Not just to Fairhope, but *through*. The first one said go into Greenville. The second one said go on. So we're going on. It's a hidden place, a safe place. For you," Dorothy says, "and hopefully for me too. But we have to follow. It's meant."

"We have to go to Fairhope," he says.

"Hope," Dumb Willie adds.

Dorothy shakes her head. "It's not meant yet."

"You're saying we don't even have a choice, Dorothy," Abel says. "We do. Nothing's *meant*." He holds out his cast. "Is this meant? Is me being a cripple all my life meant? Having nobody wanting to see me because I'm too frail and ugly? Poor Dumb Willie having to get chained up in his garden to work and get thought of by everybody as special in a way *special* don't mean? Please don't tell me any of that's *meant*, Dorothy."

Far away, a whistle calls. Abel lifts his eyes toward the sound but finds Dorothy does not. Her gaze is settled on him alone.

"You got will, Abel Shifflett. Outside you may be small, but inside you're a giant wrapped in brittle bones that stretch to bursting. Folk can get far on will. I've seen it. They'll put themselves in chains of their own choosing for just about anything, but the only way they can do that is because they start out free.

"You're right. There is choice. But behind all that choosing is a design that not even freedom can reach, and those are the things meant. There's no turning away from it that doesn't end in despair, and that's why we have to go. Your daddy'll still be where he is. The road is ever long, but we'll get there. I won't let it be otherwise."

Abel's voice is soft and breaking. "It's my choice what I do, Dorothy. I don't care what's meant. I don't want to hide nowhere. I'm scared and I miss my momma and I got to find my daddy. I got to keep Dumb Willie safe, and I'm scared I won't. So we got to keep going. Please? Maybe we can *change* what you think's meant. How you know we can't if we don't even try?"

"Because I have tried, Abel. I have, and now we're all in trouble. So will you trust me? I will keep you safe, and Dumb Willie. I will bear anything to keep you well."

She leans in now, tilting her head, and all of Abel's fear and worry is cast aside at the touch of Dorothy's lips soft upon his cheek. He feels that cheek blush and his stomach warm, hears Dumb Willie's "Oooh" from behind. Abel keeps his eyes wide, refusing to shut them for fear that will lessen the memory of it. Whether that kiss is given so that he will do as Dorothy asks is never entertained. Abel has heard tales of a woman's wiles, mostly spoken in the corners of the school playground where no teachers can hear. But he senses no wiles with Dorothy, because she's *very fond* of him and that might mean something like love.

-10-

They ease from the car in the darkness of early morning. Dorothy leaves first, followed by Dumb Willie, Abel in his arms.

"This track isn't a long one," she says, "and this part is a storage line. There's like to be cars waiting here when we get back. That's good, because it means won't be any police nosing around to check things. We'll just have to hope when the engine comes, it's pointing southway."

All of this is true; not a word Dorothy has spoken since they fled Greenville has been a false one. Colored, maybe, but no lies. She had no idea the train would switch tracks hours back to drop cars on this short line. The fact that it had only convinced her further that the letters Abel carried were more than words from his father. They were *directions*. Yet while that should bring her some comfort, she finds that is not the case. Not given where they are to go next.

They cross the rails under night's cover, taking care not to stumble as they travel the steep slope downward that leads to a mass of overgrown bushes and weeds. With one more look back to the engine about to depart, Dorothy leads them on. The land ahead is mountainous, thick with trees but thin of civilization.

"It's a ways," she says. "A day's walk, but we'll be fine. Dumb Willie, bet I can get you another rabbit. Or some possum."

Not far on they trade an open sky of early morning for one shrouded by Appalachian forest. The three of them alone together now, Abel keeping his hand in Dorothy's and Dumb Willie following close, growing tired in his steps yet buoyed by the promise of food and the black hat leaning upon his head.

Too far into this unsettled land to be famous, Dumb Willie's voice breaks into stilted song. The woods fill with the sound of old hymns recounting despair turned to hope and faith in spite of the world's heavy yoke. Dorothy adds her voice, bringing balance to Dumb Willie's clipped syllables and half words. Abel looks on in a strange way as though the verses are foreign. Dorothy coaches him until he is muttering in tune, rolling a familiar word or repeated phrase as though sampling a strange yet fragrant meal.

Memories of Greenville are still fresh in Dorothy's mind, though they look to have faded in the boys'. Dumb Willie carries Abel over the rough patches in the woods as Abel uses his sleeve to wipe the sweat from his friend's brow. Dorothy remains at a close distance, held there by a burden for the place waiting on. She listens as Abel and Dumb Willie recount stories of their lives in Mattingly, each filled with that peculiar mix of regret and longing common to any place called home. It is true, she thinks, that neither boy can go back. Even regardless of Abel's death, what would wait for them should he and Dumb Willie return to stay in Mattingly would only be a life of toil and wear for Abel, the joys he would find with his momma bent by Dumb Willie suffering the consequences of the Jones boy's death. It is meant that neither of them go back, though not in the determined and freedom-robbing way in which Abel sees it. That is a small comfort, though on this morning Dorothy finds even a small comfort well enough.

The sky eases from black to gray and then blues that burst to alpenglow along the distant ridges. Deer and possum crunch unseen over carpets of browning leaves. Birds call for the sun. The trees themselves seem to groan and stretch as a mist heavy with pine and honeysuckle rises through the branches. Far from alone, Dorothy tells them they make their long way under the watchful gaze of a world set apart, one older than the one to which they are accustomed, and more real.

*

They rest along an old logging road high in the hills as morning creeps to afternoon. Dumb Willie feasts on a salad of
greens and berries, all washed down with gulps of mountain
water that gushes from a small creek nearby. He moves off to
wash in the creek, nodding in his sweet way when Dorothy
asks that he keep his clothes on this time. Abel watches him
with eyes that now shine as stars, then looks down at his cast.

"Dumb Willie's always hungry," he says.

"So I've noticed."

"I haven't eaten. Have you noticed that? I haven't eaten
since supper the night I left."

The words are given as an innocent statement, nothing more than curiosity, though to Dorothy they ring like
a klaxon. Abel is looking at her now, wanting some sort of
answer as to the reason he no longer seems to be in need of
food at all, which is an answer she refuses to offer.

"Am I sick, you think?" he asks.

"'Course not. You're changing, Abel. That's all."

True again. Abel is changing, though in ways he does not
yet know. Not just with eyes that now glow against a soul as
strong as any Dorothy has known seeking to crack the thin
shell around it, but in other ways as well. Should someone be
back at the railcars now and stumble upon the strange tracks
made into the bushes and meadows beyond, their eyes would
see only two sets—one large, the tracks of a man both strong
and tall, and another pair of footprints, these smaller and narrower, as though made by a young woman.

It is indeed meant that they find the woman at the
farm. Dorothy is as sure of this as she is uneasy of the
prospect, but Abel is right as well. They need to strike for
Fairhope soon, and Dorothy must find a way to tell Abel
that Fairhope is their journey's end. She must take him on,

as has always been Death's purpose. If not, judgment will surely come. And that judgment, however holy it will be and however fearful Dorothy imagines it, pales against the greater judgment she will levy upon herself should the thin veneer Abel wears give out and his essence be released. She does not know what will happen then, and can only guess Abel's soul will be left to wander alone in the dim mists between worlds.

"Case you haven't noticed," she says, "I ain't dined much at all. Because I'm a free spirit, you see. A rider of the rails. Like you've become. A body gets to be that of a proper hobo's, it learns to do without certain things. We store up what we can in times of plenty so we can get ready for times of want. It's like the bears, I guess. They don't do much but eat all spring and summer, because they know winter's coming."

He beams. "Really? I'm a hobo now."

"Way I see it," Dorothy says, "you're right among the best."

*

She says she's going to scout what's ahead and leaves the boys by the creek, hiking up the next ridge alone. Its top is bare but for a few scraggly pines and a narrow game trail. This is empty land, forgotten. Dorothy looks first to where they've come from. The rail is gone now, swallowed by trees. Now on, past rolling ridges backed in midday sun that appear as waves upon an ocean, to where Abel's letter leads. That place, too, lays hidden by the reaching woods. Death, here, is alone. What counsel is left to Dorothy now will be found only among the living, and from there alone must come their aid.

They will turn east. *It is a safe place*, she tells herself, and then tells herself again. *The woman will not know who I am. I was another those years ago, and perhaps she has since moved on.*

That is what Dorothy says.

Yet her thoughts whisper the woman would never leave so long as blood flowed through her, and so she must be there still, Death having not been called since to claim her.

PART VI

THE WOEMAN

-1-

They are across the last ridge when Dumb Willie asks, "Where we. *Goin'* Do-tee?"

"You might like it, Dumb Willie," she says. "It's a farm."

Abel answers, "Who lives there?"

"Don't know"—the truth—"maybe nobody anymore"—the hope—"but just in case, I guess we'll need some rules."

Forest yields to a field where deer gather and the grasses rise nearly as tall as Abel. His blond head bobs among the tangles, disappearing in and out of sight. Dorothy's thoughts wander to another boy long ago, dirty and brown-haired, reaching for her hand as screams echoed in the distance.

"What kind—" Abel starts, and then is silenced by the noise.

Dumb Willie stops and tilts his head into the breeze. He looks at Dorothy, who hears it as well—a clanging rung twice.

At the far side of the field rests a path of flattened grass and a bank of trees. Dumb Willie crosses the field before Dorothy can tell him no. He disappears into the trees and returns leading the source of the sound: a spotted cow, too emaciated and frightened to do more than make a lowing sound at Dumb Willie's tugging. A rusted bell hangs from a rope beneath its sagging chin. Dorothy looks down the path. In the distance rests a rusted, half-opened gate.

The matter seems settled now. The farm is occupied.

Abel limps to where Dumb Willie stands and reaches high to caress the cow's nose, gaping at the beast as though it is exotic. Dorothy steps wide of the path and guides the boys closer to the trees.

"Rules," she says. "Now listen, I said we might find this place empty but it ain't, so that means I got to go ask permission for us to be here. It's a powerful thing coming to a town, but it's even more when you come to a house. So be on your best behavior, both of you. Dumb Willie, you be as kind as you always are and we'll be just fine here. And, Abel," she says, running a hand over a head that may as well be made of wind, "I'll need you to keep your distance. Say nothing unless said to. Be a ghost, you understand?"

Abel slips his hand between the rope and the cow's neck. "Don't worry, Dorothy. We won't do nothing to get us in trouble."

Dorothy offers a grin she knows looks anything but happy. "Now that's fine. Not y'all I'm worried will make the trouble, though. Stay here until I call."

She eases the boy's fingers away and takes hold of the rope, clicking her tongue so the cow will follow. Walking to the mouth of the path but no farther, because Dorothy knows who will be waiting. She lifts her head slowly.

Down the path at the gate is the woman, tall and defiant. A shotgun lies crosswise in her arms.

No words pass between them. Hers is not the face Death remembers, one as young and beautiful as Dorothy's own, though less spoiled. Time has weathered her skin to ridges and valleys that resemble the land around them. Her hair is a tangled and dirty brown, unbrushed past her shoulders. She wears a plain dress that covers her small breasts and non-existent waist. The hem ends some inches above a pair of boots in worse condition than even Dorothy's old shoes. Her legs, what part can be seen, are covered with a thick layer of coarse hair.

The last hope Dorothy has is that she will be seen as a stranger. She was called here those long years ago not as a young girl but as an old man, weathered in face and calloused of skin. A farming man. The boy's grandfather.

That hope is dashed when Dorothy sees the rage settle into the woman's cold eyes.

So it is punishment, then. This may be Abel and Dumb Willie's refuge, but it will be Dorothy's own chastisement, laid out by Abel's letter and ordained by what is meant. All the power Death holds and all the dread Dorothy can summon fall away, leaving her as humbled as a child caught beneath the judging stare of her momma.

The woman's voice is one of anger and strength, slicing through the mountain breeze: "You come for my cow?"

"No."

Now her hands, hard upon the gun. "For me, then."

"No."

The wind tosses her hair, covering her eyes.

"Will you end me, woman," Dorothy asks, "and kill what cannot die? I come for nothing save your hospitality."

"And what hospitality are you owed?"

"None, I know. But I am in need of aid."

"So it looks to me," the woman says. "So is right. I would turn you away, filth, and leave you to suffer."

"Then you would have the innocent suffer as well. Is that your way?"

She raises the scatter-gun high. "That is no way but your own."

Dorothy raises the hand not holding the cow's rein. She does not believe the woman will shoot; a gun won't harm Death, nor chase it, but only waste a shell. Yet perhaps the price of shot will be worth any revenge she can manage, however small and meaningless. Dorothy turns her head back toward the field. Dumb Willie stands as a stone. Abel wears a confused look.

Dorothy motions with her hand. "Come on here."

From the corner of her eye she sees the woman stiffen and her finger move to the trigger. Dorothy's hand remains out, pleading, and there is a moment she is sure the woman means to take Dumb Willie as Dorothy herself once took all the woman loved. Yet now the woman's eyes fill with Dumb Willie stepping into the path, and the sight of his ignorant grin is enough that it looks to shake the hate inside her. Abel slides out to a spot between the cow and Dorothy, unseen.

Dorothy lays a hand to Dumb Willie's shoulder. He covers it with his own.

"This boy has found trouble not of his own making. He is in danger, and I have sworn my help. Cast me out, woman, if you must. I will go. But let him stay and rest, and the good Lord will count it to your credit."

The woman says nothing, nor does she lower the gun.

Abel says, "What's wrong with her, Dorothy? That your momma?"

"Hush now, not a word." And to the woman, "My heart is pure, such that it is. We are being chased. I'm here only because we have no choice. We were led."

"Led?" Scorn laces the woman's voice.

"We ask charity, nothing more. Grant us that, and we will leave you in peace. You have my word."

"Your word is no more than you, spoiled and empty."

Yet her gaze remains upon Dumb Willie, betraying what Dorothy sees is the softness of a heart still beating in spite of the harsh life around it. The cow lows once more, as though offering an opinion of its own.

The woman lowers the shotgun, and with it her challenge. "What is your name, stranger?" she asks.

Dorothy squeezes the shoulder of the man beside her.

"I'm Dumb. *Willie.*"

"Bring the cow," she says, turning away. "I grant you a day. No more."

-2-

Abel settles at a spot between Dorothy's left leg and the mooing cow, peering through the narrow crack between the two. The woman bows her head and turns away. Her hair moves in thick clumps for the dirt and grease that have gone unwashed from it. Dumb Willie takes the cow. He does not so much as glance behind to see if Abel and Dorothy follow. It must be because he's so dumb, Abel thinks, that Dumb Willie would so blindly follow without even a pause to judge if following or waiting is best.

"Well, that could've gone better," Dorothy says, watching where the woman goes. "Then again, coulda gone a whole lot worse. Come on, Abel. We'll rest easy and tell ourselves the hard part's done."

And yet Abel sees that it is a halfhearted three steps Dorothy takes forward, like she's testing her feet to make sure they can still move, leaving himself to remain moored to the field. The woman has already reached the gate. She pushes it wide to let Dumb Willie and the cow through (Abel hears the faint call of "*Fank. You*"), keeping the barrel of the shotgun pointed well away. That barrel trains on Dorothy instead—an act Abel believes is no accident.

"That ain't your momma, is it?" he says. "I don't know a momma in the whole world'd aim a gun at her kid. Not even Dumb Willie's momma would."

"No," Dorothy says. "She ain't my momma, Abel."

"You sure this place is safe? It don't feel safe. Guns don't make a place safe, Dorothy. Not when there's folk of bent mind about."

"She don't have a bent mind."

But Abel's watching her, how that woman moves and how her eyes are wild like an animal's, and he says what he means: "She ain't well."

"Not well don't mean bent."

"Then what is she?"

"Help," Dorothy says. "That's what she is." She takes a step back to where Abel stands. "That woman's the only soul near who can give us shelter and safety, and that's why we've come."

"You said it was meant."

"And I believe it, hard as it is. But standing here like we're having second thoughts is an insult to her kindness. Ain't a good hobo in the world wants to bring an insult, so let's get our feet moving. It's safe for y'all. I promise it."

"For us," Abel says. "You said it's safe for *us*, Dorothy. That means it might not be for you."

She looks back. Abel follows Dorothy's eyes. The woman is gone.

"Come on," she says, holding out a hand. "We'll go together."

The path is level, the grass warm in the sun. Grasshoppers and millers flit with each step Dorothy takes, making a *brr* sound as they fly away.

"She don't like you," he says. "How you know her, Dorothy? You been here before?"

"Only once, long way back. She won't mind Dumb Willie. And she won't mind you. Just keep away."

"Dumb Willie won't keep away. He thinks everybody's his friend."

Dorothy says, "You let me worry about Dumb Willie."

They reach the gate and find the woman waiting in the shade of an old elm. Abel keeps his head low as they pass, looking up only once and only enough to register her hard stare and to offer a "Thank you, ma'am" that goes unremarked other than for Dorothy's soft "Shh."

"Obliged," she says.

"Get on," the woman tells her.

She closes the gate and keeps a fair distance, the shotgun down but ready. Marching them, Abel thinks, like two prisoners. Ahead is a small rise he cannot see past, though he hears the cow's clanging bell and Dumb Willie's singsong voice on the other side. When they cross, Abel finds the remains of a wood fence leading past a small fallow field pocked with clumps of wildflowers—grape hyacinths and coltsfoot, golden ragwort. A sea of fleabane leads down to where there sits a faded and worn two-story farmhouse with its back to the green peaks beyond. Its roof is a weak red, long bleached by the sun, the structure beneath cramped and slight with wood showing far more gray than the white paint that once covered it. A leaning porch rises from four warped steps, fronted by a center door and a dust-covered window to either side. Above, an upper porch rests at the second level with three more windows.

To the side of the house rests a barn in much the same condition. The door is open, as are the windows to the loft. Sunlight struggles to enter into the darkness. Dumb Willie stands at the barn's entrance. He's petting the cow's nose and offering it a pail of water.

"This all hers?" Abel asks.

Dorothy nods.

A few chickens and a fattened sow meander about in what could be called a yard. They scatter as Abel and Dorothy make their way to the barn, the woman drawing closer, the shotgun all but forgotten now in her arms. She leans it against the front of the barn and takes the cow from Dumb Willie, at once guiding and pulling it into a pen of mud and old boards.

"There are chores," is all she says.

"We're happy to pitch in," Dorothy says. "Dumb Willie here's a strong one not afraid of work. That right, Dumb Willie?"

"I help *good*," Dumb Willie says.

The woman stares at the cow, four sad eyes meeting. To Dumb Willie she asks, "And what have you done that warrants my aid?"

"I'm fay. Mus."

"A darkness chases him," Dorothy says, "and he has none inside."

The woman grins, though only Abel can see it from where he stands at the barn's entrance. Only he can see how that grin fades to a scowl.

"Darkness has no need of chasing when it arrives on my land walking alongside you, boy. There is hay to get out and feed for the chickens and pig. See to that, then I'll see if your supper's earned." She leaves the cow and walks through their midst.

Abel asks, "Do you know how far we are from Fairhope?" as she passes without a word and vanishes into the barn. He looks at Dorothy. "She ain't the friendly sort."

"Hush now. Come on."

Dorothy follows, as does Abel, while Dumb Willie resumes petting the cow. Cooing at it as though it is his pet. The chickens draw near to where he stands. The pig snuffs at his feet. Abel glances at him without surprise. Dumb Willie has always been good with animals, not just farm ones, but wild ones too. Animals, they don't judge.

There is a stench of rot and staleness inside the barn where neither light nor wind can reach. An old truck is parked near the back, its nose pointing toward daylight as though trying to escape. To the right near the door is a small wooden table with an oil lamp and a worn Bible resting on top. A thick mat of blankets rests on the ground beside it, along with a pail of waste. Dorothy stares from there back toward the house. The woman returns from the darkness in the back of the barn with a pitchfork in her hand.

"You bed here?" Dorothy asks.

She walks past, out into the day. "It's ghosts in the house."

Dumb Willie waits by the door. The woman stands in

front of him, staring at that empty but beaming smile on his face. It is the same grin Dumb Willie offers to everyone everywhere, though Abel sees it as something the woman has not received in a long while. Maybe never. It's like that smile strikes in her a fear, making her wary. She hands the pitchfork to him without a word and makes her way alone around the side of the barn.

"Abel," Dorothy says. Her voice is both soft and hard, meant only for him. "No words, okay? It won't go well if you do. That's just her way."

"But she's talking to Dumb Willie."

"I know. She's just not used to so many people about."

"That right, what she said? About ghosts being in that house?"

"Don't you worry on that."

"But is it right?"

"She's special," Dorothy says. "That's all."

"Like me and Dumb Willie?"

"Yes, in a way. Now, I'm going off with Dumb Willie to help with these chores. More we do, more she'll accept of us. You come along. I'll let you watch, but you can't do."

"What's her name? That woman?"

Dorothy looks down. The wind plays with her hair. Abel wishes he were that wind.

"Don't know," she said. "I was only here once. Never got far enough along for names. I had to move on."

"Why?"

"Because that's what I do. And for the bad that happened. She blamed me for it, though I had no part. Now come on. She'll be expecting me and Dumb Willie get this done."

Dumb Willie says, "A Bull you. *Comin'*? We got the . . . chores."

"I'm gonna stay here," Abel says. "You go on and help Dorothy."

"Don't go far," Dorothy says. "Promise me."

"I promise."

Dorothy moves off into the barn and up a ladder hidden in back, where she begins scooping hay through the window for Dumb Willie below. Abel examines the woman's bed and her table, keeping far from the stench inside the pail. The pages of the Bible are wrinkled and yellowed with age. The cover is worn near off. He likens it to a preacher's Bible from its heavy use. Something Preacher Keen might carry. Certainly Reverend Johnny.

He keeps close until Dorothy and Dumb Willie have settled into their work, then moves from the barn and across the yard, up the house stairs. The wood boards do not creak, though they look like they should. Abel leans in close to one of the windows and peers inside. No spirits wait on the other side of the glass. There is a sofa and two chairs and pictures on the wall too covered with dust to reveal their subjects. A piano in the corner. An empty dining room table. Peeling paint and flowered wallpaper. The only thing that captures Abel's interest is the long shelf of books reaching down the hallway. Volumes of them, paperbacks and hard, thick books and thin books and books with cracked and peeling spines. They are not stacked in the exact way some bookshelves are, ones kept as mere decoration or monuments to ego and loved by the eyes alone. These are laid haphazard, some placed on their ends and others with their spines facing outward. Pages dog-eared and stained, loved by touching.

The house reminds Abel of the one he has left behind, just as the grounds call him back to the field where he counted the coming trains. There is nothing here but rot and the remains of what time can strip away, and yet Abel sees that the woman's farm does offer the safety Dorothy promised. No one would know of a place like this, so hidden in the mountains. He sees, too, the treasure that once must have flourished here. A ruined thing can only be called such if it once was beautiful, just as something can only be broken if once it was whole.

The woman, too, is a frightening thing, though in a way the house is not. Dorothy would never confess that same feeling even though Abel believes she shares it, and in a deeper way than Abel can know. Dumb Willie does not seem frightened of her at all.

He stands in front of the porch and looks away toward the barn. Dorothy has rolled up the sleeves of her shirt and tied her hair back with a bit of twine. Sweat gleams from her chest as she forks hay from above to Dumb Willie below. Abel shakes his head, Dorothy being just about perfect. She's pretty like his momma, and works just as hard.

To the side of the house are more wildflowers, along with roses that still look tended to. Abel follows a path that empties to a backyard and a garden that Dumb Willie would likely slobber over, rows upon rows of corn and potatoes and peppers and beans, watermelons and cantaloupes, more tomato plants than seem possible for one woman's care. He catches a glimpse of the woman's billowing dress, far toward the back where the leaves of thick standing oaks shake and sing in the breeze. Not wanting to trample the struggling plants, Abel follows the garden's edge as he keeps his eyes to where the trees stand. The woman stands there, silent and still. Her hands are clasped to the front of her waist and her head is bowed, looking more grieving than prayerful at the two wooden crosses sunk into the ground in front of her.

-3-

A tugging is what draws Dumb Willie into the barn not long after the hay is put out and the chickens and cow and pig are fed. It is not a tugging, but a tugging is the best he can think it. Do-tee has gone off. She said, *Dumb Willie, I don't guess I can be here right now*, and walked off out to the fields. Do-tee's sad, but Dumb Willie don't know why. A Bull went with her because A Bull can't be seen. A Bull's a secret.

That woeman ain't here. Dumb Willie knows she's a woeman because he can see it in how she walks and talks and looks. She's sad like Do-tee. That woeman got a Bible by her bed. Dumb Willie looks inside it because of that tug, even as he doesn't think he should. None of the pages inside are marked. Dumb Willie's ma always marks her pages and his da'ee marks them and that means you're a Good Christian.

Dumb Willie don't have no Bible because he can't . . . it's a word . . . reed. He can't reed so he guesses he's no Good Christian. That woeman don't have no lines marked so she must be no Good Christian too.

He thinks on this, how maybe it's why that woeman is so sad, and what Dumb Willie decides to do is smudge over a part of a page near the middle of her Bible with his finger. It's a dirty finger, it's got pig poop on it and mud and some flower smudges, but it's some lines marked in that woeman's Bible and that makes her a Good Christian now.

Outside, the cow lows. Dumb Willie goes out there and pets it. He likes that cow but it looks sad too. Dumb Willie comes up with his own word (woecow) and laughs at how it sounds. But there's that tugging again. That cow can't feel it, but Dumb Willie can. He turns and faces the field where A Bull and Do-tee have gone off, and that tug isn't going there. Now toward the house, closing his eyes because there's spuruts there, that woeman said. He turns himself back to the barn next and hopes that tug won't point him to the pail inside the door, that pail stinks, but Dumb Willie doesn't make it that far. He stops midway between the house and the barn, to an empty space leading toward the back.

That tug.

"Bye woe. *Cow*," he says, walking off as he looks away to the field of flowers on the other side of the house. A Bull and Do-tee are there. They're sitting in the flowers and talking where the field drops off big. Even from that distance, Dumb Willie can see A Bull's shine. That's his soul wanting out, he thinks—what Do-tee told him. They got to get A Bull home or A Bull will bust, and what Dumb Willie thinks is he'll be sad no matter which one A Bull does.

He tries the words "Dumb woe *Will*-ee" and "Woe Dumb *Will*" and "Will *woe* Dumb." None of these sound right to his own mind. Nor does Dumb Willie believe they should. As he moves toward the hidden places behind the woeman's house, all Dumb Willie can do is wipe his eyes.

And yet what sadness leaks out of him now is tempered when Dumb Willie reaches the backyard. It is as though he runs headlong into a wall he cannot see and so can only stand, shocked at what lies before him. He has seen gardens before, not just the one in back of his own house that he grows for his daddy, but others. Smaller ones in town and bigger ones out on the farms, gardens that grow good and ones that sprout few of anything but weeds. Yet never has Dumb Willie looked upon such a garden as this, one stretched so long and wide that it looks like the school field where the kids throw balls.

He sees corn here. And peppers. The watermelons have started and the cantaloupes and beans, those beans look good. Rows untold of potatoes and tomatoes. Carrots. Onions. All laid bare to sun and wind and the mountains that tower close, pockets of wildflowers that have sprung up along the edges. Dumb Willie blinks as the picture of it begins to shimmer and dull, then realizes he has forgotten to breathe. He does so not in gulps, but in a slow and soft way, like you do in church. This place is like a church because it's holy.

He remembers a story of a man (it's a word, Dumb Willie cannot recall the man's name) who came to a holy place and the Lord said, "You take off your shoes." That's what Dumb Willie does. He stoops, thankful to find those unseen walls around him gone, and places his boots in the grass before stepping into the garden's warm earth. Treading down the rows of corn first, casting an expert eye to their spacing and giving a light touch to the stalks. It is good corn but struggling—it'll need hilled. Bugs have gotten to the potatoes. Birds are here. They sit in the trees and come down and eat the woeman's food and so do the rabbits. The rabbit eats the leaves and Dumb Willie eats the rabbit and then Dumb Willie buries the rabbit because all things end up in the ground. Like Chris. Like A Bull. Like Dumb Willie one day and like—

It takes him remembering if there was a scarecrow in the garden but there wasn't, then Dumb Willie sees that the scarecrow is the woeman. She's standing away to the other side staring at him with a glass and something covered in her hand. The way she's staring isn't the way most people do, like Dumb Willie is a freak and they should either run or throw something at him. She's a dirty woeman. Her hair ain't combed. There's pig poop and mud and flower smudges on her dress, like what's in her Bible.

"It'sa. *Garden.*"

The woeman stares. Not like most people but like A Bull sometimes does, like a way that's sad on the ends and smiling in the middle. She comes along up the rows and doesn't look down as she steps over the plants and around the tomatoes. That gun of hers is gone; Dumb Willie had checked that earlier too, it had no shells. She stops when she gets close enough to be heard but not touched. Holds out that glass.

"I brought water," she says. "And supper. It's been earned. You hungry?"

Dumb Willie nods. He's always hungry.

"Well, here then."

He sits down in between the rows of corn. The woeman stands there for a little bit like she don't know why, holding that glass and food out, and now on her face is a smile on the ends and sad in the middle. She sits too.

"It's . . . Mozes," Dumb Willie says, now remembering.

"What?"

"Mozes found the fire inna . . . *tree.* It'sa holy. Place." He waves his hand around, covering all the land behind the old house with the spuruts inside.

She uncovers the dish and hands it. It has apples sliced into pieces and pemmican and potatoes and carrots. There's a fork to eat with. Dumb Willie uses it like he's supposed to. He's happy for the food; there's nothing to bury.

"Where's she?" she asks. "That woman you're with."

"Do-tee inna . . . field."

The woeman turns her head that way. She puts a hand above her eyes to shield the sun and her hair blows back, and Dumb Willie sees she was pretty once. Like A Bull's ma and Do-tee are pretty.

"She would go there. I cannot stop her, but let her see. She deserves to see. She calls herself Doty?"

"No A Bull. *Say* it's. Do-tee."

"Who's Abel?"

Dumb Willie stops chewing, his face feeling flush. He says, "Ain't no A. Bull," through a spray of meat and vegetables.

"That thing's name is not Doty," the woeman says. "She's deceived you."

"No Do-tee's. *Nice* she. *Good.*"

Her hand shoots out. Dumb Willie barely has time to flinch before it strikes the plate he holds, sending food flying and the crows cawing in the trees. Her face has gone from soft to thunder, her eyes two fiery holes. She bares her black teeth and screams, "*Good?* You call what she is *good?* Are you the devil then, stranger? Come to claim me since it is not . . . *Doty's* time?"

The hand again, this time balled to a fist. It strikes Dumb Willie in the chest and neck and shoulder, one fist and now two. He rolls to his side, smashing the young corn beneath him, his body pressing the plate into the soil. He screams, "St . . . *op*," as the woeman straddles him. Her hair has gone over her face and there are crawly things in it.

That woeman's a munster like Chris was a munster. Dumb Willie shuts his eyes.

"Taker," she yells, "she takes all and leaves me *nothing*," and Dumb Willie doesn't know what it is she says because he's crying now. He opens his eyes and meets the woeman's own and she stops, hand raised to block the sun.

The woeman stumbles as she climbs off, crawling on all fours from the garden. She reaches for something in a patch of wildflowers and stands, gripping a rusted hoe in one hand. On her face is all the hate in the world.

Dumb Willie struggles to his feet. The edge of the hoe's blade is shiny and sharp. It glimmers in the sun. The woeman raises it slowly—"Taker," she says—and Dumb Willie sees that munster.

His eyes narrow. His hands ball to fists. The wind sings. It rattles the leaves of the tall oaks on the far side of the garden, sweet and smelling of honey. Dumb Willie's eyes look down at the ruined stalks at his feet, pretty things that have now gone sad and broken. Those stalks got trampled but they can still be saved. *They can be saved* is what Dumb Willie thinks.

That woeman screams again, drawing his stare, and Dumb Willie has to blink because he doesn't see a munster there now. It's the woeman, she's sad not a munster, she's just a broken stalk.

He comes for her. The woeman stands her ground and raises up the hoe, swinging the blade down in a wide arc with both hands and all her power. Dumb Willie catches the shaft in his left hand. He holds on as that shaft shakes, the woeman's eyes two things of terror, then lowers the hoe in a slow motion that ends when he wrenches it from her hand.

Her fists rise once more. She hits him once, twice, smashing Dumb Willie's cheek and the side of his face. Dumb Willie thrusts himself forward, pinning the woeman's arms to her chest. She expels a gust of air and clenches as his hands move to her back. His fingers spread wide, gripping her. Holding her. Rocking her frail body as a father would a child, back and forth, back and forth, as her screams melt to tears and then to nothing but the sound of her soft whimpers and the feel of her wet face laid soft against his chest.

-4-

Abel keeps his gaze to the ground ahead and the sky above, the wildflowers that have overtaken the field and the crows and sparrows perched in the far trees. He looks anywhere but at the young woman who walks beside him, because Dorothy is too sad to behold.

Her shirt is streaked with sweat, the hollow part of her neck now flushed, all the softness in it gone. Harsh, scraping breaths leak from her nose and mouth. Her hair is a tangle beneath her black hat. And though she continues to speak in the soft tones of ease, Abel knows this girl he loves possesses no ease at all. She has worked too hard this day. Dorothy has brought down the hay and fed the animals and tended to the most dilapidated parts of the fencing, all the while telling Abel not to lift a hand and making sure Dumb Willie does as little as possible. It is as if she has worked not only to set the woman's farm to order but to set to order some hidden part of herself. She has labored not so that something outside of herself can be finished but so something inside of her can be driven out.

"Is a quiet place here," she says. "None quieter. Don't many even know this farm. The few who do don't care."

They step through the field easy, holding hands. Abel wants to say he's sorry and would, if he knew what to be sorry for.

"You see anything in that house?" she asks. Abel glances up now, sees her grin. "Seen you while we were gettin' that hay down. Glad you only kept to the porch and front window. Ain't polite, barging into somebody's place."

"There's lots of books in there," Abel says. "That's all I saw. Why don't that woman live there?"

"Show you why." Dorothy looks over his shoulder, back toward the house. "She catches me out here, might not be good. But I expect she'll see to Dumb Willie before coming to look for me."

"Why's that?"

"Because Dumb Willie's special, like she is."

"There ain't no ghosts in that house."

Dorothy shakes her head. "You're part true. Ain't nothing in there but memories, but those can haunt as sure as any ghost."

"I found something out back. She's got just about the biggest garden I've ever seen."

"I remember such."

"And there's trees. A bunch of them. You remember those?"

"I do," Dorothy says.

Ahead the field ends at what looks like a drop off the edge of the earth itself, a swath of nothingness and the base of the mountains beyond. Abel struggles over the slight ridges in the field. They are covered in grass and flowers and weeds but must have been rows in a time long past, plowed but never planted.

"You remember the graves?"

Dorothy stops. "The what?"

"There's graves back there underneath the trees. She was there. Don't worry, she never seen me. Must be somebody she knew. She looked to mourn."

The wind kicks up, sending a ripple among the tall grass.

Abel can smell Dorothy's sweat, a combination of sweet and salty.

"Come on," she says. "I'll show you."

They stop at the field's edge, where a steep bank falls away to a level place of scrub and downed wood some fifty feet below. A wire fence sags where the farm's boundary must end, though from Abel's vantage there is no one left in the world to stop the woman from claiming as much of these mountains as she desires.

"There," Dorothy says. She points down and far to their right. "See that?"

It takes a moment for Abel to recognize what it is, not only due to its poor condition, but because of the way it sits— upside down and nearly on its nose. Two rotted tires hang in the air, barely supported by a pile of rusted and mangled metal.

"What is that?" he asks. "That a tractor?"

"What's left of it. Let's sit here, Abel. I don't think I could get no closer to that even if I tried. Nothing more a good hobo likes than honest work. But the day's worn on me, and I'm tired."

He sits first and takes hold of Dorothy's elbow, guiding her to the ground. The two of them stare out over the expanse of trees beyond, the world silent but for the breeze.

"I was here once," she says. "Right here in this very spot, long time ago. Passing through. And before you go asking me how it is that a woman of the rails can be so far from one, I'll say I've been almost everyplace once and most places at least a dozen. It's what I do, Abel. You could say it's meant. This farm was something back then. I wish you could've seen it. Like something out of a picture book."

She goes quiet here. Abel looks at his bowed legs and the

cast on his arm, that wreck of a tractor, and then Dorothy last. Wanting her to go on.

She says, "Those graves is her husband and her boy. Got to be them. Can't be anybody else."

Abel doesn't know what to answer other than, "What happened to them?"

Dorothy looks down at the mass of iron and metal below. "What happens most times," she says. "Three of them woke up one morning thinking the day ahead would be no different from any other. Come supper, only one was left. It was cold that day. It's colder up here in the mountains than it is down the valley. And there was a pour."

She looks at him, wanting Abel to say the words. He knows what they are:

"Thirty-four and rain," he whispers. "Is that right? That why you said Daddy's letter sent us here?"

"That's how I took it. Wasn't no place else close we could hide awhile from all the people looking for Dumb Willie. There's hidden places all about this world. Don't you ever listen to anybody says different, that folk have found all there is and there's no mysteries left to wonder at. No magic to be had. There's places that hold great things. Great . . ." Dorothy pauses as though she's just lighted on something, an idea that until now has never crossed her mind.

"Great what?" Abel asks.

"Miracles." Dorothy stares at him. She whispers as though to herself, "There's places of miracles."

She plucks a wildflower from the near grass and removes the petals one by one, as though each of them is a memory itself—Dorothy's own ghosts.

"Thirty-four and rain," she says. "That's how it was here that day. Cold and wet. And slick. I was here when it happened.

I don't know why that man and his boy were out here on the tractor that day. Maybe it was chores, maybe it was just something to do. Not much else you can do in a place like this at the edge of winter. Either way, that man just . . . lost control. Went too far down along this bank and they went to tumbling. The woman blamed me for it. I can't begrudge her for that, though I had no hand in it. I promise you that, Abel. But she chased me off, and it's my sin that I let her. I believe that now. I knew it the second I saw her standing up at the gate with that shotgun in her hands. I shouldn't have gone. What I should've done is sit with her a bit. Help her, I don't know. Any way I could. But I left. I left because that's my way, because there are other places for me to go. I knew she would grieve, but that's what folk do. They grieve, Abel. All the time. I never forgot her. I seen so many faces, Abel, you got no idea how many. But hers never left my memory. When you read that letter on the train last night, she's the one I thought of. I told myself it'd be okay for us to come up here, but I didn't know I'd find her in such a way. Some people, they can move on when the ones they love pass. Some can't. Like her. She's nothing but a city without walls now."

She tosses the flower away. Abel can only look at the debris below. He tries to imagine that day, see the tractor along the bank and a man at the wheel, a boy on his lap. The tractor beginning to lean and then skid, then finally topple. The screams. Was Dorothy standing here when it happened? The woman? Did they run down to where the tractor fell and try to save them, or could they only stand here on the bank in shock, lying to themselves that somehow none of this was real, that any second now the woman's husband and son would appear and they would be bruised and scared but fine, everything would be fine?

"You should have told me," he says. "Dorothy, you should have said what happened before we ever left that train. Then I could have told you how that woman would be."

"I didn't know," she says, looking at him. "I thought you wouldn't understand."

"Like I didn't think you'd understand about what happened to Chris?"

The reply looks to sting her. Abel is sorry for it, though only a little. It's a hard thing, hearing the truth. It's harder still to tell it.

"It ain't just that she lost her family," he says. "It's that she's poor."

Dorothy's still looking at him, though Abel sees no understanding in her eyes.

"I'm poor, Dorothy," he says. "My momma's poor. We been poor my whole life. That's how I understand. All of us, Dumb Willie too. We're all poor. I guess maybe you don't know what that means because you've always been on the rails. But it's different for other folk. Do you know what poor is? What it really means?"

"No," she says.

"It means you don't got nothing the world wants anymore. Maybe you once did. Maybe you had dreams of things you wanted to do and a good home. Maybe you got no brittle bones or you had a job. Maybe you even had money. But then all those things got taken away because that's what the world does to you, Dorothy—it just takes. It claims and claims, and don't give you nothing back. And when it finally sees you got nothing left for it to take, that's when you're poor. That's what happened to her. That woman's husband got taken and
. . . *(her boy)* . . .
everything, and she don't have anything left now. All she

gots is this farm, but all this farm does is remind her of how poor she is." He shudders at the thought that comes next, one Abel does not put to words for the hurt of it. "Do you see?"

Dorothy looks as though her answer is no, she doesn't see that at all, or at least she hadn't until now. And though she could offer up any reaction to this sudden understanding, Abel is puzzled by the look of guilt that covers her face. She lowers her eyes and slumps her shoulders, dipping her chin.

"She scares me," Abel says. "That woman. I didn't know why, but I think I do now. That woman scares me because I think that's how my momma is now. She don't know where I went, Dorothy, or why. I couldn't tell her, because she hid those letters for a reason I don't know. If she hid those letters, she'd never let me go look for my daddy. We were the only ones we had to love. Now she's alone. Just like that woman."

"I hadn't considered it," Dorothy says, and this only looks to heap despair upon despair. "Could be." She sighs. "I don't know what I'm supposed to do here, Abel. What it is I'm to give her."

The breeze carries a sound from far away, faint and quick. It passes before Abel can judge it, though he could swear it was a scream. He turns his head back toward the house and sees nothing.

"Give her the thing all poor folk want," Abel says. "Give her mercy."

-5-

The sun drops late, turning the world orange and evening into a symphony of night bugs stirred from torpor. Lantern light plays shadows along the barn's walls. Dorothy sits by an old wagon with Abel, the two of them watching the woman and Dumb Willie upon the stack of lice-covered blankets that is her bed. She feeds him from her plate after his own is licked clean. Staring at Dumb Willie as he dips his head and says, "Fank you," drowning in his empty grin. She either does not notice or does not mind when Dorothy eases forward to lower the lantern's wick. She wants it dim in here just now, else Abel's gaze may wander from the bed to those dancing silhouettes and see they number three rather than four.

A red mark stains Dumb Willie's cheek, just above where his lip is swollen. Dorothy and Abel had come back from the field to find him patting the cow and whispering into its ear. The woman was nowhere.

When Abel asked what had happened, Dumb Willie only shook his head. His answer had been as peculiar as his appearance: "It'sa boozed. *Stalk* need . . . hugged."

Abel had pronounced that to be Dumb Willie's usual foolishness. Looking at Dumb Willie and the woman now, Dorothy believes otherwise.

Mercy, she thinks.

"What they doing over there?" Abel whispers. "It's like the two of us ain't even here. I could strip down and run right by them naked, neither one would notice."

"What's wrong? You confused about it, or are you jealous?"

"I ain't jealous," says Abel, in as jealous a way Dorothy decides a person could. The only thing she cannot decide is which of them Abel is most covetous of, the woman or Dumb Willie. "Who cares if they won't talk to me?"

"Seems you do. Way I figure it, should make you feel better they won't pay you no mind. Let Dumb Willie have this moment. It's been a long road for him, harder in a lot of ways than it's been for you and me. And as to her, I told you that story. Dumb Willie's the only one here she'd even try talking to. I'm the one she blames for what happened."

"What about me, then? She won't even look my way."

Dorothy thinks on this. "You're a boy, Abel. Like the one she lost. Seeing you must weigh on her. It just hurts her too bad, that's all. That ain't your fault, so don't go blaming yourself." She pauses. "It's none her fault either. And that's the thing."

The explanation is flimsy, but all the one she can manage. And though it seems to satisfy Abel well enough (even to the point that he backs farther against the wagon and more out of the woman's periphery), Dorothy knows the time is nearing for the three of them to take their leave. The light in Abel's eyes has grown to a light that pours from his mouth each time he speaks. They must reach Fairhope soon.

(*And then what?* she wonders.)

(*There's hidden places all about this world.*)

This is a safe place—safer than the woods, certainly safer than the areas north and south of Greenville—but there are too many things that could go wrong with the woman here. The longer they stay, the more suspicious Abel may become, and Dorothy has grown weary with her falsehoods.

(*Miracles. There's places of miracles.*)

"I'm to say my good-nights now," the woman says. Still looking at Dumb Willie, though her eyes cut to Dorothy as well. "There's hay yet in the loft. It'll make beds enough."

She rises with her plate and Dumb Willie's, ignoring the question he asks ("Wh . . . ere you *goin'*?") as she turns by the lantern and out, fading into the night at the side of the barn. Dumb Willie is left on the bed alone. He cocks his head and looks at Abel and Dorothy as though for the first time this night.

261

"We'll go up," Abel says to Dorothy. "Don't worry, Dumb Willie can carry me if I can't climb that ladder. You need to talk to her. Bet I can tell you where she's going."

"I know well where she's going. That's why I won't follow. It would be a bad time for us to have words, Abel."

Abel says, "There won't ever be a good time, Dorothy."

"Now that reminds me of something I'd think your momma would say. Maybe time on the rails has grown you on the inside, Abel"—she tugs at his ear—"even if it's done little for you on the out."

She returns his grin with a smile of her own, one so near true and full that she feels it creeping even into her dark eyes. The boy is special.

He is special indeed.

*

She manages a glimpse of the woman before she turns up the far side of the garden and out of sight. Dorothy refuses to call out and break the night's peace, nor does she follow. Instead, she remains in place, caught between the graves and the barn— between the darkness in her past and the deeper one waiting.

Never once since pulling Abel onto the train has Death pondered the spring, knowing it as a place of mere legend. Even when Dorothy learned of Abel's purpose in seeking his father, even when he spoke those soft words of his love for her, the spring was something she never considered. Now, here in this place of such despair and need, that single idea has overtaken her. She could take Abel to the spring, if the tales are true. It is hidden. A place of miracles.

Her mind and heart quarrel over such an idea as this, a thing that has never been done:

(You cannot seek it. Would be a terrible thing.)

(Would be a good thing. Would set things right.)

(What's right is what's meant.)

(The boy received a word. He said something came into that preacher and gave Abel his word. He'll find treasure and then healing, then a reward.)

(There is no healing for him but the kind the boy does not know he needs. That is the healing that is meant. That and nothing more.)

(Unless what's meant is sometimes wrong. It's just a place. And maybe it's just stories. Maybe it's not real.)

(You will seek it to your doom.)

(Better my doom than the boy's. He is special.)

(Better the boy moves on than dies twice.)

(Better the boy dies whole than broken. It's just a place.)

(You don't know where it is.)

(But I know who does. And it must be soon, else the boy's soul will fly without me and be cast off.)

At the garden's edge she pieces together the scene before her—trampled bits of young corn and unsettled earth, a tarnished hoe abandoned in the grass. Something happened here. Given Dumb Willie's condition when she and Abel returned from the field, Dorothy is left believing the dim boy had tried sprucing things up before the woman waylaid him. That conversation had progressed to some sort of violence before ending in . . . what? Dorothy does not know of feelings enough to say what Dumb Willie and the woman have come to share. She only knows Dumb Willie has done what Dorothy had not: shown the woman mercy. Abel was right in that, just as he was right in saying his own momma will be left as broken as this woman.

Death has never considered this. It walks the long edge

of the garden, marveling at the pain that thought kindles—a hurt not only for the woman and Abel's momma but for all the ones it has left behind to grieve and crumble by taking their loved ones on.

By doing what is meant.

She finds the woman at the raised mounds near the trees where two wooden crosses stand as sentinel; she is neither bowed nor mourning, but watching. Waiting, Dorothy knows, for what the woman knew would follow. For this moment that has been written down ever since Death's arrival at the path this early afternoon, a trial with the woman as prosecutor, the dead as jury, and the night their judge. Dorothy moves to the woman's side. She removes her hat and stares at the graves.

"How did you know me," she asks, "when we arrived at your door?"

"The eyes," is what the woman says. "You may change your countenance, but not those."

"I never believed I would return to this place until it was your time. You have shown us a kindness, and I am sorry. I knew you would remain in hurt. I did not know it would yet be this strong."

"You dare stand over these bones and spout your empty words. There is no room in you for regret. You are a shallow thing, callous in your deeds and empty in your feeling. You lay your waste and move on. How did you think you would find me after taking all I have ever loved?"

She bends to pluck a fallen leaf from one of the plots—her husband's or her boy's, Dorothy cannot know. Both graves look equal in length; neither cross is marked. Nor should they be. The woman would forever be their only visitor.

Yet this motion of her hand, soft and sure and caring,

brings a memory of that day long before when Dorothy was first called to this place. Of Death come in the form of an old man to find a house set perfect and gleaming in the midst of such cold and rain. A man upon a tractor, his boy on his lap. The tractor taking to the field, the boy laughing as water and wind played at his hair, his eyes bright and wide and gathering in. The boy seeing Death and waving. Death waving back as he sees the boy's lips move—*Grandpa!* The old man moving through the field, feet sinking into the miry soil. Death is the man's father, the boy's granddad. Death is whatever will bring them comfort when it takes them on.

The tractor disappears. Only the top of the man's head is visible now, a strong face made ruddy by sun and wind yet kind as a good father's should be. He plays with the boy, joshing him with how the tractor leans and pretending that his thick arms are about to give way and drop the boy down the slope.

He turns the wheel to bring the tractor back to the level field and flinches as the back tires spin in the rain. Turns the wheel again, this time in the opposite direction, wanting to gain traction as the engine sputters.

There is a flash of recognition upon the man's face, that same unyielding expression of fear and fight that the last breaths one will ever take are now being spent. It is a look Death has witnessed in so many as to be uncountable, regardless of age or creed or color.

A wail of metal folding in upon itself, a cloud of dust. A scream, half caught, rises. Now a longer one and more piercing from the side of the house. The woman comes running. Her long brown hair trails behind like a cape, her hands hiking up her dress so she may run. Yelling for her boys, her men.

Death takes the slope and moves to where the tractor

lies. The man and the boy have been crushed by the weight of the machine and thrown, landing at odd angles though near enough to touch each other as though that were their dying wish. Already they stand apart from their bodies—the man impassive, trying to understand; the boy looking at the image of his grandfather. Death takes the boy's hand. *It's all right now, boys. We're going home. You keep with me, it's only a short way.*

The woman running, tumbling down the slope. She screams even as she rolls and rises up to see her family gone, bones and blood and twisted limbs the only things left. Her eyes settle upon Death's gaze, seeing it. Some are born with knowledge of hidden things and the thinness between worlds.

In this brief time stretched out for her as eternity, she turns from a woman at peace to one in ruin. Calling out, yelling, *No!* Seeing the bodies of her boy and her man but not their spirits. Not seeing that even as they are unchained from earth and sense the coming life, both look back to the woman they leave behind. They look back, because all look back.

We must go, Death tells her. *It is meant.*

"Taker," the woman says now. "That is all you are. That is why you are so hated, why all rail against you. You come for what is not yours and what I would not yield to you."

Dorothy stares at the graves. "I can only be what I am and only serve the purpose handed me. Would you hate the snake for striking, or the hawk for descending upon the innocent young?"

"I dug their *graves*. With my bare hands I dug them, and with my own tears I covered them back." Dorothy withers beneath the woman's glare. "Yes, I would hate you. I would hate you forever. Not for what you've done, but for what you are. You left a wife abandoned and a mother barren. To forgive you would be to despise myself and cast aside their memory. Their memory is all I have left, and though it chains me, I will not yield that to you as well."

I'm poor, Dorothy. My momma's poor. We been poor my whole life. That's how I understand. All of us, Dumb Willie too. We're all poor. I guess maybe you don't know what that means because you've always been on the rails. But it's different for other folk. Do you know what poor is? What it really means?

Dorothy does. Standing in this dark place with this woman, Death knows.

"Where are they?" she asks. "Will you tell me? Are they well? Is it bright there?"

"Where they go, I cannot," Dorothy says. "It is meant only that I carry them there. But there is more—that I know. And I know it is a bright land with no remembrance of tears, and the fields there are long and green and bursting. Should there be a comfort for you, it is that." She thinks now of Abel's momma. "It is meant."

"Not by my will." The woman shakes her head slowly. "A comfort, you say. Only one worse than the devil would speak such words."

(There is a place, the stories say. A special place.)

(Would be a good thing. Would set things right.)

(Better my doom than the boy's.)

(You don't know where it is.)

(But I know who does. And it must be soon, else the boy's soul will fly without me and be cast off.)

Dorothy nods to the ground in front of her.

"I cannot undo this, but I may make amends. You are fond of the boy. I saw you feed and tend to him. Dumb Willie is in danger, but I can save him and what he loves most. You can see to his safety, if you give us what you have."

The woman stands silent. Dorothy thinks she may not have heard. Finally she speaks. "You take all I have," she whispers, "and yet you ask for more."

"Not only will you save Dumb Willie and what he loves, but you may well have a hand in my own ruin."

The woman squats down over the first mound. Rises. She says, "They wish to know what you would require of me first."

"We must get to Raleigh. We arrived by train, but there's no time to wait for another."

She bends again, settling her soiled fingers against one grave and then the other. Smiling now.

"They tell me yes," the woman says. "But only if it is as you say. If it will save the boy and end you."

-6-

The street is quiet, shaded to the left by pear trees and willows and dogwoods that stand perfectly spaced and well tended, as though they were planted in some long-ago with only a hope of the loveliness they would someday provide. Beyond sits a baseball field. Cars and trucks ring the diamond of dirt; bicycles lean against telephone poles. The sweet smell of grass freshly cut reaches through the rolled-down window. Parents cheer their boys, their girls. Two sets of bleachers behind each dugout gleam in the sinking sun to her right. The fading light is captured by a small forest that mixes shadow and shine, giving the impression of a world blinking in disbelief that it has found Lisa Shifflett here, at this place she vowed never to go.

Her little Honda putters past the cheers of happy folk.

She tries not to stare, keeping her gaze instead to the field not far on. Here is what appear to be acres of crops, most familiar to her but many that are not, all laid out in neat rows without even a single weed to spoil the view. The wooden sign set into the edge of the field reads *Fairhope Community Garden, Mon.–Sat. 1 pm–7 pm.* Past the sign is a turnoff to the left. She takes it and finds a parking lot, mostly empty, in the shape of a backward L. Ahead is a single fence, tall and imposing and worth more than Lisa has ever made, will ever make. Just beyond the fence is a main building of wood and glass and another sign that promises a warm welcome that she doesn't believe. Behind the building are laid out several smaller ones, apartments or bungalows, each spotted with silhouettes of the tall maples and oaks that dot the property. Beyond the fence, Lisa sees basketball courts and a softball field.

She parks in the first spot and turns the engine off, waits with shut eyes as the car sputters and spits and finally dies. Her lungs expand wide and slow. She fumbles for the pack of cigarettes in the console. Two thoughts collide in Lisa's mind, the second canceling the first: she's going to have to slow down on all this smoking, and why bother slowing down at all when the one thing you lived for is gone?

It would be a simple thing to get out and walk toward the office building, push the right buzzer (or whatever they have here), and knock at the right door. The hard part— that five-hour drive down interstates and secondary roads, Lisa clenching the wheel as she met each exit ramp and turnaround, telling herself to keep going instead of go back home—is over. Or so she thought. Now Lisa isn't so sure. Now she thinks getting here might have been an easy thing compared to what comes next.

The apron is still tied around her waist. She'd called ahead yesterday, making sure it was okay to make the trip, and decided it was better to go on into work this morning rather than sit around and worry about this afternoon. Streaks of ham and eggs, the morning's special, stain her chest. The small pocket sewn into the bottom of the apron bulges with ones and fives and tens, along with so much silver that it feels as though she's carrying another child. So much money that it would take too long to count it all.

It's been like that for three days now, ever since the funeral.

Roy said she could come back to work whenever she wanted, no rush, but she couldn't bear staying at the house anymore, trapped by all those memories. Sitting on the porch while she smoked and drank, hearing Abel mess about in his room. Seeing his face peering out from the window at her, only to fade to nothingness. She'd gone in the day after the service for only half a shift. Sheriff Barnett was the first customer. After Jake left, Lisa found a twenty next to his empty coffee cup—twenty dollars Jake didn't have but Lisa needed more. She'd cried for twenty minutes after. Cried more when those four hours yielded eighty dollars in tips and more hugs than Lisa had ever received in her life. The money didn't mean much. The love did. Both felt so fine that there really wasn't a choice in asking Roy to let her back full-time.

There have been cards from classmates who barely tolerated her boy and from teachers who saw Abel only with pity, days of headlines in the *Gazette*, and an endless stream of visitors to Holly Spring Road bearing casseroles and pies. Much of the town gathered yesterday evening to lay markers along the tracks where Abel and Chris died. All of Lisa's debts have been covered by love offerings taken up by Mattingly's churches, heeding their Christ's call to care for the least of these. It is a rare night that passes now without either a call or visit from Reverend Creech or Preacher Keen, both of whom officiated Abel's funeral. Hundreds had gathered at Oak Lawn for the burial, one day after Chris was laid to rest in the hill country. Mayor Wallis deemed it a time of mourning for the entire community.

Lisa would one day like to hear about her son's service, how beautiful it was. She is likely the only person in Mattingly who remembers none of it except for how tiny that casket looked. Like it was a child's toy that had to be plucked from some department store shelf and freed of its plastic wrapper before it could be lowered into the earth and covered with her tears.

People pass along the sidewalk near where she is parked. Some nod hello. Lisa waves, her hand reaching above the steering wheel of its own volition, habit more than intent. She opens the door. Shuts it again. Drops another cigarette from the window and lights another with no thought as to whether such a thing is permitted here.

She is emptied out. That's the best Lisa could explain to Reverend Creech as to how the last week has left her. She has been reduced to nothing more than a series of reflexes and stock replies and daily rituals that demand no thought to perform—the minimum requirements to exist and still be considered human.

The hollowness frightens Lisa more than even the bitterness that grows as a scab over the wound inside her. That is what keeps her up at night. Not the night train's song as it scrapes the rails past her house, but the knowing that what the world makes empty inside you must be filled again. This revelation came to her not when Sheriff Barnett found her son's body crushed along the railroad tracks but when what remained of Abel was lowered into the ground. When Lisa heard the soft *thunk*

(*hollow, it sounded hollow*)

of that first handful of dirt tossed upon his casket and knew that was the sound of Abel never needing her again. Sitting here on this hot evening and in the shadow of this horrible place, Lisa understands that is why she has thus far refused anything beyond the town's charity. She will take their money and their food, will even take their prayers, but she cannot bear to accept more.

There will be no grief groups, no friendships forged from her loss. Lisa cannot yet imagine a Sunday morning when she will put on her Going Out dress and accept Preacher Keen's repeated invitations to join his flock in worship. And though if asked Lisa will say it is because she cannot worship a God who allows crippled boys to be crushed by trains, that is not the true reason. The true reason is that she knows herself unworthy of anything good to be found in a church pew. Lisa Shifflett is far too broken to be healed. She loved her son more than love can mean, more than she could ever say, and so always found herself unable to express its depths. In a life defined by its failures, chief among them now is the worry that Lisa somehow failed in showing Abel how precious he was, how needed, and how she would fight until her dying breath to keep him safe and well.

He ran away. Why would he run away from her?

Reverend Creech says there will come a time when Lisa is ready to move on. It will be a slow process, but meant. Lisa has resisted this notion as well and chosen to view her pain as some form of penance. Besides, it seems life will not allow such a thing. What she repeats to her customers is true—sometimes she does hear Abel moving about behind a bedroom door Lisa cannot bring herself to open. She fears the trains that roll by her house, that one will jump the tracks and come barreling for her because that's what Lisa deserves for telling all those lies to Abel. She fears those trains and yet in the next breath wishes one would take her, because then she could be with her boy again.

There are as well the constant rumors swirling of Dumb Willie, how he has been spotted roaming the woods in Happy Hollow or in the hill country, has been seen as far north as Winchester and as far west as Greenville—clear to West Virginia—and how a manhunt is now under way along the border mountains. People everywhere are now vying for the reward (another contribution of the town, and the town's preachers especially) and vowing justice, especially Henderson Farmer, who has sworn to end Dumb Willie by his own hand so as to protect the family's good Christian name.

We'll get him, the sheriff promised Lisa after the funeral. *Dumb Willie will face judgment. You can rest on that*, and all Lisa could do was say thank you because that was the thing expected. In truth she felt even then that judgment would come to them all instead should Dumb Willie be found, and that whatever had happened that night, Dumb Willie had become an instrument of mercy as much as death. In her heart, she cannot believe Dumb Willie would ever harm her boy. Such evil is simply not in him. Would Lisa ever stand in Dumb Willie Farmer's presence again, she would be more apt to wrap him in her arms than spit in his face. His capture would not bring Abel back. And yet she knows all people must lay blame to their troubles, and always to something or someone other than themselves.

Yet it is not only Abel's memory that haunts Lisa as a

ghost and Dumb Willie's elusiveness that keeps her from moving on. It is also the thing that has brought her here to this place. She reaches into her apron pocket, past all those folded and crinkled bills, and pulls out the envelope she found in her post office box only hours ago. Mixed in with sympathy cards and the electric bill and a catalog she may now order from rather than leaf through was this, another of the letters. Sometimes they came a week at a time and sometimes more, many times less, but always when Lisa had allowed a hope to grow that they would stop, as though they were a punishment for doubting a father's devotion.

She holds the envelope to the setting sun, sees the folded paper inside. The address written on the front (*Abel Shifflett, PO Box 57, Mattingly, VA 24465*) and the return (*213 Kable Street, No. 11, Fairhope, NC 28573*).

Lisa has not read the letter. She has read them all, but this one will remain unopened.

Her thoughts return to that Sunday on the porch, surrounded by all those women in their Sunday finery that bespoke better lives. To the prayer Lisa uttered in the quietness of her heart—if Abel were found well, there would be no more secrets between them. She would tell him everything, even of his father. That his name was Gary and he was a kind man in spite of his troubles, that he worked hard at helping to build things, houses and offices, because making something out of nothing brought him a peace he had always lacked.

She would tell of the first time they'd met, inside a seedy little bar not far from this place. How Gary had said, *I can see your soul, and I've never seen a more beautiful one*, and Lisa had melted beneath the romance of those words because she had yet to know their terror. He was handsome in a way that Abel was never quite. A good man, which allowed Lisa to gloss over the drugs he took. She loved him, yes. Lisa loved Gary with that childlike ardor that crops out all those things that do not fit inside the perfect picture the mind creates, setting them aside under the foolish notion that not looking at his faults, his dangers, would make them go away.

And yet Lisa Shifflett had always been a lonely sort of girl, overlooked in many of the same ways that have

(*Had*, she corrects)

plagued her only son in life. Gary Bragg turned out to be the lonely sort as well, though for much different reasons. They grew to talk of marriage and children and a house along the river, grand plans that a mere carpenter's helper could never afford. With familiarity came a gnawing sense that something plagued this man she had come to cleave herself to, some darkness Gary could never put to words Lisa understood. "I see your soul," he would often say. *It's so beautiful, Lisa*, and that would somehow make everything better for a while.

For a while.

Dreams, Lisa knows. That was all they had. Dreams and something that feels, even these years later and even in this place, like love.

Those dreams only increased the day Lisa found herself pregnant, but they were hers alone in those long weeks afterward, not Gary's. His drug use became worse, no longer a mere joint a few days a week but one a night, then two, and then marijuana chased with booze chased with worse. Heroin. Crack.

I see your soul, he said.

And then came the end, there on some dusty highway high up in the Carolina mountains, the phone call Lisa received from him late that night, Gary crying and Lisa crying as well, her hand on the tiny bump formed by the child growing in her womb.

She had always told Abel that his daddy had died just before he was born. That was never a lie. The man Lisa had known and loved was gone by then, replaced by a stranger. She left, taking nothing but a suitcase of old clothes, a handful of cash, and her unborn child. Lisa's cash ran out just south of a little town in Virginia named Mattingly. She did Gary the courtesy of passing along her address, saying he could write. It was an act of kindness on her part to give a father back a little of the everything he had lost, though Lisa never had any intention of allowing Abel to read whatever letters were sent to the tiny trailer at the end of a dead-end road. Better her boy know a lie, she thought back then, than ever the truth.

She gets out of the car and snuffs the cigarette beneath her shoe, then closes the door behind her. The winding walkway to the main building is empty but for herself. Lisa smells fresh-cut grass and flowers, hears the trees whistle and cheers from the baseball field far away. She wonders where Dumb Willie is, if he's sorry for what he did.

Gary deserves to know what has happened to his son. Not by a phone call or a letter, but in person. And the truth of it is that Lisa longs to see his face for the first time in nearly a dozen years. It may mark a beginning. Or an end. Either way, it is the first small step in moving on.

Lisa takes the stairs and pulls at the door. This won't take long. She'll be back in Mattingly before the late news and back to work tomorrow. It will be a new day. Perhaps she will go see the Preacher Keen.

Perhaps.

She turns and looks at a deadening Carolina sky bursting

with color, the moon rising and the first stars of the night. It looks endless, that sky. It looks as though it stretches on into forever. Wherever Abel is, she hopes he is being taken care of. That he doesn't hurt anymore and he's smiling.

That someone is watching over him.

-7-

It is a fine day that greets Dumb Willie, the sun creeping over the mountains and lighting upon his face through the narrow loft window, fresh hay on his cheeks and in his hair, that warm feeling of tired muscles and a hungry belly left over from yesterday's work.

He believes he would enjoy it even more were A Bull not sick.

His face looks bad because of the light that comes from it. From A Bull's mouth and nose and eyes that light comes, and from his two ears like a leaking, and his face is whiter than the white it always is. A Bull sits by the window and he's shivering cold. He says he hasn't slept and Dumb Willie knows it's because the dead don't sleep but Dumb Willie don't say. It's a finger-over-your-mouth, but Dumb Willie knows it might not be that much longer.

"I think you better go get Dorothy, Dumb Willie," A Bull say.

Dumb Willie scrambles down the ladder. The woeman is on her bed. She's reading her Bible. She looks at Dumb Willie and wants to smile, but she's forgotten how.

"Where. *Do.* Tee?" he ask.

The woeman points through the doors and into the yard, so that's where Dumb Willie goes. He sees Do-tee at the garden thinking and says A Bull's sick. That woeman don't move when Do-tee and Dumb Willie run back inside and scurry up the ladder. She don't move but watches.

A Bull is where Dumb Willie left him by the window. His face is white with light and there's sweat on his forehead and cheeks.

"Cold," A Bull say. "I'm real cold, Dorothy."

Do-tee puts a hand to A Bull's face and holds it there. He's trying to smile but Dumb Willie sees it's a slim one, not even the half grin Do-tee always wears.

"Think I'm just tired," A Bull say. "I ain't been sleeping much. Or eating." He says it again: "Think I'm just tired."

"Maybe so," Do-tee say. "Could be it's a little thing more. But don't you worry none, Abel. You got me here and Dumb Willie too, and we gone take care you fine. Ain't that right, Dumb Willie?"

"Gone take *care*. You," Dumb Willie says. "Love you A. Bull," he says, nodding as his mouth works, even though Dumb Willie knows there is nothing he can do for A Bull and no doctor he can call. There's no doctor for the dead.

"I'm fine," A Bull say. "Just cold."

"Well now, that's good," Do-tee say, "because we gone head out if you're up to traveling. Woman's gone take us in her truck if we can get it started."

"Take us where?"

"Where you always wanted to go."

"My daddy?"

Do-tee nods. "Yes. We're going to your daddy, Abel. You just breathe easy. It's all about over now."

A Bull smiles. It's a bright smile, light comes from it.

"Come on, Dumb Willie," Do-tee say. "Give me a hand getting everything ready."

It's only when they get down the ladder that Do-tee say otherwise. It's a fear on her face as she says the words, and Dumb Willie thinks the woeman hears them too:

"We have to hurry. He's not much time left."

-8-

"You sure you're okay now, Abel?" Dorothy asks. "You ain't just wanting me to know you're brave, are you?"

That makes the fourth time that question has been asked—*You sure you're okay?*—since leaving the farm, if Abel's count is right. He's sure it is. Twice now by Dorothy, each time spoken in a loud voice so as to be heard over the wind. Twice more by Dumb Willie, though he can only turn and mouth the question through the back glass. That makes four times Abel has nodded in return. He knows another will do little good. At this point, the only answer either of them will accept is *No, actually I'm not okay and I'm pretty sure I'm bound for glory, so why don't y'all go on and bury me so I don't have to answer anymore.*

But Abel would never utter such a thing, regardless of his aggravation. It isn't mistrust that keeps Dorothy and Dumb Willie asking. It's worry, and worry is a kind of love.

He nods again—number five.

They travel in the woman's truck, an old and rusting Ford built in some long-ago before Abel was even born. He and Dorothy ride in the bed in back. Dumb Willie sits up front. He is bent low in the seat so that only the very top of his head can be seen. Sometimes he'll inch up higher, his attention drawn by concern for Abel or a bird he spots out the window, at which point Abel will watch as either Dorothy raps on the glass or the woman pushes her hand on Dumb Willie's head, sinking it back. Keeping him hid.

Abel doesn't think there's much chance of anybody spotting Dumb Willie way out here. They left the farm at what must be close to an hour ago, and still they move over narrow dirt roads that look to have received no traffic in a long while.

There's no way of telling how far they've come. An hour's drive could put them seventy miles or so closer to Fairhope and Abel's daddy were it driven on the highway. But this is no highway. And that woman, she's just creeping along. Abel doesn't know if she's doing that to keep the truck from jostling over the potholes and fallen limbs, or if she's simply scared of being so far from home. It's likely both.

"Because I already know," Dorothy says. "I already know you're brave."

He feels his cheeks blush (a welcome sense, given the shivers) and can't help but lower his eyes. Abel has been called many things by many people, but never that. And never by someone so pretty.

"I ain't brave," Abel says.

His eyes come up to find Dorothy leaning against the far bedrail. Her hat is in her lap, leaving the wind to play at what part of her hair has freed itself from her ponytail. She's smiling as much as she can—everywhere but her eyes. Her gaze is full, taking in Abel with such completeness that he feels naked. Worry clouds those eyes, and concern. Concern means love too. But there is also something else hidden in Dorothy's stare, a thing like wonderment that frightens Abel as much as it comforts. It's like he's sprouted a horn in the middle of his forehead.

"You are," Dorothy says. "You're the bravest I ever known, Abel, and with a stout heart. So you can tell me how you feel."

"I'm still cold some. That's all. I promise. Must have just been a bug. Lots of germs at that woman's farm, I bet."

Which must be true—anybody whose toilet is a pail has to have germs. Abel looks through the window to find the old woman's eyes searching the rearview. Dumb Willie has snuck back down into his seat. He may be sleeping.

Then again, Abel doesn't know of any germ that could leave him feeling as he did this morning. Not just the chills, which still linger, but that strange sensation that his skin was being stretched too tight, that his insides were trying to get out. That feeling lingers a little too, along with the quiet fear that something is happening to him. Something Dorothy either doesn't know or won't tell. Just now, Abel is leaning toward the idea it's that Dorothy won't tell. She still has that mix of worry and concern on her face, all under a smile that would normally weaken Abel's knees. That wonder. But it wouldn't take much for that wonder to melt to fear, and that is a look Abel well knows. That is the very appearance he him-self has carried through much of his life, whether when his momma takes the phone off the hook when the bill collectors set to calling, or when he hears another snap of another bone, or when he used to see Chris Jones come sauntering down the school hallway. It isn't just fear, but fear made bigger by a dread that things can't be changed anymore, only faced.

That's what Dorothy looks like.

He leans forward. "Can I ask you something?"

"You sure can."

"Are you scared?"

The question looks to shake her. Dorothy keeps her smile, but now it looks frozen rather than a thing she truly feels. She pushes the free part of her hair out of the wind, revealing a perfect ear.

"I guess I am," she says, "a little."

"You ain't gotta be scared, Dorothy. Not with me here and Dumb Willie. We'll take care a you. We're almost to Fairhope now, and I bet once I find my daddy and tell him everything that's gone on, he'll want to come back and love my momma again. I bet he'll watch over you too. It's all what Reverend Johnny said." He shrugs now, though that may be the chill that settles in him rather than a resignation to how things are. "It's meant."

"Didn't think you held to things being meant."

"This one is," he says.

"There are times, Abel, I wish I had your faith."

"I ain't got none a that."

"You're wrong there," Dorothy says. "I think you got more of that than most. You just needed an adventure to find it." That smile softens to something mostly real.

"How about I read a letter? I got one left."

She tilts her face to the sun, shakes her head. "Let that letter be. We're making our own way now. All you want to hear from your daddy can be got when you see him."

"How far to Fairhope?"

"A ways yet, but not far. That woman'll have to stay on the smaller roads so Dumb Willie can be kept safe."

"You talked to her last night, then?" Abel asks.

"I did." Dorothy runs a hand down her leg, looking for something it can do. Now it rises up and settles for twisting her ponytail. "She doesn't care for me much. That's okay, and I won't judge her for it. But it yielded fruit nonetheless. I won't say the two of us are at peace, and yet here she is, helping us on. It was a good thing you did, saying I should speak with her." She stretches out a long leg and nudges Abel's shoe with hers. "You're a wise man."

"I am," Abel says, and blushes again. Being wise is almost as good as being brave.

Dorothy nudges him again, chuckling at his answer. Her face grows still. "How about I ask you something now?"

"Sure."

She draws her legs in and leans forward into the middle of the truck's bed. In a moment of panic and ecstasy, Abel knows what it is Dorothy is about to ask. She's about to ask if he can kiss her. Dorothy's going to ask it and then Abel will, and what he'll say next is that they can't ever be apart from now on because kissing means love in ways that worry and concern will never.

He leans in as well, curling his lips like he's about to blow on a candle. Turning his eyes to the window rather than closing them, because he wants Dumb Willie to share in this moment as well, if only so Abel won't later be accused of lying. Dumb Willie isn't looking, though. Neither is Dorothy puckering. Her head is down instead, her finger drawing in a layer of dust and dirt that hasn't been taken by the wind.

"What you doin'?" he asks.

"I need to show you something."

Abel leans his head down, thinking that if he can't steal a kiss he can at least steal a whiff of Dorothy's hair, and sees what she's drawn. Two circles connected by a line, with a larger circle between them.

"That a hobo sign?"

"No, that's a map." She points to the first small circle. "This is where we are." Now to the third. "That's Fairhope."

"What's the one in the middle?"

She points to it. "Raleigh."

"Why'd you draw Raleigh? That's a big city, Dorothy. I

don't think we should be going to any big cities. Greenville turned out bad, and that was only a town."

"I'd say you're right." She straightens her back, leaving the marks to glimmer in the passing sun. The woman's truck buckles and slows before turning onto what Abel guesses is their first paved road of many more ahead. "But then I went to talk to her last night. I almost didn't. I knew she was going out to say good night to those graves, and I couldn't follow her. Not right off. So I stood by the garden trying to find my strength, and then I got an idea."

"What idea?"

"You remember what I told you about that farm? How it was a hidden place?"

Abel nods.

"And I said there were other places hidden too. That's when I got the idea. Because I know of one, Abel. Or I've heard of it at least. It's just stories told, and stories might be truth and they might not, but there's a man who'd know for sure either way. And that man is in Raleigh."

"We don't need another special place," Abel says. "We're going on to Fairhope."

"You forget something, Abel. This preacher you met. He promised you treasure, right?"

"My letters," Abel says.

"And reward."

"My daddy."

Dorothy nods. "But what's in the middle?"

The word is through Abel's lips in a whisper as another chill rushes over him.

Dorothy repeats it: "Healing."

"You said I couldn't get no healing. You told me Reverend Johnny was wrong."

"I know I did," says Dorothy. "But I don't accept that no more, Abel. If there's a chance you *can* get healed, that's a chance I think we have to take. Especially now. That woman driving up there, she ain't a woman no more. I don't know if she's even much of a person. That's not her fault as I see it, it's all what happened to her. All she loved got taken away, and now she's just sad and hollowed out. I can't bear it. And there's nothing I can do to make things right for her again. I can't bear that either. But I can make things right for you, or at least try. If those stories are true. I think it's time we find out if they are, before we get to your daddy. All that's left is to carry things through. I aim to do that, great as that cost may be to me. But it may cost you too. That's the choice you have to make."

"What cost?"

"Him," Dorothy says, looking at the window. "Because you're right, we got no sense going to a big city like Raleigh with Dumb Willie being looked for. Maybe things have died down some since we left Greenville. Maybe news hasn't gotten this far south about what he did. But maybe not. It's a chance we take, either way."

Abel follows Dorothy's gaze through the glass. Dumb Willie's head is slumped against the woman's shoulder now. She's trying to push him away and drive at the same time.

"This hidden place," he asks, "it's in Raleigh?"

"Don't nobody know where it is, or at least nobody but one. Arthur. He keeps the secret, like his daddy did and his daddy's daddy, all the way back since"—she shrugs—"forever, almost. It's his people's secret."

"What people?"

"The Cherokee."

Abel feels his mouth slide open. Indians? Trains, magic,

running from folk out to murder them, a crazy woman, and now Indians. Sick or not, these last days have been the greatest of his life.

"Was a time when all this land was theirs," Dorothy says. "This hidden place too. So I bet if those stories are right, that hidden place must be close. In the mountains, maybe. Back where we came from. Place no one is."

"We can't go *back*," Abel says. "We're so close, Dorothy, and I want to go home. I miss my momma."

"I know," she says, taking his hand. "I know that, Abel. But you're not well."

"I'm better now, I promise."

"Not for long. Don't ask me how I know it or what's wrong with you. Just believe me. Please, believe me. The miles have worn you in ways you can't know, but I can see those ways. So can Dumb Willie. It's a spring, this hidden place. And in it's the clearest, bluest water you ever saw. Special water, Abel. Just like you." She leans in again, as though to share a secret. "A place of *magic*. And if someone finds that spring and gets in it, he'll be restored."

Restored. The word shines a light in Abel's mind. "So if I get in that water, I'll be healed?"

Dorothy says nothing right away and smoothes over the circles in the dust instead. "Heal you in the way you most need, yes. Shoot, they say that water'll even bring a man back from the dead."

"Do you think it's real?"

"Stories say. Arthur will know. And if it is real, he can take us there. Most would call it legend and nothing else, but it sounds no more false to me than a preacher being overcome to give you prophecy." Dorothy shakes her head. "I don't know if that spring is there or not, but I know it can be. It can be because there really is magic, Abel. This world's covered in it, but folk can't see. Or they don't want to, because then they'd know there's things bigger than themselves. We just need a little bit of that magic. A small portion will be enough to see us through."

"This Arthur man," Abel says. "Is he special?"

"He is. Arthur knows me true."

"What happens if Dumb Willie gets caught?"

She dips her head. "He may go Westbound."

They are hard words. Abel cannot bear the sound of them.

"Everything I believe tells me we've made it all this way for a reason," Dorothy tells him. "We've been led this far, though I don't know by what hand."

"Maybe it's God's," Abel says. Not his version of God, which is still somewhat fuzzy in Abel's mind, and definitely not his momma's. But Reverend Johnny's God maybe, or the Preacher Keen's. To Abel, their God sounds like One who would take folk on an adventure so long as they stepped off their front porches.

"God's abandoned us, Abel. He turned away the moment I pulled you up on that train, because it wasn't meant."

"But then we never would've met. And you wouldn't've seen that woman again to try to make peace. And I'd maybe never get to see my daddy."

"Yes, which means we have to go on. Only way we can now is if you get restored, Abel. The story says the spring can only work once. A single time for a single person, and then those waters turn to mud forever."

"What if we get my daddy first," Abel says, "and then find Arthur?"

She says it again: "There's no time left."

"I don't want nothing bad to happen to Dumb Willie."

"Then we'll just have to make sure that doesn't happen."

"And I don't want nothing to happen to you either, Dorothy."

"My judgment's coming, but it won't be now. This is the thing you've always wanted, Abel Shifflett. Longer even than wanting your daddy. And I can't bear to see pain anymore. Not yours, not anybody's. There was a time I could look out on this world like it was all just pictures. I roamed and wandered and went where I was called. I saw more faces than you can count. That's all folk was to me. Faces. I've learned from you they're more. So much more. And because of that, I want to give you more than your life back. I want it to be a grand life. A joyful life. Being a family, having your daddy there and your momma too, having you *well*. That's a grand life. But only if the spring is true, and only if we find it in time."

Abel looks through the window. The woman searches in the rearview. He sees Dumb Willie's head and Dumb Willie's eyes, Dumb Willie's lips mouthing, *You oh. Kay?* And Abel is, really. He has his friends with him and they're on an adventure and he's okay. They're going to Fairhope to find his daddy, and when they get there Abel is going to tell him how dire things are and how his daddy needs to come back, how they all need to be a family, and that Dumb Willie is in trouble but Abel can tell everybody the truth of what happened with Chris.

And yet Abel also knows Dorothy is right. It's a grand life that Abel should want, not just a good one. And as long as he must carry around all these brittle bones inside him, it will not be grand. He wants his daddy to see him whole, not broken.

"Do you know what house this Arthur lives at?" he asks.

Dorothy smiles. "No. But I know where he works."

PART VII

RALEIGH

-1-

Dumb Willie cannot recall a day when he's spoken so little as this one. That woeman, she don't talk. He guesses that's because she's had nobody to talk to for a long while. All that woeman's got is her woecow and that pig, and those two holes covered up in back of the garden. The woeman might talk to them, Dumb Willie thinks, but he guesses don't none of them talk back to her. It takes two people to talk, like he does with A Bull and Do-tee.

Still, Dumb Willie is used to talking. Much of the morning has been spent with him saying whatever is upon his mind, the birds and the trees and how the clouds look like traynes but there's no rails. That woeman never did answer back. Once Dumb Willie thought maybe she . . . (it was a word, he couldn't remember it, but it sounded like *death*, like Do-tee was and like A Bull) . . . couldn't hear, and that's why she never talked. He tried yelling in her ear—"You. *Hear* me?"—and got a hand pushed against his head, so Dumb Willie knew she wasn't that word that meant not hearing.

That woeman, she's sad.

And so for much of that time he tilted his head through the back window to make sure Do-tee was still there and A Bull. Dumb Willie made sure A Bull felt good. A Bull kept nodding his head like he meant he was okay. Dumb Willie never believed that because of A Bull's shine. By then, A Bull was like a sun.

His offer to drive the truck was met with a chuckle and snort. Dumb Willie took that as a no. That woeman and Do-tee both wouldn't let him look out the window because Dumb Willie's faymus now. Do-tee would knock on the glass sometimes, and sometimes that woeman would say, "You keep your head low, or it'll get shot off."

It's the only thing that woeman said.

And so Dumb Willie talked some and some he slept. He would wake up when that woeman's hand came upon his head and pushed him away from her. That first time it was a hard shove, like she was scared and he was a munster she wanted away. Then that push got softer. By the end, she never did a thing and let Dumb Willie sleep there against her. Dumb Willie's nose couldn't help but seek her out as he drifted. She smelled like pig poop and wildflowers and hay. It was like they were taking her farm along on their venchure.

Those roads got crowded the longer they were on them. Dumb Willie liked the dirt roads and the long, empty ones smoothed out that made the truck sound to hum around him. But these crowded roads he didn't like. There was too many people, and that woeman wouldn't even let Dumb Willie sit in the seat no more. She made him get down on the floor instead so that only his head could rest. It was crowded down there, and he couldn't see Do-tee or A Bull.

"She's laying down back there," that woeman said. "Ain't fell off, which I wouldn't mind. But she can't be seen either. Ain't legal, riding back of a truck."

"Where we. At?" he asked.

"The city," is what the woeman said.

*

The sun has gone behind the trees when the woeman stops, waking Dumb Willie from his nap. He wipes the slobber that has collected on the passenger seat. His neck and back are a giant knot from having been squished on the floorboard for so long. He tries stretching and finds that only makes him hurt more. The woeman puts the shifter to park.

"Where we. At?" he ask again.

The woeman say, "Here."

She won't move, but Dumb Willie hears moving in the back of the truck. He lifts his head just enough to see Do-tee standing up in the window. A Bull's with her. He still shines.

Dumb Willie gets out of the truck and nearly falls because his feet don't work. They pinch and stab and he stamps his feet to make them wake up. Do-tee helps Dumb Willie walk and then goes to talk to the woeman. Dumb Willie helps A Bull out of the truck while the woeman isn't looking. She can't see A Bull, he's a seecrit.

"Hey A. Bull," he say.

"Hey, Dumb Willie."

"You oh. Kay?"

"I think so. Dorothy says we're in the city. We're looking for a man who knows a magic place. I'm gone get healed, Dumb Willie, just like Reverend Johnny said."

He smiles. It's a bright smile and so full of sun that Dumb Willie has to wince.

"Gone. *Heal* you?"

"Yep. And get this, Dumb Willie. That man, he's an *Indian*."

It is a marvel to Dumb Willie, all the things they've seen and the people they've met. It's fun being faymus.

It's a quiet place where they are. There's trees and birds, not like a city. That woeman talks to Do-tee for a long while. Sometimes she looks to yell and sometimes to cry, and when she's doing neither she only listens. Dumb Willie hears Do-tee say she's sorry but he don't know for what.

Then the woeman say, "Our eyes will never meet again."

And Do-tee say, "You know we must. All find an end to their path, and that is where I stand and wait."

"What they saying over there, Dumb Willie?" A Bull ask.

"They good," he say.

Do-tee comes back to the other side of the truck and holds A Bull's hand. She say, "Abel, can you walk?"

"Yes."

"Good. Come on with me a minute. Dumb Willie, that woman wants to talk to you."

They go off a little ways to wait. The woeman stands near her truck looking at Dumb Willie. He goes to her and wonders if she's going to hit him again like she did in the garden. The woeman won't say nothing right off, she's talking with her eyes.

"You keep safe," she say.

"Sape. Sape's good."

"Don't let that girl lead you to ruin. Follow her if you must, but leave her when it's time. And it will soon be time. Do you understand?"

"Kay," say Dumb Willie.

She looks off to where Do-tee and A Bull stand. "What is it you love most? What is that girl trying to keep safe for you?"

It's a seecrit, he wants to say. *A hush-hush*. Yet the woeman looks at Dumb Willie in a way he believes everyone should, like he is a man rather than a thing, and the only way he can express his thanks for this is by offering the truth.

"It's. A Bull over. There," he whispers.

She looks in that direction again. Dumb Willie knows the woeman cannot see. And then the woeman leans close in a slow way so that Dumb Willie won't flinch. He smells the stink of her skin and clothes and the wet of her lips on his cheek.

"Thank you," she says.

"Well. Come," says he.

-2-

Abel watches and wonders why it doesn't bother him that Dumb Willie has kissed a girl first. Dorothy's hand is still in his. That's pretty much all that matters. The woman waits until Dumb Willie has walked back to where they're waiting before climbing back into her truck. She starts the engine and moves the shifter into reverse, then merely stares.

Abel waves at her. "Thank you for your hospitality," he says, though the woman answers not at all. She backs away as Abel shakes his head. "Thank you," he says again, waving the cast this time instead of his good hand because the cast is brighter and easier seen. "Manners can get you far in life, you know that? That might get you more friends," but she is gone.

Dorothy squeezes his hand, though Abel can barely feel it.

"It's okay, Abel," she says. "That was very nice."

"I got the feeling she don't like me."

"It's not like that."

Dumb Willie nods in agreement. "You a. *See*crit," he says.

Abel sighs. Dumb Willie, he can be so dumb.

"Come on, you two," Dorothy tells them. "We got a little ways to walk, but it's straight on and close."

She leads them through the patch of trees to the familiar sight of speckled rocks the size of Abel's hand, crabgrass and the occasional groundhog hole, and rows of steel crossed by oil-laden blocks of wood that stretch into the distance. Abel grins in spite of that stretchy feeling still inside him. He must be a hobo now, he thinks, seeing rails and feeling such comfort.

"We gone wait on a train?" he asks.

"Nope. We'll walk it. Ain't but a mile, maybe more. Then we're there."

"Arthur work for the railroad?"

Dorothy shakes her head. "No, but these tracks go right by there."

They move as the sun turns the orange of evening and dips behind them. Dumb Willie falls away, his head turned more to what's behind than ahead.

Woods and fields stretch on to their left. To their right begin the buildings. Tall ones, warehouses and businesses and others that look little more than great hulking monstrosities.

Dorothy leads them off the rails when they reach a spot where the tracks intersect with a road. A great empty lot filled with long-haul tractors and fading trailers lies on the opposite side. Traffic is low for this time of night. That doesn't keep Dorothy from telling Dumb Willie to keep his face down and for them all to keep to a narrow strip of trees to the right of the road.

The road loops softly to the left. Abel studies the businesses they pass and the smattering of cars still parked in what must be the end hours of the business day: *Overhead Door Company of Raleigh, Dan's Glass, Inc., Compass Rose Brewery.* None of these seem to him the proper place for a real live Cherokee Indian to be working.

"Not far now," Dorothy says. She turns, holding out her hand again for Abel's, and tells Dumb Willie to stay close. With every car that passes, she angles the leather bag over her shoulder so that it obscures part of his face. "Looks like it's closing time for a lot of places here, but it shouldn't be a problem. Arthur should still be there. He stays at work more than he keeps home."

Gresham Lake Rd is on the sign they pass, though Abel sees no lake. They pass a massive lot riddled with cars and trucks but can't see the business they belong to; everything is behind a metal fence.

"There," Dorothy says. "That's where we're going, right up ahead."

Abel sees a white sign bordered in blue resting atop a tangle of vines and weeds not a hundred feet on. He squints his eyes as that sign gets closer and stops.

The words read *Rowland Landfill, Inc.*

"Arthur works at the dump?" he asks. "We're going to a dump, Dorothy?"

She turns around, still holding Abel by the hand. "It's where Arthur works, Abel."

"It'sa. *Dump*," Dumb Willie says. "Up there."

The entrance is shut, guarded by a gate. Fencing rings the property with three strips of barbed wire hanging above the top posts.

"It's closed up," Abel says.

Dorothy says, "Not to us. Come on, it's easy."

They wait until the road is empty. Dorothy slings her bag over the top of the fence, mashing the wire.

"You first, Dumb Willie," she says. "Just mind the wire. It'll hurt if it gets you."

Dumb Willie clambers up and over. It's a wonder to Abel that the entire fence didn't come tumbling down with the man's weight upon it. Dorothy lifts Abel up and over next, into Dumb Willie's arms. She climbs next with the grace and speed of a tomboy. On the other side of the fence is a long and wide paved road that leads on around a curve hidden by piles of dirt and gravel and the chopped-off half of a hill. The road is where she leads them.

"Offices are up here a ways, and that'll be where Arthur is." She waits before adding, "I hope."

Abel's expectations of what a genuine Indian would do for a living are only somewhat dampened by the sights around them. Crows caw from the tops of straggly bushes and narrow pines. The air is thick with the stench of trash, reminding him yet again of the old woman's farm. And everywhere there are machines, dump trucks and bulldozers and backhoes, all things to boys now that dragons were to boys once. Giant steel boxes hold mountains of gray and black garbage bags. A warm, stale breeze lifts bits of litter into the air like a ticker tape parade. Dumb Willie can only marvel at it all.

Two mountains of what looks like dirt loom at the horizon. At the peak of one rests a dump truck that looks to Abel like an ant perched upon its hill. A white trailer that reminds Abel all too much of home is to the left. Beside it are two trucks. The one nearest has a frayed rebel flag attached to a wooden pole stuck into the end of the bed. Both trucks are filthy. Both have guns hanging from the racks at the back windows. Three men wait there, smoking their cigarettes and watching. Dorothy lets go of Abel's hand and walks toward the trucks. Her gait is strong and confident, that leather bag swinging off her shoulder. Dumb Willie falls in behind. Abel takes his hand.

"Keep your head low, Dumb Willie," he says.

The three men are of the rough sort, their clothes streaked with sweat from long days beneath the summer sun. Their shirts are unbuttoned to near their stomachs, names stitched in cursive along narrow tags where a left pocket would be.

"Closed," one of them says. He is the biggest of the three, with a barrel chest and tattoos along both of his arms. When Abel gets close enough, he sees the tag reads *Lester.* "Y'all ain't supposed to be up in here."

"Our apologies," says Dorothy. "We're passing through and got here too late. Arthur working?"

"What you want of Arthur, pretty thing?"

"We're friends."

One of the other men—*Harold*—works a wad of chewing tobacco in his cheek the size of a baseball. He spits a runner of brown juice onto the ground and says, "Arthur have a friend looks like you, he'd've told us."

Abel squeezes Dumb Willie's hand at that remark. "They can't talk to Dorothy like that."

"Shh," Dumb Willie says.

"I've known him a long while. He around?"

The third man, whose shirt says *Lonnie*, answers, "He's still up in the office." He points around the mounds of dirt. "Right around the corner there."

"I'm obliged," Dorothy says.

She turns, looking at Abel and Dumb Willie, and motions with her head for them to come along.

"Ain't got to go nowhere just yet, honey," Lester says. "Whyn't you keep us comp'ny here a bit."

They chuckle in a way that runs a chill up Abel's back. He squeezes Dumb Willie's hand again. Those men aren't even looking Abel's way, he's so small. So much of nothing. Like a bug they could squish. It flares an anger in him that serves as heat to ward off his chill, but also a fear. Those men are big, and Dorothy is so thin and frail.

"Kay," Dumb Willie says, though Abel has said nothing. But he lets go of Abel's hand and strides forward as though hearing Abel's thoughts and puts himself between Dorothy and the men. Even among these, Dumb Willie is a giant. Their chuckle is cut short at the size of his legs and arms. To Lester he says, "You *stink* you a. Weed."

"Come on, Dumb Willie," Dorothy says. "It's okay, they're just having some fun."

"I'd like to have some fun," Lonnie answers, making the other two chuckle again.

Dumb Willie holds his spot until Abel passes by. He turns now and follows Dorothy, giving the three men his back. Showing them he's not afraid.

*

It doesn't look like an office around the back side of those dirt mountains, though that's what the sign in front of the little shack says. Two steps lead to what resembles a porch. An air conditioner grinds against the heat through the front window. Dorothy doesn't bother knocking but walks inside. Abel and Dumb Willie go along.

The air here is colder than Abel has ever imagined air can get, more freezing than winter. He wraps his arms around himself trying to brace against it.

"You oh. Kay?" Dumb Willie asks.

He nods, thinking, *Number six*. Thinking, *No, I'm not okay*.

"Almost there, Abel," Dorothy says. "You hang on."

A wooden counter, chipped and faded by years of use, extends the width of the room. Beyond is an assortment of desks and telephones, books and papers and computers. A closed door hides in the back corner. The light inside is on. Abel reads the nameplate hung from two small chains anchored to a faded yellow ceiling:

Arthur Free.

Part of the counter is hinged on top. Dorothy lifts it and passes through, leaving it open for Dumb Willie and Abel. She knocks at the office door.

A voice bellows from the other side, "Come on in."

Dorothy eases the door open. Abel crouches down to a spot to the side of Dorothy's bag and gawps.

The man sitting behind the small wooden desk is unlike any Abel has seen in his life. He is older, sixty at least, with dark skin like leather left to crack in the sun. His chest is wider than even Dumb Willie's, but he doesn't look fat. To Abel, Arthur Free looks *powerful*. Like he could take those three men outside and sling them senseless. His hair is the color of coal with streaks of gray, long and braided in the back. A necklace of polished bone and feathers peeks from the open neck of his shirt. He glances up from the papers in his hands with eyes full of knowing, two piercing black holes that remind Abel of Dorothy's. Those eyes widen at the girl by the door before softening to the color of clouds heavy with rain.

"Oh my," he says.

Dorothy steps inside. "Hello, Arthur."

His mouth twists, and for a moment Abel is unsure whether Arthur is about to cry or laugh. He can see little through the slender space between Dorothy's arm and her bag other than the walls. Hanging there are pictures of Arthur with people Abel does not know, along with a collection of artwork depicting ancient warriors. A pipe (a genuine *Indian* pipe) hangs near the door. And there are crosses. Everywhere Abel looks, Arthur has hung a cross.

"Are you here for me?" he hears the man say.

Dorothy answers, "Yes, Arthur, but only for your help. I am in need."

Silence fills the room. Only the hum of the air conditioner can be heard. Dumb Willie takes a step closer to the door.

"What would you possibly need?" Arthur asks.

Abel feels Dorothy's hand come around her back and touch him at the side of his neck. Her fingers lead him out from behind her. He sees a fleeting look of shock upon Arthur's face that is passed over by the longer, fiercer one Abel feels growing upon his own. His cheeks flush, his chin dips. And in a whisper so quiet that even Dorothy doesn't seem to hear, Abel says, "He sees me."

Arthur's hand goes to his mouth. "What is this you've brought me?"

"Arthur," Dorothy says, "I'd like you to meet Abel Shifflett."

-3-

It shouldn't be this way, Dorothy thinks, *having to introduce Abel in such a manner.* The risk of doing so is great. And yet she has long known Arthur Free of the *ani-yun-wiya*, the Real People. The man in front of her is noble and proud, Keeper of Stories. She trusts Arthur will not let on that anything is different about the shining boy standing in front of him, and will in fact hold his kind face still and his surprise to himself.

Most of this is accomplished save for an initial flare of surprise for which Arthur cannot be held guilty. The hand he extends across the desk could be better measured against one of Dumb Willie's, and the tremble in his fingers is no outward sign of some inward ailment. It is rather awe behind that quiver, which Dorothy takes as a welcome sign. The more reverence Arthur feels, the more apt he will be to take them to the spring.

He draws that hand back before it is fully extended and before Abel can move forward to accept it, shaking his head.

"My apologies, Mister Shifflett. You're not one I'll shake a hand with across a trash man's desk."

Arthur's hands move to his sides as though he is about to move his chair back. Instead, the entire chair moves with him. The quiet room is undone by the squeaking of metal and rubber as he navigates the wheelchair he is in around the desk to where Abel stands.

Dorothy looks down at the slackened face of the boy she has walked and ridden with all this way.

"A pleasure," Arthur says, extending his hand once more. "My name is Arthur Free."

Dorothy watches as Abel's tiny hand disappears in the folds of Arthur's. His eyes are no longer on the man, but on the chair in which he sits and moves.

"I ain't never met a real live Indian before," he says.

"And I can say I've never met one such as you." Arthur's smile is lessened only some at the giant he sees in the doorway.

"You oh. Kay?" Dumb Willie asks him. "You . . . broke."

Abel turns to whisper, "Don't say that."

"It's fine," Arthur says. He pats the chair. "Only half of me, my friend. And who might you be?"

"I'm Dumb. Will—"

"Abel's friend," Dorothy interrupts, though she doesn't know why. Something in Arthur's demeanor, a hint of recognition as Dumb Willie began his name. Or it could be nothing. "We've come a long way."

Abel is still staring. It's as though he's heard nothing of what's been said. "What happened to you?" he asks.

"An accident from a long time ago. I fell from a horse and landed on my back. I was okay, thank the Lord, though I'm afraid my spine wasn't."

"He's. *Broke*," Dumb Willie says, "like you A. Bull."

Arthur's eyes settle back on the boy, though he speaks to Dumb Willie: "Well, son, you look just fine to me. Abel, I expect I'm gonna need a word with your friend in private. It's been a long while since I've seen her, and we have much to catch up on. But I'll not do a thing until I see to your comfort. What do you need?"

"Nothing, I guess," Abel says.

"Good. Why don't you two go on out and have a seat for a bit. I'll be right with you."

*

Arthur rolls toward the entrance to show Abel and Dumb Willie out into the fading shadows of the larger office. The door is barely shut before he wheels around. Through a cold stare and two pursed lips, he says, "What have you done?"

"Judge me," Dorothy answers, "should you have the gall. You do not know the why of our journey here, nor can you understand all that boy has endured. What *we* have endured."

She sits in front of the desk in a worn leather chair that looks as though it's been plucked from the landfill itself, wanting to give Arthur the respect of not having to look down upon him as she speaks. He is a mountain of flesh and muscle save for his skinny legs.

"By what name do they know you?"

"Dorothy," she says, then shrugs. "It is never my choice where I come, or when, or by what manner. I appear as what brings a comfort to them for whom grace is given, a terror to those from whom it is kept." And after a silence, "The boy loved trains. He dreams of freedom."

"Do they know?"

"Only the dim one." She moves to speak again, wanting to say *Dumb Willie*, then heeds another whisper of warning to hold the name. "He is special."

Arthur's chin drops. He utters a pained chuckle of disbelief. "The boy doesn't know? Abel doesn't *know*?"

"I did not come so that you can weigh me in the scales and find me wanting, Arthur Free. I've enough of that from myself."

"Why haven't you taken him on?"

Dorothy shakes her head.

"The boy is *fading*. What happens when his body yields? Do you hate him such that you would leave him to wander?"

"I have saved him."

"You have made him an abomination," Arthur says, "and yourself an abuser."

"It is yet to be the appointed time."

"It is a quarter past the appointed time—"

Dorothy balls a fist and brings it down hard upon the desk, rattling the phone and a cup of pens and pencils, rustling some pages to the dirty floor beneath them. "I will not hear this, and you would do well to remember what I am and not challenge my kindness."

Arthur goes cold. He reaches for the two rubber wheels on either side of the chair and eases himself backward. Dorothy does not want this, for them to quarrel.

"The boy searches for his father," she says. "I cannot deny him that, nor will I deny the safety of his friend. They are the things that hold Abel's soul to this world, not me."

"What of this friend? Has he no home?"

"They are so close as to be brothers. Home is wherever they dwell together. So long as there is a choice, Abel will not leave him."

Arthur's eyes speak what his lips will not—he believes this a lie.

"And Abel's father?" he asks.

"In Fairhope. The boy has letters his father has written. The letters have guided us, Arthur. They speak of a purpose higher than his passing. But I cannot get the boy there in time without obligement. And so we are here."

"And when the boy sees his father? Then you will take him on?"

Dorothy will not answer.

"You mean for me to take you?" he asks. "Is that it? Take you to Fairhope? And what comes when the son sees the father but the father cannot see the son? You would save Abel from the knowing and pain of his death when it occurred, only to place upon him a knowing and pain more terrible when he finally reaches for all he's sought?" He raises his hands in an act of apparent surrender. "No. I will not. It is a cruel thing you have in mind. You are a shepherd, not a torturer."

"It is not cruel," Dorothy says, "and that is not what I seek from you. I'd have your knowledge, Arthur. Nothing more."

"And by my knowledge you would condemn me to perpetuate this evil."

"The weight of it will be upon me alone. You will save the boy. Both of them, if you even care. I only need one thing. Your people spoke of a place hid in these mountains. A place of magic. A spring."

It is as though winter has stolen inside the small place where they sit, even as high summer rests outside. Arthur curls himself at this request as though reduced to little more than a child. His eyes grow wide and blacker. The tremble that only moments ago lay in his hands now creeps to his lips.

"That is legend. Nothing more."

"Your dread betrays you. It is close. I would have you tell me what you know."

Arthur shakes his head. "Such a thing is forbidden."

"I am done with forbidden things. I mean to restore the boy. Tell me, and we'll be on our way."

"You cannot do this thing," he says. "It strikes against God and all that is meant. You will suffer judgment."

"It has been done before," Dorothy says. "Once. A boy and the girl he loved. They were spared when I was called to them so they might live yet a little while more."

"Spared," Arthur says, "but by whom? Who spared them? You, or God?"

Dorothy will not answer that. She says instead, "I will suffer it for the boy. For Abel."

"Will you?" He rolls forward now, gaining his strength. Arthur's face is red with anger. "What penalty will Death itself receive? Have you asked yourself that? What is punishment but the taking of something precious in payment for offense? And what does Death hold as beyond price?"

Dorothy lowers her eyes.

"Yes," he answers. "Only one thing. That day in the far distance when the gray scales that cover this world fall away and light comes to banish the night. The new beginning. That day is what you fear. That hour of joy when the sad earth will be remade in glory, and all the past tears will be fashioned into a river of peace that flows unending, because there is where your place ends. Your purpose will have been fulfilled. Death's work will be done. And what will come of you then?"

"I will be called beyond," Dorothy whispers. "To that paradise where I cannot tread."

"No," Arthur says. "Not so long as that boy roams this world as a soul unclaimed. What you wish will be taken from you. Death will fall under its own sentence. You will continue until the days are no more, and then you will be either cast down or shown the greater mercy of being extinguished. You will be a candle blown dark."

"You do not know that," Dorothy says.

"Can any hand be raised against heaven? Even Death's?"

"I mean to restore the boy."

"Have Abel's remains been found? Is he in the earth?"

Dorothy is careful here of what she says: "His remains have been found. Yes."

"And if Abel has letters, wouldn't his father know the boy has passed? You would restore Abel's life only to present him to one who knows him dead."

"We were *sent*," Dorothy says.

"By whose hand? Would God set you free to go against what is meant and bring the boy to me? To lay upon my shoulders this weight? You struggle against the order of things to your own undoing, and the boy's. I will not take part in it." Arthur's voice is one of defiance and growing strength, his will summoned. His face flashes with a warrior's fierceness to bring even the stoutest heart to its knees. "Such a thing is not meant, and I command you leave this place."

Dorothy bends toward him—"You . . . *command* . . ."— and places her hands upon the desk. Her voice grows deep and low, falling into a tone unnatural to human ears, the words shaking the very walls of the office as though buckled by a mighty wind. The thin form wrapped about her slips away. Arthur moves backward into his chair, pale and lifeless as he beholds Death's true nature, this haunting specter of emptiness clothed in nightmares of old and young. "I will not have your insolence. I ask you to give what I can *take*."

Spiderwebs as black as the deepest cave ease forth from her fingertips, leaching into the wood of the desk. The surface begins to crack and splinter before turning to dust that rains down upon the floor at Dorothy's feet, a steady line that inches to where Arthur cowers.

"You cannot claim me"—his voice a babe's—"it is not my time."

"None know the time until that time has come. I am Death, Arthur Free of the Real People. I followed your olden kin on their long walk of weeping. They suffered me, as will you. I may not take you before your time, but I will see that you and all these you love gaze hard into my face. I will make it such that you will beg me to come swift and sure."

Tears flood the proud man's eyes, making the dry beds at his cheeks rivers that quench the fire Death spews. The ghostly fingers that reach for him recede. The desk between them topples and sinks into the ashes. Death relents as it beholds the face beholding it, the fear and despair with which too many have looked upon it for too long. Dorothy's frail figure sits in front of him once more.

"I will speak of madness," says she. "I will tell of folly." Her voice drops. Dorothy wipes her eyes to chase the weariness but finds she cannot. The tired in her is deeper, unable to be reached. "It is me, Arthur. My purpose. How many have I taken on? How many children have I torn from their mothers' breasts and how many of the strong have I cut down? How many have I plucked from this life to be either lifted up or cast down, and how many of those whom they love have I left behind to rend their hearts and struggle on alone? And for what? For what good does Death teach life's value only at life's end, when its lessons are made meaningless and its wisdom empty? How long must I endure taking hold of the gone only to see them turn their eyes back in shame and regret for the lives they leave behind? I am a shepherd merely to those as you, Arthur, the learned and holy. I am but Death to the rest. I am what comes so that they may know they have never lived. I could not bear that with Abel, nor could I abandon his friend. And so I will save the boy. I will dip him in those waters and restore him so that he can be a light to others."

"The boy is not even of my people."

"The boy is of all people," Dorothy says. "Can't you see that? He is in you all, as you all are in him. Abel can teach them what I cannot—that only by standing in my shadow will there be life. Such a thing cannot be forbidden. We have been *drawn* here. For this moment. The boy is being guided by hands other than mine toward an end I cannot see. Abel was led to me by a man. A holy man."

"The holy ones are scattered. The world bends toward night."

Dorothy shakes her head. "No. This man is one. Abel said he was a preacher come visiting. A traveler. He gave Abel wisdom in a way no man can, and I believe him. Abel says this Reverend Johnny is touched."

"Reverend Johnny?" he asks. "John Mills?"

Dorothy's heart, such that it is, feels to flutter and then move. Whether floating upward or sinking, she cannot tell. "You know of this man?"

Arthur lowers his face. He raises a hand to his forehead. "Yes."

-4-

It's a lot of noise going on in that office, Abel thinks, *especially for two people who are supposed to be friends.* Dumb Willie must be thinking along the same lines. He's gotten up to put his face against the frosted glass, trying to catch a glimpse of the other side, but there's nothing. He looks as tired as Abel feels. It's been a long way they've come.

Dumb Willie jumps away and settles back into one of the desk chairs as Arthur's door opens. He wheels himself out first, holding a piece of paper upside down in his lap. Dorothy is behind him. The look on her face is enough to tell Abel their conversation hasn't gone well. And though the reasons for that could number many, what his mind settles on is the worst reason of all.

"What's wrong?" he asks. "Dorothy? Is it the spring?" He tries to sound brave because Dorothy knows he is, tries to have faith enough that his chin doesn't tremble and his eyes do not water. "It isn't real, is it? There's no magic water."

Arthur positions himself at the apex of a triangle made up of him, Abel, and Dumb Willie. He doesn't speak, only looks with those dark eyes. Abel thinks he sees sadness there. Fear too. It's the same look Dorothy had in the back of that woman's truck for much of the morning.

"It's not that, Abel," she says. "Not that at all. It's real, and Arthur says he'll even take us."

Abel's eyes are still watering, though no longer from sadness. It's relief he feels. Those tears feel sweeter.

"Well, that's great, then. Right? When can we go?"

Dorothy says, "Come on with me, Dumb Willie. Let's sit out on the porch awhile and let Abel and Arthur talk."

Dumb Willie rises with a worried look. He follows Dorothy, but not before pausing at Arthur's side. Wanting a look at that paper, Abel guesses. Or maybe it's Dumb Willie trying to get a whiff of him, wanting to know if Arthur stinks.

Dorothy lays a soft hand to Abel's head as she goes. She bends down to whisper, "Gonna be okay now, Abel. And I'm sorry."

"For what?" he asks.

"Wait outside," Arthur says. "Both of you. Should Abel still seek the spring after we speak, come back in an hour. I'll need to make sure things are locked here."

"How far?" Dorothy asks. "Abel hasn't much time."

"He has what time he needs. It is not far."

Dorothy stands there, looking at Arthur and now Abel. She leads Dumb Willie back through the gap in the counter and out the door. Abel follows him with his eyes. He sees those three men standing way out near those big piles of dirt, watching.

Arthur doesn't move any closer than he is, though he's smiling now. It is a thin smile that stretches no deeper than his lips. Like the way Dorothy used to smile, before Abel said he loved her and before she started acting like she loved him back: a grin that cannot hide the pain beneath.

"She told me what it is you seek," Arthur says. "I can't blame you for that, Abel. Not even a little bit."

"Y'all fighting in there? Because it sounded to us like you were fighting."

"I wouldn't call me and her friends. We've known each other a long while, just as she knew my father and grand-father and all my olden kin."

"They must'a been awful olden," Abel says, "since Dorothy's so young. We're almost the same age, really. I know this guy back home, he lives in the trailer down the road from us. His wife's clear twenty years older'n him, but they're still married. It happens."

"And is that why you came to me? Because you'd like a wife one day? You want the promise of brighter days ahead?"

"I guess," Abel says. "But I think Dorothy loves me. She don't care I'm the way I am. The only reason we come all this way is because she helped us. I ran away because me and my momma are dire. That's why I'm gone get my daddy and bring him back."

"What if your father doesn't want to come back with you?"

"He will. He has to."

"Has to?" The old man's black eyebrows rise. "That doesn't sound like solid reasoning. People seldom do what they have to."

"He'll come back," Abel says.

"Then you believe the only way your daddy will come back is if he finds his boy healthy and whole? Because that I doubt. It seems to be you are a brave and noble young man. Dorothy has said as much. That blood must come from somewhere, wouldn't you think? Passed down from father to son."

"I got letters. They're from my daddy. He's nice in them."

Arthur tilts his head in that way old men do, like he's caught Abel in the middle of an important lesson. "So if it isn't for love that you came here, and it isn't for fear of your daddy, what is it? I can't imagine what else it could be. Love and fear are the two greatest forces in life."

"Guess they are. But I was promised. Promise is a force too."

"And what promise was that?"

"Healing. I was to get treasure and healing and a reward. I already got the treasure, and we got to get to Fairhope and back home with my daddy for the reward. Dorothy said the only way I'll get healing is if we come to talk to you. I need healing, Mister Arthur. I got a condition."

He grins. "Don't we all."

The *hum-tick* of the air conditioner fills the gaps in their silence.

"Knowledge of the holy place has been held by my people since the world was yet young," Arthur now says. "It is passed from parent to child among a single line of my tribe. You call us Indian. Some say Cherokee. But we are the *ani-yun-wiya*. The Real People. And we have held these lands as our own since time immemorial. The Real People are its guardians. And my line is guardian to the hidden places."

"So it's real?" Abel asks. "The spring ain't just a story?"

"You would be unwise to see it as mere story. There is great power there. And great danger." He looks off toward the open door. "Just as there is danger with her."

"Her name isn't Dorothy," Abel says. "She said she's got no name, so that's the name I gave her."

"What sort of person has no name?"

It's a trick, a question asked because the answer is known, if not to Abel then surely to the man sitting in front of him. Arthur's face is steady. His eyes invite an answer that will not be judged.

"I've seen magic. It was up at this church back home when I seen it. And then Dorothy saved us. I think she's magic some, but small. The real kind. She's not tricks."

"All the magic you've seen is small, Abel. That's all this world can hold right yet. The big magic waits. It yearns and it waits. Has she spoken to you of going home?"

"I wouldn't let her take me," Abel says. "I got to get to my daddy first. I won't go back before then. There's some trouble."

"What sort of trouble?"

"I won't say, if you'll excuse me. And it don't matter anyway, because I was sent."

"You weren't, child. You were not sent. Would you know me for more than a night, you would know I speak only truth. Go no further with this, Abel. Tell Dorothy you want to go home. Let her take you."

"I can't."

"Because of the trouble?"

Abel bobs his head. "Dorothy only wants me better."

"Turn away, Abel."

"No. I'm supposed to go on."

Arthur sighs. "I have been in this chair long, Abel. I offer myself no pity to the men I employ here. They would see that as weakness, and weakness is a thing they would abhor. But it is only you and me here, and so I will tell you the truth. I hate it, being trapped in this chair. This feeling of helplessness. Of not being able to do those things I always did before, run and play. I can't even be with a woman now." He taps his legs. "No feeling. No pleasure. And so in many ways, my life has been harder even than yours. You have never known things to be any different than they've always been. I hold memories of what I once was. Do you understand?"

Abel can. He understands helplessness very well.

"Belief has not healed me. I have belief. The Real People have always had that in abundance, which is why we have survived so many trials for so long. We once worshiped the old gods. Some still do. Not me. My mother taught me religion. I have sought the Lord's healing for longer than you have been alive, and at every seeking, that answer has come as *No*. I will be in this chair until I pass from this world into the next, but I will live a good life. I will have joy and purpose that wash away my tears. But still I seek healing. I seek it wherever it may be found. I risk my heart breaking and being broken. Some would call me gullible, if they knew. Though I think you understand."

Arthur reaches for the paper in his lap. It is thick and glossy and does not bother Abel so much as the manner in which it is turned over; Arthur will not look at him. Abel's throat catches at the black-and-white picture. The same hair, the same skin and build. The same grinning face.

"He came through this way," Arthur says, "not two years ago. It was at a little church way out from the city."

But Abel cannot hear the man speak. His eyes are too full of the picture, Arthur standing upright on a stage, hands raised in victory, his left one stretched toward heaven and his right clasping Reverend Johnny's wrist, a wheelchair toppled over on its side in the background. Like it'd been kicked that way, just as that old farmer had kicked away his walker inside that hill country barn back home. It's the same wheelchair Arthur sits in now, again.

"My healing, if it can even be called such, lasted a mere day. I went home, Abel. I walked to my bed and gave such thanksgiving to the Lord as no one ever had before. And when I woke up that next morning, my legs couldn't move. They were slabs of meat. Nothing more. Reverend Johnny Mills is a shyster. He is filth."

All the noise of this place, the buzzing of the air and the song of the evening bugs outside, the imperceptible hum of the earth's turning—Abel knows these not as the music of night but of his own heart breaking.

"It's not true," he croaks. "You didn't see him. You didn't see what happened. Something got in him."

Arthur hides the page away as though trying to save further pain. It does not matter. That picture is in Abel now and will never fade.

"I have letters"—his voice is cracked and jagged as he reaches into his back pocket, spilling the folded papers like pieces of discarded trash, like something Dumb Willie would hide in his pocket or Arthur would bury in his dump—"he told me I'd find treasure and I did. Now I'm going to be healed. You told me the spring is real. Reverend Johnny knew it was, that's why he sent me. He wants me to find my daddy."

"He?" Arthur asks. "Or you?"

"It's a lie. You're *lying* to me."

Dorothy and Dumb Willie peek through the open door.

"I'm not lying, Abel. I speak the truth. It is not meant for you to go on. You must keep from the spring. I promise only death waits there for all you love. You must go *home*."

Abel screams, "No!" as a wave of cold grips him with a fierceness that seems to strip away his skin, and here is Dorothy come into their midst, driving Arthur back with a look that isn't Dorothy at all but something terrible. Dumb Willie looks upon them not as one ignorant but as one straining beneath the knowledge of too much. Arthur yelling, "I did not harm him," and Abel feeling his body tilt and sway as the picture Arthur holds falls to the ground in front of him, the one of him and Reverend Johnny smiling.

-5-

He watches the three of them move off around the piles of fill dirt and refuse, back toward the gate. They will not be gone for long. An hour is all Arthur told them to wait, and he suffers no illusions that his words have reached deep enough for Abel to ask Death to lead him home. The boy is too stubborn. Too loyal.

The big man carries Abel as a father would a child or a dimwit his pet. Patting the boy's head, as though that alone will quiet Abel's tears.

No, they will return. In an hour the three of them will be either at this very door again or at the gate, and Death will demand what it will. Arthur cannot stand against a power such as that. No people can, not even the Real.

And so what is left? What choice does the Keeper of the Stories have open to him now?

Arthur turns his head to see three stragglers still lingering after the landfill's closing. Harold, Lonnie, and Lester are making their way from one of the tanks to the front of the office. Lester leading them, as he always does.

"Boss. Everything all right?"

"Yes, Lester. It's all fine."

Lonnie asks, "Them two friends a yours?"

"Wouldn't call them that."

"I'd call that young thing a friend," says Harold, "if I wasn't married."

The four of them stand watching as the girl and the big man (as well as the shining boy whom Arthur knows only he can see) blink out around the corner. That big man. Death didn't give that big man's name. Arthur knows why. That face has been on the news all week.

"Y'all got anything going on the next little while?" he asks.

"Don't guess so," Lonnie says.

"You up for a little overtime? Pays good."

"How much is good?" asks Lester.

Arthur grins at them. "How about twenty-five thousand?"

-6-

"It's true," Abel says. "I seen it myself. It's Arthur standing with Reverend Johnny. *Standing*, Dumb Willie. Arthur got healed but it didn't take. It was all a trick, like my momma said."

The tears are gone now, all cried out, and all Abel can

manage is a whisper that sounds more like a bark through a nose still running with snot. He wipes it with the edge of his cast. They have not gone far from the gate. Dorothy says they shouldn't in case Arthur decides to sneak away, though she adds she doesn't think he will. Abel got the feeling Dorothy scared him, though Abel can't see how that is possible. She's too pretty to scare anybody, much less a genuine Indian.

Real Person, he corrects.

They've taken refuge in a clump of trees across from the landfill's entrance. Dorothy sits away from them and stares at the locked gate, not crying. Abel has never seen her cry, but she looks like she could.

Dumb Willie says, "That *preecher's* . . . magic."

"No, he ain't. Reverend Johnny's just a trick." Abel wants to cry again now.

Dumb Willie shakes his head, refusing to believe such a thing. "I seen that. Preecher he's . . . magic."

"You don't know, Dumb Willie. You believe everything 'cause that's your way. Ain't nothing wrong with it. But I shoulda known. I shoulda seen it."

"What we gone. Do?"

It hasn't been easy coming all this way. Their trip from Mattingly has been an arduous one, fraught with dangers aplenty and some sadness too, but those dangers and that sadness have always been softened by the bright times and the fact that, in the end, Abel knew they were all being led. Every step they took and every mile they rode was paved clear by a hand he could not understand or define but only believe. Now that hand has been taken away.

"I don't know, Dumb Willie. I don't even know what I'm supposed to do now. Or even if I'll find my daddy. If Reverend Johnny's a fake, there ain't no sureness whether I can bring

Daddy back home with us or not." And this thought, which is even worse and which Abel can barely speak: "Or even if we *can* ever go home again."

From the trees ahead comes a single soft word: "No."

Dorothy has turned her head. Her hat sits on the ground beside her and her ponytail has gone missing, leaving her long hair to dangle and curl around her face. The last rays of the day's sun lights upon her, and in her eyes is an unwavering that speaks not of truth, but of hope.

"What do you mean, no?" Abel asks.

"I mean no. You will go home, Abel. I don't know when. You want it to be soon, but I don't. I want it to be as close to forever as you can make it, because I want you to have time to learn and grow and discover and love this life. But you will go home."

"It's fun being a hobo," Abel says, "but not forever, Dorothy. Home's where I belong. You can go with me."

Her smile is a sad one. "I don't know if that's true. But I know what is. Your Reverend Johnny."

"He ain't true. You seen that picture."

"I did. And that picture doesn't matter. It doesn't matter a thing."

She rises and walks to where the two of them sit. Dumb Willie scoots aside to make room.

"Let me ask you something, Abel. Do you believe in magic?"

"Yes."

"I mean really believe. Not tricks, not the way you make stuff appear and disappear and how you can make folk laugh and go wow. I mean magic, Abel. The big and the small."

"Yes," he says again. "Maybe not before, I didn't. But I do now. All this way we've come, everything I seen. Having you with me and Dumb Willie. That night we spent at the pond and then at that woman's house. Meeting Arthur, who's nice. I believe it."

"Then believe a little more. Reverend Johnny didn't heal you, Abel. He gave you a word. Those two are different things."

"But it's the same tricks. I bet all he wanted was to break my heart like he did Arthur's."

"That might be what he set out to do, but that's not what he ended up doing. Was that really him who give you that word, Abel? I wasn't there, so I don't know. Dumb Willie wasn't there either. It was just you, so you're the only one who can answer it."

Abel has to admit, "I ain't ever seen a trick like that. Not even on the TV."

"Let me tell you something," Dorothy says. "Something I've learned. It's a ruined world we walk upon. You take a look at all you see and everything that happens. The air ain't clear no more. Can't hardly see the stars because of all the lights there is. People die because of earthquakes and hurricanes, die because of a disease they get from being bit by some flying bug. Everywhere you look, it's like there's something either dying or dead. But then you look close, you see it ain't all spoiled. You see mountains like we passed on the trains, how pretty they are and how unspoiled. You step at the ocean's edge and feel that wind in your face and that sand in your toes, or you walk through a field of wildflowers on a summer's eve and let your nose fill with honeysuckle. You watch the sun set and you watch it rise. You do those things, you'll know it isn't *all* ruined, Abel. There's a spark of beauty still. There's a sense of holiness. There's magic."

Dumb Willie mutters, "Magic."

"Yes," Dorothy says. "And it's the same with folk too. Don't matter how ruined folk are, there's still that spark inside them. And that spark can't be killed no matter the bad they do or are, because they didn't put that spark in themselves. They were born with it. That spark, it's like a door that can open up inside folk to give them a glimpse of places they forgot was there. It lets them see there's more to things than they think. And sometimes that door opens so others can see that very same thing."

"So you think that really wasn't Reverend Johnny's trick he did?" Abel asks. "It was that door inside him swinging open for me to see? Or hear? So I could get that word?"

"I think, Abel, there's more than the three of us know. And I think it'll take faith to see us the rest of this way. But that way's not back. That word you got was a shield." She looks across the empty road to the landfill's gate. "And you know how to hold a shield, Abel?"

"In front of you," Abel says.

"That's right. And you know what that means?"

Abel grins. "Means it only works if you're going forward."

-7-

Dorothy doesn't have to lead the boys over the fence another time. Arthur is there when they cross the road, waiting. He unlocks the gate and swings it open without a word, then locks it behind them.

"We'll have to take your truck," Dorothy says. "We came by rail."

"No need for a truck," he answers.

He wheels his chair around and pushes it down the dusty

road that leads into the landfill. Abel and Dumb Willie trail at a distance.

"He is fading," says Dorothy.

"I know he fades."

"How far must we go, then?"

"I would rather dine with the devil," Arthur says, "than lead you on." As to her question, he will not answer.

Dorothy glances back, making sure the boys remain close and yet far enough to be spared the hearing of their words. "You promised your words to Abel would be kind."

"My words were as kind as I could make them. It is no easy thing to tell a child he has built a foundation upon sand." He rides on, the wheels crunching gravel. "And I spared him from the worse truth that he drifts at the boundary between worlds. That will be yours to confess. There is time yet, but little."

He looks a beaten man through the soft light of evening, pale and weakened. To Dorothy, it is as though Arthur Free has surrendered his heart to the belief that he goes to a place from which he will not return. That may be true, and not for him alone. Perhaps they are all moving toward legend, one a protector of the hidden places and one a shepherd for the gone, a boy passing into the veil and his friend the imbecile. And there in the midst of the sacred, Dorothy believes true they will each leave some part of themselves that can never be reclaimed.

"I tell you as I told the boy," she says. "It matters not what you say or what is in your picture. We are here now, and we have been led by a voice other than a charlatan called Johnny Mills. That is what matters now."

Arthur grins. They move beyond the trailer and dirt mounds, back toward the office and farther into the landfill's bowels. Heaps of brush and trash surround them. "You think I don't know your heart, but it is laid bare before me, and I curse you for it. You may have cared for Abel and his friend. You even may have thought once that the path to free the boy's soul lay in finding his father. But no more. All that counts for you is to return Abel to the living. And not even that, if I speak true." He looks ahead. "The voice that has led you is none but your own, and dripping of your own arrogance. You want only to rage against what you are. For that, you would have me betray my people to soften your own pain, and you would fill the boy with lies so that you may ease your own burdens. What have you told him? That the waters will heal his brittleness? That it will leave him more acceptable to a father who never wanted him? It will do neither. It will bring the boy back to the world, and with him will come all the troubles he faced while in it. You know that."

"The spring will do all I want," Dorothy says, "all that matters. I will make it right to the boy afterward."

"And how?" Arthur asks. "You would tell the boy of his death only after he is restored to a life no better than that from which he was taken?"

"I would see him live a long life before I take him."

"Why?" Arthur asks, and in such a strong voice that Dorothy hears Abel calling from behind, wanting to know if everything is okay. "It must be paradise. Yes? Abel is bound for *glory*, yet you would rather him keep to this poor world and let him suffer as we all must suffer. It is rest we seek, whether any of us know it or not. Have you ever considered that when you are called? That those you take to one path or the other only seek a rest from their worry and their fear? Their pain?"

"It is not a poor world," Dorothy says.

Arthur pushes his chair on, turning those wheels with his hands. Turning them and turning them. "Such a thing can only be said by one who merely visits here rather than dwells."

Dorothy wonders how many times Arthur pushes his own half-broken body in a single day, and how wearying it must be. How that single, repeated act must steal a bit of his pride each time. "I have not seen what lies beyond the path, Arthur Free, though I know it is paradise truly. It is rest and more. But does that paradise make this world somehow less? Does the eternal life you and Abel will find cheapen the mortal life you live now? If this world and all in it mean nothing, then why do they look back as I take them? Why do they all look back? I would just once have someone only look forward as I take them. That would soothe me, knowing but one soul has lived such that it knew the beauty of this world rather than dwelled on its brokenness alone. That is all. It is not such a terrible thing, seeking rest from what has always ailed you. Or have you forgotten what drew you to the Reverend Johnny that night?"

Arthur keeps his eyes forward, on through the paths and avenues of the landfill. "It is," he answers, "when what you seek to end your own pain only brings more upon the innocent."

*

It is Abel who asks, "Where we goin', Arthur?" though that same question has wormed its way into Dorothy's mind ever since they crossed by the small office building and on into the deep chasms of the dump. They've passed several trucks, both large and small. They stand as shadows in the darkening sky.

"Where we must, Mister Shifflett," Arthur says. "Where we must."

He rolls on. Dorothy pauses and lets Abel pass her. She stops Dumb Willie and says, "Dumb Willie, you seen anything?"

He shakes his head. The motion pops a small bubble of spit that had been lodged at the corner of his mouth.

"It's munsters. Here," he whispers.

"But you haven't seen anything?"

He shakes his head again. Dorothy turns, watching Arthur and Abel go. "Dumb Willie, it might come to you alone to get Abel where he needs to be. Do you understand? If I can't, it has to be you. No matter what, you get Abel into that spring."

"Kay Do. Tee," he says.

"Good. Now come on, let's see what Arthur's up to."

They only have a few steps to catch up. Arthur's arms are strong but it has been a long way from the gate, and Abel is shining such that the brightness has seemed to sap the little strength he had. They are coming to what appears to Dorothy as a monument to human waste: a labyrinth of ancient refrigerators and freezers, washing machines and dryers, old televisions, all of them arranged in a mound of mazes.

Dorothy puts herself in Arthur's path, making him stop. "You gave your word you would take us," she says. "Now here we stand little farther from where we've come, and I am left believing your preacher is not the only one who knows how to play tricks."

She spots a glimmer of Arthur's smirk in the dusk. "The way is hidden. I protect it well."

"You promised you'd take me," Abel says.

"And I've kept that promise." Arthur raises a finger toward the monolith of metal ahead. "The spring is inside."

"That spring's in there?" Abel says. "You keep a miracle in a dump?"

Arthur turns both his head and his wheels. What Dorothy sees in the old man's eyes is a sadness that shakes her, and a despair of things lost and never to be had again that she knows well.

"Was not always a dump, Abel Shifflett. This land was once an Eden, but now that Eden is gone. The spring is all that remains. What better place to hide a miracle than among all that people discard and call useful to them no more?" And when Abel says nothing, "You think I work at a landfill for the pleasure of it?"

Abel peers past Arthur and into the stacks and rows of appliances, where a narrow tunnel has been made. He grips Dumb Willie's arm. Bright smudges are left on the big man's sleeve. Dorothy bears witness to the flood of hope upon the boy's face, and a recognition that it is this place of dirt and stink where they have been meant to come first, not Fairhope, and the hidden spring within it the thing he must meet.

He walks forward with Dumb Willie's hand in his. Dorothy comes alongside, leaving Arthur alone.

The three of them stop near the entrance when the old man calls, "No, Abel. You cannot do this thing."

Dorothy raises her voice. "Your task here is done, Arthur Free."

"Soon," he answers, "but not yet."

Dorothy feels a pull upon her, a summoning that speaks of betrayal. Power enters as a dark current through the crown of her head and down, flooding Dorothy's arms and chest and legs, tingling her feet. She sees the faint distance shimmer and yield to dual roads leading into the distance, one wide and leading downward to blackness, the other narrow, following ever on.

"What have you done?" she asks.

Arthur tries to sit tall in his chair. He draws a pistol from the small of his back. "What I must. This place was laid not for the likes of you, Abel. You are a good boy, but your time is gone."

From either side of the mound walk the three men Dorothy knows from the trailer when she and the boys first arrived. They carry weapons in their hands, shotguns and pistols from their trucks. Dumb Willie lifts Abel into his arms. His face is white with panic as the men encircle them.

"End this," Arthur says. He looks to Abel rather than Dorothy.

Abel's eyes are lanterns, his face shivering.

"I will ask no more," the old man says.

"You call down your own judgment, Arthur Free," says Dorothy.

"And you may take me, but I will not go alone." He points the gun toward Dumb Willie and shouts to the men, "It's this one with the price on his head."

Abel screams, "No!" too late. Dumb Willie has already made his last act, no different from all the ones that came before it since that first day upon the school playground. He turns Abel's hand loose and places his body in front, wanting only to save a friend already dead.

Gunfire rings, searing the stillness of the landfill and of Dorothy's own mind. Arthur fires wide, but one of the men does not. A shotgun's blast drives a hole into Dumb Willie's stomach and chest, sending him backward to the ground.

"No!" Dorothy yells, with a force that trembles the very

dirt beneath them. Rats scurry from their hiding places among the refuse.

Arthur drops the pistol in his hand as the noise moves over and through him. The men's eyes grow wide, beholding their end. Dorothy steps forward, putting herself in the center of their circle as Dumb Willie stumbles toward the dark path made between a stove and a doorless refrigerator, Abel in his arms. A streak of blood is left in the place where they disappear.

Dorothy turns. The thin form about her slips away.

And here in this quiet corner of Raleigh, Death is loosed.

*

Twelve years Harold Franklin has lived in these parts, and he has never known a day without want. He knows what poverty can do to a man. How it strips dignity and worth. His daddy dug coal in the West Virginia mountains. For thirty years, Tobias Franklin spent more of his life below the ground than above it.

It was the only way he knew to provide for Harold and Harold's momma, and for that Tobias grew to hate the very earth that kept his family alive. He loathed the stench of the mountain's bowels and how its gray dust clung to him, to his soiled clothing and his white hard hat and the ridges of his cracked skin, even to the soft lining of his lungs, turning them black with sickness.

Harold was seven when his daddy died. It was a Saturday in January and there had been blowing snow, and Tobias said he could see the angel of death standing over him as he wheezed his last.

It was a meager life that awaited Harold and his momma

after, leaving her feeble before her time and him to vow a better life for his own family. He ran to Raleigh, where he found Darlene. She cuts hair in a little strip mall near the city's center while he buries trash all day, having forsaken the mines that killed his daddy. He takes their boy Harold Jr. to school each morning rather than letting him on the bus. Those bus kids are ornery cusses, picking on Harold Jr. for how worn his clothes are and how his feet are growing out of his shoes. Kids these days, they're awful—raised wrong and spoilt all the way through.

And so when he'd been standing near the office with Lonnie and Lester and heard Arthur say that big stupid man was the one killed them kids up in Virginia, all Harold thought of was that reward money. Even split three ways (Arthur said he didn't want none of it, which Harold thought foolish but which meant more for him and Darlene and Harold Jr.), that was more than the landfill paid in half a year.

He never entertained the thought that retard would get shot. Even when Lester said he'd do it, Harold thought otherwise. But he did, that shot rang out over the dump like Death's raging bell, and now . . . and now . . .

It's as if that girl is an iron pot left lidded over a flame. Harold stands, feet frozen to the hard dirt where his body will soon lie, horror-stricken as the girl's insides look to bubble and shake and boil over with neither clatter nor spit but a roar of "NO" and "*NO*." Her stretching in height and breadth, dark hair turning to a black like dark clouds marshaling to storm. To Harold Franklin, they have all been caught inside an explosion in reverse: not that girl blowing outward but somehow *gathering in*, consuming the very night before releasing it as woven shadows that slither from her feet, searching.

The wad of tobacco set in Harold's jaw slips free. He cannot feel it rolling across his tongue, does not sense it moving back toward his throat. His eyes do not see the retard Lester shot scampering toward a hole between the appliance pile, too full are they of the terrible truth that the pretty young girl's skin is but a blind for the terrible thing hid beneath.

The tobacco catches in Harold's gullet and hardens, making his throat gasp and his eyes bulge, robbing him of breath. Those black fingers of night crawl for him. He cannot run. The shotgun in his hands falls. The ground races up. The trees fade to a thin gray fog. His lungs die first as Harold clutches his throat.

The rest of him dies following.

Light blooms in warm peace. Harold rises up to find himself alone. Lonnie and Lester are nowhere; Arthur has wheeled off. Even the girl has fled from the approach of a shine truer than the sun. Before him lies the world split open in a long pathway that rises gently into the beyond. And at the mouth of the path, Harold sees his daddy waiting. Tobias Franklin wears his Sunday finest rather than the soiled mining clothes that were his second skin, a suit of deep blue with a starched shirt the color of mountain snow beneath. Smiling, grinning at his boy.

"Come on, now," he says. "Been waitin' on you, son."

Harold gazes down at his own fallen body. His mouth is hung open, lips a powder blue. The neck and chest of his work shirt, washed fresh and ironed not a day ago by Darlene, are stained with brown expectorate.

"We got to go on now, Harold. You come on with me. Joy waits."

He takes his daddy's hand, as strong and solid in new life as it had been in the old. Together they walk the path.

Harold's gaze moves from the light before them to the night they leave behind, casting a final look at where he fell. His daddy watches. In his eyes Harold beholds a sadness not of his father, one that expresses a feeling Harold cannot put to words. He never should have come to this place. Darlene and Harold Jr. already had all the reward that was needed. They all had each other. Harold wants to say it, tell his daddy, but such wisdom is too late now. It would only fall as ash from his lips.

*

Lonnie Patterson hardly has time to see the girl rage before the aneurysm that has gathered in his brain for months bursts, ending the world with flashes of red and orange. It is warmth that wakes him again, morning in his eyes and the rough feel of a tongue on his cheek, a wet nose pressing against him.

The yellow Labrador was called property of the United States military, but to Lonnie and all the men in his unit, Scout was his alone. The two of them were inseparable during those first few months he was in the mountains and valleys of Afghanistan. He defended her with his weapon; she defended them all with her nose. Wasn't a dog in all of Helmand Province so adept at sniffing out IEDs as Scout. Wasn't a thing missed that dog's attention except for the Taliban sniper round that felled her. Scout has since been as much a source of misery as one of longing. In the long years following Lonnie's return home, he has lost a wife and both children in the divorce. As painful as that was, the loss of Scout hurt more. He had never had a friend more true, nor has Lonnie ever found a surer source of love.

"What you doing here, girl?"

The dog barks, tail thumping against Lonnie's knee. Scout licks his cheek again and now Lonnie's nose, Lonnie wincing as he struggles to draw in breath he finds he does not need. He rises from the ground and sees himself lying there still. Scout bounds off toward a path that rises shining in a soft angle toward the sky. *That path wasn't there before,* Lonnie thinks, *wasn't no place. Path like that don't even belong in the world.*

"I think I died," he says. "When I do that?"

Scout calls with a bark. She turns in a circle, jumping, chasing her tail.

Lonnie steps forward and leaves himself behind. He turns and sees Harold isn't here anymore. Lester, too, is gone. What has this cost them all, the promise of quick money made easy, the killing of a slow boy?

"Can't leave'm," he says, turning back toward the night. "Har'ld? Les? Where y'all at?"

He turns at Scout's whimper, a mournful tone too real and felt for even a noble beast to manage. The dog comes forward and sits on her haunches, pink tongue hanging. She nudges Lonnie again, then opens her jaws to set her teeth into Lonnie's arm that way she used to do when he was about to step in a bad place. Tugging him. Trying to save.

Lonnie faces the path once more. He leans his head in as though to gauge its distance, see if he can spot his friends farther along.

"Where's that go, girl?" he asks.

Scout turns him loose. She bounds to where the path begins and turns, tail wagging so hard it looks to hurt.

Lonnie grins and follows. Thinking as he does about those old days when it was just him and his dog and the cold

Afghan night. Back when everything was scary but fine. Yessir, everything was fine.

Sure is good, having that dog again.

*

Last thing Lester Harmon needs is to still be at work when there's more work to be done next day, but it ain't no thing killing a retard. 'Specially when there's money to be had in it. 'Specially upon remembering the words that retard said when they passed on their way to Arthur's office.

You stink. You a weed.

Don't nobody call Lester Harmon that. Don't nobody who wants to live. And now what Lester thinks is after he puts one in that child killer, he'll maybe have himself a turn with that young woman.

He fires, sending the retard on to the hereafter with a load of buckshot in his belly. The girl shouts out, setting Arthur's hands to his wheels and buckling Lester's knees, and as he swings both barrels around he knows he should have pulled on that girl first, corked all her blubbering. Should—

The scatter-gun wavers in Lester's hands as that girl turns into something not human, a thing with red eyes ablaze and a horn that sprouts from the crown of her battered old hat. Her face twists into that of a lion, a bear, a demon's spawn, her legs thickening, hoofs breaking through the toes of her dusty shoes. And in that girl's hands, a heavy chain slicked with blood.

Lester turns to flee and trips over an old car battery lying on the ground. His head lands hard on the rock beside, splitting both with a wet cracking sound. Blood fills Lester's vision. His arms and feet no longer work. He is fading, fading, the night calling him as the demon trundles forward. Beside him a hole opens in the world, black and swirling. From it grope shadows of bone hands and thin, hoary legs of beasts born in the dark places beyond nightmare, spider eyes that glow yellow and gargantuan.

In Lester Harmon's last moments, he sees that demon hold a look of something near mourning. His dying body rages at the hollow life it leaves behind, all that emptiness both trailing him and waiting on, shadows reaching for his ankles and legs, his waist, the blackness pulling, taking him, taking him.

*

Dorothy has time enough to glimpse Arthur racing away, his arms pumping at the tires on his chair. Dumb Willie and Abel are gone. The only evidence of their escape is the blood left where the maze of metal and rust begins, and there is where Dorothy races. Her hair and shirt are left sticky and stained red. Her hat falls at the entrance.

Abel. All that matters is Abel.

No water waits on the other side. There is nothing but black and the smooth sides of doors and polished steel. The uneven ground threatens to send Dorothy sprawling. She uses her hands as eyes, groping the way forward.

"Abel? Abel, where are you? Dumb Willie?"

Dorothy's echo is all that returns.

-8-

That man he shot Dumb Willie that man's a munster, and Dumb Willie thinks Do-tee took that man to the debbil. He isn't sure Do-tee did; Dumb Willie didn't see. He had to get A Bull to the wadder because that's what Do-tee said. She said, *You do that no matter what, Dumb Willie*, and so Dumb Willie did. He loves Do-tee and A Bull, but Dumb Willie's bleeding now.

It's dark in this place, and scary, but not so much that Dumb Willie turns around and runs back, because what's back is scary more. There's paths all laid out inside and he don't know where to go.

"Go straight," A Bull say. "Just go straight, Dumb Willie, that way we won't end up back where we come."

So Dumb Willie goes straight.

It feels endless, this cavern of old things that remind Dumb Willie of what his ma and da'ee have in their kitchen and in their barn and buried out back of the north field.

"Run, Dumb Willie," say A Bull, and Dumb Willie tries, but it's a hole in his stomach and his feet can't move good.

Dumb Willie puts a hand in the wide space between his chest and hips. His overalls feel hot there, and sticky. He carries A Bull on into the dark. It's a

(word it's a . . . word)

tunnel here and A Bull's screaming, "Go!"

The path branches off to the right and to the left, but Dumb Willie keeps straight, taking them deeper. In this darkness, Dumb Willie cannot see how the old junk here looks older, how the knobs and buttons and sleek lines of the washers and ovens and refrigerators at the entrance of the mound have faded to the hard angles and box-shaped appliance machines of another age, and how even those yield farther on to walls made of old wagons and churning buckets, porcelain washbasins streaked with grime, and large wooden wheels.

A Bull say, "Hurry up, we got to find it," and Dumb Willie is trying to hurry, but he can't. Because of the hole in him, that hole is bloody and it hurts. There's guts in there. He feels them with his hand it hurts so bad.

"There," A Bull say. "Up there, Dumb Willie. You see it?"

He does. Ahead rises a faint light that grows with each lumbering step Dumb Willie takes. The shine alights upon the walls to either side of them, chasing darkness to reveal crumbling hope chests and pieces of a barn. Here their path begins to widen as it makes a gentle curve leftward.

And here at the end of that curve comes what feels to Dumb Willie as the end of their journey, or perhaps merely his own.

Hidden deep beneath the mound is a cavern with a high ceiling of interconnected pipes and machines, and in the cavern's center rests a pool of still water colored in a blue beyond any sky or mountain, sparkling as sapphires, drowning the chamber in a light that would outshine morning.

A Bull twitches in Dumb Willie's arms. He kicks like Dumb Willie is a horse he rides on, but Dumb Willie can't move fast no more. He can't breathe and it hurts. He sees little of the light around him, it's just dark and darker, but he sees that pool of wadder, it's pretty, and Dumb Willie knows it will be good to die here.

"The spring. Dumb Willie, there's the spring. Reverend Johnny was right. He weren't no fake."

Reverend Johnny's a. Taker.

Dumb Willie merely thinks these words. He cannot speak them.

"It'll heal," A Bull say. "It'll make everything right."

Dumb Willie carries him to the pool's edge and falls to his knees. A Bull spills from his arms but it's okay, A Bull's bonez can't be hurt because he's dead but not for long. But now A Bull's looking at Dumb Willie all wrong, like it's snowed on his face and turned his skin there all white.

"Dumb Willie, you been shot."

There's blood on Dumb Willie's hands and his shirt. It's a hole there. Dumb Willie thinks it's a hole, but he can't see. It makes bubbles on the front of his overalls that swell and pop each time he tries to breathe, sending tiny drops of blood to gather in the soft earth.

"Inna wadder. Make you . . ."

It's a word. Dumb Willie doesn't know.

A Bull looks down at that hole; there's blood and bone too, those red bubbles go *pop pop pop*.

"Inna wadder A. Bull."

A Bull crawls along the spring's edge and grabs hold of Dumb Willie. His eyes are wide and shining. Light comes out of his nose and ears, from the tips of his hair. His lips tremble. "We're gone get you out of here, Dumb Willie. Get you fixed. We'll take you to a doctor."

Blood spills from Dumb Willie's lips. His head tilts, his shoulders, the feeling in them gone. His body is now as dumb as his mind.

From the tunnel comes a call of "Abel?"

It's Do-tee say that, but A Bull is not the one she's come to claim. Not Do-tee but Death dressed like her. Another light shines. Dumb Willie sees a path in the air ahead and how that path is like home, like fields plowed and ready to bloom a garden that will never wilt.

Do-tee call out, "Get in, Abel. Jump in the water. Jump in now."

"Will it work, Dumb Willie?" A Bull ask. "Do you really think?"

"Make you. *Better*," are Dumb Willie's last words. He can't breathe and it hurts and he don't see no light, only that path. It's warm. There is no pain now.

A Bull stands as if to jump in and turns his light to Death's darkness. Dumb Willie shudders a final, shallow breath. Behind a curtain of haze and numbness, he feels a tugging. One eye is black and dead. The other glimpses A Bull pulling with what small measure of his strength remains. Pulling and pulling, his good arm and his casted one each filled with Dumb Willie's sleeve. He strains not with that faint shadow of brittle bone and thin muscle but with the light inside him instead—with his soul, bright and bursting, and a will just the same.

Dumb Willie's body falls forward. Blue diamonds rush toward him. Do-tee's distant scream of "No!" is swallowed as Dumb Willie falls through.

Water envelops him, splashing A Bull's feet and knees and a bit of his chest. Dumb Willie sinks. He urges his arms and legs to move but they cannot. That one eye remains open and blank to the sea beneath the cave, a hidden place under a hidden place, laid clear as glass and swarming with lights.

Streaks of blue and white and crimson and yellow swirl from the edges, gathering him up, and he sees these lights have wings.

They pour into the holes made through his chest and stomach. Pain that had been brought to unfeeling now bursts to pain once more, and now to a bliss so pure and deep that Dumb Willie's mind cannot contain it.

His lungs begin to burn. Dumb Willie thrusts his hands upward, first his right and then his left, like he's climbing a ladder. His feet kick with the single longing to live. He breaks the surface with a gasp of sweet air and reaches for a world he nearly lost.

Do-tee and A Bull stand at the pool's edge, their faces wet with tears. And though Dumb Willie has been healed merely in body alone, his mind is strong enough that it knows they weep for him. One cries in joy for what has been restored, while the other mourns for what has now been lost forever.

Water clouds his vision. It pours into his mouth, tasting spoiled and brackish, gagging him. When he looks, the blue waters are gone. There are no more lights. Dumb Willie now treads in the brown waters of a mud hole.

-9-

It was the spring did it. So says Dorothy as the three of them limp from the mouth of the pile of junk and walk among the bodies. It was the spring that took those men Arthur brought, a holy place that would not abide the evil of men's hearts.

There is no blood. The three men lying upon the ground look at peace save the one Dumb Willie called a weed. The terror with which the man called Lester died is now frozen upon his face. Dorothy hides Abel's eyes from that sight as they pass, though she looks. It is not Death's place to judge, only to take, yet some of her hopes Lester bore witness to the sadness upon her as he was dragged away. It would be a kind of mercy, and one that she never could have offered before finding Abel.

Dumb Willie holds Abel against his soaked chest until they are well clear and near the landfill's gate. Here they rest at the trucks the men left behind. Arthur is nowhere. Dorothy gives no thought to pursue, knowing they have pursued too much for too long—her a respite from the toil allotted her; Abel his daddy; even Dumb Willie, who has chased a happy end for them all ever since being thrown upon that night train rushing through Mattingly. And for all that chasing they have found not redemption, but the very emptiness from which they had fled. Dorothy is overcome by feelings that rush in such a mangled surge that she can do nothing but buckle beneath them: a grief of her own futility in saving Abel, and a rage—not only at Arthur's betrayal but at Dumb Willie for being saved, and at Abel for saving him.

It was meant the boy would die. Death knows that now. What has been done can never be undone, even where there is love.

The three of them sit leaning against one of the trucks when a metallic groan comes in the distance. Dorothy stands and tries to see, but the way is too cluttered. The ensuing noise forces them all to cover their ears. The great dome of junk overtop the spring collapses in a crashing sound so loud and deep that the echo carries through every wall and hill and pile of the landfill. And after, silence but for Dumb Willie's panting.

"What'd you see in there, Dumb Willie?" Abel asks. "Down in that water?"

"It'sa. *Lights*." His clothes still carry a sheen of blue that drips from his elbows and boots. Grass has begun to sprout where the water puddles in the dirt road around him. "It's lights. In'ere." He looks one way first and says, "Sorry Do. Tee," then looks the other way. "Sorry A. Bull."

"It's okay," Abel tells him.

Dumb Willie resumes his silence. To Dorothy it is as if what has happened to him was a thing not so special, nor what he saw beneath those waters anything of wonder. All things hold wonder for Dumb Willie, and she knows that is why the deaf and blind call the boy Dumb.

"What do we do now, Dorothy?"

"Nothing to be done." She looks at him. The boy's glow is all but gone for now, though it will return. If there is any light to be found in the darkness that is this night, it is that the splash of Dumb Willie being tossed into the spring reached enough of Abel to hold his soul a bit longer. Just long enough. "Time we get home now."

"I can't go home."

"Abel, there's things you don't—"

"I can't go home," he says again, making her pause. "Dorothy? We have to go see my daddy. If we don't, then all of this will be for nothing." Abel's top lip disappears, as though he is trying to chew back tears. "That water fixed Dumb Willie. It restored him, just like you said. That means Reverend Johnny was right. He said there'd be healing. He was right about that too. Then he said I had to go find my reward. That's in Fairhope."

The big man with them shudders. "Got to get you. Home A. Bull." There is water in his eyes. Dorothy doesn't know if it's from the heart of the spring or the heart of Dumb Willie.

"There's nothing for you in Fairhope, Abel. Leastways nothing that can fix things."

"There's one letter left. You said the letters were pointing to where we needed to go. They told us to go to Greenville and to the woman at the farm, so we did. But coming here was your choice, Dorothy, and now you're sad. Because those letters didn't say it. So let me read this last one. Let's just go a little ways more. Just a little ways, and then we'll be done."

Dorothy leans against the truck and looks up to where the stars lie. No words come. She has not the strength left in her.

-10-

24 March 2013

Dear Abel,

I guess I usually start off these letters by saying everything here is the same, but I can't say that this time.

All week there've been people working on the street outside. You should hear all the racket. Not that things around here are ever really calm and peaceful. Folk go to great lengths here to make it seem like it's just that, but it isn't. It's never been peaceful to me. I look out my window and I see what anyone else would and a good deal more of what no one else can. All week I've seen the street blocked and those men in hard hats standing around with their shovels. I watched them bring in big machines and dig up and scoop out and move what's not really anybody's to move at all.

Do you know what all had to happen just to get one inch of soil on top of the ground, Abel? About five hundred years. I read that once in an article. It said one inch of topsoil is five hundred years of weathering. So I've spent this whole week looking out my window and watching men who probably make nine bucks an hour go tearing up what amounts to about six thousand years' worth of history and not even know they're doing it. Not even care.

Do you understand what I'm trying to say? I hope you

do, Abel, because nobody else does, not my friends and not anybody. They might have said it's noisy outside but that's all, and when they saw me staring out the window at all that digging up, they said stuff like Gary, don't be acting like that. But I had to, Abel. I don't know how to explain it other than that, and I couldn't tell nobody because then I'd be in trouble.

Then it happened, right this morning. What I heard was the town needed a pipe replaced at the end of the street because of all the rain, so they dug down to get the old one out and then dug down more. That's where they found it. I knew something happened because right then everything just stopped. You should have seen all the commotion. I don't know why somebody bothered to call the squad, but they did. The fire department came too (just so they could be nosy, I bet) and then the sheriff. By then, there was more people out on Kable Street than I've ever seen, and that's when they started hauling up bones.

I know now that's why I got more and more upset all week at watching those men work. There's things you just don't know and I can't tell you even in a letter. I thought the reason I was getting so sad was because all that history was being tore up inch by inch and it's not supposed to be that way. Things in this world get laid down just so, Abel. That's what people don't get. There's a pattern to everything that happens and we can't see it because it's beyond our knowing, but it's there and we just have to let it. It's like a wind that stands against every living thing, and we can either bend to it or let it snap us. But that's not all about them digging those bones that got me. I guess I knew all along there'd be a body under there even though I never seen a thing before them bones got dug up.

Sanders (he's the guy they pay to keep everything around here safe and square) told me awhile ago that nobody knows about those bones. He said they look plenty old to him and had to have been down there a long time, maybe centuries. Folks from the university came to take everything away for study. They even took a bunch of the dirt, if you can believe it. I'm glad they did. That dirt's now as much a part of the bones around it as the bones. Sanders heard some of those professors talking. They said whoever it was sleeping down there went to glory a way back when it was just the first settlers. Maybe even before. The Cherokee were here before anybody else. Did you know that, Abel? Anyway, whoever it was had a hard end. Sanders said the skull had a hole clean through it, like it'd been beat in with something sharp like a stone. He said it's not ever a good thing to disturb the dead. I told Sanders he's right. There's no greater sin than not letting those who've passed go on their way. They got to lay in peace.

I'll tell you this, Abel, and it's no secret because plenty of people saw me after all that. Even Sanders did. I cried over those bones. Nobody else but me did, but that's okay. I cried over whoever that was and how death must have come so violent and lonely. I cried for the ones that person left behind and all the things that person had left undone and unsaid. I guess it was his time or hers just like someday it'll be everybody's. This world is both too beautiful and too terrible to keep a good hold on any of us long.

But there was selfishness in my tears too. I was thinking about myself as much as that poor person they dug up because I realized one day I'll be the same. I'll be bones and nothing more, and I don't know what happens after that. I know it's something, but I don't know if it's greater or less than what this world provides. All I know is that every page in the great story of our lives is different except for that last one. That last one is the same for every one of us. Death makes us all equal. It's maybe the only thing that really does.

So, Abel, what I'm telling you this time is to always make your life the kind that leaves nothing unfinished. Make sure you do every day all the things you need and then a little extra on top. Make sure you laugh and love and stop to watch the sun fall. Keep your eye on the things that matter and don't, and learn to know the difference. Most people die every day in some way or another. It's the good ones who only die once.

Love,
Dad

PART VIII

FAIRHOPE

-1-

Dumb Willie drives.

It is the only way out of Raleigh that Dorothy can find; she believes Arthur may well be on his way to the police. Even if not, the police may well be on their way to the landfill to investigate what must have sounded like an airplane crash to those inside the few homes nearby. Raleigh is no longer safe for the three travelers.

Nor can Dorothy risk taking them to the rail yard to jump a train. Too dangerous, too many eyes. Better to take one of the trucks and move away from the city, find a lonely track and wait out the night for an eastbound train that could take them to Fairhope. And they must hurry now. They must before Abel's soul begins to free itself from its prison once more.

This time there will be no means of hemming that soul back.

There is a concern (a small one stacked against the many larger worries that now plague Dorothy) that Arthur knows of Abel's father and Fairhope. It is well within his power to alert the law of where the three of them will likely turn next, leaving Dorothy to trust Arthur will hold that knowledge as secret. He will call the men's deaths an act resulting from the collapse of a rising mound of household appliances that should have been buried long ago and not tempt fate further than he already has this night. More than most, Arthur must understand there comes a day when all must settle the accounts of their lives and lay their own hearts in the balance. Perhaps it will be to Arthur Free of the Real People's comfort that his judgment does not fall to Dorothy. But that comfort will be tempered by the understanding that none can hide from Death. No, not one.

She turns the letter over in her hands, Abel's proof that where they go is right—meant. The few smudges and squiggles Dorothy can make out offer her little assurance. Only pain waits for the boy in Fairhope. Only a father who will not see the face of his child even if that father is found, at which point Dorothy will take Abel home. There will be no choice in that, not now. Abel will leave and will leave Dumb Willie to face the cold world alone, and Abel will look back.

He will look back as they all look back.

Abel rummages through the glove box and finds a plastic card that he hands back to Dorothy. He says this truck is owned by a man named Harold Franklin of Raleigh. Dorothy knows the face as one of the two she took to the path.

"Don't think that man will begrudge us the use of his full tank of gas," she says.

Dorothy believes her words to be true. Harold will

understand, seeing as how he has been reunited with his own daddy now.

-2-

Every so often Abel will turn and grin at the wonder that has ruined Dorothy's melancholy, if only for a while. Only twice since their meeting has she looked caught in genuine surprise. When Abel said he loved her was one. Then tonight, when those men came bearing their guns and shot Dumb Willie. Abel suspects he could count what happened after as well, though it hadn't been surprise on Dorothy's face when Dumb Willie got put in that water. Her expression then had been something more, and worse.

But that's okay now. Dorothy doesn't know, but it is. They are on their way to Fairhope, and everything is going to be fine.

"See?" Abel asks, his grin so wide that he feels the back of his scalp flexing. "Told you Dumb Willie could do it. He drives all the time."

Not that Abel (or Dumb Willie, for that matter) held the belief that maneuvering a real vehicle over real pavement could ever be akin to steering Henderson Farmer's tractor over empty fields. But surely the principles of operating a dead man's truck must work just the same, and Dumb Willie's going is made smoother with Dorothy to offer direction and Abel to tell which signs mean stop, which mean look-before-you-go, and how fast the state of North Carolina says they can proceed with a degree of safety. Abel subtracts ten from every posted limit and keeps an eye on their speed.

To his credit, Dumb Willie responds as a champion. Whether through luck or will or the presence of some extra something in that water, he keeps the car's nose to the center of the unmarked road they travel and only runs off the shoulder three times—none of them to harm. Even these cannot be laid to Dumb Willie's blame. He is distracted by Abel's presence, asking, "You oh. Kay?" and "We oh. Kay?"

Yes, Abel thinks. *Everything is fine.*

*

They dump the truck near midnight in an algae-covered pond not far from a stretch of lonely railroad tracks, along a dirt road none of them believe leads anyplace in particular.

Dumb Willie sets the gear to neutral and pushes hard on the open door, guiding the truck down a slight incline. He scatters to safety as the front end crashes into the water. Abel and Dorothy watch at a distance. The three of them wait in silence as the pond roils and gurgles, swallowing the wheels and windows and finally the tip of the antenna.

Dumb Willie officiates the burial. He thanks the truck for bringing them here and the man named Harold Franklin for filling up the gas tank before he died, and then he lifts a final petition that they will find Abel's daddy and his daddy will have hot food.

Abel thinks it a fine prayer.

They walk a mile or more and find an open space along a bend in the tracks that Dorothy says is good for waiting. There's no telling when the next train will come, and they'll have to wait for an eastbound. That should get them to Fairhope, hopefully by morning.

Dumb Willie curls his head atop Dorothy's bag and drifts

to sleep among dewing grass and the flicker of a thousand lightning bugs. The air is warm. They go without a fire.

Abel is on his back, staring at a great swath of Milky Way above. Dorothy lies next to him. Crickets sing, a distant frog. From far away comes the night song of a lonely mockingbird.

"Dorothy?"

"Yes?"

"You mad at me?"

He cannot look at her as he waits for the answer, too afraid of what he may see. His momma got mad at him sometimes, like when she found out what Abel did with Chris and like with that money he gave to Reverend Johnny. Lisa never looked angry. She never pursed her lips and puffed out her cheeks and yelled. Her eyes never turned cold and flinty. Never once did Abel's momma bare her teeth at him but to smile. What she would sometimes do instead was drop her shoulders and put her head low, or breathe heavy as she pressed her hands to her temples. Sometimes, when it was really bad, Abel's momma wouldn't even look at him at all. Abel never thought those things meant anger. He reckoned them more as disappointment, and seeing that in his momma's eyes was always harder to bear. Having to see those same things now with Dorothy would be even worse. Abel doesn't think he could see those things and not cry, no matter how brave he is.

"I could never be mad at you, Abel," she says. "No matter what."

"Because you looked mad. Back there at Arthur's place. And when we left. You looked mad."

"Maybe I was, but not at you. Mostly at me. You were the one supposed to get in that water, Abel. Not Dumb Willie."

"It wasn't meant for me to get in that water. I thought it was, but now I know it wasn't. I had to put Dumb Willie in."

"Sometimes we have to sacrifice a lot to get a taste of the things we want most," she says.

"Not that much. Nothing I'd ever want would be worth letting Dumb Willie die. I had to save him, Dorothy. He saved *me*."

"That isn't a debt that should have been repaid in such a way. You gave up too much, Abel. More than you know. It was your only chance to be made well."

"It weren't a debt," Abel says. "That's not why I did it."

"Then why?"

Abel shrugs his good shoulder, though he knows Dorothy can't see.

"Because it's what folk do," he says. "I don't guess you know that, seeing as how you always been all by yourself and alone. But folk take care of each other. That's how it's always been. It's the only way anybody can ever get on. Dumb Willie was dying, Dorothy, but he was still trying to get me in that water. All I saw was him in trouble. I had to help. Just like you helped us."

She goes quiet. The stars shine down.

"Abel, there's something I got to tell you."

"Let's have it wait."

"I don't think it can."

"I do. Let's have it wait, Dorothy. Just lay with me here, and let's look at the stars."

She goes quiet again.

Near dawn, the train comes. It begins with a low whistle far off to their right and deep shadows that cut through the thin night like a needle, and by the time that train reaches them it has slowed to such a speed that Dorothy and Dumb Willie do not clamber on but merely climb, Abel in Dumb Willie's arms. There is no boxcar, though an empty cattle car trailing at the end is far from the eyes of the conductor and engineer. The side door is swung wide, welcoming them. Straw lines the wood floor inside.

To Abel, it is as though the train was sent for them alone.

-3-

They wait out that ride in the way each of them has now grown accustomed, sitting side by side at the wide-open door as the world flies by, their feet keeping to the edge so as not to be discovered. Beyond them the sun awakens to shine over the corn and tobacco fields of the Carolina coastal plain. Abel has never seen land such as this, so flat and wide. There is neither a mountain nor a hill to be seen.

"I never did see the ocean," he says. "Not in my whole life. You ever seen one, Dumb Willie?"

He shakes his head as though that word is foreign.

"Ocean's not far from here," says Dorothy. "Though I don't suppose we'll get quite that way. Our road ends not far on, Abel." She lays a hand to his knee. "We're almost there. Fairhope's not far."

Not far.

Fairhope. The word remains as beguiling now as it was when Abel first read it on the front of that envelope. He only wishes the expectation that has carried him all this way could carry him these last miles as well, making him float to town rather than feeling as though he and his friends stumble toward it.

"Thank you, Dorothy," he says.

"For what?"

"Bringing me here. I know you didn't have to."

"I did," she says. "I don't know much of life, Abel, but all I have seen has told me there is little sweetness to it deep down. Every breath drawn holds promise and passion both, but it's all tinged with a measure of sadness that the things folk hold on to carry as much sadness to them as they do joy. At the end of it, all people are is restless. They always go searching but seldom find, even as the thing they search for is most often right in front of them. I didn't want that to be the same for you. I wanted you to find, and here we are." She bends down, putting her face to his ear, whispering, "Are you still excited?"

"I am," he says, though Abel does not say he is only excited some. His anticipation is great no more. Not gone, but tempered by the knowing that the end of their adventure is near. *All things must end sometime*, he thinks. *Even the good things.*

Just as all that comes after is to bow to what must be.

*

They jump for the last time near a crossing where the train slows and whistles its warning. Abel stands in the center of the track and watches the last car fade. He takes Dumb Willie's hand and Dorothy's, putting himself in the middle as they follow the rails a few miles more. Houses begin to rise at either side. Roads appear, stocked with vehicles that look like ants marching. And in the distance, a town rises.

The mark Dorothy finds farther on is their first since Greenville, carved at the bottom of a welcome sign with *Fairhope, NC, est. 1787* burned into the wood. Abel kneels to see it. The symbol looks like a rectangle with its bottom portion missing and a dash scratched upward from the top line.

Dorothy runs a finger over the grooves. Her lips move

but no words come, and her eyes, wet and unbelieving, shine as glass.

"What is it?" Abel asks. "What's wrong?"

Dorothy shakes her head. "Don't believe it is all. Thought we was cast off, but we weren't. We never were." She lays a hand against the sign and dips her chin as if praying. Dumb Willie does the same, though Abel doesn't know why.

"What do you mean 'cast off'?"

"Tell you soon enough, Abel. But this is the way we're to go. Always was. Ain't no hobo made this mark."

"Then who did?"

"Something other. Beyond. I'm a fool, Abel. Thought I was leading you all the time. Turns out, you were leading us."

She rubs the symbol again. Softer this time and only after wiping her hand on the leg of her jeans, as though she caresses a holy thing.

Abel looks at Dumb Willie, whose head remains bowed.

"What's that sign say, Dorothy?"

She looks up to him, smiling even with her eyes.

"Says, 'Here. This is the place.'"

*

Few things of this world exist in as much perfection as they are dreamed of in the heart. Fairhope is one. The town is not only all Abel imagined, it may even be more.

The first homes are a smattering of Cape Cods and farmhouses that have worn well in old age. An elderly woman sits in a rocker on her front porch, her company a steaming cup and the morning's paper. She looks up to smile and wave. Dorothy and Dumb Willie return good mornings as they pass, leaving Abel to stare and wonder about how things could have been. Their road becomes a street not far on, rows of mailboxes and flower beds, American flags tilting from porch posts or waving from aluminum poles. A yellow ribbon is cinched around an oak, the words *Come home soon, Johnny* written in crayon on a cardboard sign beneath. A child's bike sits on its side in fresh-cut grass, the front wheel turning slow. Long backyards. Swimming pools.

"Is a nice place, Fairhope," Dorothy says.

Abel agrees. Aside from the flatness of this place, it's as if they've not left Mattingly at all.

They walk on, none of them speaking. Abel suspects the same is true of Dorothy and Dumb Willie as of himself: nothing they could say would approach what they feel. There is no need to ask for directions; nothing has been left unsaid. And isn't this itself, Abel thinks, a kind of enchantment? One no less and no more than any he's found on their long way?

Doesn't everything and all hold its own small magic, waiting to be revealed to one who merely bends close enough to behold it?

They do not wander Fairhope's streets but walk with slow purpose, keeping themselves as ghosts. Passing storefronts with doors wide to the summer air, smells of fresh bread from a diner not unlike Roy's and fresh petals from a florist, the thick scents of rubber and grease coming from a busy mechanic's shop. The sidewalk grows from somewhat empty to mostly full. Dorothy keeps them away from the center and into the shadows cast by the awnings. Those who pass do so quickly. Some rub their bare arms; others sigh beneath wrinkled brows and looks of fleeting worry.

Cars idle at a lone stoplight. Birds sing from the trees rising from the pavement's edge, making Dumb Willie cock his head and listen. Abel's eyes are to every street sign, reading the letters with such intensity that he feels his lips moving with each word—*Sunset Street, Kinley Boulevard, Maple Circle*. All through the town of Fairhope they move, from one border of quiet neighborhoods through its center filled with shops and newspaper vans and street sweepers and on, until the bustle of early morning yields once more to the stillness of fields and homes.

And here, two blocks down and at the end of a quiet lane shaded by dogwoods, Abel spots a slender metal pole sunk into the ground. Two signs rest at right angles. The one parallel with them reads *Barterbrook Rd.* The other, pointing left, is what stops Abel with a suddenness that would have made Dumb Willie barrel into him were it not for Dorothy's outstretched arm.

The words on that sign read *Kable St.*

"We're here," Abel says. "Dorothy, we're here."

A smile creeps in, a burning Abel cannot push back and so allows to bloom and consume him.

Dorothy shields her eyes and peers through the traffic toward the opposite side of the street. "Kable?" She stands motionless except for the slow rocking of her knees, the hand over her brow trembling. Abel watches her. It's as though she reads in this sign not words but a portent of their ruin. "Does that say Kable?"

"We made it"—chuckling now, Abel yielding himself to joy. *Yes*, he thinks, *joy*. That was what he had felt on that old wood bench outside Principal Rexrode's office so long ago, that tingly feeling he couldn't quite explain. And on the heels of this revelation he finds another, more powerful one, that what he'd felt while talking to Miss Ellie and waiting on his momma wasn't joy at all. That had only been joy's shadow, some poor imitation of a thing he now believes had passed by the short days of his life, never to be experienced. He smiles again, thinking of that word—*joy*. Feeling it now and finally, reveling in the knowing that its fleetingness cannot in any way dim it. "I can't believe we're here."

Dorothy says, "Wait, Abel. I didn't know this place was Kable. I didn't *know*—"

But Abel has had too much of waiting, and he knows time is short. He takes Dumb Willie by the hand and they run, leaving Dorothy to beg them to stay. Into the street and across, weaving among squealing tires and bellowing horns as Dumb Willie waves and hollers, "Koose. Me," then scurrying down the empty side street cooled by morning shadow.

Pear trees and willows and dogwoods stand to their left, green in the sun. Beyond sits a baseball field. A pile of bicycles rests against one of the light posts, their owners children who have already gathered for the day's pickup game. Abel inhales the smells of summer, grass freshly cut and flowers blooming in sweet dew.

On they run, Dumb Willie struggling to keep up and Abel refusing to slow, propelled by his stumpy legs and uneven hips in a speed near unimaginable to him, driven by love. He turns to see the grin on Dumb Willie's face and Dorothy charging from way behind. Her hair flies. The leather bag bounces at her hip with each stride. Upon her face is a look not of joy but of fear. She is yelling.

Past where the children play and hit and catch is another field, this not of chalk lines and bleachers but flowering crops. The garden is larger than any Abel has ever seen, bigger even than the woman's, and here he stops at the call from behind.

"Sparra," Dumb Willie yells. "Sparra A. Bull."

Abel turns. Dumb Willie's face has gone bright red and

he heaves, bending to put his hands on his knees. He points toward three sparrows turning in the air over the field.

"It's. *There*," he says.

"Come on, Dumb Willie. There ain't no time."

"No A. Bull it's. *There*."

A sign not far reads *Fairhope Community Garden, Mon.– Sat. 1 pm–7 pm*. Men work in the field, all of them dressed in jeans and denim shirts rolled past their elbows to ward off the morning heat. At the sides of the field stand two more men, watching.

"Abel, stop," Dorothy calls. She's past the ball field now and closing in, her run turning to a loping jog.

Abel goes back to take Dumb Willie's hand. "Come on," he says. "I bet my daddy's right up the road. There's another lane."

He pulls (an act Abel knows is useless given Dumb Willie's size, but one that at least peels the big man's attention away from the birds) and moves them both on. At the side of the field rests a bank of trees. Past there is a turnoff to the left, where they find a large parking lot. A fence, barbwired just as Arthur's had been, encircles several buildings. Abel sees tall trees, a basketball court, a softball field.

"My daddy lives here," he huffs, working one long leg and the other shorter one. The world tilts from one side to the other and yet remains so perfect. "You ever seen a house that big, Dumb Willie? My daddy's *rich*."

Dumb Willie walks beside. His hand remains stuck in Abel's. He grins and echoes, "He. *Rich*."

Nothing matters to Abel anymore, not how far they've come or all they've endured, even all that's happened to him in the last day. What counts is he's here, and his daddy is here. The rest can wait a bit. All the bad and the tears are coming, but they are not now, and now is where Abel chooses to live. Now is—

He stops at a sign fastened at a spot where the parking lot begins. The three words printed steal Abel's thoughts, his very breath.

FAIRHOPE CORRECTIONAL CENTER

He lets go of Dumb Willie's hand.

"A. Bull what'sit . . . *say?*"

"Abel?" Dorothy calls near. She's walking now, that leather bag motionless against her hip, hair no longer flying. "Abel?"

He turns away from the sign when Dorothy's hand settles upon him. She looks to have grown older in the short time since they left her back along the main road.

"My daddy's here? Why's my daddy here, Dorothy? This is jail."

"I don't know, Abel."

"He said he could look out his window and see Kable Street. This is Kable Street. This is the only place. Here," he says, digging into his back pocket for an envelope. "See? Two-thirteen Kable Street, number eleven." He points to the marker by the sign. It reads *213*. "This is the place."

Dumb Willie keeps his eyes to the sign, as though waiting for enlightenment.

"Did you know he was here, Dorothy?" Abel asks. Tears sting his eyes as he turns and shields them from the sun. "You said you know Fairhope."

Dorothy bends to a knee. "I do," she says, "but all I know is ways, Abel. Not streets. I can't read. I would've said if I knew. I promise it."

Abel rubs his eyes. The water from them shines like lights in his hand. He flicks the tears to the hot blacktop of the parking lot, close to a pile of smoked cigarettes. The sight of that pile only makes him cry more. Those cigarettes are the same brand his momma smokes. "I ain't ever gone see him, Dorothy. They won't let me in to see my daddy."

"We ain't got to take one more step, Abel," Dorothy says. "Not a one. We can turn right now and talk things over. Important things. Stuff you got to know. Dumb Willie," she says, "why don't you help me with Abel here, let's get . . . Dumb Willie?"

Dorothy cuts between Abel and the sign for the correctional center, halting the spell those three words have cast. He blinks. When Abel turns, he finds Dumb Willie has gone off far to the other side of the lot, heading toward that garden.

"Dumb Willie," he calls, "where you goin'?"

The big man turns. He yells over a shoulder, "You ain't a. Bass . . . *terd.*"

"We got to snatch him," Dorothy says. "Nobody can find Dumb Willie, not here. He's wanted."

"No." Abel walks past her and through the lot. "I don't know what Dumb Willie's doing, but he does. He's gone 'long with us enough. Time we go 'long with him now."

*

Dumb Willie turns again, though only long enough to make sure Abel and Dorothy follow. He doesn't break his stride until meeting the line of trees between the prison and the field. Now he slows and slips in between the branches with a hunter's stealth.

Abel sneaks in as well, Dorothy just behind. She tugs on

Dumb Willie's sleeve and asks, "What in the world are you doing, Dumb Willie? They catch you, you're done."

Dumb Willie purses his lips. Shakes his head. In a whispered voice that reminds Abel of the way his momma would talk when trying to get him to understand a thing a child could never, he says, "A. Bull. Ain't. A. Bass. Terd."

"We have to go," she says. "Right now. This place isn't safe."

"Wait," Abel says. He's looking out from their hiding place and into the field where the men work. Some are weeding, others working a hoe or staking tomato plants. Hilling corn. All in the same sort of dress, those jeans and denim shirts. The two men across the way stand with arms folded and sunglasses gleaming in the sun, joking with each other. Barely paying attention. Abel thinks he understands now. Dumb Willie didn't come here because it was a garden to look at.

"Those are prisoners out there. People from the jail, Dorothy." There are thirty of them, maybe forty. All spread out over that wide space of rows. "I bet my daddy's out there."

Dorothy is silent.

"I can find him," Abel says. "I just don't know which one he is."

The three of them squat in a line from right to left—Abel, Dorothy, and Dumb Willie on the end. They look out into the square of dirt to study faces, careful not to stick their heads beyond the thick limbs. One of the guards breaks away and makes a slow walk around the far side toward the front. He nods to a few of the prisoners, lets one show him something on one of the cucumber plants. The man doesn't look afraid of the people he guards, nor they him.

"I bet this ain't no regular prison," Abel whispers. "There's some like a supermax, that's where the worst people go. Like terrorists and serial killers. Then maximum security and medium security, those can be bad too. But then there's *minimum* security. That's where prisoners who ain't dangerous go sometimes. I bet this place is one a them."

Dorothy looks at him. "How you know that?"

Abel shrugs. He taps his cast, his legs and chest. "It's hard to break a bone if all you're doin' is holding a book."

"But we don't know which one's your dad," she says, "or even if he's out here. And even if he is, those guards will see."

"They won't see."

The guard straddles the midpoint in front of the field now, looking and nodding. Abel and Dorothy inch closer, trying to see. A radio squawks. Across the garden comes the garbled sound of "Hey, Sanders, how's it going?"

"Sanders," Dorothy whispers. "Your daddy's letter mentioned a Sanders, didn't it?"

The man plucks a radio from his belt and pushes a button. "Clear and good," he says. "Be some good supper over here a month or so."

"Abel," Dorothy says, "I could go try to talk to him. Your daddy said he looks after things. Sanders'll know where your daddy is."

She moves off, back toward where they came from. Abel looks at the empty place where Dorothy sat and finds another empty place beside it.

Dumb Willie's gone again.

"Wait," he whispers.

Dorothy turns, her eyes counting one where there should be two. She groans.

Far down among the tangle of oaks and pines, Abel

catches a smudge of blue. He crawls off after his friend before Dumb Willie gets himself shot, Dorothy right behind. Sanders remains at his spot in front of the garden and then moves off again, easing his way toward the far side, where he and the other guard turn to watch the kids playing baseball in the field beyond.

"Abel," Dorothy whispers, "we have to get him *out* of here. I need to talk to Sanders."

Abel doesn't answer, too focused on the knotted maze ahead. He hears a chirp and sees Dumb Willie standing at the narrow edge between the trees and the garden. Not twenty feet away, three sparrows hop in and out of a row where a man stands silent, a hoe limp in his hands. He is thin and blond-haired. Stubble rings his cheeks and chin. His clothes look too large for him, as though his body has lost weight. Bent forward, head low.

Dorothy comes along behind Abel. "Get Dumb Willie," she whispers. "I'll swing back around and see if I can talk to that man Sanders."

"No."

"Abel, that man knows where your daddy is."

Abel nods. "So do I."

-4-

He moves from his hands and knees to his feet and weaves among the trees to where Dumb Willie stands. The walk feels like forever. Like how walking down the hallway to Principal Rexrode's office had felt, but more. Longer than forever.

Abel vows to relish each step.

Dorothy comes alongside and whispers they have to wait. Abel keeps moving. He reaches the spot where Dumb Willie stands (that's his name, the thing everyone but Abel's momma has always called him, though in these last days Abel has come to believe his friend anything but that) and is met with a grin. There is no emptiness in it.

"Sparra," he says, "*showed*. Me."

Abel watches the man in the row. Gary's head—*That's his name*, he thinks, *that's my daddy*—remains low. The sparrows flit and bob, searching the ground for food.

Dorothy asks, "You sure that's him?"

"Dumb Willie says it is."

They stand together, watching.

"Abel—"

"I can't go over there," he says. "Can I, Dorothy? My daddy won't see me if I do. Just like everybody in Greenville never saw me, or that woman at the farm. There's not many ever seen me. All I am's a cripple boy. Country trash. Don't nobody want to see nothing like that. It makes them feel too bad. It reminds them there's something wrong with the world deep down, and they'd rather pretend there ain't. That way they can go on without thinking it's up to them to do something about it. To help."

"That ain't . . . ," Dorothy starts, but then adds nothing. Because Abel believes she knows that's true. Dorothy knows that's right.

"But they always look at me," Abel says. "Looking's different than seeing, and folk always like to look at something worse off than them. My momma did that. She'd slow down whenever she seen a wreck along the road and she'd bring home a newspaper every night from the diner to see who died. Folk always want to know where they stand in life.

They like knowing who's above them and below. Only folk don't even look at me no more. Just you and Dumb Willie and Arthur. You said they're special. I didn't know what you meant. Not until we went in the place at the landfill where that spring was." He pauses. "I think you're special too."

Dorothy's words come as stilted and garbled as Dumb Willie's might: "Ain't nothing special about me, son."

"Yes, there is. And it ain't got nothing to do with how I love you. Even if I didn't, you'd still be special. You know that, Dumb Willie. Don't you?"

Dumb Willie won't answer, he just walks away. Farther off toward the back of the field, where he stands watching the man called Gary.

Abel nods. "That's part of the secret you been keeping together all this while."

"Abel," Dorothy says, "I got to tell you something."

There is a hitch to her voice and a strain that Abel cannot bear, and so he saves Dorothy from saying it.

"When did I die, Dorothy? Was it when Chris got me at the tracks or when I tried getting up into that boxcar?"

He lets these words fade in the breeze and wonders if he will go like that—not so much a breaking off as a wasting away.

Dorothy says in a soft voice, "Was the boxcar."

He looks away from his daddy to Dumb Willie and asks in a quiet voice, "Does he know?"

"Dumb Willie never asked. And I never told."

"Never do. Okay, Dorothy? Tell him it was Chris did it. It'll be hard enough for Dumb Willie now. I don't want him knowing he killed me trying to save me."

Gary picks up the hoe and makes a little hollow in the dirt.

"I just wanted to see him," Abel says. "Just this one time. I guess it's my reward, like Reverend Johnny said. I'm sorry I brung you such a long way for something that you might think is so little. But it's not little, Dorothy. It's just not. That's my daddy right there, and it ain't no little thing."

Dorothy's soft hand settles at the back of his neck. "Abel, you of all folk got nothing to be sorry for. I could go over there for you. Talk to him, maybe. Say I knew you once. That you loved him and thought on him often. Maybe even that you got some of his letters. Anything that'd help. He looks awful 'lone."

"No. That might draw attention. I don't want Dumb Willie caught. And I got you to worry on too. Just keep here," Abel says. "I'll be right back."

The first step is hardest. Abel must force his foot to lift up and out and down, not because he's dead, but because of what he feels—fear and longing and still that joy, though now tempered by a lingering sadness. Another step and another, leaving Dorothy behind. Dumb Willie looks to battle a hidden urge to move forward and take these last steps with his friend.

Abel moves along the rows, past the eyes of convicts who look through him but see nothing. There are other sparrows now, hopping and singing. They do not scatter but leave room for him to walk, as though they are aware of the presence of some felt but unseen other. Abel slows as he reaches his daddy's row. He looks back once to Dorothy, then over his other shoulder. Dumb Willie grins as only he can.

His father, so close. Inches away. It occurs to Abel that it never mattered he thought this man dead for so long and has only known him alive these last days, that never a moment passed when his father was not there. He lurked sometimes in a place of longing hidden deep inside Abel's own heart, was there at every train, a vague form without eyes or face. He'd always wondered what his daddy looked like, what part of him had carried over. Now he knows. Abel wants to touch that hair so much like his own, thin like wisps of silk, like the fringes of an angel's wing. He comes near and rises up on his toes, strokes the crown of his daddy's head and down its side, caresses an ear.

The hoe drops.

Abel jerks his hand away as the sparrows take flight, coaxing an "Oooh!" from Dumb Willie at the trees. And the man's face—Gary's face, Abel's daddy's—begins to tilt leftward. Here is Abel's own narrow chin and slender nose, a small mouth ringed with pale stubble. Two eyes that hold not the pale blue of Abel's own sickness but the red of wail and mourning.

Those eyes blink. Blink again. His daddy's mouth sets to trembling. His body goes rigid. And in this moment Abel realizes what is happening, this last bit of small magic. Because there are those whose souls and spirits are so tuned to the world far off and to come that they are not fit for the world here and now, and they are blessed because they see and know, but cursed by those who are blind and ignorant. Called dumb. Called crazy. Called—

-5-

"Daddy," says the shining boy, and what Gary wants to do is shut his eyes because it's not real. It's not. And if he acts as though it is, there might be trouble and he'll be sent away.

The boy is white beyond white, a color so bright and clear

that it is beyond Gary's description. He has never seen a color like that.

He turns and looks through the field, all those men spread out before him. There are yellows there, blues, tinges of orange and crimson and a black belonging to a man here because he swindled all those people out of their money. Gary looks across the field to where the guards stand watching the kids at play along the ball field. One is a purple. The other, Sanders, the calm color of deep ocean.

But this boy is not merely a color. He is not just white and shining. This boy looks as Gary did once, long ago when the world was darker.

"Daddy?" he asks again. "Can you see me?"

"Abe . . . ," is all Gary can answer, the rest swallowed by a rush and tears and a feeling that his body will rend itself apart. He holds himself tight, overcome by a rush of cold. "Abel?"

"It's me. You're my daddy. I came to see you."

"Are you real? You can't . . . you . . ."

The boy reaches out. There is a cast on his hand, yellow and shining as though it will fall away at any moment and explode into a million tiny stars. As though the arm it encloses is about to break free. He takes Gary's fingers and eases them up. They touch Abel's cheek, his two lips. They feel real, though barely. It's as though Gary's hand skims the frail surface of water.

"It's me," Abel says.

The years fall away, those endless memories that have followed Gary all this way now cast in murky shadow. Echoing voices in constant murmur of his own failures, chasing him down the long and dark path that led to this tiny place in Fairhope. Those walls, that fence.

"I see you," he says. "I see your soul."

That day flashes bright in his mind—a cold October Saturday when Gary was sixteen and he was out riding four-wheelers with his friends. Bouncing along those rocky fields. The wreck, the feel of himself flying. The darkness that followed. Waking days later in a hospital bed with his head wrapped and bleeding and a tube in his mouth, seeing the doctor and his parents there.

They were yellow, green, and a gray like clouds before a storm.

He could see them, could see their souls.

"I came to see you," Abel says. "Me and my friends."

The shock of it, seeing the most private parts of everyone, every friend and every enemy, every stranger, laid bare. The beauty of most, the horribleness of many. *A by-product of the injuries* is what the doctors said, though even then Gary knew that wasn't the case. It was as if some tiny door inside him had been pried open to reveal hidden things meant for no human eyes.

"That's Dorothy over there," Abel says, pointing to a pretty girl standing afar, "and the man over there"—he looks over his shoulder to where a big man in overalls waves and yells, "Hi. Gay"—"is Dumb Willie. He's my friend. We come awful far."

A voice from across the field calls out, "Gary?" Sanders has turned around again. He has his blue hands on his blue hips and is speaking from his blue mouth. "You okay, buddy?"

Gary ignores him, ignores everything. Because his boy is here. His boy has come all this way.

"I found your letters," Abel says. "They sent me."

Those letters. Ones Lisa said to write but to never call, never reach out, because their child mustn't know. She would spare Abel the grief of knowing his father was a convicted drug smuggler but never allow him the truth of why, how Gary had turned to drugs after his accident because drugs made the colors go away. The weed and the meth, the heroin made the colors go away, and all Gary could see when he was high were the white and black and brown of skin. She had a beautiful soul, Lisa. That's what he had told her the first night they met. Lisa had the prettiest orange Gary had ever seen. With her, he did not need to be high. He loved that color. It was the blacks and grays and deep browns of the lost that always grieved him, sending him back for another fix, another respite.

"It was treasure," Abel says. "That's why I had to come. Reverend Johnny said I'd find treasure and I did, then he said there'd be healing and a reward."

This boy, this beautiful boy he and Lisa had made. The one already three months growing in her womb when Lisa told him she was pregnant, back when all the work Gary could find was construction and Lisa was waiting tables at the Shoney's. They had no money. What little they kept went to fuel a drug habit already spiraling out of control, straining the love they shared and the future they held. Gary began selling, believing that to be a way out. Then transporting. He was in the mountains when they caught him with two thousand tablets of MDMA bound for Kentucky and Tennessee, leaving him weeping in front of a judge who glowed a pale yellow and who took pity, sending him here to Fairhope for his sentence rather than having him serve hard time at Taylorsville. His life gone, his wife and child run off.

"I had to see you, Daddy. Something's happened."

"I know," Gary says. He keeps his hand to Abel's cheek, to the surface of that water. "Your momma came."

"Momma came here?"

"She told me, Abel. I'm so sorry. I'm so sorry what happened."

"Is she okay?"

"No, 'course not. She's sad. We're both sad, Abel. You were our boy."

Sanders again: "Gary, you need some help?"

He's coming over. Sanders is coming to take me away.

"I prayed so hard. I always prayed just to see you and I didn't think I ever would. I thought you were gone from me, but then Lisa came and now you. It's like a family, Abel. We're like a family. Did you pray?"

"No," Abel says, "all I did was die."

Sanders's hands are soft on him, trying to lower Gary's hand. Gary pushes those hands away. Abel backs off, frightened. The girl and big man are gone into the trees. Gary pulls his son close again.

"Abel, where have you been? Have you seen it? What's next?"

"Dorothy hasn't taken me. That's Dorothy over there, hiding in the trees. She didn't tell me what happened to me, just Dumb Willie. She couldn't say because I had to find you. Dorothy's kind."

"But is it real?" he asks, then asks again as Sanders again tries to still him, reaching for his walkie. The other guard is running over the rows, smashing corn and potato plants beneath his boot. "What have you seen, Abel?"

Abel smiles. "Magic, Daddy. I seen magic."

He hears, *This is Sanders, all available personnel to the garden,* but only Abel's words register. They sink deep into bones long dry and a heart long brittle as Sanders grips him hard, ripping Gary away.

"Come here, Abel," he shouts,

("His kid," Sanders tells the other guard, "he just found out his kid's dead. Gonna be okay, Gary, I promise, we're gonna get you inside for a bit.")

"come to me."

Abel runs. He runs on two legs that look unfit for his body and Gary feels him in the arm Sanders cannot reach, feels the softness of Abel's hair and lets his scruff tickle Abel's cheek. He fills his nose with the scent of his son.

"I love you, Daddy," he says. "I always loved you," as Gary feels hands upon him and hears that girl talk, those hands yanking him away toward the trees and the fence.

"I'm so sorry, Abel. So sorry for everything."

"It's okay, Daddy,"

("It's okay, Gary, you just relax and come on—")

"I'll see you again. Dorothy says so, Daddy. Dorothy's always right, she's special—"

"I love you, Abel," screaming not in anger but with joy because it's real, all Gary has seen and sees and will yet see, all of it. "I love you, son."

"I love you, Daddy."

They are pulling him away, Sanders and the other guards, the blind carrying the sighted. The other convicts in the field look on. Some bow their heads. Others shout words of encouragement, telling Gary to hang in there, it'll get better. And yet to Gary Bragg, none of them are here. The soft earth is gone and the tall trees and sky above, the pretty girl and the big man with the vacant stare. It is only himself and his boy here, the two of them linked by the smile upon their faces and the lightness in their hearts that may bear all things, a secret passed from son to father that the cares of this world mean little because beyond is another place called Home, and there the two of them will one day say hello again and never good-bye.

Never good-bye.

-6-

Dorothy does not so much watch the children at play as she does Abel beside her. Dumb Willie stands to their right. His fingers are laced between the metal diamonds of the chain-wire backstop and he is hollering out, alternating between "Atta. *Boy*" and "*Nice* . . . one" as each of the pitcher's warm-up tosses slaps into the catcher's mitt.

There is no reason they have ended up here at the ball field down the road from where Abel's daddy calls home, other than the gleaming bleachers offered the closest place to sit. As it is, the three of them make up a rare crowd for the day's pickup game between a dozen of Fairhope's youngsters. Half are spread out in the field. The remaining six huddle near the first-base dugout, waiting their turn at bat.

To Dorothy it is a scene wholly opposed to that from which they've fled, one representing all of what grieves her in mortals and one so alive with joy and holding all she adores. It occurs to her that Abel likely never partook in this part of growing up. The boy always had to be so careful, weighing every action against its potential consequence. Some arrive in this world already old.

"Always liked this game," she says. "Something about it, pure and youthful."

Abel watches the first batter, a boy no bigger than himself with dirty knees and two dulled scabs on his elbows. The bat in his hands appears as long and heavy as a pole.

"Me and Dumb Willie used to play catch sometimes. Out back of my house, or on the playground at school. We always had to use a tennis ball. I never did catch good, and I was always scared what a real ball'd do if I got hit. Dumb Willie can hum it."

"I bet he can."

The boy swings late at the first two pitches, putting him in the hole and bringing moans from Dumb Willie and cackles from the team in the field. The boy's teammates urge him to choke up on the handle.

He stands in once more. Dorothy and Abel are quiet. Even Dumb Willie stops his roaring as the ball is delivered in a white blur, the boy swinging from his heels, eyes clenched with effort. They fly open at the sharp *tink* of the aluminum bat striking true. A chorus of screams rises with the ball, launched in a lazy arc that ends in an empty right field.

Dumb Willie hops, hands shaking the fence, yelling his joy until his cheeks turn crimson. The boy straddles the first-base bag and tips his cap. Abel looks caught in a place somewhere between cheer and grief at this boy he will never meet, this boy who may have called Abel a friend had things been different, had he been born in Mattingly or Abel in Fairhope, had Abel come from his momma healthy and whole. But in this world of what must be, Dorothy knows that Abel can only call the child standing tall in the field a surrogate for the life he was never granted.

"My daddy going to be okay, you think?"

"Seemed a good place over there," Dorothy says, "and good people to look after him. Things got a way of working out in the end no matter what you do. End's only thing that counts, really. Yes, Abel. Your daddy gone be just fine. He got something now I don't think he ever had."

"What's that?"

"Hope," says Dorothy. "A knowing that something's waiting for him farther on."

"What happened to him, Dorothy? Momma said he died before I was born. Maybe that's not a lie. Maybe whatever he did killed the person my daddy was, and the person he is now is somebody different."

"I expect most folk become different," she says, "the longer they go on. Sometimes better, sometimes worse. I bet he's better. He seems a kind man."

"You think he knew I'd be born broke? Somehow they did some test, and my daddy found out? You think that was what made him do something bad?"

Dorothy looks out over those kids playing and running and throwing. Toward the trees and the road past them, cars and trucks and the people they hold and past even there, way out to where the world stretches on.

"Everybody's broken, Abel. Ain't a soul stands otherwise. Only thing makes you any different is you know you is. That puts you well ahead of the rest."

"You think I'm special, Dorothy?"

"I think ain't a one like you ever." She smiles as best she knows and leans back, settling herself against the bleacher behind them. Putting the two of them as equal. "That's why things gone the way they have, I guess. I couldn't take you on, Abel. Couldn't bear to tell you the truth of things because I couldn't bear knowing the same. I wanted different for you, and that makes you special. You even made me want different for myself, if only once. Got it in my head maybe I could make things right as I saw them. Thought I could bring you all the way back at that spring. Leave you here for a good long while, then come to fetch you again when you're old and gray and ready." She turns her head, sees Abel's face. "I didn't want you looking back when I took you on."

There is another clip of the bat, more cheers. Dumb Willie shakes the fence once more and pronounces what he has just seen a genuine murcle. Dorothy doesn't look. Nor does Abel.

"What happens now, Dorothy?"

"Got to head on from here. That's our first order of business. Longer we keep to Fairhope, more folk might figure out me and Dumb Willie don't belong. They still looking for him, Abel. Might be more now, if Arthur don't say those three men died when that mound collapsed."

"Did you do that?" Abel asks. "Be honest. Wasn't the spring killed them, was it?"

"Was their time," is what Dorothy answers. "Was meant, one way or another. But none of that makes a difference. World's closing in on us, and we ain't safe. And you ain't got much time left. We need to settle on things, Abel." She nods her head toward Dumb Willie's voice. "Him most of all. Got to get you gone from here. Dumb Willie can't follow yet. There's nowhere for him to go."

Abel thinks. Now he grins.

"Might be."

PART IX

HOME

-1-

Abel sees it as something of a rest, this final stretch of their long journey. They do not flee Fairhope as they did the town of Greenville, which now seems so far away. Farther even than Mattingly. It is rather that they travel slow and purposeful instead, keeping to Fairhope's edges and hidden places so as not to risk Dumb Willie being spotted. They wait in a copse of trees along the tracks not far from town and mix quiet talk among silences that are equal parts peace and sadness at this, their adventure's close. The train that comes is bound for Raleigh. From there, Dorothy says, they strike north and west.

They sense no danger now, no strain of going against what is meant. That long trip is spent with the three of them talking and laughing, recalling that first night Dorothy saved them and all those times after, when their saving was done by Dumb Willie or by Abel. And times as well when their way forward looked bleakest, when all the saving they needed was done by the bond the three of them had come to share. The sense that they have also been led by something greater than themselves (greater, even, than Death) does not go unsaid. Dumb Willie puts it best early this afternoon as he looks out upon the passing world and then to the faces of his friends:

"It's. *Magic*. Did it," he says. "*Hebbin* . . . magic."

Somewhere west of Raleigh and in the shadows of the high mountains, Abel performs his last magic show. He has little left in the way of props, just the deck of cards in his pocket. Still, there is common agreement that his tricks are among the best Dumb Willie and Dorothy have ever seen. He bows at their cheers and blushes at their applause and wishes for no greater an audience.

They laugh, they talk, they look upon one another and remember. That long ride from Fairhope is a quiet one that Abel feels holds nothing in the way of excitement, nothing that he believes would form a memory for him to hang on to. Yet he knows now and finally that the quiet times are indeed the ones that come to define one's life. Our wasted moments are anything but.

At a flat place along the tracks where the train picks up speed for the steep hills beyond, Dumb Willie grants Abel a final wish. He stands at the edge of the boxcar's door with Abel's shoes wedged against his own, clutching the back of Abel's neck. Dorothy watches with a grin as Abel leans himself out of the boxcar and into the rushing wind. His face tingles and his hair flies wild. Beneath him, the wheels clatter against the rails. The air feels charged as he shuts his eyes and leans back his head, arms extended to either side.

Abel laughs. He is flying.

He always wanted to fly.

*

Long they walk, all this early evening and far into the night, through lands Abel thought long behind and never to be seen again. Dorothy keeps them to the deep woods. She warns Dumb Willie there can be only whispers here, and only when they warrant. The fire built for their rest is small and barely fit to cook through the bullfrog Dumb Willie plucks from a stream. Dorothy watches the trees as they prepare for their final push, ears cocked for any noise out of place.

It's a dangerous thing you'll try, she had told Abel before the great engine had uncoupled from the cars and left them in silence. *No telling it'll work even if we make it there.*

Abel had known the truth of those words then. He knows it more now, watching as Dumb Willie commits the last bit of frog to the same earth meant to claim all things. But it must work. That is the end of it so far as Abel is concerned. He will not move on with Dorothy otherwise.

Rather than dwell on the peril of their journey's final miles or the question of its success, Abel chooses instead to do what he knows he should and relish these last hours with his friend. The stars are gone this night, hidden above a thick layer of summer clouds.

Dorothy knows the way without their guidance. "I could find it with my eyes shut and my feet bound, should it come to that. It's an irony."

"I. Nee," Dumb Willie says.

Abel explains the term in a way she finds nearly poetic:

"It means it's Dorothy's grief that leads us to your hope."

Ridges and hollers lie before them in frozen roil. Hulks of trees rise like hardened shadows. The pines green even in this darkness. Abel finds himself wishing for even a pale moon to see by, if only to take in this land. He wishes to see the faces of Dorothy and Dumb Willie, the two who have rescued him. He finds he even longs for a final look at the muted yellow cast slipping from his right arm, his crooked legs and tilting hips, if only as a reminder of what he leaves behind.

Dumb Willie ask, "Where we goin' A. Bull?" in whispers that grow in tone and frequency the closer they look to get to the world's very edge.

Abel's reply is the same each time, and each time given with the same patience and kindness: "Just a little ways more, then you'll see."

They come to the field and the path of flattened grass that marks both end and arrival. The single light burning beyond the open door stops them.

Dorothy removes her hat and lays down her leather bag. She says, "Guess y'all best keep here a minute. I'll go on, see what I can do."

Dorothy walks forward as a figure steps out from the barn. A shotgun is settled against the woman's left hip. Abel can see her mussed hair in the lantern light, her gaunt figure, the weariness upon her face.

"What we *do*. A Bull?"

"Need a place where you're safe," Abel says. "People want to hurt you, Dumb Willie. I can't let that happen, but I can't stay here and watch over you. Dorothy can't stay neither. Me and her got to be heading on."

"Home," Dumb Willie says.

"Yeah. We're going home. But you can't go with us. Dorothy's seeing if maybe you can stay here. You'd like it,

Dumb Willie. There's animals and mountains and quiet. And that garden out back."

"It'sa. *Woeman.*"

"I know. But maybe she won't be so sad now. Maybe you can keep her safe and help heal up her insides. Like you did for me."

Dorothy is talking. Abel hears quiet rather than yelling and considers this a good sign. The shotgun is no longer on the woman's hip but tilted toward the ground, hanging limp in her hand.

"You goin'. *Home.*"

"Yeah. You think you might like it here, Dumb Willie? Please say yes. It's a good place. You'd be happy. That woman won't beat on you or call you stupid. Maybe you could even get her to go back inside the house. It's nice in there, better than that old barn. There's lot of books. I bet plenty of them got pictures to look at. That woman thinks there's ghosts in there, but there isn't. You can tell her that. It's empty is all. Sometimes empty can feel like ghosts."

Dorothy turns away. She's walking back with her head low as the woman watches.

"Please say yes, Dumb Willie."

Dumb Willie thinks long before offering his answer: "It'sa big . . . garden it'sa good. Woeman."

Dorothy waits until she's close before she lifts her chin. Her face betrays no hint of what has been said. The woman stands, waiting and still, like a thing hollowed out.

"What'd you tell her?" Abel asks.

"Told her everything, like you wanted. She says there's room enough. Plenty of work to be done. More'n she can bear alone."

Abel shakes his head. "He can't just be a worker, Dorothy.

She can't be treating him like another cow or pig, or we'll be bringing him to a place no different from the one he left."

"More than that," Dorothy says. She glances behind. "What she feels kept her from giving the words, but she's thankful. I know it. I can't replace the ones I took from her, but I can give her to Dumb Willie and Dumb Willie to her. It'll bring a healing." She shakes her head in an unbelieving way, like the words feel too pleasant to be true. "Death will bring that woman life, should Dumb Willie want it."

Abel feels Dumb Willie reaching for his hand. He squeezes.

"You take care of her."

A tear tumbles from Dumb Willie's eye to his cheek, mixing with the slobber there before falling from his chin. "Kay." He then lets go, moving past Dorothy and toward the barn, looking back only once to grin at Abel's good-bye.

"Love you, Willie."

"Love you A. Bull."

Dorothy places her arm around Abel's shoulder. They watch as Willie dips his head and waves to the woman in a shy way.

"They'll be fine," she says. "Don't you worry a bit. Might even be the happiest they ever been."

"You sure?"

"Feel sure. That's sure's I can get. Them two graves out back won't be three for a long while. Won't be four for even longer, should somebody stumble by after those many years. And when I come for them, it will be in peace. They'll both go knowing there's somebody waiting for them at the end of the path. That'll be an end worth finding."

Willie turns, saying, "Bye A. *Bull*," and "Bye Do. *Tee*," waving once more. The woman does the same. She raises a hand to the woman Abel knows she sees and the little boy he knows she doesn't, and in her eye is a smile she does not yet know how to speak but someday will. *Yes*, Abel thinks, *someday she will.*

Willie always did know how to make folk beam.

-2-

The morning train cuts through Mattingly in the early dawn of Wednesday, the twenty-eighth of June, near three weeks removed from the night Death chose to turn away from what it believed was meant only to fulfill what had been meant all along.

Dorothy counts three as the engines slow near the curve. Their landing is soft and sure. In the corner of the boxcar they leave behind rests a worn leather bag and three crumpled letters that are needed no more.

At the field's edge where gravel yields to grass, a plain white cross rises from the ground. Bouquets of flowers surround it, some store-bought and wrapped in cellophane, others plucked from the field itself, tied either by their roots or with pieces of twine. Another cross rises farther down at the edge of the tracks. Here are flowers as well, cards and small signs written by the hands of children, even a tiny toy train left to rust in the rain and sun. Dorothy allows Abel to linger. They stand at Chris's marker first and then Abel's own. She asks Abel to read aloud every good-bye and wish for rest.

"You think they saw me all that time?" Abel asks. "Not just Momma and Principal Rexrode or Miss Ellie, but everybody?"

"I'm sure they did. Anybody knows you even a little, Abel Shifflett, they know you're hard to miss."

Abel looks back toward the other cross—taking in those parts of themselves people left there, grinning at Dorothy that his own pile is bigger.

"You took Chris? That night you saved me?"

"I did."

"How? You were with us the whole time."

"You think ain't nobody in the whole wide world passed since we been gone?" Dorothy shakes her head. "Ain't the way it works. Even now I'm here and elsewhere, going as I'm called. I'm a wife long passed, leading her husband on. I'm a daddy and a grandmomma. I'm an angel clothed in starlight. I'm a shadow dressed in night. And I'm Dorothy the hobo, who calls you friend."

"What were you for Chris?"

"The angel," Dorothy says. "Glowing pure and white with its arms spread wide to show him a goodness he never knew."

"He was spoilt."

"He was broke, no less than you and no more than anyone. And now he's broken no more."

They take the field back to the curve and Chris's marker, to where there lies a clean view of the tiny white house at the dead end. The windows are shut, as is the back door, the shades drawn tight. The sliver of driveway Dorothy can see is empty.

"You want to go on down there a bit?"

"No," Abel says. "There's nobody home."

"Think your momma'd be down there? Late in the morning, past time for her to leave."

He shrugs. "Thought maybe she would be. She'd be . . .

waiting. Or something. I'd like to see her one last time. Daddy said she's sad."

"Ain't no last time," Dorothy says. "This is many things, Abel, but it isn't good-bye. Your momma mourns you. Looks to me the whole town does. And that's a fine thing, because it's more than you they grieve, it's the light gone out from the world by your passing. It's no choice for them but to go on as best they can. Your momma'll cry her tears, and maybe she'll find when those tears finally dry she can see new things now, things maybe she never thought on before. And that'll lead her straight back to you."

"What if she ends up like that woman?"

"So much the better. Woman's got Willie now. Your momma's got a whole town of folk to see her through."

"She don't believe, Dorothy."

"There's time yet. It ain't her end. And the end's—"

"All that matters," Abel finishes. "You think that's true? I'll see her?"

"I think she's being looked after fine."

"By the town?"

"By more," Dorothy says. "I got caught thinking I could go against what's meant, Abel, because I thought what's meant isn't what's best. I have never loved, do you know that? But I think I've come to have something of that for you and Willie, as much of it as I can, and I thought that love would be enough to restore you. But I couldn't, and do you know why? Because there is a love far greater, ever bright and never fading, calling all things back to itself. Calling all things home. And I wonder at that love, because it carries a depth measureless and beyond my reaching."

"You got to promise you'll be kind," Abel says, "when you call on her. My momma."

Dorothy says, "When it's her time to take the path, it'll be the one she loved most who shows her. I'll make sure of it."

She sees the light spilling from Abel's eyes as he takes in all that is around them, green fields speckled with yellows and blues and reds, trees that sing in the breeze, hills and mountains. Abel looks at the house and the tall weeds around it, down that dirt road stretching toward town.

"Reverend Johnny said I'd find healing. Which I did, but it was for Dumb Willie more than me. Because I put him in that spring and left him with the woman. And he said there'd be reward, but that was for my daddy, I think. I think we got sent there for him, not just me. But it was good for me too. It was real good."

"But no reward?" Dorothy asks.

Abel shrugs a shoulder. "I'm just wondering is all. What my reward is."

And Dorothy smiles. With her mouth and her cheeks, with her eyes. "Come on," she says, "I'll show you."

They take hands as they turn toward the tracks, moving slowly between the ties. Abel grips her as he hops onto one of the rails, wobbling to find his balance. He talks of Preacher Keen and how nice he was, and the mystery that was Reverend Johnny Mills. Finding the letters. Their first night on the train and the ones after, all their grand adventure.

He looks at her, blushing. "I never knew Death could be so pretty."

"I can be," she says, "to some."

"You need to be kind to Arthur too. He never meant no harm, really. He meant to kill Willie because he wanted me to get free. I didn't, but Arthur saved me. Like Willie saved me, and my daddy. Like you saved me, Dorothy."

"Okay. I promise." She nudges against him. "But only because I think you saved me too."

Talking and laughing, acting as friends will. Traveling toward where the rails rise up as a golden path in the long distance and where the sparrows swirl and sing their songs. It is to Dorothy's joy that the boy does not look back as they make their way. Abel's eyes remain down to help balance his feet upon the rail. Now forward to the way they go. Now to her. Smiling as they move down that long stretch of rail toward where the sun will arc high and then down, and then farther on, where there waits a place where the shine never fades.

Bound west, toward home.

DISCUSSION QUESTIONS

1. When most of us consider the character of Death from books and film, our first image is usually of the Grim Reaper type rather than someone like Dorothy. Did her character change your view of death in any way? Have you ever thought of Death as an entity, a force, or merely an event that must come to us all?

2. The driving force behind much of the story is a notion of what is and is not "meant." To Dorothy, the events of our lives are laid out from beginning to end. All we must do is follow. For Abel, our choices are what determine our destinies. What value, if any, do you subscribe to the notion of free will? What weight do our choices carry in the stories of our lives?

3. In what ways does Dumb Willie prove himself to be anything but dumb, and in fact show himself to be perhaps the wisest character in the story?

4. Lisa Shifflett long vowed to keep the truth of Abel's father from him. Assuming Abel had never found the letters, do you believe she was right in doing so? What are the lies we tell our children, even for their

own good, and what can be the consequences they suffer by them?

5. What sort of life do you think awaited Abel had he never gone to find his father?

6. An important moment of the journey comes when Dorothy informs Abel that he isn't the only one "broken," everyone is. What do you think she meant by this? Do you agree?

7. There were at least two reasons why Abel played his trick on Chris Jones: one to get even from Chris's constant bullying, the other to be punished. This last reason stems from Abel's hatred of being known as "special." In spite of our desire to stand out, what is it that drives us in equal measure to be like everyone else?

8. Reverend Johnny refuses to heal Abel after the service in the hill country by saying Abel doesn't have enough faith. Do you think Reverend Johnny possessed any healing ability at all, or was he a charlatan all along? Do you believe that faith is a necessary part of healing? If so, what degree of faith do you believe is needed?

AN EXCERPT FROM
THERE WILL BE STARS

PART I

HEAVEN

-1-

Sometimes, if he was not so drunk or the twins so loud, Bobby Barnes would consider how those rides to the mountain had become an echo of his life. Night would fill the gaps between the trees with a black so thick and hard the world itself seemed to end beyond the headlights' reach. No future. No past. Only the illusion of this single moment, stretched taut and endless. He loved the lonely feeling, the nothingness, even if the road upon which he sought escape from town was the very road that would return him to it. All living was a circle. Something of Bobby had come to understand that, though its truth remained a mystery too deep for his heart to plumb. Life was a circle and the road a loop, and both flowed but seldom forward. They instead wound back upon themselves, the past leaching into the present and the present shrouding the future, reminding him that all could flee from their troubles, but only toward and never away.

One of the boys said something. Matthew or Mark, Bobby

couldn't tell. The pale orange light off the radio made the twins appear even more identical, just as the music made them sound even more the same. Carbon copies, those boys. When they'd been born—back when Carla still wore her wedding ring and the only future she and Bobby envisioned was one they would face together—Bobby had joked they would have to write the boys' names on the bottoms of their feet to tell them apart. Now Matthew and Mark were eight. Still the same, but only on the outside.

The other boy joined in, something about a movie or a cartoon, Bobby couldn't hear. The deejay had put on "Highway to Hell" and Mark asked Bobby to turn that up, he liked it, though not enough to keep from fighting with his brother. He felt the seat move as one twin shouldered the other, heard the sharp battle cry of "Stupid!" Bobby pursed his lips and said nothing. Being a good father involved knowing when to step in and when to let things ride. He relaxed his grip on the wheel and gulped the beer in his hand.

Night whisked by as the truck climbed the high road above town, the engine purring. No vehicle in Mattingly ran so fine as Bobby Barnes's old Dodge. Let the town speak what lies they wished, no one could deny that truth. He eased his foot down on the gas, felt the growl beneath him and the smile creeping over his face. His ears popped, followed by the come-and-gone sound of a lone cricket. The headlights caught flashes of reds and yellows on the October trees and the glowing eyes of deer along the road, standing like silent monsters in the dark.

"Tell'm, Daddy," Matthew said beside him. "He's so stupid."

"Am not," Mark yelled. "*You're* stupid. You're *double* stupid."

Another shove, maybe a slap, Bobby couldn't know. He did know if things got out of hand and one of those boys spilled his beer, he'd have to get the belt out when they got home.

"Ain't nobody stupid," he said. "Matthew, you got what you think, Mark's got what he does. Don't mean either one's right or wrong. That's called an opinion. Y'all know what opinions are like?"

"Butts," Mark said.

"'Cause everybody's got one," said Matthew.

Both snickered. Bobby toasted his parental wisdom with another swallow. He finished the can and tossed it through the open slot in the window behind them, where it rattled against the other empties in the bed. The sound echoed back and mixed with the boys' laughter and the guitar solo over the radio, Angus Young hammering on the ax as Bobby's eyes widened against a heaviness that fell over him, a chill that formed a straight line from the middle of his forehead to his nonexistent gut, settling in the bottoms of his feet. It was as if he had been struck by some pale lightning, pulled apart and pieced back together in the same breath.

"Whatsa matter, Daddy?" Matthew asked.

Bobby reached for the last of the six-pack on the dash. "Dunno," he said. "Think a rabbit run over my grave. Like you get a funny feeling? Like you done before what you're doing now."

"That's 'cause we take a ride every night," Matthew said.

"Ain't that. *Know* that. 'Member this morning when we was going out to Timmy's and we seen Laura Beth sashaying like she always does down the walk? 'Member I whistled to her and said I knew she'd be there?"

Mark said, "You always whistle at Laura Beth."

"I'll have you know I ain't never whistled to Laura Beth Gowdy before in my life, boy. Why'd I ever wanna do such a thing? Little Miss Priss. Been that way since high school." He took a sip. "Didn't whistle 'cause she's comely, I whistled because I *knew*. Felt that rabbit and I *knew*. Like Jake? I knew he'd be at Timmy's, too, wanting one a his words. And that woman preacher."

"You said you bet she'd be outside the church," Mark said, "but she weren't."

"No, but I said Andy would be pushing a broom when we went to get gas."

"Mr. Sommerville *always* pushing a broom," Matthew said.

"But Junior ain't always been there. And I *knew* he would be. Remember? And your mom called this afternoon."

Mark rolled down the window and let his hand play with the cool mountain air. "Momma's way finer than Laura Beth Gowdy. Daddy? Laura Beth paints her hair. Momma's looks like that on purpose."

That sense (Bobby couldn't name it, something besides a rabbit, French or what he sometimes called Hi-talian) had left the soles of his feet. The worse feeling of his son's stare took its place. He kept his eyes to the road. He'd never say so out loud and risk hurting Mark's feelings, but sometimes the boy got to him. Mark could nudge his daddy in directions best not traveled.

"Your momma found somebody else to love on her, for what grief that cost us all and what good that does her now. Pondering Carla's fineness does me no good service."

For a while there were only the sounds of the big tires and the songs crackling over the radio, the classic rock station out of Stanley. Bobby felt the truck drift past the center line and corrected. Matthew leaned his head against his daddy's shoulder, drifting to sleep. Mark hummed along with Axl Rose about patience. Bobby fell into old thoughts of things lost that could never be gained again.

"Maybe we should get up here and go Camden way," he said. "All these rabbits could mean Lady Luck's on my side. Could go up to that 7-and-Eleven, get us a scratcher. What y'all say?"

Mark looked Bobby's way. "You won't."

*

Ahead loomed a T in the road, a marker that read 237 and an arrow pointing right and left just ahead of the stop sign. Bobby intended to roll right through—few traveled those mountaintops in the night, which was why he chose that road to ride with his sons—but then he felt his foot pressing harder on the brake. A chill rushed through him again. The truck stopped along a line of newer pavement and the cracked asphalt of what everyone in Mattingly called the Ridge Road.

He looked down and saw the left blinker winking. Left, on through the mountains and then down again, back to the valley and the shop.

His hands, though, gripped the wheel as if to turn right for Camden.

Matthew's head was still pressed against Bobby's shoulder. "'Nother rabbit get you, Daddy?"

Bobby reached for a beer not there. "Guess it did."

Mark stuck a skinny arm through his window and pointed. "Let's go this-a-way," he said. "Daddy? Let's get us a scratcher."

Bobby opened his mouth to say sure and heard himself say, "Guess we won't. Can't be wasting money on fanciful wishes. Ain't like old Laura Beth Gowdy's husband is calling up saying he's gotta build onto the bank 'cause of all the money I got there. We'll just take our ride."

Mark's finger still pointed. "You said that last time."

Bobby chuckled—he always did when he didn't understand a word Mark said—and turned left. Farther into the mountains, higher, higher, because up here it was the three of them and no one else, no one to call Bobby "pervert" and "drunk" and "rooned." Because up here in the dark of road and forest, Bobby Barnes possessed all the world he needed.

He turned left as Mark's pallid face kept toward the empty stretch of road to Camden and brake lights flashed far ahead. Bobby leaned forward, wondering if those were from a car or from the six-pack he'd drunk since leaving the shop.

"Ain't nobody should be up here."

Matthew yawned. "We up here, Daddy."

The radio popped and hissed and then went clear as the truck crested the ridge. Barren trees let in a view of the valleys below—Mattingly's few lights on one side, Stanley's crowded ones on the other.

"I love this song," Matthew said. "Crank it, Daddy."

Bobby didn't. A war had broken out inside him, one part sloshing from the beer and the other bearing up under that heavy feeling once more. Two parts becoming a whole. He fixed his eyes ahead, where that flicker of lights had been, and wondered who that could be and why he felt like him and the boys were no longer on a ride. He let off the gas and fumbled with the radio dial.

Matthew began to sing, a pale imitation of John Fogerty's voice, a bad moon a-rising and trouble on the way.

The car ahead. Brake lights disappearing around the sharp S in the road. Matthew singing, his voice high, almost warning that they shouldn't go around tonight because it's bound to take their lives, that bad moon on the rise. Mark saying something Bobby couldn't hear.

The truck thundered forward as though pulled by an unseen force toward the curve in the road, and now that feeling again, that French word Bobby couldn't remember, seizing him. He took the middle part of the S and found empty road on the other side. Matthew strummed at a guitar that existed only in his mind. The moon shone down over the broken outline of the trees. Shadows danced through dying leaves. Bobby looked at Mark and smiled. He winked even if he thought Mark couldn't see, because Mark Barnes might be too smart for his own good but he was Bobby's boy and so was Matthew, and Bobby would be nothing without them.

The truck took the bottom part of the curve. Bobby opened

his mouth. "It's—" was all that came out. The rest became swallowed by the terror on Mark's face.

Matthew screamed.

Bobby turned to headlights in front of them. He stood up on the brake, mashing it to the floor, but time was all that slowed. The truck continued on. He heard the sharp screech of tires locking and felt the waving motion of the back end loosing. One arm shot out for Matthew's chest, but Bobby had nothing to hold Mark in place. His youngest (youngest by thirty seconds) doubled in on himself. Mark flew in a soundless gasp: one leg pinwheeling out of the open window, a bit of thick brown hair standing on end, the fingers of a tiny hand. And those headlights, blinding him and blinding Matthew, glimmering off the unbuckled seat belt none of them ever used.

Metal scraped metal, a crunching that folded the truck's hood like a wave. Matthew floated toward the windshield. Bobby felt himself thrown forward. He lamented that of all the things he needed to say, his last word had been so meaningless. And in his last moment, Bobby understood that he had been in this place times beyond counting and would be here again uncountable times still. He heard glass shatter and felt the steering wheel press into his chest. He heard himself scream and scream again. There was pain and loss and a fear beyond all he had ever known, and as blackness deep and unending took him, a single thought slipped through his life's final breath:

There will be stars.

The story continues in
There Will Be Stars by Billy Coffey.

ABOUT THE AUTHOR

Photograph by Joanne Coffey

Billy Coffey's critically acclaimed books combine rural Southern charm with a vision far beyond the ordinary. He is a regular contributor to several publications, where he writes about faith and life. Billy lives with his wife and two children in Virginia's Blue Ridge Mountains.

*

www.billycoffey.com
Facebook: billycoffeywriter
Twitter: @billycoffey